"AN EXHILARATING, PSYCHOLOGICALLY PENETRATING WORK . . . CHARACTERS AND SITUATIONS WE CAN UNDERSTAND AND IDENTIFY WITH . . . BRILLIANT . . . DAZZLING!"—*The New York Times Book Review*

"Three sisters who are as believable and engaging, as full of human strengths (and shortcomings) as any characters I've encountered in recent fiction . . . can be absolutely hilarious . . . rare and unforgettable!"—*Washington Post Book World*

"I envy the way Candace Flynt slowly reveals the immense intensity and drama in her characters' utterly real lives. *Mother Love* is a novel I won't be able to forget."—Pat Conroy

"Commands interest and attention!"—*Publishers Weekly*

"Wonderful . . . the novel comes together as the best sort of 'popular fiction.'"—*Library Journal*

"This well-written, realistic novel steers clear of melodrama and shows that life holds plenty of painful choices but few easy answers."—*Booklist*

CANDACE FLYNT is the author of two highly acclaimed novels, *Chasing Dad* and *Sins of Omission*. She lives with her family in her hometown of Greensboro, North Carolina, the setting of all her books.

MOTHER LOVE

Candace Flynt

A PLUME BOOK

NEW AMERICAN LIBRARY

NEW YORK AND SCARBOROUGH, ONTARIO

NAL BOOKS ARE AVAILABLE AT QUANTITY DISCOUNTS WHEN USED TO PROMOTE PRODUCTS OR SERVICES. FOR INFORMATION PLEASE WRITE TO PREMIUM MARKETING DIVISION, NEW AMERICAN LIBRARY, 1633 BROADWAY, NEW YORK, NEW YORK 10019.

Acknowledgements

Lines from "The Second Coming" by W.B. Yeats, reprinted with permission of Macmillan Publishing Company; Copyright 1924 by Macmillan Publishing Company renewed 1952 by Bertha Georgie Yeats.

Lines from "The Love Song of J. Alfred Prufrock" by T.S. Eliot, reprinted with permission of Harcourt Brace Jovanovich, Inc.; Copyright © 1963 by Harcourt Brace World, Inc.

SIGNET, SIGNET CLASSIC, MENTOR, ONYX, PLUME, MERIDIAN and NAL BOOKS are published *in the United States* by NAL PENGUIN, INC., 1633 Broadway, New York, New York 10019, *in Canada* by The New American Library of Canada Limited, 81 Mack Avenue, Scarborough, Ontario M1L 1M8

Library of Congress Cataloging-in-Publication Data

Flynt, Candace, 1947–
   Mother Love / Candace Flynt.
      p.   cm.
   ISBN 0-452-26076-0 (pbk.)
   I. Title.
[PS3556.L95M6 1988]   87-30686
813'.54—dc19   CIP

First Plume Printing, June, 1988

1 2 3 4 5 6 7 8 9

PRINTED IN THE UNITED STATES OF AMERICA

To my husband, Chuck,
to my children, Elizabeth and MacAulay,
and to my sisters, Dee and Mary Mac,
with love

I have written here that I have recovered.
I mean it only in a worldly sense because
I do not believe in recovery. The past, with
its pleasures, its rewards, its foolishness,
its punishments, is there for each of us forever,
and it should be.

—LILLIAN HELLMAN

Part One

MOTHER

CHAPTER

1

"Whose turn?" asks Jude, the sister who is driving.

She makes a sharp cut with her station wagon through the white brick columns that mark the entrance to the graveyard and speeds up the hill. The instantaneous change from daylight to dusk is just now occurring. In the front seat with her are her two sisters. In the back are the empty car seats of her two babies, who are presently being watched over by their grandfather. They are running late. A sign warns that the gate will be locked at sundown, but no one worries: in these two years they have never seen a gatekeeper.

Neither sister answers her question. Instead, they keep talking about whether Louise, who has naturally curly hair, would benefit from a permanent. Neither may remember whose turn it is, but it is not Jude's. Last time they were together, she told the story about Mother reading her palm at her rehearsal dinner and predicting that she and Cap would get a divorce. They had all laughed, she most of all. The story has become less horrible than it once was. And, after all, Mother was right.

She edges over to the curb and kills the motor, which knocks for many long seconds before it finally dies. Her station wagon, bought pre-divorce, is a battered, untended car which lately has been looking as if it's about to collapse. She could buy a new car with her inheritance, but she doesn't want to spend her mother's money like that. Even when she started thinking of it as her own money—about a year ago—she knew she would spend it for something glorious.

Louise opens her door and, as if she never heard Jude's

question, says, "It's my turn to tell a story about Mother." The cold Christmas air quickly fills the car. Louise turns up her palm, testing for snow.

"You sound like you've prepared," Jude says, leaning forward to see past Katherine.

"Not really. I didn't think of it until today."

Jude opens her door. "A Christmas story? Those are always good. Those are always the *best*."

"No. I thought of it when I saw Max's pool."

"A swimming story . . . ?" Jude tries.

They are all out of the car. "Shut up," Louise says, starting across the grass ahead of them.

Max is their stepfather. Before they set off for the graveyard, they stopped by his house to wish him a Merry Christmas. He'd been alone, partially drunk, and had turned down their invitation to accompany them. But he kept finding ways to make them stay with him, which is why it is almost dark now. Several times a year the sisters drive forty-five minutes to get here: on Christmas Day—ostensibly their mother's favorite day; on her death day, and on Mother's Day. They don't observe her birthday because she did not. Pretending it didn't exist made her feel she wasn't aging, she explained to them. Made her feel that although time in general went on—anniversaries, Christmases, their birthdays—her time did not.

"Aren't you going to wear your coat, Weezie?" Katherine calls before shutting the door. When she doesn't answer, Katherine and Jude follow her in the direction of the grave site. After a few steps, they catch up.

"No, 'Mother,' " Louise mutters.

Katherine does not respond, though inwardly she wishes she could utter the enormous loud irritated sigh she feels.

The graveyard has no tombstones, only flat bronze markers. Two of the sisters' grandparents, one of whom died in 1948, the other in 1970, are also buried here. At the top of the hill is a bell tower almost obscured by overgrown holly trees. Otherwise, the graveyard is well-tended. Down the hill lies a natural pond, where many years ago the sisters brought Fleedlefoot—

the only Easter duck which survived them—to live. Several weeping willows stand motionless in the cold air. Fleedlefoot's descendants and the descendants of other pet ducks sit huddled for warmth at the water's edge.

"I forgot the flowers," Katherine says. The other two wait while she returns to the car for the three yellow roses that she always brings. They are live roses, hard to find this time of year, these ordered from a nursery in South Carolina. The yellow rose was their mother's favorite flower; now it's the flower that all of them like best, too. Katherine hands one to each sister. Both say to remind them to pay her for it. She has never reminded them; they have never paid. It's her contribution. The flowers will be frozen in an hour, but they would never put anything artificial on their mother's grave.

By the time they reach her plot, the graveyard is dark, which makes them pay more attention to each other's face. Each sister is always intent on what the others are thinking, although Katherine and Jude pay less attention to Louise because she is still so young. They are both approaching thirty, Katherine just ahead of Jude. The two older sisters are tall, chesty, slim-hipped, and leggy, built like the women on their mother's side of the family. Any exercise they do is devoted to flattening their stomachs. Any exercise Louise does is aimed at slimming her thighs. She is built like the women on their father's side of the family: narrow shoulders, small breasts, and thick hips. Katherine and Jude have squarish faces which they each soften by wearing their hair to their shoulders. Louise's face is round, innocent, and open, her naturally curly hair full around her face. All three sisters agree with their mother's long-ago assessment that Louise is cute, Jude is beautiful, and Katherine is striking. But both Jude and Katherine believe that Louise will eventually outgrow her cuteness and become pretty. She's only twenty-one.

"Wouldn't Mother give her eyeteeth to still be here?" Katherine asks.

"Hell, yes," Jude answers.

"Don't talk like that," Louise says.

Katherine frowns. "Jesus Christ, Weezie."

"*Stop* it," Louise says shrilly. "We're in a graveyard. You ought to have a little respect. For God, if not for Mother."

"We're at our very own mother's grave," Jude says. "We're just being natural. We're talking exactly the way she would talk. You ought to try it sometime, Weezie. Stop always thinking about what you're *supposed* to do. Do what you *want* to do." She pauses. "God *isn't* here."

"You both make me sick," Louise says. Her cheeks are flushed; her eyes accusatory. Accusing them of being too much like their mother, Katherine thinks. Which, perhaps, they are, Jude especially. "I don't want to argue," Louise continues. "We're standing on her grave."

"Not *on* it," Katherine says.

"Yes, we are. Where do you think the casket is? Under that postage stamp? She's here. Under our feet." With the growing dark, the sense of graveyard has become stronger. Louise thinks that if there were tombstones here her sisters might be more reverent.

Katherine's face suddenly brightens. She stretches informally, ending the gesture by placing a hand on each sister's shoulder. Neither of them relaxes under her touch. "She's not under our feet. She's right here with us," she says, looking pointedly at both expectant faces. "No, she isn't." She grins with the knowledge that they all share. "If she were here, nobody would be having any fun."

Louise steps away so that Katherine's hand drops off her shoulder. "Why do you always cut her like that?"

"I'm not cutting her. Look, Weezie, this is what we decided. We aren't going to rosy her up. We're going to remember her as she was. No purple haze. We agreed to that two years ago. It's not disloyal." Katherine's voice becomes husky. "We're her daughters. If we're going to spend time remembering, we should remember her for how she was. She was a pain in the ass."

"She was also wonderful," Jude says.

"She was horrible," Louise suddenly blurts. She is half laughing and half crying. "At least she was horrible in this story I'm about to tell." She giggles and her cheeks perk up. "Does anybody know about the cheese toast?"

Giving a little curtsy, Louise lays her rose on the bronze grave marker. Katherine and Jude do the same. There is a sudden tender moment among them.

"I'm getting cold," Louise says, vigorously rubbing her arms.

"Want to share coats?" Katherine asks. The three sisters draw together again, two coats for three—each a little cold, each a little warm. Katherine thinks of the ducks.

"Why weren't we ever like this when she was alive?" Jude asks in a rare soft voice.

"She wouldn't let us be," Katherine murmurs.

"We *were* like this when she was alive," Louise says. She moves out from under their coats until she is standing behind the grave. "Sometimes we were friends; sometimes we weren't. You can't make everything her fault."

"Tell us about the cheese toast, Weezie," Katherine says in a soothing voice which is also intended to warn Jude off. But then, to make sure the truth is stated, she says, "Of course we were friends. But none of us was happy. She kept us from being happy." They weren't really friends, Katherine thinks. Being sisters is not the same. But she can't deny *everything* Louise says.

For several long moments Louise does not speak. Finally she says, "I was happy. I've always been happy. Almost." She looks at Katherine, who lowers her eyes to avoid comment. "I guess I loved her more than you two did."

"That does it," Jude says. She kneels, picks up one of the roses, and walks quickly away from the grave. All Katherine and Louise can see is the bobbing white fur collar of her coat. They wait to hear the car door open and slam, but the sound doesn't come. Suddenly Jude is back with them.

"I don't know why I did that," she says to Katherine. In the dusk, her expression is indiscernible, but both sisters hear the trembling in her voice. "I don't know why I took away the rose." She kneels again at the marker. She begins peeling away the petals of the flower. She scatters them around the grave.

"That's pretty," Katherine murmurs.

Jude says, "Some of the time, Louise, Mother made us unhappy. Don't you remember?"

"Yes, I remember," Louise says quietly.

Cars that are passing on the street beyond the gate have by now turned on their headlights. Across the valley hundreds of empty apartments begin to light up, suddenly changing character. The air is growing distinctly colder. Each sister feels fine pricks of ice begin to hit her face, but no one comments. Even if it were snow, which they all love, no one would comment, Katherine thinks. No one is happy enough to mention something pleasurable.

In a dutiful voice, Louise begins: "I was having a back-to-school swimming party. It was when I was about nine, I think." Her tone picks up. "The twins—ugh! how I hated them—came, and Marylou and Carla—all my growing-up friends. This is so typically Mother . . ." She gives a slight shivery giggle. Jude continues to squat by the grave. Katherine considers offering to share her coat again but decides against it.

"Mother was in a mood, of course. She'd dressed up for my party in her Greek Isles caftan and gold high heels. That morning I had gone with her to the grocery store to buy Cokes and potato chips, but all of a sudden she yelled out the Dutch door, 'How many pieces of cheese toast should I fix?' Carla Covington looked at me like Mother was crazy. In a very nice voice I called back that no one was hungry, although we'd all just gotten out of the pool to eat. I didn't know what to do. My friends didn't want *cheese toast!* What I suggested was that everyone lie down on their towels to sun-dry for a while and then we'd all go in and get our refreshments. I hoped maybe Mother would go upstairs or something.

"I remember wanting to explain to them but not knowing what to say. But at the same time I also believed that whatever Mother did was going to turn out right. And that when it didn't, it wasn't because she was mean or out of control or just nuts. It was because *I* didn't know the whole story. I still sort of feel that way. That I've never known the whole story about Mother."

There is a long concentrated pause, something like a silent prayer at church, Katherine thinks. Weezie always poses a question like this. It used to be that she wanted Jude or Katherine, Katherine in particular, to try to answer it, but she seems to have realized that they have no final explanations, only more stories than she has because they're older.

"Then out she came," Louise says in a fresh, amused voice. "For effect, I suppose, she slammed the Dutch door behind her. She marched toward us, carrying a platter in one hand, her other hand on her hip. I stood up. She was so tall—"

"You were just short," Jude says.

"No, she always seemed tall to me."

"She was tall and she carried herself beautifully," Katherine says.

"But she didn't scare men," Jude adds.

"Men couldn't be scared then the way they can be today," Katherine says.

"I mean, she was proud but also very vulnerable."

"I know exactly what you mean."

Louise looks from one of them to the other, pouting. So often, her sisters mutually remark about things she never even noticed about Mother. Mother had always seemed big and fearsome to her. But she didn't scare men. What does that mean? Suddenly she notices the quiet. They're waiting for her to continue.

"She was so tall," Louise says. "She towered over me. She shoved the platter under my chin. She said, 'Here's your goddamn cheese toast.'"

"As if you'd asked for it," Jude says, chuckling.

"And that it had been a pain in the ass to fix," adds Katherine. "'Here's your goddamn cheese toast,'" she repeats, hooting.

"Watch your language," Jude says, cutting her eyes at her younger sister. This time, Louise is able to laugh.

"What did you do?" Katherine asks. She is struck once again by the original ways their mother found to pain them.

"I ran up to my room, crying."

"You should have said, 'Thank you, Mother,'" Jude says.

"I know that now. Then I was nine."

"What happened to the party?"

"It went on," Louise says simply. "A few minutes later I

heard Mother come upstairs and lock her bedroom door, and I went back down. She'd sent someone in to get the Cokes." Louise pauses before adding softly, "Everyone ate the cheese toast."

"They did?"

"They liked it better than potato chips."

"At that age, did you realize Mother was loaded?" Jude asks.

"Of course not."

"What did you think was wrong?"

"I didn't know. I guess I thought I'd done something to make her mad, but I didn't know what. Or maybe I thought . . . How do I know what I thought when I was nine? Besides, how do we know what had to do with drinking and what didn't?" Louise rubs her arms again.

"It *all* had to do with drinking," Jude says.

"I think you're wrong," Katherine says. "It was more complex than that."

"Bye, Mom. Bye, you two," Louise says, starting toward the car. "Although I want to hear what you're saying, I don't want to catch pneumonia."

Jude blows a kiss in the direction of the grave. Katherine tilts her head and then begins to follow. She had almost started to *explain* the complexity. They catch up with Louise to share coats.

"Did you swim the rest of the afternoon without a lifeguard?" Jude asks, which is something she would think of now that she has children.

Katherine answers for Louise: "I don't think they had a lifeguard before *or* after the cheese toast."

"I wonder what the other mothers thought," Jude muses.

"They probably didn't know."

"Someone could have *drowned*," Louise says in a suddenly angry voice. Although it was her story, she hadn't considered the implication of five nine-year-olds swimming unsupervised.

"But no one *did*," Katherine says.

They crowd back into the front seat, where Katherine always insists they all sit so that no one will miss anything. This time, Louise is in the middle. Jude starts the car and turns the heat on high.

"One of my friends could have drowned and it would have ruined my life," Louise repeats heatedly.

"You didn't even think about it until I mentioned it," Jude says. "Save your tears for something that *happened*."

"Of course, the possibility's horrible," Katherine says. "But nobody ever drowned in our pool."

"How do you feel about Carla Covington now, anyway?" Jude asks.

"I'm glad she's not *dead*," Louise says. She giggles. "I guess I'm glad. Carla wasn't exactly my favorite person. She told the whole fourth grade that we had spiders in our pool. Everybody who *has* a pool has spiders in it. And she pulled up my dress one day when we were standing in the lunch line. That was in second grade." Louise's voice grows more faraway. "And then in high school she sneaked and dated Billy." Billy was Louise's boyfriend from the ninth grade through her sophomore year in college. "I drove by her house one night, innocently, and his car was parked there. He always said he was visiting her brother. Maybe he was," she adds softly. "If somebody had drowned, though," she says, returning to her indignant tone, "it would have probably been Marylou, which I really couldn't have endured."

"No one *drowned*," Jude says in a thoroughly irritated voice. "Aren't you warm enough yet? I'm suffocating. How is Marylou, by the way?"

"Turn it down," Louise says. "I'm having lunch with her on Thursday. Do you remember when the professional baseball team came to town? You and Katherine had already gone away to college. Marylou married the first baseman."

"Are they happy?" asks Jude.

"Yes, they're happy," Louise says, her voice growing defensive again. It's a question her sisters always ask. *All* her married friends are happy. She's sorry, mildly sorry, that they can't say the same about theirs.

"I don't know a single person now that I knew in high school," Katherine says.

"I was always closer to my college friends," says Jude.

Louise wonders if they are criticizing her again.

"The first friends I ever made, I made in college," Katherine says. "But my *best* friends I've made since." The truth is, Katherine is not close to anyone right now. Secrets she might confide to potential friends she never does, thinking that the people she really wants to tell things to are her sisters. But she doesn't. "I never trusted anyone until after college," she continues. "Until after Frank, really. There's no set pattern, is there?"

They are not criticizing her, Louise decides. She hardly has any friends, anyway—from high school *or* college. Even Marylou is just someone from her past. They haven't talked to each other since Mother's funeral.

Traffic on Interstate Highway 85 is slow, partly because of the sleet, which is coming down steadily but not sticking, but mostly because of the Christmas travelers. Beginning with their parents' divorce fifteen years ago, they've each traveled this road hundreds of times, sometimes together, sometimes in pairs, sometimes separately. When their mother was ill those last seven weeks of her life, at least one of them traveled the road every day. Now they are on this road maybe five times a year.

The sisters are quiet. They can be comfortable together in long periods of silence, as long as no one begins to think that one of the others is being quiet for a reason. If that happens, then the possibility of an argument exists.

Of the time she spends with her sisters, Louise likes it best when they are like this. She can feel close to them now and not have to listen to their ideas, which are almost always identical, and try to reconcile them with her own. Between them, her sisters have persuaded her not to quit college, to go abroad for a year, and to dump Billy, who because he didn't go to college had become less and less suitable for her. "You've outgrown him, or you soon will," they'd said, although she could never have outgrown his sureness in the face of all her uncertainty. And now in less than six months she will have a degree in history from college, which is supposed to be important, as no doubt she will someday realize. Her sisters have lengthened her skirts, forced her to let the blond grow out of her hair, wiped off her blue eye shadow. But they *do* know so much, and it seems silly not to take advantage of their experience. And she hasn't had someone better—a mother—since she was nineteen, and, really, she may never have had a mother at all. The story most recently acknowledged by her sisters is that their mother fell in love with Max just after she married their father—when she was twenty-one and walked past him on the post-office steps. So what real mothering, except perhaps from Katherine and Jude, had she ever had? Three kids and seventeen years of marriage later for Mother, five kids and twenty-seven years of marriage later for Max—they found a way to be together. They'd waited all that time. True love, forever love, someday love was what she'd felt for Billy, so, to an extent, she's always understood what Mother went through. But it hadn't helped *her*. Motherless, she, too, now believes that Billy might not have been right for her.

She had a sort-of boyfriend, Gérard, the year she spent in Paris on Hollins College Abroad. Even though she was still taking birth-control pills, and she knew that Katherine and Jude would have said to go ahead and go to bed with him, she'd decided not to. It wasn't that Gérard wasn't handsome or that his English wasn't the sexiest English she'd ever heard. It was that she knew her sisters would have thought she should have the experience. How long will it take her, she wonders, to choose to act even if they agree? On the other hand, how long will it take her to stop doing what they say? She'll always regret not going to bed with Gérard. And she'll always remember that her sisters never knew he existed.

Of the time Katherine spends with her sisters, she likes best when the conversation is honest and careful. She loves her sisters as she would love different children, each for different reasons. As perhaps their mother loved each of them. Katherine knows she was their mother's favorite. It was Mother's talent that Jude and Louise probably thought the same thing. But Mother also hated her the most. And that was the difference. What Katherine loves about Louise is her solidness, which she used to regard as Louise's naïveté. Louise will not make many mistakes, because she won't take many risks. There's virtue in that, Katherine is beginning to realize. Jude, on the other hand, will do anything, which Katherine admires, too. While neither sister is totally her favorite, Jude is the only one who can truly upset her.

She knows so much about these two sisters of hers, and though they don't realize it, they know so little about her. When she assumed the position of surrogate mother so many years ago, she encouraged them to believe she was invincible, but she's surprised that they still think her so. They're all grown up now. How can they accept without question what she offers about herself? More than other daughters, they should realize that those bulwarks of strength—mothers—are not what they seem. Last October, at a dinner party she and Frank gave, Jude, drunk and behaving obnoxiously to the date they'd gotten her, announced that Katherine was the sanest person she has ever known. The tone of the remark brought it close to an insult, but Katherine knew Jude meant what she said. Being so sane, she can't tell them the dangerous thing that is going on in her life. For one reason, she fears they'd never recover from losing their belief that she has everything under control. It gives them hope that one day they will, too. For another, it would do *her* no good. They aren't old enough or experienced enough to give her advice. They're her sisters, though. Why don't they sense that something's wrong?

Of the time Jude spends with her sisters, she likes the sparring best. Not that she likes to fight—well, maybe she does—but mostly she likes the mental exercise. She's so much nicer to her kids, she's noticed, when she's spent some time with her sisters. She's more persuasive than either Katherine or Louise, and she feels a certain power over them when she's able to make more sense.

She knows more than they do, because, through no fault of her own, she's endured more. She lost the world that she always expected to possess—the secure world of marriage and family—and survived. Her sisters are scared. Scared that something might happen to them, too. But she's no longer scared. There's nothing left to be scared of when everything you thought you had is gone.

What happened was she finished high school and went straight to the same college as Cap, where they got married, and with family help she finished her education, because no one wanted him to grow away from her. Instead, she grew away from him because—though hardly anyone knew it (she'd taken pains to keep it concealed)—she was smarter and more ambitious than he and she wanted to be somebody. Except that she doesn't want those things anymore. It's all right that Cap's gone. What's been hard is no longer living where all her friends live, not having any money, not going to the country club every Friday happy hour, not doing all the things she'd grown up planning to do. But, thank God, she doesn't care about those things anymore. She's in the process of looking around to find out what she does care about.

Talking to her sisters, especially to Katherine, helps her define what she wants and she's discovered she doesn't want the same things her sister does. For years she would accede to Katherine's wisdom. But Katherine is no longer wise. She's become like every other married person: complacent, self-righteous, and boring. Safe, too. But she's also the sister that Jude at one time would have died for. Katherine is one of them, yet not quite. She's intense, too intense, when she ought to be so relaxed. Jude tries to fit her into the married slot—angrily, on account of how happy Katherine acts—but deep down she knows that Katherine doesn't completely fit. Katherine is octagonal, and the married slot, everyone knows, is round.

Sometimes Jude believes that the whole six years—hell, the whole twenty-six years—she lived in the manner of her parents—was a huge mistake, her trying to be someone she's not. It's hard for her to remember being ordinary or being happy being ordinary, but she knows that for all those years she was both those things. She's now as flamboyant as she was dull before. But was she really dull? She remembers trying to be dull. She remembers never saying about half the things she felt like saying. She remembers wondering if she really belonged, although what she and Cap had had was everything she knew she'd ever wanted. She is finally herself now: wild, free, open, exciting. Smart, independent, available. She hopes someone will notice.

"Are you doing anything tonight, Weezie?" she asks.

"Why?" Louise answers groggily. The sway of the car has made her doze.

"Never mind."

"I didn't even hear what you said," Louise says. "I was asleep."

"Lucky you," Jude mutters. She puts both hands on the steering wheel, instead of the casual hand she normally steers with. "I wanted to know if you'd come home with me and help me put the kids to bed."

Louise waits too long to answer, so Katherine says, "I will."

"I don't want to keep you away from Frank," Jude says. The comment is made without rancor, but Katherine knows her happy marriage has made Jude feel abandoned. She forgets how alone Katherine was those years Jude was married and she wasn't.

"You won't be keeping me from Frank. He can take care of himself for another hour."

The exit to Greensboro, North Carolina, their home, looms ahead. Jude takes it without slowing. She is a fast, purposefully reckless driver. Katherine, who is a fast, accidentally reckless driver, does not mind riding with her. Louise, who is a slow, careful driver, does. It's a two-mile-long exit ramp because of some politically motivated highway construction, and Jude travels it faster than she did the highway. Louise's body stiffens. She puts her knees together and folds her hands in her lap. Katherine considers intervening on her behalf but decides not to.

"I really don't feel I got to see enough of them today anyway," Katherine continues. Their earlier schedule was hectic: celebrating at their own homes (except Louise), celebrating with their father, sending Jude's children to ex-spouse and ex-in-laws, getting them back, leaving them with Daddy to go see Max, visiting Mother's grave. She's hardly seen her niece and nephew. "What's Christmas for?"

"Christmas is for families," Jude says sarcastically.

Louise draws herself up to say something, but Katherine discreetly elbows her. "Has it stopped sleeting?" she asks.

"Yeah, Katherine, it's stopped sleeting," Jude says. "I don't want you to come home with me," she adds curtly.

"Whatever," Katherine says. If she insists, Jude will resist more firmly.

"I'll be happy to help you put the children to bed," Louise says. "I haven't seen enough of them, either."

Jude doesn't answer. Katherine leans forward slightly to catch a glimpse of her face. She is squinting because of the headlights of an approaching car.

"All right?" Louise asks.

"Sure. Whatever suits you."

The next thing Louise is going to say is that if Jude doesn't want her to come, then to forget it. That she's doing the favor, and Jude should be appreciative. With all her powers of concentration, Katherine silently begs Louise not to say those things. She touches Louise's arm with her fingertips.

Louise turns angrily, but when she sees Katherine's imploring expression, dramatized by the passing headlights, she withholds the comment she was going to make. She feels the way she's always felt: that she just doesn't know the whole story. Maybe it's wrong to be so acquiescent. Maybe it means she has no center, which is how she so often feels. But maybe she's not old enough to have a center yet.

Jude has curled both arms around the steering wheel. She looks so tired. Almost involuntarily, Louise puts her arm lightly around her. Katherine, sensing the gesture, puts her arm around Louise. Tears that she is proud of fill Louise's eyes. Katherine is flooded with relief and gratitude and, once again, hope. Jude says gruffly, "What's all this?" But she feels that someone has wrapped her in the red velvet comforter Mother used to tuck around them when they were sick. The feeling is reflected in her voice.

CHAPTER

2

"When's the funeral?"

The quick shock on their faces that her daughters immediately conceal is what she has been waiting all morning to see. It's unfair, she knows, to make them suffer this way, but it's absurd for them to think she doesn't know. She's going to die this afternoon. She knows it, so why shouldn't they?

"There's not going to be a funeral, Mother. Look at you. You're sitting up for the first time in weeks." That is said by her oldest daughter, Katherine. If just Katherine were here, she thinks, they could talk about this approaching death openly. She could ask: When's the funeral? And Katherine would answer: When would you like it to be? She could say she wants to wear the burgundy negligee she wore the night she married Max, and Katherine would say: Fine. She would then add: Closed coffin, of course; and Katherine's face would relax, the idea of the negligee having not been quite appropriate in her mind, yet undeniable since it was the wish of a dying woman. She could say she wants lots of yellow roses, and Katherine would roll her eyes impatiently, since that was something she hadn't even needed to mention.

Perhaps she could have this same conversation with *each* of her daughters individually. It's when there's a crowd that things like this can't be discussed. But she *knows* she could have the conversation with Katherine, which somehow makes a difference in how she feels about her. Katherine *is* her; the other two are her, too; what Katherine is is *more* than her. Which is what has always so undone her. She tried to say it to Katherine once and then wished she hadn't tried. The day Katherine got married to Frank, she sent her a dozen long-stemmed roses. On the card she wrote: "I love you even though you are older and smarter." It was a joke, she said later, but both of them knew it wasn't.

She would like to ask Judith and Louise to leave so she can tell Katherine these things, and if she wasn't going to die, she would. Normally, she asks anybody to do anything she wants. But today she shouldn't. Today she should behave. They will always remember today. They'll pick every detail apart. They'll remember how they walked into the intensive care unit and found that she'd been moved into a private space, how they'd felt a sense of hope, even though for several days now the doctors had said they could no longer stop her lungs from filling up with fluid. They'll remember how she was sitting Indian-style at the end of the bed, not at all like an ICU patient, at least not like any of the ones she can see through the glass dividers. But they'll also remember that she let her legs show, her poor blue hairy skinny legs. She let them show so that they wouldn't think other than what was true. And they'd looked because they knew how proud she's always been of them. Beautiful legs, she once had. The narrowest, most delicate ankles. "Even your feet are beautiful." That was what James had told her on their wedding night. She'd been seventeen years old. Dear, sweet James. He was somebody she would like to see today, but protocol wouldn't allow it. *He* wouldn't allow it, so bound by protocol was he. Her daughters will remember that she grinned at them, her famous knowing grin, the one that lit up her eyes and made her whole face feel alive. She'd grinned and asked, "When's the funeral?"

Her youngest daughter, Louise, not so calm as Katherine, had cried out, "Mother, don't *say* something like that." It's *she* who's in pain, but Louise still thinks of her own hurt first, as young people do. Louise is only nineteen, with a face that will never look over twelve. Not like her own face. Or Judith's or Katherine's. A baby face, soft, pliant. Why shouldn't she think of the pain she feels on her mother's death day?

Louise will not suffer the most at her death. Judith will. When she asked her question, her middle daughter said nothing. Judith's jaw dropped, but the very personality in her eyes seemed to falter. Judith will think she did not have to die. Judith will think that someone didn't do enough. Judith will blame the doctors. And Max.

When later today she does die, Judith will think that even in death her mother remained true to form. Even in death she forced the issue. *She* would rephrase, if she could be here to rephrase, that even in death she insisted upon the truth. She insisted upon herself.

There must be many ways of knowing one is going to die, but this is the way it was for her. First of all, she awoke this morning feeling suddenly strong, as if some sort of life force were gathering in her arms and legs. They felt tingly, bristling. She felt her heart beating faster, an itching in her bottom. It was the first time she had felt well enough to contemplate sex in months. She was sorry she would not have one more chance at sex. Sorry that the last time she and Max had made love she hadn't realized she would never make love again.

Then the doctor came by to see her. They communicated with their eyes all she needed to know. On the scratch pad which in the last seven weeks had become her voice, she wrote that she would like for him to take her off the respirator machine. He had answered, "Right away." If his avoiding yet honest face had not told her so much, she herself could almost have begun to believe that she was at a turning point. And if she could believe it, knowing what she knew, no wonder it was so hard for them to see her and not hope. That was why she asked, "When's the funeral?" It was the only appropriate question.

The other reason she knew she was going to die was that she'd wanted to brush her hair. Brushing one's hair—truly brushing one's hair, she thought—belonged to the young and healthy. Bending over so that your head hung to your knees, electrifying your scalp with long serious strokes, and then flipping the hair back, training it the other way, distributing the oils so that every single strand glowed with health. She could have misread the desire to brush her hair, too. It could have meant that she was growing strong again. But her favorite nurse had handed over the brush with a freeness uncommon to the spartan ICU. Doctor's orders: Give the dying woman what she wants. She'd bet she could have a glass of vodka if she would only ask.

But then, despite her surging energy, she had not really been able to give her hair the workout she wanted, had instead had to enlist Gloria's help. And then she had had to force Gloria to brush harder, harder, harder, until finally the bristles dragged her scalp. It had hurt: her skin was thin and delicate from these long weeks of illness. She had wanted it to hurt. She had wanted something else to hurt besides the parts of her that had hurt for so long. She had wanted fresh pain to prove to herself that she was still alive.

When she raised her bowed head—not bowed between her knees as she would have liked but only barely inclined toward the mattress—Gloria had had tears in her eyes. Although by then the respirator had been removed, she did not speak. But with a long, lingering gaze she told Gloria that she appreciated her willingness to accommodate want rather than need when, in this terrible place, need so mercilessly predominated. Later she called Gloria back to make the ponytail. Her hair had not been washed in seven weeks. It would be washed tomorrow when there was no longer any fear of aggravating her lung infection.

One of them—she is not sure who—has asked her a question. "I was daydreaming," she says. "Did someone say something?"

"I said your hair looks neat," Judith says.

"Thank you, I guess," she answers. They must find it odd to hear her talking, although this raspy bubbling sound she makes can hardly be called a voice. It is good that they can *hear* her before she dies. Their last communication does not have to be with pencil and paper. She thanks her doctor.

In her life her hair has looked exotic, beautiful, crazy, in disarray—but never neat. She rather wishes Judith had not used that word. Perhaps she finally does look neat, but her hair, her whole head, feels humming with unneat energy. She has always worn her hair full around her face. Now it is as thin as a pencil mark.

"I know you can't wash it now," Judith murmurs by way of apology. "I'm just glad you had someone comb it. Doesn't it feel better?"

"It does," she says. She bends her head low so that with as little effort as possible she can reach her nape. With a violent tug that reverberates from her fingertips all the way to her heart, she yanks off the rubber band. Around her face her hair loosens, rises, comes alive.

"That's nice," Judith says.

She doesn't know why she made a ponytail in the first place.

She feels prettier now that she has loosened her hair, and with the feeling of prettiness comes that old desire to outrage them. With a single action she knows she has reclaimed the grip she has had on each of them since birth, the grip that never relaxed even the slightest until seven weeks ago, when suddenly they realized she was not immortal. Seven weeks for Judith and Katherine; maybe not as long for Louise, who even now might not really believe that her mother is going to die. Who, when it happens, will probably view her death with astonishment.

She sees in their faces that she looks more nearly like herself than she has in weeks. No respirator. Vitally brushed hair. And her own terry-cloth robe, which she now stretches carefully over her legs. She rubs her hands together, looking them over like something she has forgotten about. They have had a bluish tone for weeks. Now, even to her exacting gaze, they have taken on not a pink but at least a red glow, as if chapped. Can they be chapped? She thinks that this is July. No, they can't be. But they might be sunburned. All the hands of her daughters are tanned, she notices. Not as tan as they could be, since they have taken no beach trips this summer because of her illness. But still tanned. That's evidence that they have gone on living: one of them working, one mothering during her summer vacation from teaching, one relaxing after a difficult second year in college. Managing to visit her almost every day. Yet still they are going on, have hardly slowed their lives at all.

Could *she* go on living if one of them was dying? She thinks she will tell them the truth, which is no, no, a thousand times no. But mothers are fools that way for their children. And children, daughters at least, are never fools for their mothers.

She picks out Katherine and says: "If one of you had died before me, I could not have lived." All of them are silent. Tangling with a dying woman is something not many people are willing to do. And she has announced her death. She announced it prematurely, she realizes. Right now her body feels as if it has reached a plateau, a plateau she perhaps will stay on forever.

"Wouldn't you have lived for the other two?" Louise asks.

There is a stricken look on Judith's face. Because she has one child and one on the way, Judith understands exactly what she is talking about. But she doesn't turn the question over to her middle daughter, the only one who can answer from a mother's point of view. "Katherine?" she says.

"What exactly is the question?" Katherine asks coldly, although she knows very well what it is.

"The question is: Why would parents die for children and children not die for parents?"

"Nobody would die for anybody," Katherine says in an almost inaudible voice.

"That's not true," Judith whispers.

Louise begins to cry. "Why is she doing this?" she asks her sisters.

She stares intently at her youngest daughter. Louise cannot look her in the eyes. Instead, she glances back and forth from Katherine to Judith, with a beseeching expression. "Look at me," she commands. The strain of her anger makes her lungs shudder. She had hoped not to have to be suctioned while they were here, had endured a lengthy and intense suctioning just before they arrived. She takes several short breaths, trying to calm herself, trying to stave off this drowning feeling. She imagines her lungs filling up like a compartment in all those submarine movies. Will the sailors be rescued in time? In the movies they are. She thinks that someone might come take her arms and pull her out of her own liquid, someone like Max. Or perhaps she could simply lie out in the sun—the way she used to spend so much of her spare time—until all the excess water in her body evaporates. But she knows once more that a rescue is impossible: she is wet through and through.

Katherine puts a hand on Louise's arm, which gives Louise the courage to face her.

"It's just a question that I want to know the answer to," she says to them all in a steady voice. "I don't *blame* you. I just want to know the answer before I die." In fact, she doesn't blame Louise, who is too young to know, at all. If she blames anybody, she blames Katherine for just now saying, "No one would die for anyone." Isn't that what life is all about? Dying for other people? Not literally dying, but making choices that are sorts of deaths. That's how she has lived. She cannot bear that Katherine might think she's lived wrong. Or to think that Katherine might not believe what she believes. Or even to think that Katherine might never have understood. Katherine is her. Katherine is a better her. An older, wiser her.

Louise, in tears, lays her head on Katherine's shoulder. Katherine sends her outside to the water fountain. She expects her two older daughters to tell her, as they always have, to go easy on Louise, but instead they are each looking at her with frightening intensity, two entirely different visages.

Judith's always half-hostile eyes are filled with a sullen kind of fear. She is angry with the truth, as she always has been. Her delicate eyebrows draw up over her eyes.

A thousand questions fill the elusive haunted eyes of her oldest daughter, a thousand questions that she will never get to answer. But they are questions that could not have been asked before now.

"Let me talk with you one at a time. Judith first," she says, never taking her eyes off their faces. A look of panic that she easily interprets crosses Katherine's face. "I won't die before it's your turn," she says.

Katherine's anxious expression relaxes. "Be sure you don't," she says, grinning the lopsided grin that they share. Katherine's lips on her forehead are extremely warm. For a moment she wonders if Katherine has a fever. For only a moment . . . Louise returns, no better composed, and Katherine takes her arm. They stop to speak with Gloria, who for weeks has told all of them that she has never let herself get so close to a patient. Once Gloria even said she felt like a fourth daughter, which had brought polite smiles from the other three. She has already asked Gloria if she can have all the time she wants with her daughters. She expects that Katherine is making the same request.

The intensive care unit has been emptying in the past few days. One death, but also a number of surgical departures. Now only she and the old people and the man who was shot seven times by his girlfriend's husband are here. Frightening-looking people, those who come to watch the still-unconscious lover. At first she examined them for the lustiness that she was sure must dominate their lives, expecting to feel some sort of kinship. But she found only meanness in their crude, thin faces . . . and stupidity.

"Mother?" Judith says.

Her mind is wandering, as it tends to do when she's not getting enough oxygen. She takes several quick breaths, since she can no longer inhale deeply. "I'm okay," she whispers, though a great lurching feeling has just swept through her. Is she off the plateau for good? She feels the need to rest but doesn't think she has time. With a fierceness, she draws up her shoulders, straightens her back, opens her eyes wider, flexes her hands. Her mind summons all her mental energy. It returns, but feels tenuous.

Judith is the daughter for whom she used to feel happiest but now feels saddest. But she feels less sad than she once did—when Judith and Cap first started having problems—because Judith feels so sad for herself. Like her father Judith chose a sort of tenure-track existence by going to a proper college, by marrying the son of an important family in town, by choosing the right neighborhood to live in, by planning for two children. Through similar proper channels, James rose to vice president of the bank during their marriage. Now, despite the divorce, he is president. Both his and Judith's lives were totally describable long before the lives were ever lived. But then, for James, the unexpected happened. She forced change on him. Most people want to live without change. Or if it comes, they think they can deny it or defeat it. But in her experience those who resisted it most were struck hardest by it. Things always change. That's the only truth she knows. She thinks Judith and Cap will separate not long after this second baby is born.

Judith is now as fragile as she was once confident. Perhaps, when her bitterness leaves, her strength will return.

"I'm going to miss you," she says.

Judith's warm brown eyes—so identical to her own—stare unresponsively. She puts her hand to her mouth. Her lips move in myriad rapid ways. "Are you really going to die?"

"I am."

"I don't want you to."

"I know you don't."

"You're too young to die."

"I was always too young to do everything."

"That's different from dying."

"No. Actually, it's very much the same. I more or less chose to die, you know, by the way I lived. I always believed that I might go at any given moment. Not many people have something like that constantly on their minds, but I knew any day I was going to be hit by a Mack truck. So I lived the way I wanted to. It sounds crazy, but it was really very free."

The long paragraph has made her light-headed. What she has said is not really the way it's been. She did not choose to die. She thought, in fact, she would never die. Only careful people died. She'd chosen to live spontaneously, precisely so she would not die. So why is she dying? That's what she has been trying to figure out these past few weeks.

Earlier this morning, when Max came by to visit on his way to work, she had casually asked him whether he thought it had been worth it—losing so much to have each other and then her dying in no time at all. She was trying to make some sense of things. She watched him carefully as he answered, wanting nothing but the truth even now. Especially now. He'd ridiculed her words: "Worth it." He'd said relative worth had never applied to them. He'd looked at her with his searing blue eyes. She saw the awareness in his face that he could not make her live. He who had always been able to do anything.

He talked. She listened. Max could make her listen like no one she had ever known. It was as if his was the only voice she'd ever totally comprehended. It didn't even matter what he was talking about. His words went to her core and touched her spirit. It had always been that way. The shock was that it had never faded.

He said: "To me, you are the sun. You're undeniable, unquenchable, irresistible. You're the sun." He'd said it standing above her, not touching her, his hands in his pants pockets, making his summer jacket flare back roguishly. He'd said it in a soft, dry, unemotional voice, the only way words like those can be said. "You're life. My life is over when yours is through. I won't die, but I will die." He choked slightly, but then he smiled at her. "I've had the sun, buddy. How many people can say that?"

Raising her hand like a student in school, she whispered, "One more."

She had not told him that today is the day, and she is not sure whether or not he knows. But he hadn't commented about the respirator being gone. He'd pulled the curtain around the bed then and straightened her pillows and lifted her by her arms to a more comfortable position. She began pointedly watching him as he walked around the bed, tucking, straightening, patting the sheets. When he was through, he looked at his watch. Time to go to work.

"Lean close," she said, and when he did, she cupped his impassive face in her hands. He was the handsomest man she had ever seen. Unshaved, fat, or bleary-eyed—ways she'd often seen him, too—he was still the handsomest man she'd ever seen. It had something to do with how he could be vulnerable and unreachable at the same time. Hers, and not hers. She had known since she was a teenager that the real lovers of this world—of which they were two—came into being because of how someone walked up some steps or whispered when they talked or bent at the waist to pick up something dropped, rather than for any such reason as social or economic compatibility, which was why she had married James. Something ignited between two people and was never extinguished.

With her thumbs she put just the slightest pressure on the unbearable soft skin of the pockets under his eyes, feeling at the same time the roughness of his beard in her palms. She could only stand to look directly into his eyes for a moment. She moved her hands to his shoulders, whose breadth always surprised her, a breadth not remarkable to the casual glance but very noticeable to the spread of her arms. Finally, with one hand she reached into the curve of his body and felt tenderly of him. He had not smiled.

"I didn't mean I *chose* to die," she says to Judith, who has summoned Gloria. "I really chose to *live*, which has its own implications." With unexpected briskness, Gloria rolls over the oxygen tank and hands her a mask.

She suddenly realizes that by sitting up without support she is wasting energy she might need later. "Help me change position," she says to Judith, her voice thick. Gloria's raised eyebrows ask if she wants to be suctioned, but she shakes her head. Her legs come totally uncovered as Judith lifts her. She is amazed that in such a short time they can have lost all semblance of beauty. The skin is blotched and marred by bedsores.

"I don't look very good anymore, do I?" she asks. She wonders briefly if Max was moved by her touching him this morning or horrified.

"You look better than everybody else," Judith says, with a cursory glance toward the other beds.

"Frankly, I thought I'd be going to heaven in a little better style."

"We'll make sure you look good," Judith says. There is a startled moment between them.

"So you believe me."

"Always."

"Do you have anything to say?"

"I love you. You know that. I don't know what I'm going to do without you." She begins to cry.

"I hate that I'm not going to get to see your baby."

"So do I," Judith says, her whole body giving in to her sobs.

From this time on, she suddenly thinks, she will no longer have a separate relationship with each of her daughters. They will become a little group with a collective inaccurate memory of her. She resents in advance that she will be discussed, that they will develop certain uniform views about her, that she won't be here to make her case. She resents that she will become one *way* in their memory, a personality without the ability to strike a new course. It is maybe the *frozenness* of death that she hates most.

She touches Judith's arm. She's about to tell her to stop ruining their last few moments together, but Judith has stopped crying. Whispering, she says, "I've always loved you the best because you were the most like me." Faint pleasure glimmers deep in her daughter's eyes. Watching it grow, she adds, "You won't tell Katherine I said that, will you?" Judith barely shakes her head. "Or Louise." She wishes she'd mentioned Louise in the same breath.

"I think you'd better go get Katherine," she says. "I'm really . . . tired." She places the oxygen mask over her nose and mouth and leans back on her pillow. Judith briefly touches her limp hand, and then is gone.

When she senses that Katherine has arrived, her eyes are closed as if she is asleep. "Ask me," she says without opening them. She knows that Katherine is relieved. It was a practical joke to pretend she was asleep for their final conversation. Would Katherine have dared to wake her? She wishes she'd thought to give her the opportunity. The oxygen is making her feel alert again. As if she has on someone else's stronger glasses.

"All right," Katherine says. Her eyes are shining and nervous at the same time. "How can you . . ." She falters. When she begins to speak again, her voice is barely audible but intense. "How can you"—she averts her gaze—"claim that you would die if one of your children died, and yet when I was sixteen years old you abandoned me? How can you say that?"

"I never abandoned you," she says. She feels blood beating in her head. A loose trembling feeling spreads all over her body. "You abandoned me."

"You told me to leave."

"*No*. One night, you got mad at me and walked out the door and never came back. The next day, I found out that you'd gone to live with your father."

"You *told* me to leave. Don't you remember?"

"Of course I remember. I was angry at you. I didn't mean for you to leave for good. Yes, I remember. Don't ask me if I remember. We'd had the same fight five thousand times. What gave you the right to take the last one literally? I told you to leave because I was mad at you. I never told you, 'Don't come back.' In fact, I begged you to come back."

Katherine is silent. She is not beautiful the way Judith is beautiful, or cute like Louise, but she has grace and presence. Her blue eyes have looked sad since she was born, before she had reasons. Her mouth registers everything ever said to her and everything she would like to say. She's the most passionate of her daughters.

"I'm right. You know I'm right." She takes a breath from her oxygen mask. In a mollifying tone she continues, "I told you you could ask whatever you wanted. Ask now. This is your last chance." She is gasping shallowly, but Katherine doesn't seem to notice. "I'd prefer that you not attack me any further," she adds. "You're my favorite person in this whole world, and I'm about to die."

"The only thing I want to know is why you abandoned me," Katherine says in a careful voice.

She looks steadily at her daughter . . . at herself. "All I can say is that in my heart I never abandoned you. I made a choice to live with Max instead of your father. I made a home for you. And because you decided to take seriously something you'd never taken seriously before, you never lived in that home." She pauses. "Doesn't how you feel about Frank explain that to you? Wouldn't you make certain hard choices to keep him? It wasn't a choice to leave *you*. It was a choice to leave your father. I thought by now you would understand that."

"I've always understood how you feel about Max versus Daddy. I'm not talking about them. I'm talking about you and me. Why did you tell me to leave?"

"I'd told you to leave so many times," she says, shaking her head. "It was the way we fought. Why did *you* decide that one day you really would? Why, when I begged you to come back, did you say no?" She locks into Katherine's eyes with a sudden intensity. "We have the exact same questions," she says. "We always have." She hugs her arms around herself and closes her eyes. Softly, she weeps. Into her shoulder, so that Katherine cannot hear, she whispers, "I'm not ready to die."

"If it was the way we fought, it shouldn't have been," Katherine says.

"I know."

The silence between them is long and—because it has to be—accepting.

"I have another question."

Her forehead wrinkles. She would like to put her hair back into a ponytail because it's feeling itchy. "Spare me."

"You won't mind answering this." Katherine pretends to conceal a grin. "I want to know why you act like you never loved Daddy, when I know for a fact that you did."

"How do you 'know for a fact'?"

"I remember."

"You *don't*."

"You're right, I don't. But I know *you*. And I know you wouldn't have married him if you didn't love him. I don't think it's right for you to tell us you *always* loved Max."

This is just the type of question she expected. "Of course I loved your father. He was so competent and helpful."

"And tight."

"Very tight. I just happened to meet somebody who swept me away. I wasn't even looking. I've *said* I fell in love with Max when I was twenty-one, but that was just how old I was when

I met him. I was twenty-one when I found out I *could* love him. I didn't ever expect to be with him. And then all of a sudden the time was right. Right, not necessarily for you three or for his children. But right for us. I guess I've said I didn't love your father in order for you to understand the contrast. Men like Max hardly ever come along." She looks to see if the praise rankles, as it usually does. "Max is not a particularly *good* man. I don't think he has a thoughtful bone in his body. None of that applies. When I married your father, I was marrying a man who would be sweet to me." She looks momentarily away, wondering if she will get to see her husband again. "It was as if Max and I were two waves rising up to meet each other. It never changed."

She lies back down on the pillow. "Could you lower the angle of the bed a little?" she asks.

"Should I get Louise?" Katherine asks anxiously.

"Probably." She feels so overpoweringly sleepy. Oxygen would help. She hardly has the energy to hold the mask to her face, but she owes it to her youngest daughter.

They are all three standing above her and Katherine is asking a question that she doesn't understand. Louise's eyes are swollen, all the makeup washed away. Judith's face is drawn. The question is: Does she mind if they all come back in while she talks to Louise? She wonders if Louise is afraid of her or if they know these are her last few moments. She shakes her head.

Hoping for a rush, she tries the oxygen again. This time it gives her energy to open her eyes and smile at Louise. She takes more breaths. "You're my baby," she says. "And you know mothers always love their babies best." She does not expend the energy to look at Katherine and Judith, although she would like to see their expressions.

"I want you to do me a favor," she says. Louise nods, her tears flowing again. "I want you to tell your father goodbye for me."

"My father? You mean Max?" Louise's tears stop abruptly.

She grins. She regrets the use of energy, but she grins broadly anyway. She can't help imagining how the message will be received. How not only James but also her own daughters will always wonder what she meant. They'll think she still loved him even at the end. She did. But never the way she loved Max.

"*Mother?*" someone says sharply. They are calling her back, and she is so close to sleep.

"Yes?" She doesn't really see them, but she knows they are there. "The answer is yes," she says, her gurgling voice audible, she fears, only to herself. "The answer is always yes."

Before she lapses into a coma, she feels their hands touching her. She hears their sobs.

CHAPTER

3

Max, their stepfather, pauses as he always does before concluding the mealtime prayer. Around the table the sisters, seated among their men, open their eyes and look carefully at one another. His pause seems to hang in the air forever.

So falsely pious, Jude thinks, steeling herself for the coming words, which are always the same—guilt words. She wonders if after all these years Max is still ashamed of taking their mother away from their father.

Katherine directs the irritation in her eyes toward Max's bent yet, in her view, unhumble head. He is a large, heavy man with thick hands and wrists. His hands are folded on his plate. The plea he will make, she thinks, has something to do with the reason Mother is limping today, reportedly because she fell off the stepladder in the kitchen. Katherine forgives Max for hurting her mother, but she wants him never to forget that she knows it goes on. That she sees the broken locks, splintered doors, odd scars, and spills on the walls. Max does not routinely hit her mother. Mother asks for it and asks for it, and finally he breaks down and delivers, which is probably the worst shame she can make him feel. She wins their fights by making him use unequal weapons—wrecking his manliness. But he's weak enough to be wrecked. On Max's praying face is a look of true pain. At least he's sorry he hurt Mother. She sees that Mother is watching her—an accusing look that comments on Katherine's irreligion—and bows her head again.

Louise brushes her knee against Billy, who out of reverence, she supposes, does not nudge her back. Is it because he's a Baptist, too, that he doesn't find this kind of prayer discomfiting?

How could anybody be a Baptist, her sisters have asked ever since Mother married Max. She has told them that Billy is not the same kind of Baptist as their stepfather, but he is. She's just afraid for them to know it.

Max finally speaks: "And, finally, Lord . . . please . . . please . . . forgive us of our many, many sins."

Although his praying tone is known, expected, its tenderness always surprises Katherine. Max does not converse with them often, and when he does, it's with a strict, removed tone as if after ten years he doesn't really know them, as if he is outside their lives by choice. Nor has he ever spoken much to the various men they've brought home over the years, with the current exception of Katherine's new boyfriend, Frank. Maybe Mother and Max are only worried that she'll never get married. But Max seems able to talk to Frank. Frank is older than all the rest of them—in his mid-thirties—and well established in a legal career.

The silence continues. Does he expect a direct response from God?

"Amen," Katherine mutters.

Max lifts his head and looks directly at her. Mother's eyes snap open angrily. Baptists end their own prayers. Her Episcopalian sisters add faint reflexive "Amens" of their own but give no real support. Around the table, everyone changes position.

"That was typically rude, Frank," her mother says. "I hope you know what you've gotten yourself into."

"She's just hungry," Frank says. "Look at this spread." Everyone looks gratefully at the fat ham, the slightly scorched turkey, the big hunks of sweet potato, green beans, corn bread, the mound of cranberry sauce. Katherine sees a suppressed grin on Cap's face. Billy's eyes are wide. Neither of them can believe how easily Frank defuses Mother. She can't, either.

A moment of confusion overcomes her. Should she allow her boyfriend to interpret her, for the sake of peace, or should she be honest? She's not "just hungry." She was irritated by the embarrassing length of a prayer that after ten years is still foreign to her.

So far this Christmas Day, Mother is in control of herself.

Her hair is arranged on top of her head, not simply repaired, and she's dressed attractively in white wool. Sometimes when she welcomes them at holidays, the smile on her face only barely covers her general anger. But today her eyes open normally, and she seems not unhappy that they are here, troubling her at her invitation.

"I'm *not* just hungry," Katherine says. She wants Max to know that Mother's limp has not escaped her notice. She wants Mother to know that, although she likes Max, she still finds him very strange. She also wants everyone to know that she has Frank's full support for however she behaves.

"We *know*," Mother says, scowling at her, while Max begins to carve the turkey. "We know you're rude. We're just sorry Frank doesn't."

Katherine dares not look Frank's way. Will he be angry at her for keeping the fight going? Probably not. But it might make him guess at other things she doesn't want him to know. She waits to see if Max will say anything, but it seems, because of her mother's leg, that he won't. Jude stands up quickly, pushing back her chair and hurrying away from the table. She is barely pregnant and sick a lot.

They arrived in separate cars about an hour ago, an hour later than they promised Mother they'd be here, which meant she might be an hour drunker. But she wasn't. The house is decorated with all the sad artificial wreaths that used to be so pretty when they were children but are worn out now. A scrub pine from the woods sits decorated in a corner. Mother's taste used to lean toward the elegant; now it's early American, like Max's.

The men at the table, in addition to Max and Frank, are Billy, Louise's boyfriend since ninth grade, a slim smiling young man who wrestles in the 132-pound class for the high school team, and Cap, Jude's husband, a lanky would-be basketball player who, out of college, became a sports writer for the *Greensboro Daily News*. Neither has much to say, although when they do talk, Billy says kind things about other people and Cap makes jokes about Jude.

Everyone is to spend the night here, Jude and Cap in one bedroom, Billy and Frank in another, and Katherine and Louise in the third. It's unfathomable to Katherine that she will suggest to her baby sister they make a swap for part of the evening, but somehow she knows it will happen. Louise won't accept that Katherine is sleeping with Frank so early in their relationship—unable to understand how things speed up so quickly from age eighteen to age twenty-six—just as Katherine thinks it's dreadful that her baby sister, still in high school, is making love with a boy. They will swap anyway, because, for once, their desires supersede their interest in protecting each other. Although Louise doesn't know it, last week, after four months of dating, Katherine moved in with Frank. She thinks they will marry soon. She doesn't particularly care about marriage, but she's not against it, either. Frank, who has a position in the community, cares about it a great deal.

Jude returns to the table and Katherine stands to pour the wine. She can see her mother's face actually soften. Frank grins at her—his face is too impish to wear something so serious as a smile—so evidently she has not embarrassed him. She smiles too, glad not to have ruined Christmas lunch, but also pleased with what Frank looks like. He's adorable: thick hair, darker than hers, with cowlicks all over, and light-colored eyebrows which soften his face. He's only an inch or so taller than she, making them fit together, not just in bed but however they're together. Her other boyfriends have always been tall. She's more aware of Frank's face than anyone she's ever gone out with. It's a wonderful face. He's a wonderful man. She can't understand why no other woman has latched on to him. He's such an easy target—a *believer* in people. But he's never been seriously involved, he says, with anyone but her.

Raising her glass, Katherine makes a toast: "To Mother and Max on Christmas Day. I apologize for being so hungry for this wonderful food that I hurried up the blessing. Really, Max," she adds, her eyes finding his. He gives a brief, accepting nod. Mother glances at him and acquiesces. Crisis ended.

"I bought a couple of boxes of pigeons," Max announces.

"If anybody wants to shoot skeet, I thought we could go out after lunch." Behind the house the land falls gradually to a creek and then rises again to a wooded ridge. It is across the meadow that they aim their guns at the clay disks.

Neither Katherine nor her sisters could be called sportswomen, but they grew up knowing how to ride, swim, ski, and, since Max, shoot. They learned shooting as an apology, Katherine thinks, from Max to her. She'd been spending a weekend with Max and Mother about five years ago, when she was still in college. The two of them were in the living room yelling at each other about Mother's flirting at some previous cocktail party. Katherine came out of the kitchen to go to her bedroom just when Max hurled a set of keys across the room. Mother didn't duck; he simply missed. The keys caught Katherine's temple and dropped her, dazed, to the floor. Max never apologized, but soon afterward he told her he had something he wanted to teach her. She'd already sensed when they were helping her stand up that some permanent debt had come into being. It was only a bonus that she became an excellent marksman and that she loved to shoot.

"Do you target-shoot, Frank?" Katherine asks, aware that she doesn't know everything about him the way her sisters know everything about Cap and Billy. Frank is an exerciser instead of a sportsman.

"No, but I can learn." This is what she loves about Frank: his constant openness to new things. His parents probably sat by a fire and drank sherry and read poetry Christmas afternoons when he was growing up. Frank is from Rhode Island, a convert to North Carolina since the week he arrived at Davidson College. He'd planned to receive a gentleman's education in the South and then return North for law school, but he never even applied to his father's alma mater, Yale. Instead, he went to Duke.

"Ever shot a gun at all?" Max asks. There is criticism in the question but Frank doesn't notice. Max identifies with other men, Katherine knows, based on what he senses of their virility, their love of God and country, their experience with the armed services, and how much money they make. He appears genuinely astonished that Frank, a man successful in his work, a man he's felt comfortable with from the moment they met, might never have held a gun.

"Nope," Frank says. Many Southern men would want to lie if they couldn't answer that question affirmatively. But Frank is happy to be who he is. He'll probably find it strange that Katherine can average eighteen out of twenty pigeons with a .410-gauge shotgun. "Guns have never interested me," he continues.

Max's facial reaction to this statement is a little less subtle.

"I can sail," Frank says.

"Magnificent," Mother says. "We finally have a gentleman in the house."

Mother is walking a careful line, Katherine can tell. Is Max going to continue to accept Frank or not? Max begins chuckling at himself. Sometimes he realizes when he's being impossible.

"So I pass?" Frank asks. He hasn't missed a single innuendo.

"You pass," Mother says. "You get a higher grade than Katherine."

Billy, Louise's boyfriend, is a fine shot, which is the type of thing that makes Max say—through Mother—that everyone should give him a chance with Louise since he's not grown and no one can predict what kind of man he's going to turn out to be. Even at eighteen, though, Billy exudes a sense of unworldliness in which Katherine and Jude think he will insist on staying stuck. Louise is unworldly herself, but she won't be forever. Katherine plans to see to it that she's not.

Cap hardly ever connects, because he's too lazy to aim carefully enough. When Jude got pregnant in October, Mother joked privately that she was surprised Cap was accurate enough to cause the conception.

"How did Cap manage?" Mother asked over Thanksgiving, extending the joke to Jude. They'd had only one round of drinks, which Jude had refused. Cap was outside, getting another log for the fire.

"To what?" Jude asked. Mother reached over and patted

her stomach. Often Mother's tone alerted one to coming criticism, but this time both Jude and Katherine were unprepared.

"Make *this*."

Jude understood immediately. Katherine flushed, ashamed that she'd laughed earlier at the joke. Jude uttered a single word, "Chance," and looked at Katherine with tears in her eyes.

"Don't look to her," Mother said. "It was *her* question." Katherine shook her head that it wasn't. Later she tried to explain.

Everyone but Jude and Mother, who never eats, is steadily consuming this reasonably tasty Christmas dinner. Food helps their dispositions, Katherine thinks. It takes the edge off hunger, but also the edge off other kinds of desire. On a full stomach they'll feel less like arguing. But they won't want to aim a gun as carefully either, which is one of the reasons Katherine, who's also maintaining a svelte body for Frank, stops eating.

Max eats the way Katherine imagines he makes love—voraciously, although he doesn't and has never appealed to her. Besides the fact that he's her stepfather, he's past the age he could appeal to her. She thinks that at twenty-four she could be interested in a man as old as forty but no older. There's a sense of faded desire in men past forty, and at her energy level she couldn't be interested in faded desire. Max does not appeal to her at all. He's too rough and crude and unrefined. He knows how to *behave* exquisitely, but he has a lack of natural refinement that is innate to her father and Frank. Max is unreachable, too. He can't be possessed, not even by Mother. What Katherine has always longed for is a man whom she can possess body and soul and who also possesses her. Not a weak man, but one who finds her irresistible. For a man to be good at what he does and also adore her is all she has ever wanted. Max is good at what he does—a self-made plastics manufacturer—and he adores her mother, but he holds part of himself back. Frank is good at what he does and adores her and holds nothing back. She wants Frank. She's going to get him. She's already gotten him. She hasn't showed him her whole self, but she's decided it isn't necessary to show him her whole self. Frank thinks she should be happy all the time. She'll never be happy all the time, but he won't know it. She's going to let him see her as a lover and as a wife. But she's not going to let him see her as someone who's sometimes sad.

The devouring is over and everybody moves slightly back in their seats, except for Billy and Max, who are still picking a few last morsels from the serving dishes.

Cap says, "Oh, hell, I'll have one more potato," rejoining them. He always wears a slight smile, to put himself in a separate world from everyone else. It's his protection from Max and Mother, Jude has told Katherine.

"Through?" Max asks Frank.

"Stuffed," Frank says. He nods and keeps nodding to indicate how good he thought the food was. "I'd like to learn how to smoke a turkey."

"Nothing to learn." Max decides to load his plate again. Katherine thinks he's showing off. Gluttony, she might point out some time, is an uneducated way to show off, since it leads to heart attacks. *Would* Max fill his plate again to show what a man he is? To show how much more of a man he is than the other men here? Can he be that hungry? Katherine is proud of Frank's trim, athletic figure, his slim hips—slimmer than hers— and flat stomach.

"Make a fire under a bed of wet cedar chips. Cook the turkey slowly all night long," Max says. "Get up every couple of hours to stoke the fire and replenish the wood."

Frank nods and adds, "Fall asleep over lunch." Frank often has a distracted way of listening that makes one feel he has lost interest in the subject being discussed, but he is always highly attentive to Max.

"Not really," Max says, a twinkle in his eyes.

"I could stand a nap," Cap says.

An instant elapses—an instant in which everyone thinks how lazy Cap is—and then Mother says, "You know where the bedrooms are. You always have." Everyone pretends not to hear. Jude's stomach is too upset for her to stand up for him.

Max says to Frank, "Come help me set up the trap." He is

justified in not inviting Cap to participate, but not Billy. Louise stands angrily.

"Need some help?" Billy asks before she can say anything.

"Always can use some help," Max says, not even looking in his direction.

Cap, long used to being ignored, takes his plate to the kitchen. He comes back for Frank's plate, but Frank says, "I'll get it." Everyone except Max, who is still eating, rises.

When they pass each other, Cap says to Jude, "I'm serious about a nap. Join me?" Jude doesn't smile.

"Maybe after a while," she says.

Mother slips away, which is something none of them used to understand. Everyone but Louise and Billy, who are underage, is drinking: why doesn't she stay with the party? Except that once Katherine followed her to her bedroom and saw her retrieve a bottle from under the bed. She turned it up and drank for ten seconds without stopping.

The men leave, Cap deciding for sure to take a nap. How he'll be able to sleep, with the shotguns blasting outside his window, everyone wonders. Mother hasn't returned from the bedroom. "How about washing?" Katherine says to Louise. She and Jude always make Weezie wash because they have dry skin and she doesn't.

Jude begins wiping off the table, although she feels like lying down herself. If she joins Cap, she'll only further isolate them from the family. On the other hand, joining him might help perpetuate the myth that they're still in love. Actually, she does still love her husband, sort of, even though it's hard, incredibly hard, to keep loving someone who no longer loves you. Even if you're pregnant. The trouble with her and Cap, she's finally beginning to figure out, is that they started dating in the eighth grade and screwing in the tenth. When she was sixteen, she hadn't understood the meaning of passion. Or she'd understood that it meant fucking felt good. But fucking so young had eliminated the chance of real passion between them. By the time they got married, right after college graduation, it was simply comfortable—not a good way to enter marriage. How she wished she could tell about a million young girls what she knew.

Katherine is trying to find room in the fridge for what little wasn't eaten. Mother's refrigerator is a health hazard, as was their grandmother's refrigerator before it, as are Katherine's, Jude's, and eventually, presumably, Louise's. To their knowledge, this one has not been cleaned in the ten years Mother and Max have lived here.

Katherine feels some but not much guilt as she shoves the cooking pots onto the shelves. A woman with a minimal sense of homemaking skills would put the leftovers into plastic containers and wash the pots and pans. The last pot Katherine shoves in knocks over some jars in the back.

Weezie leans back from the sink, soap suds on her arms. "Are you really going to leave that mess for Mother?"

"God, Weezie, give me a chance," Katherine says, feigning innocence. A jar of maraschino cherries without a lid has overturned, and the liquid is dripping down four shelves.

"What we ought to do is clean out her refrigerator for her," Louise says.

"On Christmas Day?" Jude asks. She's resting against the counter, watching her sisters. If anyone asks, she doesn't feel well.

"It would take fifteen minutes."

"It would take two days," Katherine says. "I ought to wipe up this cherry juice, though." Louise passes her a sponge.

Louise returns to the dishwashing at a quicker tempo, her mouth stern. They are always against her. They never do what she suggests. Why do they think alike? Why doesn't she think the way they do? She wishes she did think like them, but she doesn't know how.

"Girls?" Mother has changed out of the white wool dress she wore at lunch and into some ratty blue pedal pushers. She is barefoot, and when she steps from the living-room rug to the hardwood floor of the kitchen, she has a quick moment of imbalance. She has taken down her hair, which at lunch was arranged in a French twist, letting it fall to her shoulders in thick unbrushed strands. "Girls," she repeats as if she doesn't see them only ten feet away.

"Here, Mother," Louise says without looking up.

"Max said to come outside." With an awkward step, she turns to leave.

"We're not finished with the dishes," Jude says dully. She's still leaning against the counter.

"Let's clean out the refrigerator," Louise whispers.

"*What?*" Mother says sharply. "What did you say, Louise?"

"Nothing. It was a joke."

"What did you say about me? This is my house. Tell me what you said about me." The voice, only a few minutes absent from them, has turned surly.

"I didn't say anything about you." Louise keeps washing the dishes. She never gets mad at Mother; she just walks out. "I thought we might do you a favor and clean out your refrigerator today."

"Keep your nosy little faces out of my refrigerator. Don't touch my refrigerator. Any of you. Get out of my kitchen. I told you Max wants you all outside." She moves toward them. Louise turns off the water. Katherine shuts the refrigerator door. Jude throws her dishrag on the counter. They start in her direction. It takes her more time than it should to turn around.

"Where are *you* going?" Jude asks in an arch voice.

"The same place you are." Mother's voice is deadly. She leads them crookedly across the living room.

"You don't have any shoes on, Mother," Katherine says.

"I know that, bitch."

"It's cold outside, Mother. It's Christmas Day."

Mother turns angrily, her hand raised to strike Katherine, but Katherine is too far behind. The fury on her face is undirected, as if there are enemies in the very air. On one hand, Katherine is embarrassed that Frank is going to see this. On the other, she's perfectly willing for Mother to show him what she's really like. Her stomach suddenly goes hollow. She doesn't understand why she never gets used to this. As they reach the hall, Jude slips away toward the bedrooms. Mother, miraculously, turns toward the steps leading to hers and Max's. Katherine and Louise look tentatively out the back glass storm door. Boxes of shotgun shells and clay pigeons sit on the driveway. Max, Frank, and Billy have got the portable release set up. Each man is holding a gun.

Spotting them at the door, Frank motions for them to come out. Katherine's whole body warms. Frank's presence protects her from Mother, but somehow Cap's and Billy's do not protect Jude and Louise. She should marry him for no other reason than that. They put on their coats, which are hanging on pegs by the door.

"I'm not going out there if she's coming out," Louise whispers.

"Max won't let her touch a gun."

"He hasn't stopped her from drinking. I think Billy and I will just leave."

"Don't do that," Katherine says. "She'll get mad at us for whatever you do, and then the day will be ruined for everybody." Louise says nothing. "Please, Weezie. Try to ignore her. Just because she's looking for a fight, you don't have to give her one. Pretend like you don't hear her."

"That won't work," Louise says.

"Try it."

"I'll try it once."

"Try it twice," Katherine says, sarcasm edging into her voice.

She opens the door. Is it possible for her to smile at Frank? She forces an artificial one onto her face, although she knows more or less what's going to happen. "Accentuate the positive," Frank would say if she told him how melancholy she feels. "What positive?" she would ask. But the exchange will not take place.

The transparent winter sun has vanished behind the clouds, which will make hitting the birds easier. But it's gotten colder. She doesn't shoot as well when her hands are cold. When she and Louise join the group, Frank puts his arm around her waist. Max probably thinks that's unmanly too, but he's wrong. Again.

"Show us your stuff," Frank says. "I've been hearing about your expertise with a shotgun, of all things."

"Why do you say 'of all things'?" she asks.

"You're just so feminine. I've never imagined you with a

gun in your hand. Have you ever killed anything?" There's a combination of horror and wonder in his voice.

Katherine feels uneasy. Can't she have different aspects? Can't she be feminine and kill a rabbit or squirrel or dove? She doesn't get a thrill out of shooting animals, but she's never felt sorry for them either. It's the way she grew up. *Won't he let her be sad?* "I've killed something before," she says, her voice solemn enough to make him think she didn't enjoy it. "But I prefer shooting pigeons. Clay ones," she adds quickly, and Frank's mouth forms an "O."

"Well. Ladies first?" she asks. Billy is holding the .410. She takes it from him and breaks it open. It's loaded. "I'm ready," she says to Max, clapping the gun closed. One of the nicest things about her shooting, Max has told her, is her liquid style. She doesn't aim at the sky, waiting for a pigeon. Instead, she holds her gun loosely, swings the barrel as if following the flight of the bird, and fires on the move. She doesn't know why she's such a good shot, but Max says she's a natural.

Her stepfather releases a pigeon. Should she for some reason miss? Her desire not to is too strong, and the clay bursts into a hundred pieces.

"Bravo," cries Frank. She has already signaled Max to release another bird, so there's no time to say thank you. She connects again.

They are in rhythm now, a rhythm established over five years of back-yard target practice, so Max releases the pigeons without her signal and she knocks them out of the sky and reloads. She feels tempted to add a flourish or two but resists. The beauty of her style is its simplicity. Max stops after twenty, her share, and with a flush on her face, she quickly passes the gun to Billy.

"That was incredible," Frank says.

"Good job," says Max. "I hated to stop you, but maybe this was the day you wouldn't miss."

What if it *had* been the day she didn't miss, she wonders. If so, they should have kept on, even if she shot all hundred and fifty birds. She could ask Max to let her continue, but now her momentum is broken. "Twenty was enough," she says.

"Do you ever *miss?*" asks Frank.

"Of course she misses," Louise says. She's standing hugging her arms, legs tight together, knees slightly bent. "She was lucky today."

"I was lucky," Katherine says.

"Lucky, my ass. She's good. She's damn good." The unexpected voice startles them all.

"Hey, buddy," Max says softly.

Mother has added socks, shoes, and a thin windbreaker. Her face looks suffering and exposed in the outside light. She smiles hopefully at everyone. Her lips are rough and uncolored. Because she has stood still for a moment, her next step—toward Billy—is another awkward one. She reaches for the gun he is holding.

"Not today, buddy," Max says.

At the same time Louise blurts, "You're too drunk." She's embarrassed that Mother considers Billy the line of least resistance.

Billy doesn't know whether he's expected to withhold the gun or not, but when Mother's hand closes over the barrel, he lets go. At least it isn't loaded. Or shouldn't be, if Katherine loaded nine more times and shot twenty birds.

Max reaches for the gun. Mother smiles a sheepish but engaging smile, but when he almost has possession, she jerks back her arm. He steps steadily forward as she steps back, grinning. Katherine glances at Frank, whose face is quizzical and slightly pale. Mother's not going to *shoot* the gun, she wants to explain to him, although she thinks it's something he ought to realize himself. This is a game. This is nothing. There's no threat of violence now. There's no threat of violence when no one is really mad about anything. Sometimes at this house there *is* a threat of violence, but it always relates to deep, passionate matters, not jokes. She's angry at Frank for being frightened. He's hardly had time to get to know her family, but he ought to realize—simply from knowing her—that there's nothing to *fear*.

Mother yields the gun to Max, her haughty gaze sweeping over them all.

Katherine hooks her arm through Frank's. There was anger between her mother and father, but never the threat of violence she's always felt between Mother and Max. When she was younger, it frightened her, but now she knows why it exists: between them the emotion has never been killed. Instead, it's grown stronger and less controllable. If one day, for example, Mother shot Max or Max shot Mother, she would not be entirely surprised. She would tell people that yes, they adored each other, and by that she would mean that murder was not out of the question.

Mother has begun to shiver from the cold, and Max asks Katherine to take her in by the fire while he gives Frank some pointers on shooting skeet. Louise has disappeared, pulling Billy down the driveway for a walk. Katherine wishes she wouldn't apologize to him for the way they are.

"Come on, Mother," she says. Mother is staring vacantly over the valley, her shoulders slumped. She can be guided now like a child, but Katherine doesn't want to take her arm. Why is she drunk on Christmas Day, when all the people she loves are around her? Why isn't she happy?

"Come *on*," she says again. Mother takes a vague step forward, not in the right direction. Katherine walks briskly toward the house, expecting the click of her shoes to attract her mother's attention.

"Katherine," Frank calls.

She turns. The two men are looking questioningly at her as if she has bypassed a crying child.

"Could you help your mother?" Max asks.

Mother is his responsibility, Katherine wants to say. He wooed and won her, so now and forever she is his responsibility. Behind him and Frank, the light is beginning to fade. Dusk will drop quickly because of the thickening clouds. The valley is as quiet as one of their never-lived-in bedrooms.

Mother turns finally and begins to follow her, and without a word Katherine again reverses her direction. This time, her step is not brusque but soft. The anger inside her has already begun to break down, but she takes a sharp breath to reconstruct it. She waits for Mother to catch up. They walk side by side, their hands occasionally touching. The feel of the sad chilled skin should soften Katherine's heart but doesn't. She does not love her mother, because it is too dangerous to love her mother. At any moment her mother's love can turn to hate. Mother seems so helpless, though.

Katherine's anger continues to crumble. She may be unable to maintain it, but she won't let love replace it. She'll be neutral. It's what she's promised herself since she was sixteen years old and Mother told her once and for all to leave. She fails at this promise over and over, but one day it will stick. She *will* be neutral. In a similar way this is how she is becoming the love of Frank's life. By not being real. By never being sad or melancholy or even desolate. By being happy . . . all the time. Frank is in love with her, she knows. He is in love with a mirage. It's a mirage she intends to be for the rest of her life.

She and Mother climb the brick steps together. The house is quiet except for the buzz of the forgotten oven timer, which Katherine heads for, leaving her mother at the living-room doorway. Suddenly she remembers her superb marksmanship. Did Mother see her perfect score, or was she just rebuffing Louise?

The barest feeling begins to build again in Katherine's heart. This is not love, though; it's gratitude: she is grateful to her mother for noticing her skill with a .410-gauge shotgun. You cannot love someone who hates you, even if they hate you only some of the time.

Mother has disappeared when Katherine returns to the living room. The noise of a shotgun filters through the house. One blast, and then nothing for a long time. Then another. She wonders how well Frank is doing, but instead of going out to watch, she sits on a knee warmer in front of the fireplace and stares at the orange coals. A little flicker of light appears and then vanishes, and then the coals begin to go gray.

CHAPTER

4

"I really didn't expect your father to be so nervous," Mother says. "I had no idea he was a . . . V."

"*Virgin*," Louise quickly supplies, since she knows the abbreviation was made for her. She is lying on the sofa in Mother and Max's bedroom, looking at the ceiling, while Katherine, Jude, and her mother are arranged in various positions on the king-size bed. "There's nothing wrong with that word," she adds. "It's better than the opposite."

"What a mouth," Katherine mutters.

"Shut up," Louise says.

"*You* shut up," Jude finishes impatiently. Is she going to be asked whether or not Cap is a virgin? How will she answer?

Mother sits cross-legged on one side of the bed, her hair loose around her face, an unlit cigarette jerking in her mouth whenever she talks. The bedroom is an enormous room, big enough for a graceful table for two at which Mother and Max often breakfast, a small tiled fireplace, the elegant high-backed sofa where Louise has planted herself, two plush armchairs, and an exercise bike.

Katherine lies on Max's side of the bed, her head propped on a pillow. Every few minutes she sits up before a small magnifying mirror, which she holds between her knees, and plucks another hair from one of her eyebrows. It was her idea for them to spend Jude's wedding weekend at Mother's. A girl ought to be with her mother the night before her wedding, she thinks. She ought to have an afternoon of girl talk with her and her sisters. Katherine promised Jude that she will watch Mother and not let her get drunk and spoil everything. Even though Mother is drinking a beer, she is not worried. Secretly, she is certain that the importance of the occasion will keep Mother sober.

They arrived yesterday morning in time for the bridesmaids' luncheon. Mother had been at her best, charming in the way that she, of all people Katherine knows, can be. Mother never moves from person to person at a social occasion. She finds someone and listens to him and asks him questions and before it is over she is the person's best friend or at least the confidence that the person has shared with her is "best-friend" confidence. And Mother means it. Lots of people who don't know her very well love her. After the luncheon the three of them sat around the pool for a couple of hours while Louise went bike riding. Mother had been perfect there, too—making knowing but not pugnacious comments about their friends' parents. And Katherine had first begun to feel correct in her intuition. It was right for them to be here.

She watches her mother smoking, eyes half shut in laughter. Sometimes Mother says something so apt that it becomes an effort to stop laughing. Sometimes Mother is so attentive to them that she is amazed. This morning Mother brought Jude breakfast in bed. For lunch she fixed Jude's favorite: tomato sandwiches, which she made far enough ahead for them to get real sloppy. After lunch she presented Jude with an ice-blue peignoir set, more beautiful than the one Jude herself had selected for tomorrow night. It makes Katherine wonder if they were wrong to have left here. Should she have forgiven Mother and come back? What have they missed? But then she remembers that she *did* come back once. She didn't come back the *second* time. And she remembers that these times with Mother never last. Though the bedroom is warm, a cold nervousness begins to fill her. It's always when she remembers that the good times don't last that Mother begins to change.

Jude sits at the foot of the bed, her legs stretched straight in front of her. She lies flat every few minutes and raises her toes toward the ceiling. Her hair is rolled around large plastic curlers that keep having to be rerolled because of her exercising. Mother has been fine all day, but she's started drinking a beer. Just one beer, Jude reminds herself. Her shoulders shudder reflexively. She laughs aloud at a funny story Mother is telling about their next-door neighbors. She seems to have forgotten the subject of Daddy's virginity. Mr. Underwood serves his guests cheap whiskey poured from a bottle with a premium label. He serves the good stuff to himself out of a decanter. "But people do have taste buds," Mother adds. "I can tell that this is a Schlitz," she says, holding up the can. She knows she is making them uneasy.

Louise rises up from the sofa into a back bend. Then she lets it go and falls flat. She is bored that they are here. Somebody ought to be home with Daddy. If she were home with him, she could also be with her friends. She's not interested in a description of her parents' wedding night. The thought grosses her out.

"Go get me another beer, Louise," Mother says.

Mother is trying to get rid of her the way she always does when she wants to tell Katherine and Jude something "grown-up." They think she doesn't know anything about sex, but in fact, just a moment ago, she proved she does. A virgin is someone who hasn't had any. She learned everything at her fourteenth-birthday pajama party last spring. At first it was hard for her to believe what happens between a man and a woman. Then it was harder to believe that anyone would enjoy something like that. But Carla Covington had finally convinced her. The source itself made her slightly sick.

"*I* want to hear about you and *Max*," Louise says, so that everyone will know just how informed she is. Mother and Max, *not* Mother and Daddy, are the ones who have an exciting sex life. She knows from hearing Katherine and Jude talk.

"That's rude, Louise." Mother's tone is more abrupt than Jude expects, considering how well they've all been getting along. But then her voice softens. "I promise not to say another word until you get back."

Louise wonders if she ought to take the time to say what her best friend at camp told her about getting eaten by her boyfriend. Again, the idea has been more than she can visualize, but she has come to realize that people do some very gross things. Not her.

Jude stops her legs at a halfway point in the air, straining for the sake of her stomach muscles. "Go on, Louise," she says. "We'll save the dirty stuff for you."

Louise leaves willingly. Jude grows attentive. Despite her reluctance to spend this weekend here, she's feeling closer to Mother than she's ever felt. She thinks of herself as in the process of bypassing Katherine. She's about to become a married woman. When she does, she and Mother will have something in common that Mother doesn't have with Katherine. Next, she will have children. She'll become as different from Katherine as they are now alike. And perhaps they will never be the same again. Yesterday Mother confided to her a worry about her sister: "Why do men leave Katherine?" Jude has never thought of it that way. She had always thought that Katherine hadn't met the right man. But both Katherine's last two boyfriends broke up with her. Maybe something *is* wrong. She lets her legs drop to the bed.

"Your father was very suave," Mother says, her eyes focused on some spot across the room. Her face is buoyant because of the presence of her three daughters. This is the way she would like for it always to be: to have them here with her. But no matter how she entertains them, they never stay. They don't love her enough to stay. Even when she gives them everything she has.

"He slid my straps off my shoulders and let my gown drop to the floor," she says. "Can you imagine your father doing that?"

Neither of them answers. Katherine can perfectly well imagine her father making a sexy move, but it's so embarrassing to hear about it. By the end of the story—worst of all—everyone is going to be angry. Jude thinks her father would be a very tender lover. She is touched to be hearing this.

Louise's footfalls sound on the stairway.

"I can't say the rest," Mother whispers.

"You told them something," Louise accuses. She has brought Mother's beer.

"No, she didn't," Katherine says. She still hopes that Mother will tell only the first half.

"He looked me up and down and said . . ." Mother pauses

to find a church key in the drawer of the bedside table, since Louise has forgotten to open the beer.

"Don't stop now," Jude says in mock lasciviousness.

Mother jacks open the can. "He said, 'Even your feet are beautiful.'"

Jude's eyes close. She holds her legs in midair again. She hopes Cap will say something like that to her. She hopes he'll say or do something to make their wedding night special. Not about her feet necessarily. If Cap told her her feet were beautiful, she thinks she would probably laugh. What difference does it make what her feet look like? But Cap may not think of anything to say at all. They've been doing it so long she wonders if there's anything new he could think of.

"That's the kind of man I want," Katherine says. "One who tells you even your feet are beautiful." She hopes Mother might admit what a lovely comment it is.

"No, you don't," Mother says.

After a silence Katherine says, "Please don't start criticizing Daddy. Not today."

"We'll all leave if you do," Jude offers. It's a hollow threat, since not long from now they'll have to start getting ready for the rehearsal dinner, but Mother gives a look of acquiescence.

Then her face changes. "You asked to hear the story," she says. "You need to know about your father. All of you need to know."

Jude can't remember asking to hear the story. She looks angrily at Katherine because she's not helping. "Daddy and Cap have nothing to do with each other," she says.

"They certainly do."

In a cajoling voice Katherine says, "You promised you'd be nice, Mother." Then she adds seriously: "This is Jude's wedding weekend. I think we ought to try to make her happy. Really. Let's all do everything for Jude. Think of her and no one else." She doesn't look at Mother as she speaks. The idea may have appeal; it may not.

"I just worry that she's making a mistake," Mother says. She looks challengingly at Jude.

"*Katherine!*" Jude implores, rising from the bed.

"*Mother!*" Katherine says.

"At least Judith has the *opportunity* to make a mistake," Mother adds.

Jude glances at Katherine, wondering what Mother means. The slightest change, a sort of widening of the features, comes over her sister's face. Jude realizes what Mother meant. But, now, what difference does it make that she's getting married first? In Mother's view, her marriage is a mistake. How can a mistake be better than not getting married at all?

Louise stands up and walks without comment out of the room. It's so easy for her, both Katherine and Jude think.

Suddenly Mother winks. "Now I can tell you the rest of the story." She motions for Jude to sit back down. "I'm not going to say anything bad about Cap. I promise."

Jude hesitates. Did Mother call her wedding tomorrow a mistake just to get Louise out of the room? She studies the smiling, seemingly unaware face. Then she looks at Katherine's tight expression. The air she is breathing seems suddenly to go thin. Should she denounce Mother's unfairness or ignore it? She supposes she can endure any insult if the final result is that tonight Mother behaves.

"Have I ever told you what he wore?" Mother asks.

Jude sees Katherine nodding. Katherine has been told everything at some point or other. Sometimes Jude thinks it's because Mother loves Katherine best, but most of the time she knows it has nothing to do with love. Mother grins. She has a lopsided grin that is very endearing, very youthful. Katherine often has the same expression. Not now, of course.

"Black silk pajamas," Mother says, as if the memory is pleasant. "With a red dragon embroidered on the back of the shirt." She looks at her fingernails, which are brightly painted for the weekend. "When I was seventeen I thought they were dashing."

"But now you think they're silly," Katherine offers in a brittle voice. She takes off her glasses, which she is wearing to rest her eyes from her contact lenses. When her glasses are off, she tends to talk more frankly. It's because she can't see the expression of the person she's talking to. At the same time, she also feels physically vulnerable. She would not be able to avoid a slap.

"Not silly. I thought they were an excuse," Mother says.

"Do you have to get into that?"

"An excuse for what?" Jude asks. She might as well know what Katherine knows.

"It's just more criticism of Daddy," Katherine says. "It only makes us mad at you, not him. You can't make us feel about Daddy the way you do. You can't make us love Max either." Katherine puts her glasses back on. Is she trying to orchestrate a smooth weekend or would *she* rather fight, too? "We love Max and we love Daddy," she says strongly. "Just let us love them both."

"I'm not criticizing your father. I'm just trying to warn you against passive men. You and Jude particularly. Neither one of you would be able to live with a passive man."

"Cap isn't passive," Jude says.

"Daddy isn't passive," Katherine says.

"He was afraid of me. He didn't know what to do. He would rather have worn the pajamas than take them off."

"Did *you* know what to do?" Katherine asks.

"I expected him to have intuition. I expected him to want me."

Katherine's cheeks burn fiercely. This is too personal, she wants to say. Also, it isn't true. She knows innately that her father is some sort of lover. Not crazy/wild, necessarily, but tender, even careful. "I'll bet you were a wonderful bride," Katherine says. "I'll bet you made Daddy feel like a real man."

"A real man doesn't have to be made to feel like one."

Katherine's shoulders suddenly go limp. Why does she ever believe that Mother will behave any differently than she always has? Why does she think she'll be strong enough not to rise to the bait? If Jude's wedding is ruined, it will be all Katherine's fault, because she had tried to think how she would feel if she were the mother of the bride.

"Jude's old enough to know about this," Mother says.

Old enough? Jude wants to say that in a way she's older than Katherine.

"There's nothing else to tell," Katherine says, suddenly wondering if there could be more to the story of Mother and Daddy's wedding night than she has heard. Mother is bluffing, she decides. Long ago, she first heard this whole manipulated tale. Nothing has ever been left out.

"Get me another beer," Mother says to Katherine.

"You don't need another beer." Can she be finished with number two already? When did she drink it?

"Do it."

Which is worse? To get the beer or to have Mother send Jude, who will be afraid to refuse? How is it that when she is away from Mother she feels that she has some measure of control over her, but when she's here she feels totally powerless? Why doesn't she remember how things are, before she comes? And why is she hurt when Mother remarks that Jude is getting married first? She has settled all this in her own mind. When Cap and Jude decided to get married last fall, she was dating Paul May, who was in med school at the university where she'd just graduated. Although they were basically only sleep-together friends, she idly considered really going after Paul with letters, tiny gifts, and stronger sex, so that she and Jude could get married at the same time. But Paul was too single-minded to be interesting enough to marry. And he would never adore her. She does not mind that Jude is getting married first. In a way, it fits: the "mother" getting everyone taken care of before she takes care of herself. She's going to have a long wait with Weezie, though.

"I'll get the beer," she says. She can get the beer slowly. She can pour it into a mug, which someone told her makes it less potent. She can even run the can under hot water before she brings it upstairs. Mother won't drink warm beer.

And then she suddenly thinks of Max. Won't he keep things under control? Can't he make Mother do what he wants? It shames her to want Max to *make* Mother behave, because she

57|

has an idea how he does it. But this time she wants him to, anyway. She'll even ask him to.

The thing she least understands about her mother is why she doesn't try to please. Don't people who love people try to please them? It's not enough to be whatever you are and expect to be lovable. You have to be good; you have to be the best you can be. Has Mother never loved Max enough? Or them? Is that what's wrong?

As she leaves the room, Mother is telling Jude that Daddy bought the silk pajamas in Japan while he was on the world tour that his parents arranged to get his mind off her. The part about abandoning the tour is a story they all know, but Jude is nodding as if it's fresh material. From the Philippines, Daddy cabled home that he'd seen enough of the world. Next on his itinerary was Hawaii, but included in the cablegram was his suggestion that Hawaii would make a better honeymoon spot. He would "save" Hawaii for her, he said. In three days he was back in North Carolina.

"I still think that's the most romantic story I've ever heard," Jude says. She is glad Katherine has left. Sometimes she thinks that the only reason Mother is difficult is that Katherine makes her that way.

Mother smiles. "I know you do. Of course, your father was a fool."

Jude has heard this comment before and dismissed it. This time, though, she tries to understand what her mother is telling her.

"We had the rest of our lives to be married. Besides, it didn't even turn out." Mother puts another unlit cigarette in her mouth.

"But he loved you more than anything."

"Sometimes that's not what you want in a man." The cigarette bobs.

"I don't understand how you can say that." Jude is wondering how much Cap loves her. More than anything? Would he come home from abroad to marry her? "*Max* loves *you* more than anything," she suddenly observes.

"That's true. But it's different. Your father was too devoted to me. I sometimes even think it might have worked if he hadn't come home. I was disappointed in him. Can you understand?"

Jude shakes her head disbelievingly.

Katherine has been standing just outside the door, not able to break away. She sticks her head back in the bedroom. "You couldn't have felt that way," she says. "You were seventeen years old. You *had* to be thrilled."

Mother stares at her without speaking. Jude has a critical look on her face. It's as if they each feel she has interrupted a private conversation. But she was part of that conversation only seconds ago.

"It got so he couldn't make a decision without me," Mother says quietly to Jude.

"Isn't that what people want?" Jude asks, in an equally intimate voice. "That's the way I want Cap and me to be." She does not glance again at Katherine, and Katherine decides to leave to get the beer. Jude never realizes when she is walking into one of Mother's traps.

Jude watches Mother contemplate her question. She hears the steps creak and knows that Katherine is finally gone. From the forthright way Mother is talking to her, she feels that Mother, too, is beginning to feel this same sense of connection that she herself is feeling. They will both know things that Katherine will not know, not for a while and, if Mother is right about Katherine and men, perhaps not forever.

"I don't think I can explain subjugation to you," Mother says. "You'll just have to see for yourself. Your father stopped acting like a man. I know that's what women say they want nowadays. For men to be *people* instead of men. But I want my man to be a man. Or at least not to melt into me so much that we become one person instead of two. It takes away the compellingness of the other person, don't you see?"

Jude doesn't agree, but she nods anyway. "Cap's very unique," she says. "I think we're about as good a balance as two people can be. I'm serious; he's sort of crazy. He's relaxed; I'm sort of ambitious. Don't you think that's good . . . to be different from each other?"

"Sure," Mother says.

"You don't mean it."

"It just wasn't what I was talking about. Sit closer," Mother says. Jude moves within reach, and Mother takes one of her hands between her own. She wonders if she should feel suspicious, but she really trusts her mother right now, trusts her to speak to her best interests. Her own mother could not speak any other way.

"There are really no rules about love, honey, except that maybe people end up always wanting what they don't have," Mother says. "I think you and Cap are going to do great together. I don't think he's the most exciting man I've ever known, but you need to remember that I compare everyone to Max. It's not fair, but I do. And Max, as a man, probably wouldn't even catch your eye. I'm not speaking literally. You know what I mean. Max thirty years younger wouldn't appeal to you." She watches Jude carefully. "Would he?"

Max thirty years younger is something she can't imagine. Besides, Max is sort of mean and quiet and doesn't have much sense of humor. Cap says the funniest things she's ever heard. "I can't imagine him young," Jude says.

"But he's *so* young," Mother insists. "Not even he realizes how young he is," she adds in a faraway voice. Changing tones again, she says, "I shouldn't have even asked the question. I knew you couldn't answer it." Mother stares at her.

"He doesn't appeal to me," Jude says.

"Nor does Cap appeal to me."

Jude's eyes suddenly well with tears. They have each answered the same question, yet her answer was only honest and Mother's was hurtful. Everyone knows that Max is an exciting man; why won't anyone say that Cap is? No matter what Mother says, she loves Cap anyway. She will always love Cap. Once they are married, they will become closer and closer until they are like two halves of one person, which is the way everybody *else* in the world thinks it ought to be. Mother is just from a different generation. She first thinks of men as men rather than as people. That just shows how narrow her relationship with Max must be.

"Cap is cute," Mother says.

"So is Max," Jude adds quickly.

They are trading wary smiles when Katherine returns with a beer for each of them. It's occurred to her that Mother might be continually angry at them for never drinking with her. The appearance of the multiple cans delights Mother, but Katherine can see the concern on Jude's face. It's just an idea; maybe it will work, maybe it won't. Mother's eyes are sparkling. She looks as pretty as the bride-to-be. If there still *is* a bride-to-be.

"What *time* is it?" Jude suddenly cries.

"Five forty-five," Katherine says.

Jude hastens to her feet as if she feels the pressure of time. In fact, she feels only an unexpected desire to get away from her mother. She is partly worried about how Mother will behave tonight, but she is suddenly more upset about what they've been discussing. Has Mother been telling her not to marry Cap? She's afraid to ask.

"I'm going to start getting ready," she says. She carries her beer with her, not looking at her mother or her sister. She's mad at them, and they, she guesses, are mad at her.

This is a handsome house that Max and Mother built for all of them, large, but also small, in that there is only one huge great room to live in, the expansive master bedroom, and a separate sleeping wing for the three of them. Katherine walked out on Mother six months before Mother and Max got married and they were all scheduled to move here. She'd made Jude and Louise leave, too. She told them they wouldn't be able to bear the fights with Mother if she wasn't around to protect them. She even warned that Jude would be the new target of attack. But that implied that Mother attacks indiscriminately, which Jude no longer believes. Mother really attacks only Katherine. If Jude had stayed here, she believes she and Mother could have gotten along. They're getting along now. It's just that they don't agree about Cap.

She passes Katherine's bedroom, an "adult" room, and continues to her own bunk-bedded room. Just seven years ago she was a full-fledged tomboy. Had she actually remained here, the bunk beds would have given way to a canopied double bed, the throw rugs to white carpet. She loves having *been* a tomboy, but now that she's grown-up, she wants her room at her mother's house to show it. The present decor only serves to remind everyone of that painful time. When two years ago she asked that Max and Mother redecorate her room to suit her age, though, Mother had responded with a bitter "Why?" So perhaps the anachronism will last forever.

After a while she hears Katherine coming down the hall, passing her own room, passing Jude's, and pausing at Louise's door. For the past seven years Katherine has "managed" Louise, telling her to do her homework, to get dressed, to eat. She also shops with Louise, makes her doctor and dentist appointments, and tries to keep her from making too many mistakes regarding her personal appearance. "Someone has to take care of her," Katherine says, but Jude thinks Katherine likes the power.

"Get dressed," Jude hears Katherine say. "You brought your pastel striped dress, didn't you? Wear that and stockings. You have to wear stockings. We're going to church and to the country club. You *have* to wear them."

Of course Louise argues.

Katherine says, "Think of someone besides yourself for a change." She closes Louise's door firmly.

At Jude's room she stops to say, "Mother's fine. She's in the bathtub, and she didn't even drink all of that third beer. I think she liked it that I drank some with her." After Jude had left, Mother had even toasted the bride and bridegroom, but Katherine decides not to tell Jude that. It seemed more like a curse than a blessing. "I asked her please to behave tonight and tomorrow, for your sake, and she promised she would. Don't worry. I can't stand to see you so worried."

Katherine's face shows no emotion. She's upset about the way they excluded her, Jude knows. Jude hadn't meant to be that way: it just happened. "If she ruins my wedding," she says, "she would have ruined it whether we were here or not."

"Not necessarily," Katherine says. "I sometimes think that just asking her to behave is what makes her misbehave. Sort of like asking Louise to wear stockings. Only you can't trust *not* asking her."

"Louise is fifteen. Mother's forty-two."

"I don't know if it makes much difference." Jude has a stricken look on her face. "I *am* sorry," Katherine continues in a lower voice. "I talked you into coming here. I had this romantic idea of how things ought to be."

Jude begins to weep, yet she keeps her eyes opened wide, focused on Katherine. "Do *you* like Cap?" she asks in a stricken voice.

"I *love* Cap," Katherine says without hesitation. "I think he's wonderful and warm and funny, and I think you're lucky to be marrying him." She forces herself to walk to Jude and take her in her arms. She rocks her back and forth. Jude smells just like a bride-to-be: light perfume and faint soap. "You don't ever learn, do you?" she whispers. None of them ever learn, she reminds herself, forgiving Jude's shifting loyalties.

"She can't ruin tonight. She can't ruin tomorrow," Jude says in a stronger voice. She pulls away from Katherine and looks out her door. "I'm going to tell Mother she may not come to my wedding at all."

"Wait a minute," Katherine says.

Jude turns. "I don't want her there. I know what she's going to do. Something *horrible*."

"She'll be fine," Katherine says. "I'll talk to Max and tell him how worried you are. He'll help us. I know he will." Katherine is certain that Max will be sympathetic. But she doesn't know what he'll be willing to do.

Jude's face calms the slightest bit. "Shouldn't *I* talk to him?" she asks.

"No. It's my job."

She'll talk to Max based on when he hit her with the keys last year. She'll adopt that same tone of intimacy he has occasionally offered ever since he accidentally hurt her, so he'll understand how important it is that he do as she asks. She has never told Jude about the accident, Jude always being suspicious of "accidents." It was Jude who first showed Katherine evidence that Mother and Max's fights were physical as well as verbal. But another reason she's never told is that she never wanted any pressure from her sister about when she was going to "collect."

This is the first moment important enough to remind Max of his debt. He has to do more than be nice to her and teach her how to shoot a gun.

I know how you and Mother fight, she is going to say when he gets here. And I don't want to cause another argument. But you've got to make her behave during this wedding. And I don't care how you do it.

Will he understand all the hidden messages?

"I'll handle everything," Katherine says, a surer tone in her voice. "Don't worry anymore. I've figured out what to say."

She goes to the great room and sits in the dark, so that she can intercept Max when he arrives. Soon she hears his car and rises and stands in the shadows, ready to appear when he opens the door. She is so anxious to make no noise that she scarcely breathes. Max opens and closes the door. Did he slam it? He walks into the entry. Is he stomping? She steps out of the shadows, a finger to her lips, when he is taking off his coat and laying it over the banister. Her appearance startles him.

At the same time, a groan comes from the direction of the bedroom.

"Buddy," he suddenly cries. "What's wrong?" He takes the six steps to his and Mother's room in two strides, disappearing from Katherine's view. It sounds as if he's stopped her from falling. Then Katherine hears an indecipherable murmuring. No words are clear, only Max's gentle persuasive tone. Mother is sobbing.

"You just can't stand to see your daughter—" she says. The rest is garbled in a fit of coughing.

She waits to see if Max will come back down to talk to her, but the door closes and she hears the dead bolt fall into place. She doesn't really need to talk to him, she realizes. By seeing Mother, he will know why she was standing here. She just won't be able to remind him of what he owes her.

Why isn't he angry at Mother, she wonders. Doesn't he care if she embarrasses them all? Perhaps, though, she begins to hope as she tiptoes down the hall to dress for dinner, Max is in the bathroom with Mother now. He may be making her throw up, bathing her in cool water, laying out her clothes. Katherine makes a prayer to Max, a prayer that—like all her prayers—skips God. If there were a God, she decided long ago, her mother wouldn't exist.

She goes to Jude's door. Her sister's face is clear, happy, sure of Katherine's ability to make everything all right. She is taking out her giant plastic curlers. Her makeup is complete, but she would be glowing anyway.

"Mother's fine," she says. What else *can* she say? "Max just came in." She turns, as if she's in a hurry to dress, before Jude can thank her. All her sisters ever do is criticize her; maybe she deserves it. She turns back to say, "Cap's a great guy. Really he is." But her voice sounds funny. She's begun to wonder if Mother is right.

CHAPTER

5

The August heat hangs throughout the upstairs. Katherine is sitting at her desk, which, when school got out in June, she converted to a dressing table complete with mirror, bright lights, and all the makeup she has bought to give herself a natural look. She is fifteen years old and not very pretty. She hates makeup, but according to her mother, she needs makeup, so she practices with it daily. She does have nice legs, like her mother, and a better than average bust, but her face is squarish, which she is trying to compensate for by wearing a pageboy hairstyle, and her nose is too large and her eyes too small, all of which she is altering by her growing expertise with colored creams.

She shares this room with Jude. At least, she does right now. It's a large room with space for a bed for each of them, Jude's desk, Katherine's dressing table, and a large chest of drawers, which they share. Mother says that she wants Katherine to move to the downstairs guest room so she can have some privacy. But Katherine doesn't want privacy. One weekend when they were off visiting Daddy, Mother moved her clothes to the downstairs closet. Katherine had slept in the guest room for a few days and then, without saying anything, moved back upstairs. Mother had not commented.

For the fifth time in an hour Katherine dabs at her face with astringent. The breeze from the attic fan, which feels only warm to the rest of her body, feels ice-cold to her face. All three bedroom doors—hers and Jude's, Louise's, and their mother's—are open. One window in each room is cracked to create a draw— just like a fireplace, as their father used to explain at the beginning of every summer. He didn't say it this year, though, because he's living in his own apartment. So the night when they'd first needed the fan, way back in May, Katherine said the words herself: "Remember, everybody, it works just like a fireplace, so raise one window, just one in each room, about five inches." Mother had laughed. It was the first time she'd laughed gently about something regarding Daddy in years. For a moment Katherine wondered if she might miss his company, but deep down she knew Mother didn't.

Also, now there is Max. Max isn't supposed to exist yet, since separations must last two years, but he is there at the end of their long driveway waiting to pick up Mother, who these days takes many long afternoon walks. Or there waiting on the telephone while one of them fetches "Mrs. Patterson" in from the pool, where she lies in awkward positions trying to perfect her tan. Or there at a restaurant where they have gone to eat and unexpectedly run into "my friend Max," no last name. Katherine knows. She might not have known, but she knows because their father told them.

"Your mother has a boyfriend. *Has* had," he said the night he took them to see *Where the Boys Are,* a movie much too adult for Louise, though Daddy hadn't seemed to notice. Then he drove them home and told them good night, and they all got out of his car and walked to the rarely used side door, where, oddly, Mother had left a light on for them. They had forgotten to kiss him goodbye, and just as they reached the porch, he tapped the horn lightly. The sound might have been meant to summon them back, but all three of them—as if they were one person—only threw a single arm behind. Nobody turned around, not even little Louise.

At first, Katherine wasn't sure Daddy knew what he was talking about. In all her and Mother's walks up and down the driveway, Mother had never mentioned that she might love somebody else. That night she sneaked Louise into their room. In bed in the dark she told her sisters that if it was true Mother had a boyfriend, *she'd* never heard about it, and she heard *everything*. She'd expected to have to soothe them, but instead they were excited. Jude hoped that Mother's boyfriend had lots of money. Louise hoped that he had a daughter her age. Although she didn't say this aloud, Katherine hoped he could calm her mother down. She'd thought that Daddy's leaving would make Mother less agitated all the time, but it had not. Daddy was right about Max, Katherine found out the next time they ran into him at a restaurant. He'd called them each by the correct name: it was a dead giveaway.

Because the bedroom doors have to stay open in the summer, all of them are more aware of one another now than in other seasons. Katherine and Jude have more fights with Louise. Mother comes by their rooms more often to glare at them. Or, if she is not glaring, to gaze blankly at them as if she were looking at strangers. Katherine knows, though, that if they *were* strangers, her expression would not be blank but engaging and curious. No one but them sees the real her. Katherine and Jude actually have fewer arguments in the summer than they normally do, for the same reason: open doors. It's because they want to keep their arguments, which are usually about Mother and secondarily about Louise, a secret.

Louise and Jude are out somewhere in the neighborhood, perhaps around the corner at the Garrisons' playing Kick the Can or No Bears Out Tonight. Katherine is willing to play Kick the Can, but she hasn't played No Bears since last summer when Mr. Garrison, who was the Bear, grabbed her by the waist from behind and pulled her butt tight against his crotch. The worst part, though, was how he growled in her ear like a bear and kept growling until all the people who hadn't gotten caught came out of their hiding places. By then she was fighting to free herself, only succeeding, she realized later, in looking like a bad sport. She has told Jude and Louise not to play No Bears, but she hasn't told them why, because she's afraid they'll blab.

It is seven o'clock. They are having no dinner tonight. If they were, Mother would have appeared by now at Katherine's door and asked her the same old question: Did Katherine think the dinner was going to walk upstairs? To which Katherine had recently answered yes and received a hard slap across her face.

She and Mother had been standing on either side of the threshold of Katherine and Jude's room. Jude was sitting on her bed picking her toenails, her amusement over Katherine's remark suddenly frozen on her face. "It was a joke, Mother," Katherine said in a voice devoid of pain.

Her grief over many things was once boundless, but she has learned not to feel pain. Sometimes she's proud she can't feel it. She has thought for a long time that her ability to be sad is dead.

After Mother's slap, she'd instinctively turned her burning cheek against her shoulder, but then she brought it back into full view. Mother didn't apologize, but Mother teaches that apologies are false. How she behaves is who she is, who she will always be. She does not intend to change, even if she could. She isn't sorry. Either you like her or you don't. Although Katherine realizes that this kind of thinking is arrogant, she has always believed her mother had a point.

All afternoon—until about an hour ago—Mother's room has been quiet. With the noise of the fan, it seems impossible that Katherine can make enough noise to disturb her, but still she has picked up and set down her makeup tubes and bottles with great care and moved about her room on tiptoe. Once she picked up a straight pin with her bare foot and did not cry out. As soon as her sisters come home, she'll go downstairs and they'll all have cereal or soup. She'd go now—she's hungry enough—but something keeps her here. A dangerously balanced truce exists: if she stays in her own room, she believes Mother will stay in hers.

In the last forty-five minutes Mother's noises have been neutral noises. She would open a drawer, let the handles drop, close the drawer softly. Or she would go into the bathroom and turn on the water, let it run softly for a minute or so, close the handle carefully. Or she would flip the pages of the telephone book, find a number, close the book, and set it back under the phone, which makes little dinging sounds when she moves it.

But in the past few minutes she has opened a drawer and flung it shut. Seconds ago she slammed down the telephone receiver when this time and the one before there wasn't an answer. Now Katherine hears her jerking something out of her closet. Hangers screech across the rod as if they are being thrown to hell. Most of Mother's clothes these days show evidence of some sort of mistreatment: a tear, a stain, a missing button.

Katherine feels her face go ashen. Her stomach knots and her arms feel weak. Nothing is going to happen. Responding in advance like this only draws Mother to her the way a dog advances to bite you if he smells that you're afraid. Katherine tiptoes to her bedroom door and closes it. The breeze in the other two bedrooms will increase, but she hopes Mother won't notice. More than anything in the world, she wants to lock the door, but she doesn't.

She hears her mother in the bathroom again. Something glass drops on the floor and breaks. Katherine sits down at her dressing table, taking deep breaths. She picks up a blue eye pencil and with a wavering hand makes a heavy mark under each eye. She coats her eyelashes with mascara. After the mascara has time to set, she will feather her lashes into thickness with a toothbrush. She'll tissue away the excess pencil.

Something hits a wall in her mother's room. Something that's been thrown. It sounds like the telephone book. Katherine jumps up from her dressing table. A bottle of nail polish falls on its side, making the tiniest clunk. She takes a deep breath and walks again to her door. Mother is coming down the hall. With a shaking arm, Katherine quietly turns the bolt. She doesn't breathe. She doesn't move. Her stomach waits. The doorknob turns quietly. Then it rattles like money in a can.

"Open this goddamn door," Mother shouts. She shakes the handle and the door shakes. She beats on the wood. She shakes the handle again. "Katherine!" she yells.

Katherine tiptoes across the room to her dressing table. She will speak to her mother from there. But then she remembers that the door is locked. She hurries back to it. Quietly, she unbolts it, and then leaps in two giant steps back beside her dressing table. She picks up the old toothbrush that she now uses on her eyebrows, holding it so tightly that her fingers hurt. "It's unlocked," she calls. "Come on in."

Mother opens the door and stands holding the handle, her arm as stiff as a stick. "Why was your door locked?" she asks.

"It wasn't," Katherine says. She tries to look neutral, innocent, while her heart slams in her chest. "You just didn't turn the handle all the way."

Her mother has on underwear and a full slip. Because of the weight of her breasts, her bra straps cut like ropes into her fleshy shoulders. She looks pleased that Katherine has lied. Katherine tries to maintain a steady expression.

"Do you expect supper to walk upstairs?" Mother asks in a mocking tone.

"No, Mother," she answers, equally mocking. She can't tell if her mother is joking with her or not. But perhaps so.

"Where are your sisters?"

"I don't know."

"And you don't care, either."

Katherine doesn't answer. In a sense, she supposes her mother is right. She has not, for example, told Jude and Louise about Mr. Garrison. And she doesn't really mind if he does to them what he did to her. In a way, she'd rather they be disgusted by him the way she was than be terrified about some future encounter.

"You don't care, either," Mother repeats. "*Do* you?"

"No, I don't care, either." She debates whether or not to add the next sentence. In an impassive tone she says, "I hate my sisters. Everyone knows that."

Mother comes into the room and sits down, in profile to Katherine, on Jude's bed. "You've always hated them," she says. It's as if she's talking to herself. "Which they don't understand, but I do. You hate them because they're prettier than you are and because they're nicer than you and . . . because they don't put out for boys."

Katherine's heart goes dead in her chest. She has heard the other two accusations many times, but the third one is new. She can hardly go on standing.

Without looking at her, her mother says, "You screwed J. T. Thomas in the back seat of my car last weekend while I was at the movies with Peggy. I know you did, so don't say you didn't. I found the empty pack of rubbers. Your boyfriend's pretty careless, Katherine. The package wasn't even *tucked* anywhere."

Mother pulls a rubber pack, black with gold writing, out of her bra. Katherine easily recognizes it since she was the one who went in the men's bathroom at the Phillips 66 service station to make the purchase. Mother twirls the pack in the air and then tucks it away again. "I have no real interest in what you do with your life," she continues. "What I want to talk about is what I'm going to tell your sisters."

"About what?" Katherine asks.

Mother turns and looks at her for the first time since she sat down. Katherine's lungs heave, yet she feels she is suffocating.

"You *can't* tell them anything. Why would you *want* to tell them anything?"

Mother smiles in a strange way. "Oh, I wouldn't tell them about you and J.T. . . ."

"It's not even true," Katherine inserts.

"I'd be too ashamed to tell them about you and J.T. I just hope *you're* too ashamed to tell your friends about you and J.T. Because once you tell them, you won't have them anymore."

"It's not true," Katherine says. "I wouldn't tell them anyway, but it's not true. I don't know anything about that pack of rubbers. I've never even seen a pack of rubbers." Then a brilliant thought strikes her. "Maybe it's *your* pack of rubbers," she says.

A furious look comes over her mother's face. Although Katherine is frightened, she still thinks that she might be right. Maybe J.T. got rid of their pack, the way he was supposed to. She knows that her mother didn't go to the movies with Mrs. Craven. Should she say that?

"You need to learn to lie better," Mother remarks.

Katherine lowers herself to the stool in front of her dressing table, feeling with both hands to pull it under her. What has she admitted? Nothing, really. She could be this upset about Mother threatening to tell her sisters something terrible about her that wasn't true.

"Look, Mother, I didn't do anything," she says, her arms

hanging limply at her sides. "Even if I wanted to, J.T. wou——"

"Even if you wanted to, J.T. wouldn't," her mother mocks.

"He really wouldn't," Katherine says. Her voice has become almost conversational, she notices. Sometimes Mother can be wooed away from a fight if one is careful and interesting and not condescending. If one makes it absolutely clear that if Mother *wants* to fight, the fight will continue.

Katherine is not sure this will work, but since she's getting older, maybe they can tell each other the truth more often. Maybe if she says, "You weren't out with Mrs. Craven Saturday night, anyway," then she can explain how she just wanted to try sex, that it wasn't raging desire but curiosity that made her talk J.T. into going all the way. J.T. isn't speaking to her now, anyway.

"*What* did you say?"

She didn't know she'd said anything. "I said you weren't out with Mrs. Craven last Saturday. She called here wanting to know where you were. I covered up for you. I said you were next door."

Katherine stares at her mother, waiting and hoping. She has not thought this out, but some elemental instinct tells her that she cannot take the time to. The same instinct tells her that if she thinks at all, she will fail to act. She reads perfectly the expression on her mother's face. It is both surprised by her daughter's perceptiveness and vulnerable to her criticism—an open, waiting face. What Katherine wants to say is that whatever Mother does is just fine.

She rushes to the bed and sits beside her mother, covering Mother's hands with her own. Her eyes show all the hope that she feels. She thinks how so much about them is alike. They look alike. They think alike. Maybe they love each other. She is not as tall as her mother yet, but she hopes to be. Maybe she will also be as strong. In an impelled yet quiet voice she says, "You're right about me and J.T., Mom." She notices how incongruous the word "Mom" sounds. She wishes she could call her mother by name.

Mother sits slack-faced, unjudging, but her hands lie stiff. Is this the best approach, Katherine wonders. She fumbles to intertwine their fingers, but Mother's hands are unresponsive. It may be shocking, Katherine is beginning to think, to find out that your fifteen-year-old daughter is no longer a virgin. But it happens to everyone sometime. Just a little earlier than usual to her. Not as early as it's happened, for instance, to her friends Penny and Delores and Frances, and for a different reason—they're going to *marry* their boyfriends—but early. Not *too* early, she thinks. If she can just explain to her mother that going all the way with J.T. didn't mean anything, that she was simply ready to find out what grown-up life was like so she could get on with her individual experience, she is sure Mother will understand.

Should she say that it was an interesting sensation with no great pain or pleasure attached? Should she say that it felt not at all the way she expected the first time to feel—a slight stretching of herself to allow the entry of a slick fish? She'd always imagined that an erect penis would somehow be comparable to the wild eels they had caught as girls on vacation at Morehead Beach. But J.T.'s penis, at least, had not been like that at all. It grew enough to make its way inside her, but otherwise was as quiet as a carrot.

Her mother's hands seem suddenly to explode. "You cheap little whore," she says. "Look at the junk on your eyes." One hand catches Katherine's stomach. The other travels wildly in the air. They appear to move involuntarily, but Katherine is aware of the purpose in the hand that has struck her. Frantically she grabs at her mother's arms, but her mother raises them high, out of reach. They each stand. She hears what Mother is saying but knows she doesn't mean it or won't mean it as soon as she understands.

"Let me tell you why," she says, finally seizing her mother's shoulders. Her tone is brave and pure. She knows that Mother will accept what she has to say. If she will just listen. "Let me explain," she says in a more insistent voice.

Mother grows silent for a moment, as if she is going to listen. "Let go of me," she says quietly.

Katherine stares, her hands like clamps on her mother's cool flesh. Then she lets her arms drop to her sides. "I want to explain," she says.

"I don't want to hear it," Mother says. She seems to be matching Katherine's countenance in the opposite: her eyelids heavy, her chin lowered almost to her chest, her face heavy with scorn.

"It's not what you think," Katherine says, her voice wavering. Suddenly she hears Jude and Louise pounding up the stairs. "Wait," she says. "I don't want them to hear this."

"Why not?" Mother asks. A strange gleam fills her eyes.

Jude steps into the room behind Mother. She has on shorts and a bandanna shirt. Her skin glistens with dried perspiration, which Katherine can smell. Louise passes through the hall to her own room.

"Jude's here," Katherine says in case Mother hasn't noticed.

Jude sits on the bed and begins to examine one knee, which is dirty but not bloody from where she has fallen down. Not so long ago she would have retreated to Louise's room during one of Katherine and Mother's fights, but lately she stays. It is less to try to protect Katherine, Katherine thinks, than to see for herself how the fight progresses. Doubt about Mother's meanness has sprung up between them. Katherine is not sure why, but she suspects Mother talks about her to Jude. Jude has been questioning Katherine's descriptions of their arguments. She criticizes Katherine for not being more compliant. She says that Katherine knows Mother is not herself right now. But when has Mother ever been "herself"?

"I don't care who's here," Mother says. Her brown hair stands almost artificially about her face. It is thick luxuriant hair which has always made her look younger than any of the mothers of Katherine's friends.

"Please be careful what you say," Katherine says.

"Famous . . . last . . . whorish . . . words."

"*Mother!*" Katherine yells, but it's too late.

Jude stretches her knee straight ahead of her as if to test for soreness. Her face is blank, but it's the blankness of intense concentration.

"This is the last straw," Mother says. "I'm through with

you. I'm not going to have you in this house anymore being this kind of example to your sisters. You can't live here. You have to leave." Her voice, which has loomed almost like God's, suddenly becomes very specific. "Now," she commands. "I want you to vacate these premises."

Katherine waits for the change of mind which so often comes after her mother has said something terrible. But Mother's face is like a mask. She doesn't look as if it's pained her to say what she's said. Jude brushes at her knee. Another member of this family who's totally unaffected. Katherine and her mother stand like stone pillars.

Finally, in a soft but slightly triumphant voice, Katherine asks, "Did you hear that, Jude? Mother's throwing me out. I just want to make sure you heard."

Jude does not look up from her knee. "I only heard the last part," she says in a faltering voice. "I didn't hear what *you* said to *her*."

Katherine stares at her sister, but Jude will not look up.

"You have ten minutes," Mother says. "Jude, I want you to go in Louise's room while Katherine gets her things together."

Jude rises quickly, still not looking at Katherine. "Why don't we all just go downstairs and have some supper?" she asks. She's beginning to look less pleased with herself.

Mother grabs her arm and pulls her through the door. Jude's eyes flare wide in amazement.

"Leave her alone," Katherine says, her voice finally rising. Mother pulls the door closed behind them. As loud as she can, Katherine yells the same words again.

"Why are you hurting *me?*" Katherine hears Jude whimper. Then Louise's door opens and slams shut.

Katherine turns and looks around her room. Not many minutes ago it felt like her only refuge. Now, suddenly, the room isn't even hers anymore. It belongs to Jude, or soon will. Now, suddenly, she doesn't mind leaving. Her sisters don't know what it will be like here without her. They have no idea.

This is just a fight, she tells herself. The worst fight they've ever had, but still just a fight. Probably before she even has time to get her suitcase out from under the bed, Mother will come back in and ask her to stay. Whether she asks or not, though, Katherine is leaving. She'll walk out the door with her suitcase hanging from her fingers. If a neighbor slows his car to ask where she's going, she'll explain forthrightly that her mother has just told her to leave home. Where she's going, she doesn't know. That's the truth, isn't it? And she's decided at this moment that she's going to live by the truth. Yes, she went all the way with J.T., if anybody wants to know. She wanted to see what it felt like. Not much. She's also been drunk before. She's also made straight A's, and she can play the flute beautifully. She's even a good mother, although her sisters would deny it. Yes, she's leaving. And she'll tell her mother, or anybody who asks, that she's leaving this time and she'll return once, probably tomorrow. But if Mother ever makes her leave again, she's never coming back.

In case anyone does see her, she decides to pack her less obvious beach bag, as if she's going on an overnight. In it she puts underwear, a nightgown, and shorts and a shirt. She stops at her dressing table, but instead of putting her makeup in the bag, she rakes the tubes into the top drawer. She doesn't even like makeup. The beach bag is only one-third full, but she can't think of anything else she wants to take. If she had a picture of Jude and Louise, she'd throw it in and show it to them on her way out to remind them that she loves them. But all the family photographs are in a drawer in Mother's room.

She tightens the drawstring of the bag and slings it over her shoulder. It's a bright turquoise color, so jaunty that no neighbors will think she is running away with it. She's not running away, she remembers. She's doing what she was told.

She opens her door and the attic fan pulls a blast of surprisingly cool evening air through the room. Both Louise's and her mother's doors are closed. But then Louise's door opens, changing the air currents again, and two faces peer out at her.

"Where are you going?" Jude whispers.

"I don't know," she says in a distant voice. She plans to walk down the hill to the curb market and call Daddy.

"Don't go," Louise says. She is pouting as if a doll she doesn't like very much is being taken from her.

"Want to go with me?" Katherine asks.

"No," Louise says emphatically. Then she smiles broadly as if she's joking. Of course, she doesn't want to walk out the door and into the summer dusk. All sorts of scary things, including Mr. Garrison, are out there. She wants to stay in her own safe pink-and-white room. Katherine wonders if Mr. Garrison has touched either of them.

She does not ask Jude to go with her, which they silently acknowledge to each other in lingering gazes. In a serious warning whisper, though, she does say, "Stay away from Mr. Garrison. Just do it because I told you to." They do not even look curious. Then Mother's door opens, and Louise and Jude quickly close theirs, and the air in the upstairs hall abruptly shifts again.

Without looking at her mother, Katherine trips down the stairs. She feels both pain and exhilaration, but more of the latter. In the foyer she pauses to listen, but Mother is not following. She starts through the house toward the kitchen and back door but checks herself and moves intently toward the front double doors.

The only times both doors were ever open that she knows are the three times Mother and Daddy brought a new baby home from the hospital. In the home movie of Katherine, Mother wore a fitted black dress with a white polka-dot collar and black-and-white spectator pumps. Even though she had just given birth, even though she was carrying the baby in both arms, she still moved like a model. The grainy film did not obscure her sparkling eyes. After she walked grandly into the house, she turned back to Daddy and waved. Then, for the camera, she hugged Baby Katherine tightly.

Katherine stands on tiptoe and then kneels. She undoes all the levers and locks and opens both doors wide. An attic fan cannot work with downstairs doors open, Daddy always explained to them each year. She leaves the doors standing wide and walks out. She arrived so many years ago by way of the front door, and she will exit the same way. For good luck, of course. To her sisters, who she knows are watching her from the upstairs windows, she throws up a hand and gives a hearty wave without turning around. A mosquito immediately bites the back of her leg, and she thinks that another thing she should have packed in her bag is a pair of slacks. But, no matter. She is on her way.

CHAPTER

6

It's the morning after their parents' annual pool party, and Louise, who is six, heads for her sisters' bedroom because Mommie and Daddy's bedroom door is locked. She has already been downstairs and sipped horrible-tasting stuff from the glasses scattered everywhere, and even gone outside and walked all the way around the pool, which she's never allowed to do alone and never *can* do, because usually all the doors are locked. She knows how to pour her own cereal and milk, of course, but she would rather Katherine do it for her. Katherine will wake up for her. Jude won't, and neither will Mommie or Daddy, not this morning anyway, but Katherine will. And then Katherine will wake up Jude so she'll have somebody to talk to, and Louise will get to listen to all they have to say. They talk about Mommie and Daddy a lot, and she knows that they will again this morning because of the big fight Mommie and Daddy had last night after all the guests left.

The party was a Hawaiian luau, and Mommie had made all three of them wear grass skirts and leis over their bathing suits. Actually, she'd only had to *make* Katherine and Jude; Louise thought it would be fun to dress up like Mommie, who also had on a grass skirt. Katherine hadn't wanted to be "another tacky decoration" at the party. She'd told Mommie that she didn't like the fake palm trees or the signs on the fake palm trees or having to wear a bathing suit and carry hors d'oeuvres around. She was too old to do that, she told Mommie. Mommie said that if she was so old, maybe she ought to find her own place to live.

The sign that Katherine wanted Mommie to take down said, "We don't swim in your johnny; please don't 'poi' in our pool." When Jude told her what it meant, Louise laughed. For a while Jude had thought it was funny too, but finally she decided she agreed with Katherine—the sign *was* embarrassing—so Louise was the only one Mommie helped to get ready.

Mommie had brushed her long dark curls into two ponytails on each side of her head. She had bobby-pinned a real orchid over her ear. When Mommie played "Little Brown Gal" on the stereo, Louise, only Louise, had danced the hula story which Mommie had taught them all. She ran her hands over her figure to describe the little brown gal. She put her fingers together in the shape of a house to describe the little grass shack. She swooped her arms out by her sides to illustrate the land of Hawaii. Everyone told her she looked adorable.

She didn't remember going to bed, but late that night Mommie's and Daddy's yelling had pulled her out of a deep sleep. She had tiptoed to her door and opened it at the same time that Katherine and Jude opened theirs. Katherine had beckoned her to come across the hall to their room. The fight wasn't scaring her, but Katherine must have thought it was, because she cuddled her in the bed and whispered about all sorts of things right in her ear so she couldn't hear what Mommie was saying. Jude, standing at the door, had done the listening. This morning, when Louise awoke, she'd found herself back under her own covers.

She opens her sisters' bedroom door and surveys the room. The spreads for both beds are lying on the floor, and Jude and Katherine are asleep on their stomachs, Jude under her pillow, Katherine pillowless. There's a funny smell in the room that Louise can't identify, a sort of human smell that isn't the smell of sweat. Perhaps one of her sisters is sick.

She crawls into bed beside Katherine and thinks how she let herself be cuddled, whispered to, tended last night even though she didn't really need those things, even though she would as soon have stood at the door with Jude and listened. Mommie and Daddy's fights don't upset her, although they make her sisters cry. She almost wishes Katherine hadn't seen her open the door because she would have liked to listen all by herself. But then it was so nice to be hugged and told all the funny things about the different guests at the party. Something she found out last night was that once, when Katherine was playing across the street at the Pendletons' house, she'd walked in on Mr. Pendleton peeing. He was naked. Of course, she'd only seen the back of him. But what she wanted to know was why he didn't have any clothes on in the middle of the day. Louise had no idea.

"I'm hungry," she says aloud.

Katherine awakens easily, stretches, pushes Louise out of bed, follows. She goes straight to the bathroom, Louise behind her, and then Louise sees what has made the bedroom smell so funny. Someone—Katherine, Jude, a guest?—upchucked in the commode last night and didn't clean it up.

"Who did that?" she asks.

"I did," Katherine answers shortly. She finds a toilet brush and a can of Comet and begins methodically scrubbing the dried-up vomit. Louise watches the movement of the brush, afraid to look at Katherine's face. She knows that her sister is not genuinely ill. In a way, she wishes she were.

Katherine finishes cleaning the commode, flushes it, pees, and flushes it again. She brushes her teeth long and thoroughly. She washes her face and looks carefully at her eyes, turning her face from side to side. Louise, who has finally grown brave enough to watch her, notices that her eyes seem to have no color. Even after her face has been washed, the skin looks stale, almost dead. Her lips are pasty and wrinkled as if she has been in swimming for a long time.

"They're going to get a divorce," she says.

"Who?"

"Mother and Daddy." She begins brushing her hair, which is so dirty that it doesn't move between strokes. "Daddy went to sleep at the party, and after everybody left, Mother woke him up and said they were going to get a divorce."

"Are you sad?" Louise asks.

"No. Are you?"

"No." Katherine hands Louise her toothbrush, and, dutifully, Louise adds toothpaste and begins to brush. "Why did Daddy go to sleep?"

"It's not *because* he went to sleep," Katherine says disdainfully.

"You said it was."

"That's what she told *him*."

"Oh," Louise says.

"She told me a long time ago she was going to make him leave."

Louise is not sure what the right question is. "Why?" she tries.

"I guess because they don't love each other."

Louise spits out her toothpaste. "She didn't tell you that."

"Yes she did. You know whenever she makes me take a walk with her? That's what she's always talking about. We walk up and down the driveway and she says, 'I don't love your father. It's something you need to know.' Then she tells me to be prepared and to get you and Jude prepared because one day they're going to stop living together." Katherine's voice turns flat. "I guess the day is today." She wets a washcloth and begins wiping around her eyes again.

"Are you sure?" Louise asks.

"Positive."

"Who will we get to live with?"

"Her, probably."

"Oh." Louise yawns. She's very hungry now. "Will we ever get to see Daddy?" Between Mommie and Daddy, she is thinking, Daddy is her favorite because he lets her stay up late when Mommie is at bridge club and he doesn't make her wash her hair if she doesn't want it washed.

"Sure," Katherine says. "It will be better," she adds, her voice perking up. "It will be real bad for a while, but then it will be better. That's what I've read." From under a towel Katherine brings forth a smile. "Believe me?" she asks.

Louise nods. "Let's cook pancakes," she says, skipping ahead.

Downstairs, Katherine first goes to tear up the sign that she found so offensive, but some guest has taken it home as a sou-

venir. Despite all the mess from the party—overflowing ash-
trays, leftover drinks, soggy refreshments that the flies have
found—the outdoors offers an intoxicating perfume of summer
flowers. It's cool and lovely out by the pool. She and Louise can
clean off the table and have their breakfast under the yellow
umbrella. She'll get things started and then go wake up Jude.
It's important, she thinks, that the three of them eat together
this morning. It's particularly important that Louise know she
has someone to take care of her.

Last night, after Jude had given her report on Mother and
Daddy's fight, Katherine had returned sleeping Louise to her
own bed and then waited on top of her covers for Jude to drift
off. For a while she was going to go through with it because she
hated Mother so much. Jude kept tossing. But then the anger
went away, and Katherine was left with the dare she had made
privately to herself while talking to Louise to keep her from
hearing what Mother and Daddy were saying. Finally, Jude went
to sleep, and Katherine became as wide awake as she'd ever
been in her life. Instead of feeling like a daredevil, she began to
sense that this was the right place and the right time. She felt
totally grown up. She could not even remember a time when
she thought of herself as a child. She'd been *born* grown up. So
why not? All her life she's been simply waiting to pass through
childhood. She was not going to wait any longer.

Downstairs at the bar she drank a glass two-thirds full of
vodka and one-third full of Coke. She drank steadily but not so
it would take her breath away. And when the vodka began to
gag her, she added ice to make it cold and soothing instead of
so medicinal. She hadn't been afraid at all. And even though
this morning she no longer feels the masochism or the anger or
the deviltry, or whatever it was—only an oozy, sick feeling—
she still feels her braveness. She feels, as she knew she would,
that she is old enough to do anything. And always has been.

If she was brave, she could take chances. If she was brave,
she could also be responsible. She had taken a chance and learned
just how brave she was. She'd chosen to get herself drunk and
had lived through the misery without one audible whimper. For

two hours, while the house was quiet and everyone dreamed their own private nightmares, she threw up and never called anyone. She was the most grown-up person she'd ever known.

Louise breaks the eggs. Katherine heats up the griddle, mixes the batter, and sends her baby sister to wake up Jude. Mother and Daddy often sleep late on Sunday morning and will today, without question. When they're asleep like this, the house always feels slightly deserted—free of grownups—but today something else is in the air. The house can be Jude's, Louise's, and Katherine's, exclusively. It won't be their parents' house at all. When they get their divorce, Mother and Daddy can both just leave. And like this morning, Katherine will be the cook, and after they eat, everyone will help clean up. Rather, Jude and Louise should clean up, since she cooked. She needs to start thinking about things like that and not set the wrong precedents at the beginning. They'll each clean up their own rooms. One day a week they'll vacuum and dust. They'll take turns buying groceries. Has it ever happened that the parents went away and left the house to the children? It's not that she doesn't love her father. It's just that she feels she can manage without him.

She would let them both come to visit. They could even spend the night—separately, of course—in their old bedroom. And when each of them remarried, they could bring the new husband or wife home. There would always be home. It wouldn't be Mother's house and it wouldn't be Daddy's house. It would be theirs: the house that they were born out of, grew up in, and maybe would live in forever. Three gutsy kids.

The only problem Katherine anticipates will be transportation, since she can't drive yet, but they live near enough to school to walk. Immediately, Katherine decides that even if parents in the neighborhood offer them rides, she will turn them down because she won't be able to reciprocate. Not accepting rides, she already knows, will cause a fight between Jude and her. But she is the boss. Somebody has to be the boss, and since she's the oldest and will have all the responsibility, it's going to be her.

Automatically, she throws away the first batch of pancakes,

though they look pretty good. Daddy says first batches don't ever *taste* good, no matter what, so don't waste good butter and syrup. She hears Jude and Louise coming down the stairs and decides to make the new batch in the shape of each person's first initial. She won't tell them today what she means by the initials, but someday, when they are all three living here, she'll say, "Remember the morning after Mother and Daddy's big fight? When I fixed pancakes in the shapes of our initials?" They'll be nodding. "That was a good-luck wish for the three of us. That we would always love and take care of each other. No matter what happened between Mother and Daddy." They will all nod that the good-luck wish—how foresighted of Katherine—had worked.

Even then, though, she won't tell them about her vow to love, mold, and care for them. Never will she let them hear from her that she was the one who had guided their lives. It's the kind of thing, anyway, that you can only know privately. Unless they are somehow able to realize it themselves, they will never know that on this day she became their mother. But that's what's happening.

When Jude walks sleepily into the kitchen, she sees a startling change on Katherine's face, some new way of thinking that has altered her sister's features. Her eyes are both fevered and discerning. Although it is impossible in a single night, her face appears much thinner. Maybe what Jude sees on Katherine's face is simply what's on her own face. There is something new in the house, something exciting. Normally, Jude is hard to wake up, but today when Louise called her name she arose from the bed immediately.

Jude carries napkins and utensils, Louise syrup, and Katherine her beneficent offering of pancakes as they move barefoot and in nightgowns out by the gleaming turquoise pool. Party flowers wired by the florist to small Styrofoam boats float on the still surface. Sitting in water, even chlorinated water, has kept them perfectly fresh. Katherine retrieves one and sets it dripping in the center of the table while her sisters dispose of a dozen or so leftover plastic cups. She is thinking that she should also have fried some bacon and that someone should have brought out butter to make a complete meal, but she'll know better next time.

"Wait," she tells Louise, who has used the syrup first and is about to taste her pancake. "Give Jude your 'L' and I'll take the 'J' and you eat my 'K.'" She is already switching the special initial pancakes around on the plates over Louise's objection. "This way it means something. Don't you see, Louise?"

"It's sort of like sharing, Louise," Jude explains.

"I want my 'L,'" Louise says. "Give me back my 'L.'" Her brown eyes, still heavily mascaraed from last night, are dully demanding.

Katherine stares at her long and hard, trying to convince her by her own seriousness, but Louise keeps asking for her "L." The idea doesn't work if there's a babyface involved. "Are you really going to act this way?" Katherine asks. She is holding her own pancake on a fork poised over Louise's plate.

Louise nods.

Katherine slams the "K" pancake back on her plate. She lifts the "L" off Jude's plate. It rips in half. She throws the two pieces toward Louise. "Take your goddamn pancake," she says. She reaches over and forcefully puts Louise's fork in her small fist. "Eat," she says angrily.

"Let's you and me trade," Jude says halfheartedly. She holds her plate across the table. Louise, her brief tears already dry, has begun to eat.

"Watch this, Louise," Katherine says. The two sisters trade plates. "The idea wasn't only to share but also to be part of each other forever. But you didn't want to be. And now you can't be at all ever. This was your only chance."

"I don't care," Louise says. Her voice is tinny, babyish. She holds up her syrup-coated fork in front of them and begins licking the tines. She grins self-consciously.

The trouble with having always been grown up is that you have a hard time understanding other people's childishness. "You *will* get to be part of things, Louise," Katherine says. "I'm sorry I said you wouldn't." But *is* she sorry? There's a recalcitrance in Louise, even now, that seems to Katherine to have nothing to do with age. If Louise were fourteen, if they were *twins,* Katherine thinks, Louise would still have said no. How is she going to be a mother to Louise if Louise doesn't want to cooperate? At least Jude listens to what she says.

"Anybody want more?" she asks in as detached a voice as possible. They have each silently finished the doughy-tasting pancakes. Katherine had hoped to feel a sense of unity with Jude as she was eating the "J," but because of Louise she feels nothing. The pancakes don't even taste very good.

Jude thinks that later she might suggest to Katherine that the three of them mix their blood in a planned elaborate ceremony. Then Louise might be caught up in the mystery instead of thinking—as a six-year-old would—that someone was trying to take something away from her. She herself wasn't totally clear about what Katherine had in mind, but she went along because she always goes along with Katherine. At every end with Katherine there's always a reward, even though the journey might be totally obscure. What *had* Katherine meant? That they were to *become* each other? If only Katherine would explain. But Katherine expects you to know the meaning of the things she does. To have to admit you don't is embarrassing sometimes, so Jude always goes along. She trusts her sister completely.

Nobody wants any more pancakes. With a sort of deadness in her eyes that she hopes Louise will notice, Katherine stacks the plates, the glasses, the syrup, and the utensils and heads with everything in precarious balance across the patio. So what if Louise is only six? It's time she realized that every situation is not resolved according to what the baby wants.

Doesn't Louise see who is nurturing her? Don't either of them understand how much they need her? Perhaps not yet. All that is predicted has not come to pass. She's told Louise that Mother and Daddy are getting a divorce, but it's not the same as having it happen. When it does happen, she plans to protect her sisters by becoming their mother. They will resist, she is beginning to see, the way all daughters resist. But she will persevere.

The sky is cloudless, the deck already hot enough to make her feet automatically seek shade. Sometimes on hot summer Sundays they all—Mother and Daddy included—come to breakfast in their bathing suits. Daddy often does laps before he eats. After breakfast Mother will wade in to her waist. She never swims, but sometimes on very hot days she scoops handfuls of water onto her fleshy chest. Mother is tall and slender, but her shoulders are hefty—out of biological necessity, Katherine has always thought, to support her huge bust. After getting wet, she lounges in the sun, readjusting her position every fifteen minutes. She returns to the water often.

Katherine is wondering how she will manage to open the screen without dropping all the dishes, when suddenly the door swings open. Before her stands her mother, wearing only underpants. One arm holds the door; the other, clamped across her chest, supports and attempts to conceal her enormous breasts. Her eyes are tight, weary, but the expression on her face is uncritical.

"Thanks for feeding the girls," she says.

Katherine often fixes breakfast on Sundays, cereal anyway. What's new? Could her face show what's new? She places the pile of dishes in the sink and returns the syrup to the pantry. Mother is preparing what is known as the family hangover cure—two of them—a glass of tomato juice with a dash of vodka ("to kill the tomato taste," according to Mother), a whole egg carefully broken to preserve the yolk, a heavy shake of Worcestershire sauce, and a spoon of sugar. Katherine has prepared the concoction for them when neither felt well enough to get out of bed. The one time she eliminated the vodka, they made her bring the whole bottle upstairs.

Mother does everything one-handed, still clutching her breasts with her left arm. What does it mean that she's fixing *two* cures?

"I'll take one of those," Katherine says, allowing a bit of mystery to enter her voice.

"*You'll* take one? For what?" There is instant knowledge in Mother's eyes.

"Just kidding," Katherine says. A blush creeps up her throat like hands. "My head hurts," she adds. "It was a joke." Mother stares at her without expression.

Suddenly Louise presses her face into the screen door, asking, "Can I go swimming?"

"Yes," Mother says.

"No," Katherine says.

"You'll watch them, won't you?" Mother asks.

"No, I won't."

"Yes, you can go swimming," Mother says again to Louise. Katherine glares at her.

"You're responsible for watching Louise," Mother says. She puts her fingers down inside the glasses in order to carry two in one hand. "Wasn't it a wonderful party?" she asks. She looks steadily at Katherine, waiting for an answer. "Louise was the cutest thing I've ever seen."

Katherine stares. She stares at her mother's face, at the arm across her mother's breasts, at the two glasses of hangover cure. She's trying to understand, but she doesn't. No, she won't dress up in a grass skirt and perform the hula for the guests. No, she won't cook bacon. Isn't pancakes enough? No, she won't watch her stupid baby sister swim. "Why don't you put some clothes on?" she asks bitterly.

The arm supporting her mother's breasts jerks once, as if Mother wants to strike Katherine, but instead she holds herself more closely.

Katherine hears Louise splashing in the pool. "I hate Louise," she says. "I hope she drowns. She's not cute. She wasn't cute at the party last night. She's a brat, and all she was doing was showing off." Katherine walks to the far end of the room, where a rarely used side door leads to a part of the yard out of sight of the fenced-in pool. "I am not watching her," she calls. "She can drown, for all I care." She expects that her mother will come after her to threaten punishment, but when she glances back, just before the door slams, Mother has vanished upstairs.

Katherine walks down the driveway. Since she is still wearing her nightgown she cannot just take a long walk somewhere and never return, not without the whole town having more to say about their family than they already have. "Don't *poi* in our *pool* . . ." Are Mother and Daddy getting a divorce or are they not? Is she or is she not going to become her sisters' true mother?

She was going to watch them and guide them and give them all the love she has. She was going to acknowledge their individuality, their separateness from her, yet teach them all to be united. But, ahead of time, practically ahead of Katherine's own decision, Mother figured out what she was going to do. Cunningly, she pulled out the chair just when Katherine was about to sit down. Without even trying, she showed that as a mother Katherine is unfit. She's willing to let her baby sister drown, isn't she? Yes, goddamnit, she is.

For a long time she sits on a stump just off the side of the driveway. She expects something to happen: Daddy to leave in his car to try to find a Sunday *Times,* or Mother to come out and punish her, or Jude to wonder where she's gone. Nothing happens. She can't even hear the sounds of her sisters swimming. It's as if, outside of her family, she doesn't exist. Could her sisters already have drowned?

She is furious when—as she approaches the back wooden gate—she hears her sisters laughing. Opening the latch, she lets herself into the fenced-in heat. Don't they care about her at all? Could she walk away from here and never be thought of again? The answer, incredibly, seems to be yes. And she had been willing to give her *life* for them.

Mother and Daddy are sitting on the deck outside their bedroom, each drinking the tomato juice that Mother fixed. Daddy sees her and waves, but she doesn't acknowledge him. It's always horrible to watch them take the hangover cure because each one makes a point of swallowing the egg yolk whole. It passes like a rock through their throats. There. First Mother, and then Daddy.

A sour taste rises to Katherine's tongue. Suddenly she is throwing up in the bushes, throwing up the horrible uncooked pancakes that she, as mother, served this morning. She hears a chair scrape, a sliding glass door open. She doesn't have to look up to know that it is her father coming to her aid.

But in a matter of seconds both of them have their arms around her, asking what's wrong. She will not look up, but she knows that her uncaring sisters are crouching close to her, too: she sees their baby feet, the water dripping from their ruffled bathing suits. None of them can fool her. The only reason they are all standing beside her right now is because she puked. They couldn't just ignore her. Like you can't, in good conscience, ignore anything in trouble.

Part Two

LOUISE

❧❧

CHAPTER

7

Someone—one of her sisters probably—once told her that she should never leave a task unstarted. Which is why Louise has been sitting at her desk for the past two hours when everyone she knows is out sunbathing behind Tinker Dorm. The task is a graduation requirement. For her senior English teacher, a small squirrel-like woman whose hair is fastened high on her head, Louise must write a paper assessing who she is after four years of college education.

"Be specific," Mrs. Grantham had said. "Offer anecdotes which show you to be a unique individual. An individual *different from every other individual in this room.*" Each time Mrs. Grantham said the word "individual," her mouth pursed and her high bun jerked in emphasis. "I expect you to describe your intellectual growth above all," she'd continued. "But I expect you to discuss physical and emotional changes, too." The class, including Louise, had collectively blushed. Everyone was wondering—especially the girls with boyfriends—just how far Mrs. Grantham expected them to go.

Louise is not sure what to write about. She doesn't feel a whole lot different than when she was eighteen—physically, emotionally, *or* intellectually. She knows more facts, but mostly forgettable ones. What is calculus, a course she took her sophomore year, actually all about? And she has met lots of people. But, to her, the real value of college, which she can never tell anybody—especially her senior English teacher—is that it's over. Or almost over. In six weeks she will have a Bachelor of Arts degree in history. Then she is going to find a job. Not a job related to her degree. She purposely took no education courses so she will never have to teach. She's going to find a plain old job that pays the rent. Then she's going to try to meet someone like Billy but with a college education.

If she can just get this task started, she can quit. She writes "Then" and "Now" at the top of the page and draws a line between them. Eyes: still blue. Hair: still full and heavy and curly. Not frosted since her junior year in high school, when Katherine made her return it to its natural state. Features: ??? She gets up to look in the mirror. Maybe she looks older, but she can't see it herself. She even weighs the same, 115, as she weighed her freshman year, about five pounds more than looks good on her. There's no physical change at all. Oh, she's finally put going to bed with Billy out of her mind, put going to bed period out of her mind. There's the occasional throb down low to remind her, but that's something she simply has to live with. No physical change for her, Mrs. Grantham, except that sex is out of her life, which must be a reversal of how it is with most girls her age. Perhaps in her paper she can say that physically she feels more refined, which is a truth Mrs. Grantham would probably embrace with joy.

Louise wonders if this paper could dare tell the truth. Could she write that college has not changed her at all? That she views her four years here as a holding pattern before she is allowed to land in real life? Mrs. Grantham might sail through the sky over such honesty. Or she might flunk her.

Louise picks up the telephone, dials Katherine's number, and bills the call to her father. This is something she'd better get another opinion on. It would be exciting, she's beginning to think, to make a sudden splash after merely being a face in class for four years, which is how she knows she's regarded at Hollins. A professor here with whom Katherine corresponds, an old college boyfriend, has told Katherine that he doesn't know who Louise is. How can a sister of hers have escaped detection? is how the professor phrased it.

Louise wonders what Katherine would think about this "refinement" of hers. Would she realize it's all her fault? That when she made Louise break up with Billy, Louise would have no more sex. Did she expect Louise to go cold turkey? Or did she think she would have sex with *dates?* Surely, not the latter. But the former hasn't been easy either.

Katherine knows that she and Billy used to do it, not because Louise ever specifically told her, but because when they used to spend weekends with Mother, before Katherine and Frank got married, they would change bedrooms for a while in the middle of the night. Very late, after Mother had made her regular surprise visit, Katherine would touch her arm. Without a sound they both would rise out of the double bed and tiptoe to Louise's room, where Frank and Billy were sleeping. Quietly, Katherine would draw Frank out of his bunk and leave Louise with Billy. After a while Frank returned, and Louise slipped back to Katherine's bed.

Being in bed with Billy was the most wonderful feeling she ever had. Being delivered there by Katherine felt natural to her, too. It felt so natural, in fact, that she still doesn't completely understand why Katherine would have ever thought of making her break up with Billy. She thought Katherine understood how much she loved him, the way Louise understood how much Katherine loves Frank. The way they both understood that Mother would have loved to have caught them with their boyfriends but would never choose the right time to surprise them.

The phone rings and rings and rings. Louise wonders if anyone has ever called someone and let the phone ring until that person got home. She brings the phone from its spot by the window seat and lies down with it on the bed. The drone sounds hopeful. It reminds her that, not very long at all from now, she will be on her own. She would have been on her own a lot earlier than this if it hadn't been for Katherine. She would have been on her own a year and a half ago if she'd followed her instincts and packed up and driven home. But she'd listened to somebody again—her old roommate Macy—and called first her father, who'd then called Katherine, who'd called her and said, Don't go anywhere, I'm on my way. She was never able to convince anybody that nothing had happened. She hadn't had a fight with a friend; she wasn't flunking out; she didn't hate the food, for Christ's sake. It wasn't because Mother had died in July either, a theory that Jude advanced. The fact that Mother was dead made her care *less* about coming home. She'd just decided that a college education wasn't for her. Katherine helped her unpack her things.

The next semester she'd found herself in Paris. Her sisters had convinced her father that it was the place for her to go. They convinced her of the same thing, but only because she didn't know how to fight them. The same way she guessed that Daddy had never figured out how to fight Mother. She'd stayed through the summer and come back just in time to start school again, her senior—hallelujah!—year.

She hangs up the phone. Although no one answered, she feels a lot closer to home than she has in a while. Home has heard her: at least Katherine and Frank's Irish setter has. She might still tell the truth in her paper. "Why I Was Not a College Dropout" could be the title, subtitled "Through No Fault of My Own." It's probably better that she hasn't reached Katherine. Katherine might try to stop her.

"Who were you calling?"

It's Jennifer, the roommate she was placed with this year since they were both in Paris last spring when sign-ups took place.

"Trying to get my sister."

"Again?"

"She wasn't home. I call her a lot, but she's never there."

Jenn throws a canvas bag on the bed and begins to peel off her string bikini. She has the kind of figure that bikinis are made for: no bust, tiny waist, no hips. She draws a couple of envelopes out of her bag and throws them on Louise's bed. "I picked up your mail," she says.

"Thanks."

Jennifer is a popular girl, on intimate terms with almost everyone in their class, as well as a number of underclassmen. She's pretty in an unfeminine sort of way. Her deep dimples and deep-set eyes give her face a fleshy appearance, though she isn't plump at all. She has a sort of permanent forward-leaning stance, which Louise thinks comes from being told so many secrets. Louise knows that everyone considers it both odd and a stroke of good fortune for *her* that they are roommates.

But all those secrets are what makes Louise feel so uncomfortable around Jennifer. Their dorm room feels chock-full of things that Louise can never know. "Is something wrong with . . . Caroline, or Pat, or Susan, or Vicki?" she always asks. It seemed callous to her *not* to ask when a classmate has come to the room in tears. Louise thinks that maybe sometime *just once* whatever is wrong might *not* be a secret. Maybe Caroline's father has died or Pat has broken up with her boyfriend or Susan is flunking physics or Vicki has mononucleosis—problems that will immediately become "public." But Jennifer will never tell her anything.

"I'll be in the shower," Jenn says, flashing Louise a big shy smile. The smile has no purpose. It's just the fake kind of way girls here treat each other. She smiles back, a fake herself.

The silence between Jennifer and her has deepened this semester. For one reason—after serious contemplation—Louise has decided she will never share *her* problems with the World's Biggest Ear. For another, Jennifer has never shared a problem with her. Maybe Jennifer has no problems. Some people don't, although those people could perhaps be liars. But off the top of her head Louise can name four problem-free people: Katherine, Frank, Billy until she broke up with him, Max until her mother died. She wonders where her father should be placed. He seems happy *enough,* but that's not the kind of happiness she's describing. She's describing someone who wakes up in the morning with nothing terrible on his mind. Using that definition, Jude is definitely unhappy. So is she. Jennifer is definitely happy. After all, she's getting married the day after graduation, and Louise plus six girls she's counseled during her years here are to be bridesmaids.

Actually, she wishes Jennifer had never asked her to be a bridesmaid, and she wishes she had not accepted. It costs too much to do something like that as a courtesy. More importantly, though, she just doesn't want to be in a wedding. She doesn't want to have to listen to the music and hear the words and watch the tears and the smiles. It will only remind her that she doesn't have Billy.

Louise has had no communication with Billy since early the summer her mother died, which was when she had given him back his pin. It was a pin shaped liked a pair of wings that he had found at a flea market and given to her in place of a lavaliere or fraternity pin or "possibly even an engagement ring."

"Possibly even an engagement ring," she'd told her sisters, neither of whom wore diamonds, on a Saturday the June before Mother died. They'd been sitting around the glass-topped wrought-iron table in Katherine's breakfast room, eating huge bowls of ice cream. Frank and Cap were playing golf, though not with each other, and Jude had brought little Katie over for some exposure to her aunts. The reason for the bowls of ice cream was to celebrate Jude's asking each of them to be godmothers. Since they were celebrating, when they finished toasting the baby with their spoons, Louise showed them her pin. They did not admire it.

"Not that there's no diamond. Who cares about those anymore?" Katherine said. Frank had not even given her an engagement ring, only a wide gold wedding band. "But that he's already admitting defeat. There will *never* be a diamond, which means just one thing to me: Billy has no ambition at all." Katherine had been hunched over her bowl, but then she sat up straight. "I'm not saying that Billy has to be rich, Louise. But don't you think he ought to have an occupation? Think about yourself. Can you live in an apartment the rest of your life? *I* could, but *you* couldn't. You've always liked life soft. Can you be happy never having a new dress? Not you."

"Billy does have an occupation. He's a woodworker. And Mother will buy me some clothes now and then," Louise had answered.

"Woodworking isn't a job," Katherine said. "It's for fun."

"It *is* a job." Louise could understand how they might think Billy's work was not serious. It had taken months for her to understand that he wasn't simply amusing himself. "I'll also be working," she said. "We'll have two incomes."

"What are you going to do when you have children?" Jude asked quietly, the ring of experience in her voice. Because of her unexpected second pregnancy, she was not going to be able to return to teaching next fall as she and Cap had planned.

"We might not have children."

"*Louise!*" they both had said.

Of course she was going to have children. She knew it as well as they did. She'd curled her hands into fists. They could see them through the glass-top table, but neither of them chose to look. Billy wanted to have four children, he'd always said. Two little girls who would look like her and two little boys who would look like him. But how would they take care of four children on his salary? It was true: with that many at home, she would not be working. Her faith in Billy was suddenly shaken. Had he ever tried to figure any of this out himself? Often, Billy expressed the view that "God helps those who help themselves." Could he be counting on Him?

Then Katherine said the thing about Billy that her sisters always said, the thing that made her angriest but that she never knew how to dispute. "You realize, Louise, that you're already way beyond Billy. You're going to be a college graduate. Even if you haven't outgrown him yet, you will soon. I know it's hard to accept, but it will happen."

That afternoon, in a rush, with her sisters standing by, she had given Billy back his pin. Stuck it in an envelope without even his name printed on the outside. She couldn't *write* his name, she was so upset. She wasn't sure he got the pin—she'd let Katherine drop the envelope in his mailbox—but she didn't hear from him for several weeks, and then Mother got sick and they spent all their time visiting her. Once Jude ran into Billy at a gas station, and he'd acted as if nothing was wrong at all, except that he didn't ask about her. And then Mother died and her junior year began. How could he have received the pin and not called her for an explanation? Perhaps he wondered how she could have delivered it without one either.

Jennifer returns on tiptoe from showering, her short, dark,

towel-dried hair as perky as a fur pelt. She changes the towel from around her body to around her head and moves naked about the room. Louise feels uncomfortable, though she knows she's not supposed to feel uncomfortable. She doodles in the corners of the sheet of paper where she has been listing her personal characteristics, "Then" and "Now." The only characteristic she has been able to come up with so far is not really a characteristic but a state of being: "untraveled" before college, "traveled" since. She supposes she could say "Mother alive" before, "dead" since, but she doesn't want to have to explain in a paper how she's changed since Mother's death. She's so much sadder now than she was when Mother first died. Recently she's been realizing that Mother is never going to know a thing about her. Not what she becomes or where she lives or who she marries, except that she's not going to get married.

"Aren't you going to open your mail?" Jenn asks. "I think there's a letter from a guy."

Louise is puzzled. She retrieves the envelopes from her bed. No guys write her. Her father, occasionally. She takes a quick breath, recognizing Billy's boyish scrawl. She is about to tear into the envelope and then remembers Jennifer. She slits the flap methodically with her fingernail. The letter is three pages long, so it's not a request that she return his Johnny Cash album collection, which she's kept and pretended to forget about. What does Billy want? She skims the letter quickly. She knows what he is asking, but what is he really asking?

"It's from Billy," she says aloud, her voice scarily calm. "Do you remember him?"

Jennifer has sat down at her desk, which in the narrow room fronts Louise's, to give herself a manicure in the nude. She cocks her head but doesn't take her eyes off the careful strokes she is making. "The carpenter?" she asks.

Jenn has never met Billy; no one at Hollins has, since Louise would always go home for weekends instead of inviting him here. Most of her friends think of Billy as "older," since she has always vaguely described him as "being out of school." It isn't a total lie: he'd had one semester at a junior college, which he felt had not advanced him in what he wanted to do.

"Yes, the carpenter," Louise says, less calmly than she would like. "The *wonderful* carpenter." She can't help herself. "He makes furniture, moldings, boxes. My jewelry box," she cries, hurrying to her closet to bring out one of Billy's early, rather primitive pieces. The jewelry box was her twelfth-grade Christmas present. He'd used pine instead of cherry. Later he realized what kind of wood he should have used and hated that he'd expended so much energy on inferior material. Louise, however, happens to like the mistake.

She sets the box on Jennifer's desk. "It's a pretty little thing," she says, more in control. "Simply made out of the wrong wood. Billy built it when he was first learning his craft."

All of Jenn's fingers are spread on her desk. "This hand is still wet," she says. "Want to open it for me?"

Louise opens the box. Since she no longer has the wings pin, there's nothing to see except some cheap high-school jewelry. The box is lined in red velvet, which they did together that Christmas night after all the family visiting was over.

"I can't remember why you don't see him anymore," Jennifer says.

"I don't see him anymore for . . . for lots of reasons," she says. Should she tell Jennifer why she and Billy broke up? Jenn's fiancé is already a practicing attorney. More than likely, *she'll* wonder about Billy's ambition, too.

What the hell. If Billy does come for the weekend, Jennifer will have to know so that she can put him on the lists for the social events surrounding the wedding. Thinking "wedding" gives her an unexpected surge of pleasure. Only now she wishes that she wasn't a bridesmaid for another reason. She would like to be sitting with Billy when the rector reads the vows. She knows exactly when she would slip her hand under his.

"Let me read you something," she says, and then suddenly feels sick with herself. For a brief moment she thought she wanted to read Billy's letter to Jennifer. Now she doesn't. Jenn doesn't know Billy. How could she possibly understand what his letter means?

Jennifer polishes her pinkie again and looks up. "Go ahead," she says. Her flat nipples are like additional eyes on Louise.

Strangely, both the nipples *and* her eyes have an emotionless look about them. Maybe her *lack* of curiosity is what draws people to her. If she isn't so eager to know, she won't be so eager to tell. Louise can vouch that Jenn doesn't tell a thing. It hasn't occurred to her until now that she may not *care* enough to tell.

The letter has no salutation, but she says, "Dear Louise," anyway. She reads:

I have been thinking a lot about you lately because I saw your sister Judith at the hardware store. She told me that you were doing great and about to graduate from Hollins College with a major in history. I didn't realize that you were so interested in history. I've always been interested in history myself, especially the history of World War I and World War II. Did you know that they didn't call World War I World War I when it happened? (Does that sentence make sense?) It wasn't called World War I until after World War II. Judith was buying a lawn mower and I told her that she ought to get a Powerbilt. She had the babies with her, and, boy, aren't they cute? It's a shame what happened between her and Cap. I hadn't seen Charles before. Katie really does look like you. I told Jude that. Those fat little cheeks. Those sparkling eyes. The only difference between you two is that her hair is blond, and yours is—well, you know what color your hair is. Anyway, Judith thought I was totally wrong. She thinks that Katie looks like Cap's side of the family. But I don't see it. On the other hand, maybe I was just trying to see you in her.

I know how much your graduation means to you, and how happy you'll be to make your daddy and your sisters happy. I'm proud of you too. It's quite an accomplishment to go off to college and to stay there and finish. A history major too! For some reason I've always had it in my mind that you were going to teach kindergarten or first grade. Did you change your mind at some point? Jude also told me that you spent almost a year in Paris studying. She said going to Paris really helped you grow up. And that you're a totally different person than you used to be. That sort of surprised me. You couldn't have been any better than you were, so you must have gotten worse!

What would you say to me coming up to watch you graduate? I asked Judith if you had a steady boyfriend. I didn't want some guy to think I was trying to horn in. But she said that you date lots of guys—not surprising—but none of them is really special . . .

Louise suddenly remembers that she is reading this letter to someone besides herself. Jennifer's four eyes are watching her impassively across the desk. It's too late to edit out Jude's lie, but Jennifer seems not to have registered it. Louise hasn't had a date in ages, except a dreadful blind one to the UVA spring fling who was five feet two or something equally short, in a literary mode, as he described himself, planning someday to write poems about brown lung disease.

"Is that the whole letter?" Jennifer asks in a flat voice.

Louise shakes her head. She decides to continue. If necessary, she will explain to Jenn that the lie about all her dates was Jude's lie rather than her own.

> So. I would like to attend your graduation. I especially want to watch you walk across the stage and receive your diploma. Then after your family leaves, maybe we could talk a little while. By the way, I know it's way too late to be saying this, but I am sorry that your mother died. I came to the funeral, but you didn't see me, and then I had to get back to work, so I missed the part at the grave. I always liked your mother, although I wondered if she liked me. Maybe it was just Max who didn't like me. And possibly your sisters. Deep down I've always had the feeling that your mother approved of almost everybody. In fact, I would go so far as to say she probably thought it was *wrong* to disapprove of people. Unlike everybody else.
>
> Let me know how you feel about me inviting myself as soon as you can because I need to take off that Friday from the shop. I would also like for you to locate me an inexpensive motel room, *not* where your family is staying. I hope you will say yes. I am proud of you and would like to witness this very special moment in your life.
>
> Take care,
> Billy

"*Why* did you stop seeing him?" Jennifer asks again.

"Well, we went away, you know." How can she say her sisters *made* them break up? Who would believe her? She wonders if Jennifer was sent by her parents or had gone to Paris of her own accord. She's never asked. "I guess I didn't feel like it was fair to tie Billy up for the whole time I was gone," she adds.

Jennifer contemplates this. Louise realizes that she kept *her* fiancé "tied up." But Jefferson Davis Miles III was a man with a future, a man to *be* tied up.

"I remember your not seeing Billy for a long time before we went to Paris," Jenn says in a tone aware of its historical accuracy.

How could she remember something like that? Louise had scarcely known Jennifer before they were seatmates on Air France flight 343. On the trip *over,* they had talked about their teachers at Hollins and about Annie Dillard's sudden fame for writing about Tinker Creek, where lots of couples now took "nature" hikes. Louise was certain that she had not mentioned Billy at all. While they were there, they had seen each other only in classes, since they lived with different families. On the flight *home,* they had discussed Jennifer's upcoming wedding. About mid-Atlantic, Jenn had asked Louise to be a bridesmaid, as a tribute to her year abroad. It was the first time Louise had realized that "a year abroad" had happened to her, too. She'd felt enormously nostalgic. She wondered if she would ever see Paris again. She wondered if she'd noticed it carefully enough to say that she'd seen it once.

Jennifer's historically accurate statement continues to hang in the air. Perhaps she is looked to because she provides such an exact context for the life of whomever she's listening to. Jenn tests her nails to see if the second layer of polish is dry and then unwraps her hair and lays the damp towel across her pubic hair and breasts. Her eyes seem to become more engaged with the moment.

Louise resumes doodling. Is Billy's letter the letter of someone still in love? Certainly he's not angry with her. What does Jennifer think? She scratches through the "traveled" characteristic under "Now" and writes "untraveled" instead. Then she crumples the paper. Is she one or the other? The truth is, she is both. She went somewhere, but only physically.

"I'll have to say Billy sounds sweet," Jennifer says. Louise lifts her eyes but continues to doodle. One of her favorite things to do is write the entire alphabet without lifting her pencil from the paper. She can't respond to anything anyone says until she reaches the end. She does it as fast as she can, holding her breath. "Jeff is sweet to me, too," Jenn continues. "When I have my period, he brings me chocolate milk shakes and makes me take a heating pad to bed. He may just be relieved that I'm not pregnant, but still . . ."

vwxyz. Louise cannot believe her ears. Jenn has just casually confessed to having sex. No one has ever told her anything like that before. Even when she and Katherine changed rooms at Mother's, they didn't *talk* about it. Is Jenn expecting her to make a similar confession? She absolutely refuses. "Billy's the nicest person I've ever known," she says. "But my sisters think he's not ambitious enough." *abcdefg* . . .

Jennifer waits until she finishes another time through the alphabet. "I hate to tell you this, but your doodling is driving me crazy." She looks at Louise, her face a mix of honesty and good nature. Louise blushes. She feels that she is somewhere she hasn't been before with a friend. She doesn't know Jennifer at all. But that is changing.

"Did living in Paris change you any?" Louise suddenly asks. She's surprised by her own fervency. "Was it possible that you could have gone there and come home *not* to marry Jefferson Davis Miles the Third?" Is this really her talking? She's embarrassed that she's called Jeff by his whole name, the way everyone in the bridge room does behind Jennifer's back, but Jenn doesn't seem to notice.

"It was possible," Jennifer half whispers. She appears to be thinking very hard. "Which is the reason I think I *am* marrying him. I've never told anybody this . . ." She pauses and Louise uses a soberly drawn mouth to say she understands she is about to hear a secret. "I dated in Paris," Jenn says. "I dated seven nights a week. I had the most fun I've ever had in my life. I felt like a clown at a circus." Her eyes have become like a child's.

Louise looks quizzical.

"Invisible," Jennifer says in a mysterious voice. "I could do

anything I wanted. Like a clown can. There was nobody to recognize me or tell on me or stop me." A serious light fills her eyes. "It was *not wrong*," she says, as she has evidently said to herself many times. "It was the only way I could ever have married Jeff. Jefferson Davis Miles the Third," she adds.

Louise picks up her pencil and then puts it back down. It is not the time to apologize. "What if you had fallen in love with someone?" she asks.

"I did," Jenn says, a dreamy smile filling her face. By now her hair has dried porcupine-style. She shakes her head slowly. "But he was Swiss. Regarding women, they haven't yet entered the twentieth century. And he lived over there. I want to live here." She closes her eyes and stretches, her body straining against the hard chair. Louise thinks that if she had known what Jennifer was doing, she would have gone to bed with Gérard, the guy *she'd* met. She wouldn't even have wondered what her sisters would think. If only she'd known.

Jennifer snaps awake. "You must never tell," she says. "Jeff wouldn't marry me if he knew. That puts my entire future in your hands." She laughs. "Or *one* way my future could go."

One way her future could go? Louise feels suddenly helpless. "You're getting married in a month," she says in a weak voice.

Jenn reaches across the desk toward Louise's hand but stops short of touching. "I know. And I'm glad. Marrying Jeff is what I want. And I want children. Two, four, six. However it happens. Jeff will be a good provider and a good father. I love Jeff. And I've had plenty of fun. To tell you the truth, it all seems perfect to me. And I've tried to figure out how it might fail. I guess the same way your sisters have done for you. Billy's ambition and all. And I just can't find the crack in the wall or the missing brick or whatever you want to call it. I'm going to be Mrs. Jefferson Davis Miles the Third and happy about it."

Jennifer goes to her dresser and takes out fresh underwear. With the white harnesses securely in place, she looks more girlish than before.

Mrs. Billy Jones and happy about it is what Louise is thinking.

"What was his name?" Louise asks.

"Jacques Terlinden."

"Do you stay in touch with him?"

A wistful look fills Jennifer's face. "No. No, I don't," she says quietly. "It's not a good idea. He doesn't even know my address."

"It's so sad," Louise says.

"Sad?" Jennifer asks. "Why?" She stands stiffly by her bed. "Tell me," she says in a brittle voice.

Louise has been struck by a sudden insight but feels uncertain about expressing it. What if she's wrong, or what if what she thinks is stupid? "It's—it's ob-obvious why it's sad," she says, feeling that the word "obvious" is too strong. "You're in love with Jacques and you're marrying Jeff because Jeff is like you and Jacques is different. I don't know why life has to be kept so homogeneous." Her voice grows in strength. "Why can't some of us have the courage to experiment?"

"Because this is my *life*," Jennifer says. Her eyes grow brighter but she doesn't cry. "I can't marry a Swiss man."

"Why not?"

"Because then I'd have to live where he lives—in Paris."

"You said you were happier in Paris than you've ever been in your life."

"It was because I didn't know anybody there."

"That's the only reason?"

"No, but so what? Jacques and I were lovers. That doesn't relate to real life." Jennifer's voice softens. "I couldn't have Swiss babies. I couldn't be happy never seeing my family. Or Virginia. Or my *whole culture*." She looks suddenly tired.

"Wouldn't you have gotten used to Paris?" Louise persists. "Wouldn't it have been like adoption?"

"I'm crazy about *Jeff*," Jennifer says stubbornly.

"I have no doubt that you are," Louise answers. She has tried to say this kindly, but the funny nasal tone that Hollins girls use to show sarcasm has crept into her voice.

"Why are you trying to mess me up?" Jennifer suddenly asks, her voice almost beseeching.

"I'm *not*," Louise cries. How can she have any effect at all on someone like Jennifer?

"Jacques is dead to me. He's a part of my past that I recall *fondly*."

" 'Fondly' does not seem to be the correct word," Louise says. This continuing boldness is shocking to her, but she cannot seem to stop herself. It's not exactly fondness that she feels for Billy Jones, either. How could she have given him up? She looks at the precious letter on her desk in front of her. Billy's scrawl warms her heart. His words charm her. Although she cannot say why, she feels angry at Jennifer. At the same time it's an anger limited in significance: they hardly know each other. She folds Billy's letter and sticks it in a drawer. Jennifer doesn't even notice.

"I don't even think about Jacques," Jennifer says, her tone becoming chatty. "I haven't thought about him since last semester. Not seriously, anyway. I think about Jeff all the time. I really do. Christ, Louise, you're going to be in my wedding!"

In a small voice Louise says, "I don't feel right about it."

She is folding up into herself, sure of what she is thinking, but unsure, too. What does she really know about Jennifer and Jacques or Jennifer and Jeff or Jennifer and Virginia, the United States, her *whole culture*? But she knows about herself. She loves Billy. She should have done something about him a long time ago. The person she's angry at should not be Jennifer at all.

"It's none of my business," she says, her voice suddenly impersonal. "I've just overreacted. I appreciate your telling me about Jacques. It's the kind of thing I need to know so I can make my own decisions."

Jennifer looks at the towel she has left lying on the carpet. She picks it up and straightens it carefully over the back of the chair. Then with a sort of shrug she knocks it off again. "I'm going to marry Jeff," she says.

"Of course you are," Louise says. "It's the *right* thing."

Jennifer gives her a long, irritated glance.

"It's the best thing for you," Louise continues. "I was only thinking about Billy when I said all those things. I was thinking how *I* ought to be marrying him." She stands and leans across her desk toward her roommate. She feels she doesn't know Jennifer well enough to actually go to her and hug her.

Jenn folds her arms under her bra. She turns her back to Louise, bracing her knees against the low bed. In a hoarse voice which travels forward, bouncing off the wall before it comes back to Louise, she says: "That's why people always come to me to talk. Because they can't bully me into saying something they want to hear. *That's* why I have so many friends, Louise. You've always wanted to know, haven't you?"

Jennifer's shoulder blades heave upward—an angel about to fly or a no-longer girl overcome with deep secret womanly grief, Louise thinks. Or perhaps she has only taken a steadying breath.

"I don't want you to tell anybody what we've talked about," Jenn says in a wholly new pragmatic tone. "That's another rule for keeping friends—discretion." She looks over her shoulder so that her eyes meet Louise's. "What I am going to do in a month is *marry* Jeff Miles. I know what you think about it and I appreciate your honesty." Jennifer looks at the wall. "Just don't try to take back what you said. Don't lie to me. Believe in what you believe." And then very quietly: "Unlike some people."

There's a cursory knock at the door, but before either of them can speak, Mary Ruth Ellis, a fellow senior, comes in, saying, "Somebody stole my *Complete Works of Shakespeare* and I know who, and I want you to go with me and observe me getting my book out of her room in case we have to go before the Honor Council."

She is speaking to Jennifer, not even acknowledging Louise's presence, although Louise is certain Mary Ruth sees her sitting at her desk. Mary Ruth is a short, obnoxiously enthusiastic girl who carries her generous bust as if it's as important as a mountain. Mary Ruth and Jennifer, like yet unlike Louise and Jennifer, are friends for the first time this year. Unlike, because Mary Ruth didn't want to leave Hollins without making friends with the most popular person in the senior class. Louise never expected to be friends with her roommate. In fact, she realizes, she may not be.

111|

"Why don't you start at the beginning?" Jenn asks crisply. Her entire countenance is changed, all self-awareness gone. It's as if she thinks she exists to serve. Reflexively, Louise stands and then sits back down. The movement forces Mary Ruth to notice her.

"I walked by the room and saw my book on the top shelf," Mary Ruth says. "Don't ask how I know it's mine. I just do. I've never even been in that room, but I got this incredible feeling. She's a klepto. I know she stole Sandy's manicure set." This is an event Louise does not know about, but obviously Jennifer does. "And now my book. We can't let this go on." Mary Ruth pauses to smile at Jenn, an oddly cheerful smile.

Louise starts a new "Then" and "Now" sheet with a line drawn down the middle. Only an hour ago she would have been flattered that one of Jennifer's friends would speak so openly in front of her. Now she feels only contempt for Mary Ruth for ignoring her and using her roommate. Louise smiles to herself. She's not being ignored anymore by Jennifer.

"*What?* Do you not believe me or something?" Mary Ruth suddenly asks.

It takes Louise a moment to realize that Mary Ruth is talking to her. "Of course I believe you," she says.

"Why were you grinning, then?"

None of your business, she thinks, but she says, "It had nothing to do with you." She sees a gleam in Jennifer's eyes.

"Come with me," Mary Ruth says to Jenn. "I know she's still sunbathing, because Janice just came in and told me. I really need two people, though."

Louise knows she won't be asked, but decides to say no if she is. Why can't Mary Ruth *use* Janice, she'll ask. Mary Ruth continues in a musing tone: "With two observers, nobody could doubt me. I *know* it's my book. It looks like my book from fifteen feet away. I take notes in ink, so we'll be able to tell."

Jennifer is pulling a half-slip up under her armpits to travel the halls.

"Will you go with us?" Mary Ruth asks Louise. "Janice is in the shower."

Hell, no, she thinks, but she shrugs her shoulders. "Sure."

On the way down the hall, Jennifer says that to be absolutely in order they should find Greta or Marianne, the senior representatives to the Honor Council, and have them watch Mary Ruth steal back the book. But Mary Ruth interrupts that no one will dispute three people. No one will dispute three people, Louise thinks, especially when one of them is strange Louise. Strange Louise doesn't participate, and she certainly wouldn't participate in order to lie. There's an advantage to her presence that Mary Ruth doesn't realize: Louise hates her guts.

Louise has no idea whose room they are headed for. She walks slightly behind the two of them, knowing that she is not truly included. It's the way she's felt around people all her life.

At the door of Kristin Anderson's and Pam Eddinger's room, Jennifer advises Mary Ruth to proceed without any secrecy. To go in and get the book without touching anything else, while she and Louise stand watch in the hall. If Kristin or Pam should return, no one should run or in any way disguise what they are doing. Louise is in awe of her clearheadedness.

Mary Ruth knocks. No one answers. She looks up and down the hall. Louise can't help but do the same. Jennifer doesn't turn her head.

The room, bright with afternoon sun when Mary Ruth opens the door, is like every room on the hall: an entry dressing area with sinks and then the room proper with bookcases on the far wall. All three of them focus on the top right-hand shelf, where the thick Shakespeare stands.

Louise watches for Kristin and Pam. Stealing *back* offers all the thrills but none of the hazards of being a thief. Which roommate, she wonders, is guilty? She begins to wish that one of them would appear.

Mary Ruth darts out of the room, book in hand. "It belongs to me. It doesn't belong to Kristin Anderson," she says. Her face is the same white that Louise knows her own to be. Only Jenn seems calm. Mary Ruth opens the book to where at the beginning of the year she wrote her name. Although it's been inked through, her signature is still legible.

"Let's go," Jenn says, guiding each of them by an elbow.

Mary Ruth shrugs away from her. She stands in the middle of the hall, thumbing through the pages. "Do you recognize my handwriting?" she asks, pushing the book toward Jennifer.

"Wait on that," Jenn says. Mary Ruth reluctantly closes the book.

They are three abreast now, hurrying, in spite of Jenn's calmness, back to safety.

"I'm so afraid," Mary Ruth says, in a tone of voice that isn't fearful at all. "Should I be afraid?"

Jennifer shakes her head no.

"Louise is afraid," Mary Ruth asserts. It's the first time she's ever said Louise's name.

She is not sure it happens, but as they walk through the door of their room, Louise thinks that Jennifer throws a gentle elbow her way, a wordless sign of a suddenly exclusive friendship.

"Louise is not afraid," Louise says, the Hollins nasal tone sounding for the second time ever in her voice. She decides to include her lack of fear in the list she is making for Mrs. Grantham. A list that she is going to work on some more after she writes to Billy. She picks up Jennifer's towel off the floor.

CHAPTER

8

Jude sets her alarm fifteen minutes before the very earliest either of her kids has ever woken up and still wakes up ahead of it. In the pitch dark, she listens for them but hears nothing. Even the radiators haven't begun clicking. In the process of leaving babyhood and napping less, her children wake up later than they once did, and she could sleep later herself, but she does not. For the year after Cap left *they* were her alarm clock, more or less. For that year—the year she'd slept so very heavily—she had no idea how long they'd been crying to get out of their cribs when she finally heard them. It couldn't have been *that* long, since it was impossible to sleep once they really started making noise.

She's been setting the alarm since Christmas night, when Katherine, who went to Daddy's with her to pick up Katie and Charles and then came here to help put them to bed, commented that, to her, the children looked fragile, nervous, and afraid. They weren't fragile, nervous, or afraid, she'd tried to explain. They were tired. Kids are like little animals, she'd said. They pee when their bladders are full. They whine when they're hungry, and they scream and then go to sleep when they're tired. She meets their needs just fine. Still, that night she'd set the alarm for the first time. She wanted to make sure what she'd told Katherine was true.

If anyone is fragile, nervous, and afraid—she should probably have said—it's Jude. Katherine would be no different if she was one person responsible for two babies. But Katherine has decided that she's not going to have children. She mentioned it again last week. She says she's told Frank she's afraid she'll be a mother like their mother, and—though he says she won't be—he understands her reluctance.

"What do you mean, 'a mother like our mother'?" The phrase has become a regular refrain from Katherine's lips. Jude's question, though, is also a regular refrain. Of *course,* Jude knows what Mother was like. But whenever she asks this particular question, Katherine stares at her as if she's being betrayed. She should remember that Jude is their mother's daughter, too. Does that mean she's a bad mother? Is she a mother—in Katherine's view—"like their mother"? Is that the reason for the criticism about the kids? What Jude knows, now that she has children, what she *tells* Katherine over and over, is that their mother was just trying to live her own life. It was a life that conflicted with having children. Every adult life, she points out, conflicts with having children. But Katherine doesn't understand.

Since she's had her own kids, Jude has found out what mothers face. It's not, as Katherine thinks, simply her excuse not to be perfect. A girl reaches her twenties. Life is wonderful and she's having fun. She meets someone, gets married, and gets pregnant. And then it's as if she went over the waterfall. She comes home from the hospital and finds out that her own life has disappeared. What she wants to do for herself and what she has to do for her baby are mutually exclusive. So she begins to slight one or the other—almost always herself—and is miserable for the rest of her life. *Their* mother happened to slight them, but to Jude this doesn't seem so horrible as it once did. Except that even this explanation doesn't really satisfy her. Mother didn't slight them: she gave them more attention than they wanted.

Although Jude wishes it could be different, it's not just her kids she thinks of these early minutes, but also whether or not anyone is in bed with her. She does not often let someone spend the night, and she always sends him on his way before she goes in to the kids in the morning, but it's still one of the first questions she asks herself.

Nowadays she sleeps with dates arranged by friends and with guys she meets in bars. Right after she and Cap separated, she slept with three of his friends—husbands of three of the couples in her crowd—until she realized that none of the three had, as they claimed, been in love with her all these years. Number three happened to be someone she'd sort of always been in love with. But number three had no interest, in his own words, in "actually giving something up." That was when she stopped looking for a man among the neighborhood husbands.

Always been in love with . . . The phrase galls her. At this point, after all these years of thinking she knew, she has no idea what love is. But she expects somebody someday to feel it for her, and when they do, she will recognize it. She questions whether she will ever be able to feel it first herself, mostly because she doesn't know what it is. At this point she thinks she only knows what love is not. It's not commitment. It's not companionship. It's not sharing a future with your two children. What love really is, she thinks—or what it must be for people like her, who have loved in vain—is death, because you give up everything for it and then it vanishes and you have nothing left. But if it doesn't vanish—the way it didn't for Mother—you have everything, and whatever you gave up no longer matters. Mother gave up Daddy for Max. Katherine thinks Mother gave up her three daughters, too. But Jude is less sure. Nobody could make her give up Katie and Charles, she's almost positive.

Going their separate ways has probably ended up being the best thing she and Cap could have done. Still, the question of why her marriage didn't work torments her. Were they too alike or not alike enough? Was it the burden of the kids? Is love really so important? What *is* love? One of the things that has most surprised her about her divorce is how she thought Cap had never lifted a finger to help out when they were husband and wife. She'd been wrong, she found out that first exhausting, lonely year.

Peter Burns, a date arranged by a friend, is in bed with her. Before she attained complete consciousness she knew someone was, she just wasn't sure who. The alarm will go off in another minute or two, and she'll let it wake him up instead of waking him up herself. He's not the man for her, and she's not going to act as if he is by being sweet or by pretending to some sort of sexual goddesshood that she might offer someday to somebody but not him. In other words, she could wake him up by sucking on him, but why do that? It would keep him coming back for months, but it wouldn't make her want him. She's looking for someone she would die for and who would die for her. Peter Burns is a podiatrist, which eliminates him from consideration anyway. Podiatrists don't have souls. Should she share the joke?

She shakes Peter's shoulder roughly. The alarm hasn't rung, but she wants him out of her bed. She has just made a new resolution: to save herself for someone with soul. That almost has to be the step before all others. She should have thought of it sooner.

"Time to go home," she whispers harshly.

"Huh?" He turns over and groans, but before he settles back against the pillow, he is rising, clambering in a rote manner out of the bed and toward his clothes. He's done this a million times from a million different single women's beds.

That's really the secret, Jude knows by now: how they get out of bed the next day. It tells the breadth of the man's experience or philandering—whichever you wanted to call it—how she ranked in that breadth, and whether or not he would be coming back. The lovemaking itself hardly ever told anything. Or at least it hadn't with anyone she'd ever made love to. In and out in and out in and out . . . whoosh . . . wow. Always the same. And it wasn't that she didn't like sex. She liked it as much as the next guy, not, of course, the next girl.

She's had the suspicion all her life that most women don't like to make love. Those three friends of Cap's she'd been to bed with confirmed it, at least about their wives. Although the information could easily be suspect, she now thought it was the only honest thing any of them had told her. Their wives loved sex all during dating and the first year of marriage and especially when they were trying to beget, but after that they hated it. They hated the invasion, Jude knew. They hated being used, which anyone hates if they don't think they're using, too. People try to tell you that sex is mutual giving, and it is, but it's also mutual using. If you aren't thrilled, too—wherein lies the problem for so many—then you feel used. Jude wonders if number three, her favorite, had not shown more interest in her because he expected her to change into a person like his wife. That would never happen, but he'd never have the pleasure of knowing.

When she tells Peter goodbye, it's as if he came to fix the sink, or maybe less appreciative. She does not offer breakfast, a kiss, or any hope for the future, though she thinks from the way he came back to the bed before dressing that he will want to see her again. She sits up, the sheet protecting her nakedness, her back primly straight against the headboard. She smiles the way Katie smiles when it's requested of her for photographs. She does not really see Peter. He stands uncertainly, not knowing enough simply to leave.

"Did you have fun?" he asks, gesturing with his hands to show that he doesn't understand her reserve.

She looks at his hair, which is so full and thick that it doesn't move. Just the thought of touching it again revolts her. She isn't going to say no, she didn't have fun, but she isn't going to say yes, either.

"How about tonight?" he asks. Maybe he thinks she's just moody in the mornings. Maybe he thinks he can break through. His innocent unintelligent eyes seem desperately trying to say that *he* had a good time. Aren't things like that mutual?

If she felt like talking, she would say, "Good times are not necessarily had by all." She does not wish to have to hurt his feelings, but soon she will be forced to.

She puts a finger to her lips. "Sh-h-h." She presses her hands together and angles her face against them to indicate her sleeping children. "Katie and Charles," she whispers to his befuddled look. No! She doesn't want to go back to bed with him.

He breaks into a wide smile, seeming to understand everything. It wasn't that she had a bad time at all. She just doesn't want him to wake up her kids. "I'll call you," he whispers. "Elevenish?"

She nods. She'll take the phone off the hook for the hour

before and the hour after. Maybe she'll take it off until she decides how to avoid all she doesn't want, whatever that may be. With a silent wave, Peter tells her goodbye. She is still smiling.

Getting rid of him has taken almost twenty minutes, and still the children are sleeping. She decides to bathe away all remnants of Peter's invasion, realizing how, even to her—a woman who loves sex—sex can be considered one. Perhaps "meaningless," like the ladies' magazines say, is how this particular encounter should be described.

She suddenly realizes something. How can sex with a man ever have any meaning if she doesn't love the man before they do it? A person all by herself isn't passionate. A person is passionate *about* something or someone. Passion, even more than love, has direct objects. But she's expected to *show* passion before she *feels* it. As is the man.

Should she consider the man? Not a single one she's dated in the past year has waited more than two evenings to make a move on her. As a result, she's fucked lots of guys. She'd thought that this kind of going to bed would eventually feel natural, but it still feels forced. Without passion, how do you undress in front of someone you hardly know? How do you touch bodies? How do you put tongues in each other's mouth? What she is now wondering is this: Has she actually had a hand in keeping herself from falling in love? Something about this reminds her of teaching, the way she's expected to show every student the same degree of attention. The concept, she will say, works better in the classroom.

While she is running a shallow bath, she thinks of Cap—in love, she had finally gotten out of him, with another woman. He would never have fallen in love with Carolyn Welch, she suspects, if he'd simply been dating her. But married people don't get to hop into bed with someone new each night. Instead, they have to wait and watch and try not to. If Cap had had a chance to *date* Carolyn, it would be over by now. But because he was married he couldn't. As a result, he's made a decision based on incomplete information. Maybe Carolyn *is* better in bed than Jude is, but how will she be on canoe trips and taking car pools and when Cap falls asleep at night in front of the television? Can she possibly be better enough than Jude that it would matter?

Cap and Carolyn *are* still together, and they plan to get married when the divorce comes through. Carolyn—who has never been married, who is a "career" journalist, which Cap "admires" over Jude's own pragmatic teaching, who, according to Cap, has taught him a lot about "mutual respect" in a relationship—is older than they are and wants to have a baby before it's too late. Jude has wondered, not seriously of course, whether she should offer one of hers.

Although it had hurt her, she was really glad when Cap told her about Carolyn, because it showed her she could still be right about things. No, she hadn't suspected another woman. She'd believed Cap when he said he was leaving because she expected too much of him. What she'd been right about was rearranging her bedroom. Not at the beginning, but later, when she knew for sure Cap was never coming back, Jude had put the bed on the opposite wall and changed around the rugs and dressers and chairs. It was like spontaneous combustion, her favorite physics concept, except that it took effort. She'd painted the room a soft pink, replaced the photographs with posters, and bought herself a sumptuous down-filled comforter with Mother's money. She gave away their bedspread. It was not the same room, and when Cap called and asked to spend the night, as he did regularly for many months, it was so much easier to say no. The place where they had loved each other no longer existed.

Just as she finishes her bath, Charles, her younger child, begins calling her in a gurgling voice. His sock feet pound against the end of his crib—the first respectable noise of the day. Katie, agile at almost three, has proved herself able to crawl out of her crib following her afternoon nap, but she will not get out of bed alone in the morning. It's her first invented game: when she hears Jude finishing with Charles, she lies down. Jude can stand over the crib as long as five minutes waiting for Katie to open her twitching eyes, but she won't do it until she's picked up. Then she bursts into laughter. Already she has more self-control than Jude has ever dreamed of having. Or maybe it's that normal baby strength she's always telling Katherine about. Maybe it exists in a more real way than she's imagined.

All day today, Saturday, she will play with her children, a taste she has worked to acquire. It's the only day of the week that she has their exclusive care. The five days she teaches, they go to Mrs. Raynor's. On Sundays she takes them to church for the relief of the nursery. She always needs that relief after All-Day Saturday, although she has never gotten to the point that she doesn't look forward to All-Day Saturday.

While she and Cap were married, she simply tended to the children's needs and went about her business in the spare moments. But since the separation, she takes a day a week with them. It was her own idea, nothing she'd read. And nothing she'd had a model for: Mother had never played with them. She would have given it up if she'd hated it, but she'd found it's something she loves.

This morning, they'll first eat from their high chairs, which she sets up near the stove for warmth. After breakfast she'll give them baths. She lets them play for a while in each other's bedroom, and then she carries all the toys to the living room for a giant play session. At some point Cap will drop by to visit.

Although it hasn't happened yet, Cap agreed before Christmas that soon they would work out a regular visitation schedule. So far, he comes by the house only two or three times a week. He says the children are too young for him to take both overnight. He says that since Carolyn has never been married, it's too much to ask her to spend a weekend with two babies.

"I thought she'd be used to dealing with real life," Jude had commented after Cap made known his worries.

He'd been stoking a fire for her, his eyes squinting against the smoke of his cigarette. His father was dying of emphysema, albeit slowly, her mother was dead of lung cancer, and still he didn't have the sense not to smoke two packs a day, up from only one before their separation. From his bent-over position he said, "What do you mean, 'real life'?"

"Being a newspaper reporter and all," she'd said. "I thought you always told me they were the only ones who really knew what was going on in the world." Cap's most admired person is a reporter named Sam Sawyer who writes about the down-and-out, the bad, and the ugly. He's always said he would have been that kind of reporter himself if he hadn't gotten hooked on sports first.

"Knowing about real life and dealing with two babies are two entirely different things," he'd said, still not realizing how much hate she was feeling for his girlfriend.

He picked up the bellows and began to tell her the difference, but she'd interrupted: "I'd like to see *you* deal with them sometime. You need to take the kids for a weekend. Charles is almost two, and Katie is no trouble. In fact, she helps with him." She wanted to point out that Carolyn could use some mother-practice, but she wasn't ready to hand her kids over to the enemy. In a quiet way she's still furious that someone would plan to have a baby with the man she hadn't yet divorced and the someone hadn't yet married. "You can do it," she said, feeling as false as a cheerleader. "It's not that hard."

She looked at him straight on, her most earnest look, the one she'd always used to tell him his duty. Neither her father nor her mother had ever mentioned duty to her. She learned about it from Katherine, who talked about such things as the duty of having your mother at your wedding—even if she ruined it; the duty of providing emotional support for a lazy husband—even if he divorced you; and the duty of attending your sister's upcoming college graduation when Jude has no idea who will be willing to take care of the kids while she goes. Frankly, she had never believed much in duty—too guilt-laden for her—until it came to what Cap ought to do.

"There are *two* of them," Cap had said when she asked him about keeping them over Louise's graduation weekend.

"There are two of you," she'd retorted. But it appeared that one of them did not count. Was it Cap or Carolyn?

She rediapers Charles and together they go in to watch Katie's trick, which is both performed and applauded with much glee. Unlike Cap, her children always wake up happy, which may be her greatest contribution to their heredity. Even after the worst drunk she ever pulled, she still woke up reasonably civil. At least she didn't blame the world for the state she was in. But even when Cap had no reason, he woke up mad. It was the first character defect she'd noticed in him, unimaginable in the context of her family, all of whom deteriorated as the day progressed. He'd actually slung a pillow at her before their marriage was a week old.

With her two babes in arms, neither of whom is ready to be lowered to the floor, she moves down the hall. Taking care of them alone is an enormous struggle, which she confirms to the frequent askers. But what she never says is how much better her life is since Cap left. The fact that she no longer has to contend with another adult's desires is part of it, but only a small part. What she feels with her children is a unity that she has not felt since she and Katherine were girls. All her life she has wanted to love someone totally, the way she used to love her sister. She has wanted to be a sole lifeline, bread and water. Finally she has found this with Katie and Charles. That's one reason she's said so little—only enough to produce guilt—about Cap's not taking them overnight. That's one reason, when Katherine commented that the children looked fragile, nervous, and afraid— even though it was Christmas night and Jude knew they were just tired—that she's been getting up earlier than they. She *may* have a man someday—a man she would die for and who would die for her—but, until then, this is what she has. And this is what she loves.

She stands in line waiting for admission to the Fifth Season, a discotheque in the lobby of the Holiday Inn–Four Seasons. From here, all that can be heard is the bass throb of the drums, unless someone opens the padded doors, and then the music seems to erupt. The Fifth Season is the only acceptable dance spot in Greensboro, according to Missy Greer, who'd planned to meet her tonight until she got a last-minute date. Although Jude has never been here, she was relieved when Missy canceled. She'd already envisioned herself getting stuck with the type of men Missy attracts. Certain men like short, buxom, "bux-ass" women with stationary blond hair—*why*, Jude has no idea—but they're the kind of men who own their own bowling ball or have their hair styled. Not the kind of man Jude's looking for.

Her children are with a babysitter. She left school at four, picked them up at day-care, and took them home to feed. When Missy canceled, she considered canceling her own babysitter and staying home for the evening, but then she remembered how trapped she would feel all next week if she didn't go out tonight and tomorrow night. Besides, she has All-Day Saturday tomorrow with her kids. Tonight she needs to take care of herself.

At only nine o'clock the line for the disco is hardly moving. The Fifth Season holds four hundred people, according to the fire department's sign near the cash register, and when the disco is full, someone has to leave in order for someone else to go in. The people who are already in pairs are the only ones who have anything to say to each other, Jude notices, and they speak mostly by touching. Two men are standing behind her, and a girl in front of her is striking various poses, but no one talks. It's as if they are Episcopalians on Shrove Tuesday, observing their night of silence. Sort of. She hasn't thought about church in a while, and she's surprised that she thinks of it now. Maybe this line she is standing in reminds her of waiting for Communion. Only this line is a whole lot slower. And less forgiving.

The name of this place, not the Holiday Inn part, but the Four Seasons part, always calls to her mind—in an ironic way—the Vier Jahreszeiten Hotel in Munich, Germany, one of the stops when Mother and Max took them on a trip to celebrate Katherine's college graduation. "Grandmother money" from their father's side—the money that had allowed Daddy the luxury, as Mother always put it, of going into banking—had paid half their way. The other half came from Mother's divorce settlement with Daddy, which she had sought, she'd always told them, so she could give it to them. It was true, they'd found out when she died and left them what remained. Mother had not let Max pay any of their expenses. A trip like this, she said, was Daddy's responsibility to them, one he'd never meet unless she made him.

Louise had been too young to go, and Jude was sure that both she and Katherine had had "Daddy's responsibility" in mind when they made her sign up for Hollins Abroad. Although their main purpose had been to keep her in school, at the same time they knew it might be her only chance to see Europe.

The Vier Jahreszeiten was the most elegant and, she fears as she stands at the Greensboro Four Seasons, the last place like that she'll ever see. She raises her eyes to keep quick sentimental tears from welling in them. She shouldn't have had those glasses of wine before she came. But at least she knows the Vier Jahreszeiten exists. It's better to know things like that and suffer on account of them rather than to know nothing like that at all. At least she knows she will find no soulful man here. She can even smile that once she was in a place where such a man might have been and now she is here.

The line moves a little and Jude realizes why no singles are talking to other singles. If they happen to get paired up with the person who by chance is standing beside them, they'll have no opportunity to look over the crowd. There has to be *some* sort of self-determination in these kinds of situations. Of course, you're limited to who shows up.

The girl in front of her is next when a man about forty bursts through the door. The door swings shut—or did he slam it?—on the woman following him. She pushes it back open with one strong slender arm. In her other hand she carries a drink. She is short, which she is trying to combat, Jude notices, by wearing four-inch heels. She has on a straight black skirt and a peasant-style red blouse, which despite its fullness fails to disguise the size of her breasts. Mother used to wear clothes like that, but it never worked for her, either.

"You son of a bitch," the girl hollers. Her face is so painted, so Spanish-looking, that Jude expected to hear a Spanish accent, but there is only an unpleasant country twang.

The boyfriend—if he is her boyfriend, rather than someone who shut a door in her face—is headed toward the men's bathroom, but before he can reach the door, she throws her drink. It shatters into small pellets, as if it's safety glass, against the blue tile to his left. One pellet lands beside Jude's foot. Is this funny? She can't decide. No one else in the line is laughing. Maybe they're not because the girl has started crying. The bouncer, a stocky, bearded man, has already taken hold of her arm.

"I'm sorry," she wails. "Don't make me leave. I know him. Go get him for me."

"Miss?" someone calls. The girl who had struck poses in front of Jude for so long is gone.

"Hey, you're next," says one of the men behind her. The boyfriend has not come out of the bathroom, and the bouncer, who apparently won't go in for him, begins to escort the girl to the front door. Jude wants to stay and watch for another minute, but suddenly she feels—although no one touches her—that the entire line is pushing her forward. First things first.

"We've only just begun," the lady at the cash register says. Her face is also painted, except it's an old face instead of a young one. What was highlighted on the girl is actually drawn on her.

"Nice crowd," Jude murmurs.

"It's better inside," the lady remarks, raising a watercolor eyebrow. It's funny, Jude thinks, that an eyebrow will move whether it has any hair or not. The cashier, she realizes, is no more sympathetic to her than to Lolita.

Jude pulls on the surprisingly heavy door. Inside, the room is dark, as dark as the hotel parking lot. There's a spotlight on the band, Lost in Space, but it does not light the room. Individual lamps on the tables glow just enough to help her find her way around.

Whereas the people in line had looked as individualistic as the animals in a zoo, inside the men all look like walruses and the women like angelfish. She's kidding, but it's true that in this dim-lit room especially the men look so much alike. They're all dark, even the blonds, in a sleazy way. They all have vacant looks, and wouldn't you think they'd try to appear intelligent in a place like this? They also all look afraid. Not overtly afraid, but with a nervousness manifested by some extraneous motion in each of them. It makes her feel calm.

The men within range have looked her over by now, and the

ones who are passing her on the way to the john or the cigarette machine practically step in front of her, dipping their whole heads in a combination perusal and nod—yes, they'll take her if she nods back. On the one hand, she doesn't have to put up with this; on the other, it doesn't bother her a bit. She's a snob, she knows: not a person in here has the slightest appeal for her. She's a snob because she knows it without meeting them. She knows that if they're here they can't be worth much. Men with souls have other options than the Fifth Season disco; women with souls don't. So she will sit down, get drunk, and say no in various ways to anyone who asks.

She steps daintily down the steps to the sunken bar and perches on an empty barstool. Once a few years ago she ate dinner alone in a fancy Italian restaurant and blushed every time she took a bite. But she's older now and thinks that it might be possible—with the loud music, cigarette smoke, the so-called conversation swirling around her . . . and enough drinks—to actually ignore that she is here. She is *not* in a place where people come to have fun, and if she isn't here, then she won't have to leave unhappy. What *is* fun, anyway? she asks herself. What is happiness? What is love? These are the simplest questions on earth, but she can't answer them. She can give an example of what is not fun: being here alone on Friday night. What might be fun, she has no idea. She orders a dry martini.

The way not to be bothered is not to notice people noticing you, and by the end of the drink, she thinks this might be possible. Even including the earlier wine, she's not drunk, but she's getting a buzz on. Martinis are not her favorite drink, only the most sophisticated one she knows. After a while, she'll change to vodka or Scotch on the rocks. Whatever she chooses, though, she always drinks the same way: a couple of quick belts and then slow sipping the rest of the evening to maintain but not go beyond a solid high.

A five-dollar bill suddenly hangs suspended in the air above her left shoulder. The quick-moving bartender had left before she could pay. "May I?" a voice says.

"You may not," she says, taking the money before the bartender does. With only a cursory glance behind, she passes the bill back over her shoulder. She saw enough to know that he is medium-size and that his curls are plastered to his forehead as if he is wet. She has met a seal instead of a walrus, she guesses. From her own wallet she pulls out three ones and fans them on the counter. Can't she have a drink in peace? What right does anyone have to assume she is here for any other reason? He did have on a tie, she noticed. Most of the men here wear open collars and gold chains. She would not marry a man with *soul* if he wore a gold chain. This man is still standing behind her, not too close, but close enough to fend off anyone else. She can tell that he's not looking around, only waiting. He's not even staring at the back of her head—she would feel it if he were—which she appreciates. Maybe he is the best man here.

"Well?" she says. She turns around on the barstool and gives him not her best smile. He has a pencil stub stuck behind his ear. She points at it, having enjoyed pointing at things since she learned it was bad manners. "What's that for?"

He cocks his head. "Taking notes," he says. He's cute in a young sort of way, meaning that he looks about her age, without the experience. He may have an "ex," but no kids, for sure. Probably he drives a 280Z, a car her kids wouldn't fit into. His eyes are dark; they may have no color.

"It sets you apart from the crowd," she says in an ironic tone.

"I suppose it does," he says. "but I really do take notes."

All the girls ask "On what?" so she won't. A sudden flush swirls through her. She even feels it in the backs of her knees. He's another goddamn newspaper reporter.

"What's wrong?" he asks.

She turns up her glass and holds it there as if she has a drinking problem. She swabs the ice cubes with her tongue to get every last drop. "I don't talk to newspaper reporters," she says.

"Who do you talk to?" He closes the gap between himself and the bar and signals the waiter for a beer. From elbow to shoulder his arm touches hers, but if she moves even a fraction to the right she'll be touching the stranger on her other side.

"Oh, I don't know. Doctors, lawyers . . . professional people. My father. My sisters. My friends." It's one thing not to allow him to buy her drinks, but another thing entirely that he hasn't offered to order her one. "My two baby children," she adds.

"Who did that to you?"

"I did it to myself."

She's been talking straight ahead instead of looking at him, but now she turns, her face clearly disappointed. "I'd like another drink," she says.

"I didn't want to be presumptuous . . . again," he says.

"I don't want you to pay for it."

"I don't intend to."

She learns more about him each time she looks. His eyelashes are curly and he has a large mole on the cheek nearest her. His lips jut out from his face in a masculine way. Instead of a sports coat with his tie, he has on a soft leather jacket. His hands are clean but they look as if they've been scrubbed very hard to make them that way. He doesn't have on a ring.

"Are you a newspaper reporter?" she asks.

"No. Neither am I a doctor, lawyer, or other professional."

Her drink arrives. The bartender stands waiting. She makes no move toward her wallet, and in a flash he offers his five again. "I'll pay you back," she says in a low tone. "I just prefer not to do the actual transaction myself."

"So you've decided to talk to me?" he asks.

"Why not?" she says, smiling her inverted smile. She fully intends to pay him back, although at some point in the evening she knows she will begin thinking that he has more money than she does, so why shouldn't he pay. She's a teacher; he probably digs for gold. She's discriminated against; he can have whatever he wants. She supports two other people; he takes care of himself. Besides, he came here tonight planning to buy some woman some drinks. It might as well be her. "So, what do you take notes on?" she asks, as this second martini begins to flood her. It's the one question she promised herself she wouldn't ask.

"It's a writing assignment for my twelfth-graders. They have to write a description of what happened to them on Saturday night. I always do the assignments, too."

"You teach?"

"Yep. Professionally, actually."

She begins chuckling to herself. He's cute; he's really cute. She has started running her fingers through her hair from the base of her neck up, which tells her that she's beginning to get drunk. Cap used to say what a sexy move it was, which is the type of thing people should restrain themselves from saying. She still starts it naturally, but she can't continue without feeling that she's false. She continues anyway.

It's hard to stop laughing. She'll talk to anybody, she suddenly feels like telling him. But he must already know she will. Why would he hang around someone who didn't want to talk to him because he wasn't a doctor or a lawyer? Even though she'd said it to get rid of him. What kind of person must he think she is?

"So, you're here on assignment," she says.

"Basically."

"And you're planning to write about what happens to you tonight . . . and read it to your twelfth-graders."

"That's the plan." He thinks she is criticizing him, she realizes, although he has the same unruffled look. Like all dark eyes, however, his hide so much. The pigment stops her at the surface.

"Why aren't you taking notes?" she asks.

"So far, nothing's happened that I'll forget."

She raises her eyebrows and gives him a steady look. A quick grin touches the corners of his mouth and then vanishes. They have mutually acknowledged that his last comment was a line. At least it wasn't an ordinary line: it related to the conversation they were having. At least the line had grace.

"Are you going to write about me?" she asks. She's down to swabbing ice cubes with her tongue again.

"I expect so."

"What are you going to say?"

"That you're pretty." He says this without a smile. "That you seem not to belong here."

"There're lots of pretty people here," she says. She nods in the direction of a girl to their left—a much prettier girl than she. "Who belongs and who doesn't?"

"People with two kids don't belong," he says.

She stares at him. "So you're a bouncer, too. A psychological bouncer." She would point out her cleverness, if he wasn't making her so mad.

"I know things," he says.

"You know nothing about me," she says coldly. She is sorry for every bit of information that she has given him. Hell, her first visit to a place like this and she's being told she shouldn't be here. The irony is that all she'd wanted was to be left alone with her martini.

She had felt a rising interest in him, but now she only feels the sense of futility that overwhelms her during those moments when she knows her kids are not enough. She is tired. She has taught whining seventh-graders all day long, feeling her eyes actually age as the clock ticked toward 3 p.m. dismissal. Her eyes are always fine again the next day, but how long will a night's sleep rejuvenate them?

It is Friday night, Date Night Number One, as the radio announcers used to say in high school—all that wonderful conspiracy of young love, from every direction, that once surrounded her. Sometimes when the Wolf Man hummed over the airwaves for her to move a little closer to Cap, she felt as if there was a kind of instruction going on, an instruction she welcomed as eagerly as every girl before her. On dates, Jude felt lured by the Wolf Man as much as she felt lured by Cap. It was as if inside Cap's car there was a *ménage à trois*, although in high school she hadn't imagined that people did things like that. She let herself be lured because she knew—from Mother, though not from Katherine—that Katherine had done it with J.T. But what was she being lured toward? Sex with her boyfriend or equivalence with her sister? Perhaps both. Although Mother said Katherine had *lost* her virginity, Jude longed for what Katherine had gained. Romance. The meeting of bodies. The knowledge of a male. Until she found out that, unlike Katherine, who had broken up with J.T., she couldn't stop. Katherine did not date seriously again until college, but Jude was paired with the man she would marry.

Jude had loved the Wolf Man for his voice and for making her think that what she and Cap were doing in the back seat—to the beat of the records he played—was what everyone else was doing. It wasn't what everyone else was doing, though even now she thinks premarital sex is all right. The actual act, in other words, is no big deal. What she is against is what the earliness of that experience can take from a girl. In her whole entire life—she is twenty-eight years old and has been fucking for eleven or twelve years—she's never felt passion. She blames it on the Wolf Man. On her sister. On her mother, for telling her. And, she guesses, on Cap.

She picks up her blazer from where she had tucked it under the bar rail.

"You're not going, are you?" a voice says.

She'd forgotten about the black-eyed note-taking teacher, who was only interested in fucking her, too. Just a better line than most. Or maybe he didn't want to fuck her. Either way, what does she care? She doesn't know him, she doesn't love him, she doesn't feel passion for him. And the deck is eternally stacked against her. She'll never have the chance to know anyone well enough to feel passion. And once she's fucked the person, it's too late. Desire occasionally strikes her: for example, without the lecture, she would have gone to bed with this guy tonight. But it would only have been glands. There's no opportunity for anything else.

She sees more clearly than she's ever seen: she will not find what she wants.

"Would you please give me your phone number?" he asks. It's obvious from his face that he thinks he's the reason she's leaving.

"Why?" Hardly realizing it, she is already halfway to the door. Some lucky person can take her place.

"Because I'd like to call you." He's walking beside her, restraining her arm, impeding her progress.

She stops abruptly. "Let go of me," she says quietly. His mouth is tight with anger. They stand looking at each other.

"When are you coming back?" he asks.

"Are you kidding?"

"You're a very interesting woman. I'd like to know you better." The fakey words do not match his sincere tone.

"I don't like you," she says, and the truth of this makes it come out in a whisper. She relaxes, straightening up. He does the same, standing taller, too. People are looking at them. She turns her head to the right and to the left until they begin looking somewhere else. "I like you fine," she says. "I don't know you. Just like you don't know me. How could I know whether I like you or not?"

"Will you at least give me a chance?"

She still cannot breathe easily, with hopelessness squeezing her heart, making her all tight inside. She gives him her most blank look, the one without life or personality. If only he would just go away. Maybe the challenge is what makes him not back off. So she smiles—a cute, come-hither smile. She bats her eyelashes. He laughs. He thinks she's funny.

There's no hope at all, she thinks.

He asks if she would please sit back down at the bar with him, but she says that she'd rather they go to her house. He says all right, but nothing in his manner suggests that he thinks he has triumphed. They take two cars and on the trip across town she doesn't try to lose him.

After she dismisses the babysitter, he builds a fire in her fireplace so expertly that bellows aren't needed. They sit wrapped in separate blankets and talk. He is thirty years old. He's been married twice. He's considering a career change: he'd like to become an optometrist. He comes from south Georgia, where his father was an itinerant preacher and his mother sewed clothes. He went to college on scholarship.

He asks her hardly anything about herself, seemingly content with the remarks she makes. He *will* ask, though. It's pleasant, she thinks, simply to listen rather than be bombarded with questions to which the answers mean nothing right now. It is only significant that she has two sisters if he's sometime going to meet them. It's only significant that she tell him about her mother if they become serious. She doesn't like to talk about things like nuclear war or neo-conservative politics or charismatic religion with near-strangers, because she holds in no regard the opinion of someone she doesn't yet respect. She just likes to chat, hear funny stories, laugh, be quiet.

Finally she asks, "Why did your marriages break up?"

"The first because I ran around on her," he says, pulling his blanket closer to him. She is used to a low thermostat, which saves her money. "The second because she ran around on me."

"Is that a problem for you?" she asks, taking off her blanket so she can better enjoy the fire.

"To be run around on?" He laughs. He's less good-looking away from the crowd.

She doesn't answer.

"No," he says. "I don't think it would be. Not at this point." He stands and folds his blanket. For a moment he stares into the fire. The light in his eyes, though, is only a reflection. The last glass of wine she poured him sits full on the hearth. She'd thought about asking him for it when she finished the bottle but never did.

She hides her unsteadiness as she moves close to him, slipping her hands into his back pockets and pulling his hips up against hers. This is when she feels most like a woman, most like the woman she imagines her mother to have been. So compelling. So irresistible. The best lay he's ever had. It's something that a mother of two can be proud of. He kisses her once more, tenderly, and then stops.

"I'll come back," he says.

"That's not the way I want it."

"Let me come back," he says, his hands on her shoulders.

She leads him into her bedroom and undresses him and then slips out of her clothes, including the sexy garter belt she bought last week. She does everything she can think of to him. He seems to like it. The heat of her climax builds slowly—like a fire made of coal instead of wood—and when she comes she feels ripples in her thighs, in her ass, in the back of her brain. But in her heart she has closed this man out forever. A man whose name she can't remember.

CHAPTER

9

Her Yeats professor, a solidly built, morose man who kept the class ten extra minutes just to listen to his own voice, is responsible for her tardiness, Katherine tells Frank. She drops her books on the floor of the car and falls into the seat. Her eyes are moist and she is out of breath, but she could look this way because she's been running. In truth, she's stirred up because of how the poetry has made her feel. Frank doesn't like to be late, but her blustery arrival seems to have neutralized his irritation with her. She says hello, exuberantly, and receives a kiss.

At the end of class Dr. Stern read Yeats's "The Second Coming," his voice swaying, arcing, descending . . . and, as usual, showing off . . . with words she wants to read to Frank now. They are on their way to a meeting of United Way volunteers. Frank had offered to pick her up after her morning class and return her in time for her afternoon class so she wouldn't lose her parking spot at the university. He's vice-chairman of this year's campaign, and although they won't be able to sit together, he wants her to be with him at the kickoff luncheon. She's not even a volunteer.

She flips through her textbook, scarcely heeding the fragile pages. Should she read Frank this poem? Should she tell him how important it is to her? Or will its importance worry him? In a way that transcends regular life, she is suddenly in love with William Butler Yeats. This is how she was supposed to feel ten years ago when she was in college, she knows, but the time was not right. In college, she'd had excellent grades, but only by holding in her mind everything she was taught, long enough to take the tests. In college, for the first time in her life, her attention had been on friends and on dating, with—as it ended up—insignificant results. In college, she had not opened any doors. She is opening them now.

Frank is hurrying down tree-lined West Market Street to the beltway, which leads to the Holiday Inn–Four Seasons Convention Center, where local meetings of this sort are held.

"Everyone will be late," she says. "Really." She doesn't mind speeding, but Frank is a speeder who gets caught.

"You forget I'm at the head table."

It's not the time to read him poetry, but she doesn't think she can stop herself. "Will you listen to something?" she asks.

He speeds up to make a changing stoplight. "Sure."

She tucks her hair behind her ears. She'll make her voice large, resonant, affecting like Dr. Stern's. She reads:

> Turning and turning in the widening gyre
> The falcon cannot hear the falconer;
> Things fall apart; the center cannot hold;
> Mere anarchy is loosed upon the world,
> The blood-dimmed tide is loosed, and everywhere
> The ceremony of innocence is drowned;
> The best lack all conviction, while the worst
> Are full of passionate intensity.

Her chest heaves. In her excitement she closes the book, but, just as quickly, opens it again.

"That's nice," Frank says. "What's it about? Other than war?"

"It's about Christ's second coming. I should have told you that before I read it. There's more—about a new Nativity—but I can read that on the way home."

Frank nods agreeably, willing to drop the conversation or continue it, whichever she prefers. She reaches and messes up his hair, which always looks messed up anyway. His irregular profile does not suggest how attractive he is.

"Stop," he hollers.

"It makes you cuter."

"Stop anyway." He gives her hair a swipe. She pulls out a brush and begins straightening them both.

"What kind of day have you been having?" she asks.

"Reasonable. And you?"

"Same, although I think I've been waiting all my life to take this course."

"Well, well," he says, seemingly pleased.

Katherine tries to visualize the ending of the world. Instead of by fire, as she believes most people expect, she sees things Yeats's way, with the world caving in and the waters rushing to fill up the holes. *Despite* the promise of the rainbow. However the world ends, though, according to the poet, anarchy, "mere" anarchy will seem tame alongside. "*Mere* anarchy." Does it mean what she thinks it means?

Lately, Katherine has been thinking that she herself is an anarchist. She's against what society expects, against what anybody expects, really. A tiny example is this United Way luncheon, although nothing is expected of her but to be there, and only Frank expects that. But it's *not* only Frank who expects it. Society expects it too. Her presence at this meeting will not be noticed, but her absence certainly would be. In this community, wives support their husbands. In this community, wives and husbands are *teams*. When next year's campaign—with Frank as chairman—is successfully completed, a line in his victory speech will state that he could not have been successful without her help. If *she* were to address the same meeting, she would have to tell the United Way campaigners that volunteerism revolts her. Not on an individual level, she'd insist, but when it becomes group-think, group-give, group-self-congratulate. She's not upset with the Boy Scouts or the drug-action council, but the United Way as a whole angers her. She doesn't totally understand why.

Although so far Frank seems not to have noticed, she's becoming an anarchist in her marriage, too. Maybe it's because she's so sure of him. She's recently realized that she's been too sweet all her life. It was the only way she thought anybody would love her. She's especially been too sweet to her husband. But, a little at a time, she's been acting more real. If she's unhappy about something, she doesn't hide it anymore from Frank until it goes away. She's been trying out her ideas on him and making her opinions known, even insisting on them at times. She feels guilty: it doesn't seem fair to change, to start saying no when the whole four years they've been married she's said yes. But, so far, there's been no friction at all. She hopes Frank will still love her when she gets up enough nerve to say how sorry she is that he's involved in the United Way at all.

She says, "What do you make of the lines 'The best lack all conviction, while the worst / Are full of passionate intensity'?"

Frank has forgotten about the poem, she sees, but he quickly readjusts. "What does your professor say?"

"He hasn't given us his interpretation. He read to us and then dismissed us." She thinks again of Dr. Stern's flamboyance before the class: egotistical yet strangely intriguing. He's a large man whose face inclines slightly heavenward. It's obvious from his bold gestures, his forceful voice, and the way he turns, as if onstage, that he's quite sure of his good looks.

In a different tone she says: "It's funny. Dr. Stern doesn't give the answers. And I used to *hate* that in college. I never cared what other students thought. But in this class there aren't any right answers. Only more studied ones." She sees Frank smiling. "You already knew that, didn't you?" She reaches into his ribs and tickles him once quickly. "You found it out ten years ago when you tried your first case," she adds, grinning. Although Frank now primarily practices corporate law, he got started with divorce cases. "I'm just your arrested developer," she says, darting her hand at his side again. Frank fends her off. "But it's an amazing class."

"Sounds like it."

She starts to read from the beginning of the poem again. He gives no indication that he minds. She whispers, which makes the words sound frightening. This time she continues into the final stanza.

> *. . . but now I know*
> *That twenty centuries of stony sleep*

Were vexed to nightmare by a rocking cradle,
And what rough beast, its hour come round at last,
Slouches towards Bethlehem to be born?

"Wow," Frank says in a somber voice. She hopes he won't use what she's read to make a comment about babies. "I think I understand about the 'worst' being full of passionate intensity," he says. "Wouldn't you—especially if you were *bad*—be scared shitless on Judgment Day?" He begins laughing, the cackle that makes her laugh at him as well as his joke.

"I thought you were going to say something serious," she says. She puts on a smile and then begins smiling for real. What he said *was* serious, and it *wasn't* about babies. "Funny," she says. "Really. Funny. I'll mention it at my Friday class."

She was displeased, but now she's pleased again. The world needs people like Frank. It needs steady, predictable people that it can count on. Frank listens to her, he cares about what's going on in her life, he reminds her not to take herself too seriously. She's even a little bit proud of him for working on a United Way campaign. Her husband is a leader, someone who can get a complex, nonpaying job done. He doesn't have to be an anarchist just because she is. Everything he undertakes does not have to claim his heart and soul. Even law, she has come to realize, is just an occupation for him, unlike it would be for her.

The last half of the line is easier to understand than the first half. What *does* "The best lack all conviction" mean, she wonders. Perhaps, during the Second Coming, even those people who have nothing to fear shall be afraid. *All* souls are to be overwhelmed: the "best" faltering in their beliefs, the "worst" deservedly terrified. This is what she'll suggest at Friday's class.

The luncheon has begun by the time they arrive. Katherine should have realized that busy men are running this campaign. Frank hurries to his place at the head table, and she finds a single empty chair at a table near the front of the room. She introduces herself to the people sitting nearest her. The only person she knows is a woman realtor at the far end who has called her a few times to ask indirectly if she and Frank are interested yet in a house in a better neighborhood.

Two hundred people, including a small black contingent representing what used to be the black YMCA but now is open to everyone, have gathered in the banquet room. They span a broad social range, except for people in the top positions. Men in Greensboro who used to work with the Jaycees now learn leadership through the United Way. The Jaycees is no longer the place to be socially, just as for women, the Greensboro Preservation Society has surpassed the Junior League. Perhaps it's because volunteerism is so closely tied to social climbing that Katherine finds it abhorrent. Maybe she's hating the wrong thing. But it's hard to separate the two, and, indeed, no one who raises money would want to. A few years ago, the Greensboro Symphony Orchestra hit upon the idea of sponsoring a new debutante ball to compete with the venerable Greensboro Debutante Club. Although in the club's view there's really no contest, membership in the symphony guild has grown at an alarming rate ever since. Unless one is from a venerable family, no better way exists to ensure a daughter's coming out than to give the symphony one's time and one's money.

While she eats, Katherine studies Frank, who is seated next to Ken Bedingfield, the campaign chairman. Rarely does she have so much time to observe him unobserved. She truly loves how he looks: the lively brown eyes, the untrainable hair, the quick grin. Even when there's nothing funny, Frank's impish face can make you think there is. She also likes how he looks in comparison with the rest of the men, their stiff shoulders exuding self-importance. At least that's how most of them look to her. Frank is humble and generous and honest and kind. All these things show in the way he carries himself. He's also devoted to her. Just now he looks up and sees her looking at him and slows down his chewing. They have been married four years; they've just driven over here together; but his face lights up as if he's fallen in love. He leans toward Ken, whispers something, and points out the person wearing the pleated skirt and ankle-high boots—an outfit she knew would be acceptable to both town and gown. Not an anarchist's outfit, she thinks wryly.

"Who *is* that girl?" she knows he has asked Ken. After a few seconds Ken understands the joke.

She smiles in appreciation, all the time wondering if he is still going to love her if she gives him a final no about something really important. But she probably can't stop saying yes. She's been trying to please people for so long that it may be all she knows. If it's all she knows, she won't have to worry about Frank, since she won't be able to behave toward him any other way.

Still, she wonders, as she always has, how big a role eagerness to please plays in love. If you love someone, do you automatically try to please that person so he'll love you? Or do you act your worst to see if he'll love you, anyway? Are you ever just yourself? Isn't it dangerous to be just yourself? When Mother told them, "The answer is always yes," right before she died, did she mean to give in to other people and be what *they* want you to be or be what *you* want to be? "Yes" to *whom?*

So far with Frank, she's been her best. It's made him happy. It hasn't made *her* unhappy, although it seems to be making her *something*. Her mother was her worst with Max. Her mother was her worst with her father. Her mother was difficult with everyone, and everyone, including Katherine for many years, tried to please her mother. Maybe what is happening to Katherine is that she is finally becoming her worst. She may be one of the ones scared shitless on Judgment Day. Along with the woman who gave her birth.

Ken stands up and announces that he has promised all their bosses to have them back at work promptly, so he needs to go ahead and talk about the campaign. He is a tall, athletically handsome man who wears both his jackets and his trousers too short. He introduces the division chairmen, as well as Frank, asking that the audience hold its applause for one single expression of appreciation. After the round is finished, Ken himself begins clapping into the microphone. As if on cue, the other people at the head table join in. Ken is beaming. Over his clapping, which sounds very loud with the amplification, he says, "We applaud you, our volunteers. You're the people who do the work."

Ken draws himself straighter and assumes a serious expression as he waits for the room to quieten. He lifts his chin slightly and leans toward the microphone, which at its tallest is not tall enough for him. He is a model of community service, but Katherine cannot admire him the way she admires Frank. There's something so completely unfalse about Frank, even if he is doing good.

"We, the people in this room today," Ken says, "are here for one reason: to help those less fortunate than ourselves. I know that each of you works hard for what you have. You could choose to keep every dollar you make. You could provide your families with every luxury that your incomes could afford. But you are people who are givers—not just consumers. Everyone of you here—I know your faces—has shown a willingness over and over again—not simply in the United Way campaign, but throughout Greensboro—to use your resources to help others.

"If you are like me—and I'm sure all of us here think pretty much alike—you feel that God has smiled on your life. You feel that He has blessed you; you know that this community has blessed you. And you want to give back to Greensboro—as do I—a portion of what Greensboro has given you.

"Before we begin this campaign—which will help all thirty-five of our member agencies—I wish to express my appreciation for your time. Now I ask each of you to make your pledge. Make it before you ask others to give. Make it so you *can* ask others to give. A committed *soldier* can create a committed *army*.

"I ask today that you give to the United Way and keep our community safe and strong."

Someone in the audience realizes that Ken's speech is over and begins to clap. Katherine watches the glaze lift from Frank's eyes as he joins the applause. Everyone at the head table appears pleased. She allows herself a secret smile: the look on Ken's face is beatific.

Ken turns to Frank and shakes his hand, the way Katherine has seen a president do. The clapping intensifies and then abruptly halts. At the head table, Ken is reaching deep into the pocket of his trousers. He has evidently cut a hole in his pocket, because he keeps reaching down, down—almost to his knee. When he pulls out his hand, he is holding a thick roll of money. "Monopoly money," he says into the microphone, so no one will think that he in particular is rich. Mild applause resumes. He takes the rubber band from around the roll, and sure enough, except for the top bill, the money is fake.

"I just want each of you to dig as deeply as possible," he says. There is new enthusiasm around the room. Ken has made them laugh. Katherine senses that everyone would like to sing something patriotic, but no one will begin. At the head table all the men and one woman, an anesthesiologist's wife, begin to stand and shake hands. A final wave of applause crosses the room.

Frank finds her in the crowd and brushes her lips lightly with his, an action that has earned them the reputation around town of really being in love. She is pleased that the United Way doesn't daunt him. Recently, he has begun kissing her in church when members of the parish wish each other peace, an idea he got from watching a fellow communicant who grew up Episcopalian. Frank is a converted Unitarian, already tired, when she met him, of "not believing in anything," in his own words. He has embraced her faith with the fervor of most converts, wanting to be as authentic an Episcopalian as possible. He wishes he had grown up Episcopalian, he tells her, the same way he wishes he had known her as a little girl. To the latter wish she says: no, he doesn't.

A man's arm encircles her waist from behind. Before she can resent the familiarity—it's as if, since she's married, Frank's friends may touch her at will—she realizes it's her father.

"Daddy!" She turns to kiss his cheek, while he shakes hands with Frank. His sad, deep-set eyes did not change when he saw her, but he smiled. He's a taller than average man, but seems almost slight because of his narrow shoulders and small hips. Louise is the only daughter who resembles him, their faces possessing a similar softness. Since Katherine can remember, he has been half bald. The advantage is that in his twenties he looked older than people his age but hardly any older since. Because of his thinness, his clothes always seem too big for him, but they are impeccably styled. "What are you doing here?" she asks, although she knows he participates in charitable projects to enhance the bank's image.

He leans toward her and says in an undertone, "I'm helping *save* our community."

"Fum those less fo'tunate than we'ums who has wucked owah fingahs to de bone," Katherine adds. If no one else were here, she and her father would be shrieking with laughter. They both know what Ken wants to keep the community safe from. As it is, all three of them chuckle softly.

She likes running into her father unexpectedly like this. It gives her a feeling of warmth toward him that she doesn't have when they're scheduled to see each other. She feels somehow linked: a girl with a daddy traveling about town, a daddy who makes private jokes and hugs her when he sees her, a daddy identifiably *her* daddy. Although she lived with him for two years before she went off to college, she never thinks of her father when she thinks of her growing-up years. It's as if he's had no influence on her life at all, unless he's the reason she's not insane. If so, he has a significance in her life that she's not fully aware of. Perhaps because her father exists she can expect to have a sane future too. Rather, a future that is running out, to use Frank's most recent words.

"What did Ken say wrong?" Frank asks suddenly, his mouth pursed.

"We were only teasing," answers Katherine.

"He said what he really thinks," her father chimes in. "He doesn't want to help people less fortunate for *their* sakes but for *his own* sake. He wants to be protected."

Frank steps back from them. "I thought his digging in his pocket was pretty clever."

"So did we," her father says.

"Me, too," Katherine murmurs.

She hooks elbows with both of them and looks from one to the other, so they'll each know they're appreciated. "Frank's chairman of this thing next year," she reminds her father. "He's wondering what you say to generate enthusiasm without sounding like a fool." Frank lets his arm drop free of hers, so she is left standing with just her father again.

"I don't know what you say not to sound like a fool," her father remarks. "But it needs to be something more subtle than what was said." Her father has definite ideas about what money means and what it doesn't. He does not think it makes people holier.

"*You* won't sound like a fool," she tells Frank. He thinks they are being excessively critical, she knows, but at the same time he wants to avoid Ken's mistakes. He still doesn't know what the mistake was. "I'll write your speech," she says lightly, slipping her arm free of her father's. She thinks of the opportunities that writing it will give her.

She enjoys their awareness that she loves them both. She enjoys the feeling that each of them is a bit jealous. She thinks how pleased they both would be if she were standing here pregnant, instead of standing here with just the past and the present. How, if she would stop using her diaphragm, the way Frank wants, her entire span—past, present, and future—could be here at the United Way meeting. Perhaps the idea of "saving" the community might then have meaning for her. But she doubts it. She is too much of an anarchist. "Mere anarchy." Does she underestimate it?

Frank moves away to shake hands with the division leaders who might agree to be *his* division leaders next year, and her father tells her goodbye. She watches her father pick up his own solicitation paraphernalia at the door, which reminds her that he, too, has a responsibility in this campaign. And he's not a social climber. She stoops to retrieve her Yeats book from under her chair. While they were hurrying through the Holiday Inn parking lot at their arrival, Frank had asked her, "Why are you bringing that?" Her act had been reflexive but aware, since she had not had to look in her hands to know what he was talking about.

There are two possible reasons why she brought the book to the meeting. Maybe she *was* showing off, hoping someone would ask if she's a student again. Or, if she wasn't showing off, maybe she brought the book inside as a talisman against the dreadful boredom of adult life. Even if volunteering does not always have social overtones, it's sleep-inducing. Look at this meeting today. Her undergraduate education—narrow though she had made it—had not led her to think life would be like this. Not that she's unhappy. She loves Frank. She loves her family. She loves having her own home. But what is there to *do?*

On her behalf she can say that her instincts, when she was twenty, had been correct. She'd majored in communications, figuring that whatever work she did would always be exciting and never the same. Out of college she'd become an upwardly mobile receptionist at the television station and had just begun to handle a camera when she met Frank. By the time they were married and she thought again about her job, someone less distracted had taken her place. She was offered another toehold but turned it down. Camera work was no longer interesting to her. Then her mother died and anything to do with television seemed superfluous. So she quit. For the next two years, until she started graduate school last spring, she'd edited an airline magazine. Her responsibilities had been to think of story ideas and find money-desperate freelance writers to research and write them. She held on to that job six months longer than she wanted to because Frank had begun to encourage her to quit work. He never said so, but he wanted her to be bored at home so that she would want to have babies. She *was* bored. Editing the airline magazine bored her, but being bored did not make her want to get pregnant. Now that she's back in school, things have changed for her once again. But they haven't changed for Frank.

These days, Frank often asks her if she's aware of her biological clock. She always gives him an emphatic yes, but it's not the same biological clock he's talking about. He's reminding her that she has approximately ten more child-bearing years. To her, her biological clock will be ticking between now and when she reaches age seventy-two, when she expects—since she doesn't smoke—to die. That's how much time she has to become and be what she wants to be.

Of course, the problem is, she doesn't know what she wants to be. She likes to read Yeats. And she's enjoying her other course, art appreciation. Last semester she was fascinated by her intro-duction-to-theology course. She also studied the history of sci-ence. Her history-of-science course made her dream of being a doctor, but at the age of only twenty-nine, she does not have time. Yes, Frank, she's very aware of her biological clock. It doesn't give her time to go to medical school. She's thought it might be interesting to be a priest, after taking the theology course, but she's not sure whether she has the religious depth or, since she's a woman, the political bent. Probably she doesn't have time to do that, either. She's even wondered about being some kind of artist, but she's pretty sure she lacks any kind of creative talent. Wouldn't it have shown up by now? The type of artist she would most like to be is a dancer, but according to how Margot Fonteyn did it, Katherine should have started prac-ticing over twenty years ago.

Is no one awake going through college the first time? Or was it just her?

She checks her watch. Ten minutes until class time. Frank is having an intense conversation with Ken. She hopes he is not telling him their criticism. Frank's earnestness sometimes leads him to tell people things he should probably keep to himself. He would think Ken ought to know he'd made a mistake so he wouldn't make it again. He would consider that, as Ken's friend, it's his responsibility to help him all he can.

"Hi, Ken," she says cheerily. "You did a nice job." He doesn't glare at her, so she guesses Frank hasn't been talking.

"Do you think it was too religious-sounding?" Ken asks.

She thinks for a brief second about Yeats. "Not at all," she says. "Not even a little bit." What he meant was, did she think it was too evangelical? "My class starts in just a few minutes," she says to Frank.

Ken stretches in an enormous way, taking up air space twice his size. "Hey, Anne's thinking about doing that," he says.

"Going back to school?" she asks cordially. Anne Beding-field is a statuesque but styleless woman who wears her bleached hair in a French twist. Katherine cannot imagine her in a class-room. Her bracelets would make too much noise.

"She's always wanted her degree. Whaffor? I ask her. She's

not going to do anything with it, so why take up everybody's time, hers included? Do you know what I mean?"

Frank murmurs to Ken that they need to go.

"Do *you* know what I mean?" Ken asks Frank, since Katherine hasn't answered. He towers over them, his big hands propped at his waist. The United Way is a million miles away.

"Sort of," Frank says.

"No, he doesn't," she says dryly.

"You do. Both of you do," Ken insists.

"No, we both don't." Katherine turns her back. Frank tells Ken goodbye and follows. "I'm going to be late," she mutters as they hurry across the room. "For that." She hates Ken, but she hates Frank, too, for not supporting her. Frank has to maintain peace at the cost of his own belief. If he *has* any beliefs. Her hate suddenly dissolves. She knows Frank has beliefs. He's in no way like Ken. He cares about the things she wants to do. It dissolves, but for a moment, she felt it.

"Read me some poetry," he says as they get into the car. It's such a decent thing for him to ask her to do. "Read me about the beast slouching toward Bethlehem again." That's a subject he wouldn't forget.

"Not now."

"Are you mad at me?" he asks. "Because of Ken . . . ?" He doesn't start the car.

"Sort of," she says, beginning to thumb through the book. She's echoing his own response to Ken. She supposes that she should not expect him to join her battle, although "a committed soldier" can create "a committed army." Does he realize, she wonders, that part of her battle is against him? She reaches over and turns the key in the ignition, still not forgiving him. He begins backing out of the parking place.

"Turning turning turning the widening gyre," he says. "The falcon cannot hear the falconer. The center cannot hold. Things fall apart . . ."

"Pretty good," she says.

He begins humming. The tune is "Onward, Christian Soldiers."

"I hate to tell you, but you make me laugh," she says. She

lays her head on his shoulder, and he puts his arm around her, hugging her close and driving with one hand. He smells like starch and skin and utter reasonableness. "I shouldn't get angry at you because I'm angry at Ken," she says. "I guess I worry that secretly you think like he does. That I'm wasting all my teachers' time as well as my own time. As well as *your* time. That's the implication. That I'm wasting *your* time. But I'm not like Anne Bedingfield."

"Who said you were? What's Anne Bedingfield like? Do you really know? I think she's pretty brave . . . with a husband like Ken."

"It appears that I'm Anne Bedingfield's clone."

"How?"

She sighs and removes his arm from around her and begins the litany that she thought out on the way to the parking lot. "Anne's married to the present chairman of the United Way, and I'm married to the future chairman. Neither one of us has a job. Now she's going back to school . . . like me. Why does somebody like her have to go back to school? She ruins it for the people who are serious."

"You hardly know Anne Bedingfield."

"I know *enough*." Katherine tucks her hair behind her ears, works her lips. "Stop about Anne Bedingfield," she says. "I don't care about her. I only care about you and what you think. But I don't want to be minimized. By Ken or you or anybody." They are nearing campus, and since her class has already started, she won't be able to continue the conversation.

"Have I ever minimized you?" he asks.

"No. You haven't. But you could. And you might. What if I told you . . . Never mind."

"Go ahead."

"I don't have time now."

"What if you told me what?" He noses their Audi into a parking space. She reaches for the door handle to escape, but he grabs her hand. "I know you want to keep going to school," he prompts. "I don't think it's busywork. I think it's important. You can go to school and do other things too, though."

"Like having a baby?" she asks.

"What's wrong with having a baby?" he asks in a low voice.

"If you *want* to have a baby, nothing."

"Do you not?"

She pulls free of his hand and opens the door. He reaches for her but she eludes him. She stands outside the car. Frank's eyelids droop. He takes a breath and lets it out slowly.

"I want to go to graduate school," she says in a small voice.

"You're going to graduate school. Here we are."

"I want to go until I become something," she says, a little more firmly.

"You can. You can." His voice makes her feel as if she's being patted on the head.

She knows what he's going to say next, so to stop him she shuts the door. Around on his side of the car, she throws him a kiss so he won't be able to reach her again. He rolls the window halfway down. "We'll talk more tonight," she promises. "Don't worry. I'm not going to medical school."

"That's a relief, I guess."

"I would if I could," she says. "But my biological clock won't let me."

Frank looks steadily at her. The paternal look in his eyes is gone. "You may miss it *all*," he says matter-of-factly.

"All *what*?" She sidles closer to the car. He rolls his window the rest of the way down and props his elbow at the opening. She leans against the car door. Their hands are close, but Frank doesn't touch her.

"All what?" she repeats, but this time her voice is softer, humbled. She doesn't look at her watch, but by now Professor Barnes must be deeply involved in her Balthus lecture.

The metal of the car warms Katherine through her clothing. She feels so young like this: girl on college campus leaning against car of boy. She wishes she'd met Frank when she was twenty. If she'd had babies then, they'd be half grown by now. It was like unconscious art—a term Dr. Stern used all the time—to have your babies in your early twenties. You hardly knew you were doing it, and then it was done and over with. She'd give anything to have a seven-year-old son and a six-year-old daughter right now. But she would have had to have met Frank ages ago. And been smart enough—or unconscious enough—to get pregnant.

"I love you," he says.

She always automatically says she loves him too, but not this time.

"You know, we've got to face this question," he says. "It can get too late without your knowing it. One day you might wake up and feel too old to have a baby. I mean *mentally* too old. I've seen it happen to people in their thirties. *Young* thirties."

"I'm not scared to have children," she says.

"You're not?" Real surprise is in his voice.

She's told him for so long that she *is* afraid that suddenly she wants to grab some of that protection back. "Not the way you're talking about," she says. "I'm not old. I'm young. Maybe I'm too young." She searches his face. "What I most am . . . I guess . . . is not ready. You know how much I'm enjoying school." He nods as if he does know. "I just . . ." He grips one of her hands tightly.

It's so horrible that someone's happiness can depend on what another person will or won't do. Her life hasn't even started becoming what she wants it to be. But it's about to. How can she tamper with it now? And why does she have to make Frank happy with *another* someone? She's lucky, she supposes, that Mother didn't have this same choice. If she had, none of them would be here.

It's so deep inside Katherine why she won't be a good mother, but, of all the things she knows, she knows this best. The reason she will never be a good mother is that she will smother her children. Worse than smother. Destroy. She will destroy her children because she'll love them too much. To make up for her sisters. And for how her mother didn't love her.

No matter what she tells Frank, he doesn't believe that Mother didn't love them. He says that there are two types of people: those who are loved by their mothers and know it and those who are loved by their mothers and don't. He can't conceive that a mother might not love her children. He can't imagine that more powerful forces can be at work. Mother loved us in her own peculiar way, Katherine has said, but it was not the most powerful emotion she felt. Possession—an emotion as unkin to love as jealousy—was the most powerful emotion she felt. She cannot tell Frank what she suspects about her own self. Then he would know what he has to convince her away from. If Katherine has children, she fears she will possess them instead of love them. She won't know how to love them, since she was never loved. She'll possess and destroy them. Nothing can change her. Not even Frank can make her different than she was made so many years ago.

"I would be a good mother," she says. A grin cuts deeply into Frank's face. "You don't have to convince me of that. I would love our children a lot. I guess I'm worried that I'd love them too much."

"You can't love children too much," Frank says, as she expected him to.

"Yes, you can."

"Nope. No, you can't." Frank was on the debate team at Davidson College, and she sees the looseness that enters his body when he first feels he is winning advantage over his opponent. Maybe together they could be good parents. But no, she only knows how to be a bad parent. Inside, her chest freezes and burns at the same time. She tries to take a deep breath but can't make the air go down.

Women have tricked men into marrying them with "accidental" pregnancies. Has a married woman ever pretended to be trying to get pregnant? She would have to switch to birth-control pills since diaphragms have such physical presence. She would have to switch to hidden pills and not forget to take them for the next ten years.

"I'm doing more than enjoying school," she says.

He kneads her hand insistently: she feels an impulse to jerk it away. "You can do both," he says. "I'll help you. We'll hire babysitters. It can be done. Easily. Lots of people do it."

She nods. She knows that everything he says is true. He'll

help her; he always helps her. They have enough money to hire babysitters.

The color in Frank's cheeks heightens. "I think this is a perfect time to start trying," he says softly. "You should be barely pregnant during the hot summer months, and then around Christmas or after, the baby will be born. Don't think I haven't noticed how you've felt since you've been back at school. I have. I want you to stay in school. It's what means something to you. You're so curious. Which is what I love so about you. Your openness to everything." Then he makes a little joke. "Like babies."

It's not *baby* anymore but *babies*. She's so afraid. But Frank speaks so tenderly. Even if she didn't know anything about his past, she could, on a first meeting, perceive that he was a child who'd been loved by his mother and knew it.

She can make love tonight without her diaphragm but also without worry since she's just finished her period. In a timely way she can pretend to vacillate, at least until Frank catches on to her rhythm.

"We'll have the most remarkable child," he says. "He'll be impossible like you . . ."

"And reliable like you," she can't help adding.

"And curious like you."

"And tyrannical like you."

He stops laughing. "I'm not going to *make* you have a baby," he says flatly.

"Of course you are," she says.

He gives her a long, searching look.

"What do you think I'm going to miss?" she asks brusquely.

"You need to go," he says. "I need to go." He starts the car and begins to inch away. Their hands fall apart. *The center cannot hold.*

"Stop," she calls. He puts on the brakes and watches her through the side mirror. She waits. He backs the car into the parking space again.

"Do you want to say something?" he asks.

"I love you," she says tentatively.

155

He gives her a smile that is not a grin, a sad smile. But there is also about him a sense of hope. "*I* love *you*," he says.

When the car is totally out of sight, she walks instead of running to class. Frank says she is going to miss it all. When she reaches the classroom, everyone is gone. She missed the Balthus lecture, too.

CHAPTER
10

Because Louise has been looking so hard for him, they all see Billy before she does. She turns, and her black robe swirls around her ankles, then releases. The tassel bumps over the corner of her mortarboard, its awkwardness making her blush. Billy is walking toward her from Siberia, which is what everyone calls the incredibly faraway parking lot. "Oh," she says. Her hair is hot on her neck.

Louise and her family are standing outside Tinker Dorm, the place she lived her freshman year. Hollins College lies in the thick of Virginia's Blue Ridge Mountains, and trees are plentiful in the original quad section of campus. But around all the newer buildings, the landscape has been shaved and rolling fields of grass planted. Scattered in the openness are girls by themselves, girls in clusters, and girls, like Louise, whose families have just arrived, or whose families are being introduced to other families. It is a bright clear day, the blue of the sky stronger than the green of the mountains, which is the case here—Louise has noticed—far more than half the time.

It's been so long since she's seen Billy that her eyes seem to be refusing to recognize him. Who is this man walking more and more slowly toward her? One enormous change must be getting in her way: Billy is wearing a mustache, a thick blond mustache that makes him look older than he's ever looked before. He looks older than she does, which makes her uneasy. Always before, around her sisters, she and Billy have been kids together. Now he looks like someone her sisters' age. Of course, she's graduating from college today. Maybe she looks their age, too.

Before he reaches them, Katherine says, "Did you know Billy was coming?"

Jude answers for her: "Certainly she did."

Daddy says, "Well, there's Billy, what do you know?"

Frank, who has only been around Billy a few times in his life, gives a noncommittal "Hmmmm."

Jude thinks Billy looks ridiculous with a mustache—blond mustaches have always looked silly to her—and she wonders if he grew it with hopes that the family might view him in some new way. It's impossible for *her* to view him in a new way, if anybody wants to know. She regards him in the way she now regards Cap: inert and ineffectual. If that's what Louise still wants, fine. But it hadn't been enough for her, and she wishes her little sister would pay attention.

Because of Cap's inertia, because he wouldn't give her an answer about keeping the kids this weekend, she'd finally had to call Carolyn Welch. First, she'd told Cap that if she couldn't get a decision out of him, she'd get it from his girlfriend. Then, she asked him about newsroom as opposed to sports deadlines, which he willingly provided. Then, she called. It felt strange to be calling the *Greensboro Daily News,* where she'd so often called her husband, to ask to speak to her husband's girlfriend. She wondered if the switchboard operator recognized her voice. Then she wondered if the switchboard operator had known about Cap and Carolyn before she did. How many people *had,* she'd always wanted to know, although that's supposed to be a little detail that doesn't matter. It was supposed to demean Cap, not Jude, that he'd carried on with someone before they'd separated. And if everyone at the newspaper office thought—with prompting—that she must be a bitch, who really cared? She thought *they* were crazy to keep a person on staff who produced as little writing as Cap did. He'd always complained that there weren't enough sports stories in Greensboro. That was like saying there weren't enough trees.

Her conversation with Carolyn Welch had turned out to be

utterly civil, until near the end when Carolyn said how *agreeable* she thought Katie and Charles were. Thank God, Bernadette Oldham had happened to walk into the teachers' lounge and start listening. It had kept Jude from telling Carolyn to go fuck herself. "Agreeable" wasn't a word she wanted applied to her children, not by anybody and certainly not by their soon-to-be stepmother. Calling an almost-two and a three-year-old "agreeable" was a cold, cold thing, she'd wanted to scream. But because of Bernadette, she'd restrained herself and won a weekend babysitter, possibly for more than once.

Katherine can't help but smile when Louise hugs Billy. The hug begins as a superficial embrace, since it's in front of not only them but also all of Louise's classmates, but suddenly Louise is hanging on to him so tightly that she no longer has her balance. Her mortarboard falls off and bounces on the grass. Frank retrieves it. Billy, who's managing to keep them upright, looks embarrassed. In individual ways they *all* look embarrassed, except Louise. Her lips tremble, her eyes seem to stare at some other time—either the past or the future, Katherine isn't sure which—but she's not embarrassed. She even gives a slight whimper.

"God, Weezie," Jude murmurs.

"Looks like she's glad to see him," Daddy comments.

"Hi, Billy," Frank says jokingly, since there's no real way to speak to him.

Louise does not look at her family, but a sort of specificity returns to her eyes, alerting Katherine to the fact that she's looking at someone. Katherine follows the line of her gaze and sees a tall girl with short black hair standing by herself about fifteen feet away. The girl averts her eyes as soon as she realizes she's been noticed.

"Jennifer," Weezie calls out. "Come meet Billy . . . and my family." She lets go of Billy, whose eyes follow her. Katherine wonders if perhaps his visit *is* a surprise. Jude's expression is asking the same question.

First Daddy and then Frank offer their hands to Billy, while Louise is drawing her friend over to the group. Despite a perfectly congenial smile, the friend has an aloof manner, but Louise's face is worshipful. "This is Jennifer Ayers," Louise says. "She's the reason I'm not coming home this afternoon. She's getting married tomorrow in the chapel. Did you tell them I'm in the wedding, Daddy? Daddy knows because he had to buy the dress." She's as jumpy as a chipmunk.

Katherine notices that her father is about to comment on the expense of the bridesmaid's dress, so she quickly tells Jennifer how nice it is to meet her finally after hearing so many lovely things about her. She doesn't sound much like herself, and if Louise has described her at all, Jennifer will notice. But that's probably why Katherine spoke the way she did: to make Jennifer realize from the beginning that one view of a person isn't necessarily all there is.

Jude says to Jennifer, "Good luck," and although the words sound perfectly ordinary to a stranger, everyone in the family knows what tone Jude would prefer to use if she could bring herself to be a little ruder.

Louise hears Jude but doesn't even bother to look her way. She's told Jennifer to expect anything from her family and to plan in advance not to be offended.

By telephone both Katherine and Jude have heard a little about Jennifer. "By far the best friend I've ever had" has been the description. Like Katherine, Weezie has never had friends. But Katherine doesn't have friends, Jude knows, because she prefers her sisters. Louise cannot hold on to people. She'll start out with someone and then become irrevocably angry with the person, always over a matter irrelevant to the friendship. In junior high Louise "gave up" on Macy Grant because Macy's mother was sick with emphysema and Macy wouldn't stop smoking. In high school she ended a friendship with Iris Kennerly because Iris secretly dated someone else while going steady with Billy's best friend. So far, the relationship with Jennifer is too young to have "betrayed" Louise, but there's still plenty of time.

They have formed a small circle. Louise holds her mortarboard instead of putting it back on. Daddy offers everyone a cigarette, although—except for Jennifer, whose habits are unknown—he knows that no one smokes. Has he forgotten, or is he being polite? It's the kind of question that Katherine has always had about him. Half the time, Daddy seems to be one of the most aware people she knows; the other half, the most dense.

"Don't mind if I do," Billy says, stepping forward.

"*Billy,*" Louise exclaims.

"What did you expect? My favorite girl left me." He lights up, hugging her playfully around the shoulder. "I had to turn to something." Katherine and Jude exchange glances: at least Louise and Billy don't seem to be back together.

"That's no reason to smoke," Louise says primly.

"*Tell* me a reason," Billy says. Louise doesn't seem to realize that he's still teasing her.

"There *is* no reason to smoke. A reason *not* to smoke is my mother." Except for Frank, there is the slightest rift within each family member in the circle. Daddy always cringes when Mother is mentioned. Katherine and Jude both think what Weezie said is inappropriate. Their mother's memory should not be invoked over such a trivial matter as Billy's taking a cigarette. Louise sees their faces and realizes that she has said something wrong. What is it this time? She knows it has to do with her mention of Mother. But what, goddamnit, *what?* She'd like to grab Billy's hand and run away from them, and if Jennifer wasn't here, she'd do it.

Billy hurriedly puts the cigarette to his mouth again.

He appears to need its calming effect, Katherine thinks. He's brave to be here, brave to talk to them as if they'd never said an ungenerous word about him.

"You're right," Billy says softly in a voice meant just for Louise. "A good reason *is* your mother." He grinds out the cigarette under his heel, and Jude involuntarily groans.

"It was just an accident that Louise and I got to room together this year," Jennifer is saying to their father. "When we got back from Hollins Abroad last summer, everyone had already signed up for roommates. So we were put together. No choice or anything. I feel so lucky. Louise is so . . . well . . . so empathetic."

Katherine feels that Jennifer has aimed the word directly at her. Jude thinks Jennifer is playing up to their father. They both smile as if they've always thought this about their sister. Frank and Daddy—now that Jennifer has stopped exclusively addressing him—step back a bit from the circle, Daddy giving his attention to his smoking, Frank to the stateliness of Tinker Mountain.

Louise looks at Tinker Mountain, too. Jennifer's words of praise have made her quiver with good feeling. With a smile she identifies the mountain to her family as the site of Hollins College's oldest tradition, Tinker Day. She hears in her voice the ring of nostalgia, which she's never heard before. She describes the president's surprise announcement, the climb up the mountain, the picnic on top. There's no need to admit to her family that she wasn't aware Tinker Day was something she'd ever think of again. At least she's thinking of it now. Jenn is watching her wistfully. They did not spend this year's Tinker Day— their last—together. They hadn't been friends yet.

"Did you two spend a lot of time together in Paris?" Katherine asks politely.

"*No,*" Louise and Jennifer say in emphatic unison.

"She wasn't interested in me then," Weezie says teasingly.

"That's not true. We were living with different families." Jennifer's face brightens. "I asked you to be in my wedding. Actually, I asked you to be in my wedding, hardly knowing you at all. I think that says something."

"It says that you were sentimental about leaving Paris," Louise says. "You would have asked whoever sat beside you on the plane coming home to be a bridesmaid."

Jennifer smiles, a pretty smile that softens her patrician manner. "Well, it happened to be you," she says. "So aren't we lucky?"

They look at each other with the kind of feeling that Katherine wishes existed between *her* and Louise. She wants both of her sisters to think of her as their *best* sister. Jude always has, but Louise still treats her like a mother, rejecting whatever she says without considering it. Now Weezie is all grown up and educated and Katherine's mothering is over. Starting today, she'll say, she'd like Louise to listen to her as a sister.

Jude has decided that Jennifer is a fake: a fake with their father, the way well-bred girls often are toward parents, and a fake with their sister. Louise will never see Jennifer again, once she does Jennifer the favor of populating her wedding party. Louise is just one more pretty face to walk down the aisle. *All* of Jennifer's attendants, Jude would bet, will be gorgeous.

"I'm going to go look for Jeff," Jennifer says, and without goodbyes, she is gone.

"Nice girl," Frank says.

"She's wonderful," Louise says, giving Frank a grateful smile. She's so proud that Jennifer is her friend. "Didn't you like her?" she asks Billy. "Didn't *you?*" she asks Katherine and Jude. Murmurings and nodding heads say that everyone certainly did.

Katherine felt jealous of Jennifer. Great-looking *and* out-of-style for someone that age, with her short hair and her gangly body. Exactly how Katherine wishes she'd been at age twenty-two, sure of her own differentness.

Jude found Jennifer too completely predictable. She graduates from college and gets married the next day. Exactly—add a week—what Jude had done. Jennifer will be in for some unexpected surprises, she thinks.

They have an hour before graduation, an hour that Louise would like to spend sitting down with Billy and talking. She hardly knows how to behave around him. Does he still love her? She can't tell yet. She'll have to look deep into his eyes when nobody else is watching. Then she'll know.

She appreciates that Katherine and Frank and Daddy and Jude have come all the way up here to watch her graduate, but they are only furniture in her life, she's been thinking. *Antiques. Good* furniture. But still something that's there only because she has to have something to sit on. A family, she should have realized a long time ago, doesn't exist to engage or excite or delight or please you. It's only your backdrop. In a family, nothing changes. Families are like jails, inescapable jails, which would be great for the people you don't want out on parole. Her family, for example, will never have a new attitude toward Billy. She saw how they greeted him—too familiarly. Because they knew what he once was (not that anything was wrong with him), they think they know what he'll be like forever. It's unfair, she wants to proclaim. Her sisters might like Billy if they'd just look at him. They might like her, too. But they'll never look at her either. To them, she's stuck forever in the way she's always been. It makes Louise wonder if you can't really care about people you've known all your lives. At some point those people stop letting you change, become someone new, someone better. The reason she's friends with Jennifer is that they met after they grew up and they both liked what they saw. She'll never be friends with her sisters at all.

The strangest thing about this, though, is how Katherine and Jude have said that since she's come home from Paris, she's been a totally different person. They *know* she's no different since Hollins Abroad; they've just said so to keep Billy away. But she *is* a totally different person now. Although she's the same, now she's proud of who she is. It's as if Jennifer has opened the door of her jail and taught her to fly.

In fairness to her sisters, she'll admit that she would probably have quit college and gone home to get married if it hadn't been for them. And today she's graduating and everybody's proud—Billy's proud, she mustn't forget—and probably it's a big deal, although it doesn't quite feel like one to her. She has a college degree. She's lived in Paris for a year and is even sorry she wasn't there more literally. Billy's here to watch her graduate. So maybe things haven't turned out so badly after all.

In her paper for Mrs. Grantham—the paper that was supposed to describe her physical, emotional, and intellectual changes over the past four years—she'd finally figured out what to say. The most important thing she'd learned in college, she wrote, was that mistakes aren't final. She'd given two examples: her friendship with Jennifer, whom she'd misjudged, and her love affair (she'd called it a "friendship of the heart") with Billy, whom she'd turned her back on. Mrs. Grantham had given her a B+ and written the word "Amazing!" at the top of her paper. It was the best work she'd ever done at Hollins.

She tries to hold Billy's hand as they all walk toward the quad, which with its trees is the part of campus Louise likes best. But he won't cooperate. Her family lags behind as if she is a true tour guide. She wants to whisper to Billy that it was her sisters, not her, who sent back the wings pin. When he asks, Didn't you know your own mind? she'll have to admit that she didn't. When he asks, Do you know it now? she'll have to convince him that she does. She got to know her own mind starting six weeks ago when she told someone some truth that the person would rather not hear. And although it didn't change anything for the person, Jennifer, it changed everything for Louise. It made her know that, if he will have her, she is going to be Mrs. Billy Jones and happy about it.

Both her sisters look beautiful today, she has finally noticed. They wear flowing dresses, so handsome on their tall elegant bodies, and high heels, which make them seem taller—because of their long legs—than anyone here. Louise is wearing a white shirtwaist dress, a Hollins tradition, and white *peau de soie* shoes. Jude has her hair up. Katherine's hair is down, curling at her shoulders, shiny and soft. They are walking together. Frank is paired with Daddy. And she's trying, with difficulty, to stay at Billy's side.

In the quad, buildings of ancient maroon brick surround them. Her own dorm, another variety of mountain, is just across the yard. A stage, a podium, and chairs have been set up in the grass for the graduation exercises. On the ground in front of the podium sits a huge bouquet of flowers. She shows her family the stump where Jeff proposed to Jennifer just before they left for Hollins Abroad, and she wonders if there's any chance her relationship with Billy could be sufficiently mended by tomorrow that he will propose to her there, too.

She raises and lowers her eyebrows quickly at him, a flirting look of hers that he has always loved. He smiles, but there's a reticence in his smile, as if he thinks she's teasing him. She does it again to emphasize how much she means it, but then she feels foolish, because Jude, who was watching, narrows her eyes in disdain. She's just jealous, Louise tries to think, but she can't help wondering whether her playfulness becomes an almost-college grad. What really upsets her, though, is the mistrust in

Billy's eyes. He used to respond to her flirting look so whole-heartedly, but now he is timid, unsure of her. She can hardly blame him.

"Aren't you going to show us your room?" Jude asks. "That's what *I* want to see."

She's bored already, Louise can tell. She wants to see some-thing that will provide fodder for conversation, such as Louise's dorm room. Louise hesitates. Her room is personal. Seeing it will just give her sisters things to talk about. But it's where they've been headed. Not long from now she must report to chapel, and she needs to freshen her makeup and stop by the bathroom. Since it's Graduation Day, she supposes she's even allowed to invite the men inside. "We don't have time now," she says. "After the ceremony."

She wants her sisters to see her bridesmaid's dress. She wants Billy to see Jennifer's wedding dress. Jeff might be in the room, and she wants Billy to meet him and vice versa. After their hon-eymoon to Acapulco, Jennifer and Jeff are going to invite her and Billy to Richmond for a weekend. And Jenn wants Louise herself to visit "all the time." Jennifer has promised to come to Greensboro, too. Will all this ever happen? Out of nowhere, she feels her first doubt. The only thing she and Jennifer have be-tween them is lots of long, meaningful talk. And a return plane ride. And a decision, against Mary Ruth's pleading, not to go to the Honor Council. (Kristin Anderson will graduate today with their class.) But is that enough? They don't have any Paris history. They hardly have any Hollins history. But they *will* have history, she becomes sure again. They've sworn to each other to get some. Jenn has even asked her to move to Richmond. Of course, she can't.

She's been watching Billy constantly while giving this tour. Though she never signed up to be a campus guide for prospec-tive students, it's as if she has a memorized speech. She hears herself describing something and doesn't even listen to what she's saying, but the words are accurate, she can tell. Billy has always been uneasy around her family but perfectly comfortable around her. Today he seems just the opposite. He's been making conversation with her father and Frank and joking with her sisters. Every time she drops back to walk beside him, he drops back farther so that they are walking separately again. Why?

"Can you at least tell us where it is, so we can go to the bathroom?" Katherine asks.

"Where what is?"

"Your room?"

"Will you leave me alone about my room?" she snaps.

Quickly Jude asks, "Are you hiding someone there? Someone about six two with great eyes?"

"No, I'm not, Jude," she says over her shoulder in her Hollins-sarcastic voice.

Billy is about five seven. His eyes are a pleasant almond shape, but not "great eyes." His eyebrows are scraggly, which is why his mustache surprised her so. He's a regular-looking guy, but a wonderful one. Why does Jude have to make fun of him? Louise would like to make some clever biting remark aimed at Jude's not having a man here at all, but anything she would say would only make Jude think of something meaner.

"*Billy* wants to hide in your room. Don't you, Billy?" Jude continues.

Louise gives Katherine a "help me" look before remembering that Katherine is the one she snapped at.

Because he *has* hidden in her room before, Billy blushes. Even his mustache seems to change hue. Not Louise's dorm room, but her room at home, one day in high school, when they both skipped fifth and sixth periods and sneaked over to her house. It became a one-time experiment as soon as she heard the key turn in the downstairs lock and Daddy call upstairs that he'd come by to pick up some papers. Billy hid in her closet while she agonized in the bathroom. Daddy left without coming upstairs, which made her realize he knew what was going on. It was the work of a concerned neighbor, she'd finally figured out.

"Maybe Jennifer found Jeff," Katherine says shyly. "We wouldn't want to interrupt."

"You two are so *disgusting,*" Louise says, near tears. How can they be this mean to her on her day?

"Girls," Daddy says with no conviction at all.

"What a baby," Jude mutters to Katherine.

They don't even listen to *him*, Louise thinks. She's always known they don't, but it surprises her each time it happens. She wonders if Katherine listens to Frank. She suspects Jude *never* listened to Cap, which is probably why they're divorced.

"The whole thing was a joke," Katherine mutters back.

Also, they have the arrogance to talk to each other as if nobody else can hear them. They're like one person in two bodies. She used to want to be the third body of that one person, but no longer. *Never* will she want it again.

"I think we have time to go to my room," she says in a suddenly controlled voice. It may appear that she's capitulating, but she is actually making a decision. She will not *not* invite them to her room because they asked to come.

She cuts across the courtyard, leaving them behind. When she hears them begin to follow, she unobtrusively slows down so they'll be able to catch up. Everyone converges at the double-door entrance. Louise grabs the wrought-iron handle, flashes her group a smile, and gestures for them to enter. When they are inside, she weaves her way among them and heads off to the left.

"The parlor," she announces, adding before her sisters can: "Where we kiss our dates good night." Billy stops to look, but no one else does. She'll explain to him later that the remark was aimed at Katherine and Jude.

And then they are all in her room, crowding its spaciousness—a swarm of bees invading to suck her flowers. Her fuchsia bridesmaid's dress hangs full-length on one closet door. Jenn's wedding dress hangs on the other. Katherine and Jude go to the dresses, Katherine calling the bridesmaid's dress "lovely" and Jude responding that it *is* lovely but useless to anyone but a bridesmaid in a wedding. Daddy goes to the window to see what kind of view Louise has had. Frank stands at her bookcase above her desk, reading titles. Billy stops at her dresser, looking at the framed photographs she brought from home: one of Mother in a silk pajama-style outfit smoking a cigarette; one of Daddy, unsmiling, in a suit; one of Katherine and Jude when Mother used to dress them alike; and fortunately, one of him, which she'd packed in her suitcase last fall in the event that she couldn't bear not seeing what he looked like. She had not looked at it all year, because she knew how it would make her feel.

"Like it?" she asks. The room is as big as the bedroom in which she grew up, with a similar high ceiling, crown molding, and tall windows. Just last year, shag carpeting was laid to give the dorms a contemporary feeling, although the more elegant flat carpet was left in the halls and parlor. One of the funny things Jenn does is sit on the floor to study and pull the long blue-and-green strands up between her toes. When she has a good grip, a whole section of rug rises up like a wave.

"This is so much nicer than my room in college," Jude says. "We had bare floors."

"Lots of space," Katherine adds. "It reminds me of our rooms when we were growing up."

Neither of them asks her anything. She should probably consider herself lucky.

"Nice view," says Frank, who has moved over near Daddy.

Billy is still looking at the photographs on the dresser. The one of him shows him leaning against his car, his arms folded across his chest. He looks unusually muscular.

"You haven't changed much," Louise says. She's standing only an arm's length from him but feels too shy to move nearer. The photograph holds her back. It hasn't been sitting there all year, the way it's pretending to be. She had it with her, though. She didn't have to ask Daddy to mail it.

"Neither have you," he says. She can tell by the way he lowers his eyes that he doesn't want to talk about them in front of her family.

"Five minutes," she says. They really have much more time, but maybe she can somehow hurry this whole ceremony up.

"Where's the bathroom?" Katherine and Jude ask in unison. Louise leads them across the hall.

As soon as they are away from the men, her sisters completely change. They drop their mannered poise and each dives for the bathroom doorknob. Jude wins but can't get the door open. The handle has to be turned to a certain point and no farther. Louise spills into them as they try to shoulder their way through. They're all hooting with laughter. Louise reaches around Jude to force her fingers out of the way. When she gets the knob in her hand, she turns it expertly and the door flies open. They fall shrieking inside, their laughter dissipating as they move toward the stalls.

"I wish we could have gone to college together," Louise says in the sudden quiet. Her mellow voice echoes against the dividers.

"God. Why?" Katherine calls.

"So we would have had the chance to be friends."

Everyone begins peeing.

"Who wants to be friends?" Katherine asks, louder, so she can be heard.

"You and Jude are friends," Louise says.

"We're not friends. We're sisters. There's a big, important difference. You can have *millions* of friends. You only have one or two sisters. You're our sister, too, if you haven't noticed."

"I am not," Louise says, but not loud enough for either of them to hear.

Jude flushes her commode. She has made no comment. Louise waits until the flush is entirely finished, and then flushes her own bowl. She takes her time coming out of the stall, thinking Katherine is delaying, too. But when she appears, Katherine is standing at the mirrors with Jude. The silence extends on and on, Louise is not sure why. It's Jude's turn to say something, but her face is blank. Louise feels that the subject of sisterhood has just been opened.

All Katherine ever does is reapply lipstick, but both Jude and Louise retouch their eyelashes, their cheeks, and their lips. Louise puts on powder to keep her face from looking so sweaty, but Katherine tells her that it makes her look pasty, so she blots it off. Then she has to put on more rouge.

Jude breaks the silence. "If you want a friend, it looks like you've got one. Jennifer seems just your type. She accepts you, doesn't she? A sister just reminds you of who you are. Jennifer gives you freedom. A sister makes sure you can't change."

Louise looks back and forth between them. What Jude said is just what she's been thinking. Something funny is happening on Katherine's face. She's not going to cry, but her features are all loose and questioning.

"*You* know what I mean," Jude says gently to Katherine. "It's hard for sisters to be friends. They're always too busy telling each other what to do."

"You mean, they're always too busy being honest," Katherine says icily.

"No, that's not what I mean. Yes, but no. Yes, they're honest, but it's honesty from their point of view. Not pure honesty. Honesty with a goal."

Katherine's hurt look remains.

"Sisters are better," Jude says with a sigh.

Louise gets her rouge back on, but it's too bright and she has to go into a stall for some tissue. Katherine and Jude have hurt each other's feelings: she hasn't seen that in a long time. When Louise exits the stall, though, Katherine confronts *her*.

"Do *you* think sisters can be friends?"

"I would like to have gone to college with both of you," she says in a faint voice. "That's all."

"So that we could be friends?" Katherine presses.

"I guess."

Katherine has come around to stand beside Jude. They are not exactly blocking the door, but they are standing in front of it. Even when they've upset each other, it's still them against her.

She tries to force a smile onto her face, but it won't come. Or if it's there—she feels the corners of her mouth turn up—it's simply hiding her confusion. With Jennifer, she just says what she thinks. Maybe she can do the same with them. "I would love to be sisters with both of you," she says, taking Katherine's cue. "Honestly. I know I've never acted like it, but what I would most like is to be sisters with you the way you're sisters with each other." This is not at all what she's talked about to Jenni-

171|

fer, but she knows it comes from her heart. Until this moment, she thought that the only "sister" she would ever want is her roommate.

"Sisters *and* friends?" Katherine asks.

"Both," Louise says.

Jude is silent. Katherine is her sister; Louise is her sister. Neither of them offers what she needs right now in a friend. What she needs is someone who doesn't make too many suggestions, someone who more or less endorses how she feels about things. Among the world's divorcées, she's found plenty of possibilities. And it's not that they don't really care about her, as Katherine would surely suggest.

Katherine cannot understand the distinctions Jude is making. A sister is the one person who will tell you the truth when the rest of the world is lying to you. Isn't that worth any attendant pain?

Louise will be sisters or friends with whoever wants what. It's just two different words, in her opinion, for what's really the same thing. But both words are open to her in a way that she's never felt them to be. Sister and/or friend with Katherine and/or Jude.

"It's my day," Louise almost shouts. "And I want to hear a story. Who wants to tell one? Somebody try to think of something good." She sees that her idea immediately appeals to them. No one but her has thought about telling a story. But they're together. It's what they always do.

"There are no *good* stories," Jude says, her voice wholly changed. "But I know a funny one." Her body relaxes. She takes one of her feet out of its shoe and begins turning the shoe on its side, then up, then on its side. "When I first started dating Cap, we were at Mother's one night making out on the living-room sofa. Mother knew we were visiting, but I guess she must have forgotten. Or maybe she didn't forget," Jude says wryly. "All of a sudden she came tiptoeing down the stairs and through the living room completely naked. She was holding her bosoms with one arm like she always did and covering her crotch with her other hand. She didn't see us."

"Were you humiliated?" Katherine asks.

Jude laughs. "I was *jealous*. Cap never stopped talking about Mother's damn bosoms. All our life together . . ."

Mother's bosoms have always been so much more significant to her sisters than to Louise, maybe because she's so far out of the competition. "Tell me a *real* story," she says. "Something I can think of while I'm graduating. Please, something *good*."

Katherine tucks her hair behind her ears. "I know," she says. "This one will make you glad you didn't go on that trip to Germany with us. You were too young. But you got to go to Paris all by yourself to make up for it. You always luck out, Louise. Someone's always taking care of you."

"Gee, thanks," Louise says. "Is this a story or a sermon?" She's not angry at Katherine, which surprises her. "And is it *good?*"

" 'Good' as in 'horrid.' I really thought Mother was a dead woman." She looks at Jude for confirmation.

"The worst," Jude says, nodding. "Absolutely the worst of all time. Worse than my wedding. We saved this until you were old enough."

"Lucky me," Louise says.

Katherine begins: "Max had some business in Düsseldorf, and he left the three of us in Munich for the day. We were staying at the Vier Jahreszeiten Hotel, an elegant, *elegant* place. Jude and I spent the morning window-shopping. Mother was sleeping in—or so we thought. When we came back to the room, the doors to our balcony overlooking the courtyard were open. Mother was collapsed in a chair, her head thrown back as far as it would go. Farther than I thought a head *could* go. I thought her neck was broken. Her mouth had a terrible twisted expression.

"When we tried to wake her up, she didn't respond at all. She was just drunk again: no big deal, in retrospect. But what was so horrible was that we were afraid to do anything. If Mother wasn't dead and we called a doctor—which we finally did— she'd be furious at us—which she was. We didn't do anything

173 |

for ten whole minutes. She could have died in the time it took us to act, and we would have been to blame."

"Partly," Jude inserts.

Katherine smiles shamingly at her. "Jude and I had a fight about who was going to see the concierge about a doctor and who was going to stay in the room. Jude didn't want to do either thing by herself. So I finally shut the door in her face. Have you ever forgiven me for that?"

"Nope."

"Good. I haven't forgiven you, either." Katherine looks away. "It was very awkward with the concierge. I didn't want to say I thought my mother was dead, so I said that I thought something was wrong with her. *Maybe* she was drunk, but I really didn't know. She looked so much *worse* than drunk. It took forever for him to understand what I wanted.

"Fortunately, the doctor who served the hotel was there. In about five minutes he arrived at our room. What I remember about the way he came in was his total calmness, as if someone in our room had a cold. Mother began to wake up while he was examining her. He'd moved her off the balcony and laid her on the bed. He was sitting on the edge beside her. She opened her eyes and in the deadliest voice told him to get his hands off of her. I don't think she knew he was a doctor. And I don't think she thought he was a rapist. I think she thought he was someone she'd brought home. Then she saw us, and knew he wasn't.

"The doctor backed out of the room, doing us the favor of not looking our way. I don't ever remember being so afraid. Mother's eyes were wild. When the door closed, she asked us, 'Which one of you is responsible for this?' We'd drawn together, but suddenly Jude moved away from me. 'Katherine is,' she said. That's what I've never forgiven *her* for. Nothing else happened. Mother stared us into the other room and then went back to sleep. She was still asleep when Max got back. But then she woke up and we all acted like nothing happened. She may not even have remembered."

There is a long silence. Katherine and Jude are lost in their memories. Louise, who was at first horrified, is now angry at them for telling her a story like this. Then she remembers that she ought to feel relieved that she never had to face what they faced. Finally, she feels the terrible separateness that she's always had to endure. Isn't that worse than pain?

In a measured voice she says, "I wish you wouldn't tell those stories. They're grotesque. I'm never going to tell one again. I've decided. I thought I liked it, but I don't. I don't know why you want to hear them yourselves."

"Because they help," Katherine says.

"Help what?"

Jude has been listening closely. Katherine's memory for these stories amazes her. What she tells is always exactly what happened: no embellishment and no constriction. She *does* like hearing the truth. She *is* glad she has a sister who will tell it to her. A little while ago the truth was too tiring. Now it isn't. "If we *didn't* tell these stories," she offers on Katherine's behalf, "we'd have nothing to talk about. This is what's happened in our life."

"But do we have to tell every little bit?" Louise asks. "It reminds me of torture. I don't see how they help." She had tried to keep her voice an inquiring one, hiding the disgust she's begun once again to feel. People can go too far with the truth.

"I guess telling the truth about Mother helps me admit the truth about myself," Katherine says.

"What are you talking about?" Louise asks, strain beginning to show in her voice.

"If we left things out," Jude once more offers, "I think we'd begin to wonder what was wrong with *us*."

"I don't understand. I don't understand, and I don't *want* to understand. I want to hear something good. That's all we need. Don't either of you know a story that's worth hearing?"

"It's good that Mother's not here to ruin your graduation," Jude says.

Louise turns for the door. "I give up. I totally give up. We've probably *missed* my goddamn graduation."

"I've thought of something good," Jude says, opening her purse.

"We're out of time," Louise says.

"Now?" Katherine asks.

"I said we're out of time."

They look at one another and agree. Jude pulls out an envelope and hands it to Louise, who's propping open the door with her ass. "Max sent you this," she says.

Louise looks at each of them. A chill crosses her body and then vanishes. She has no idea what caused it. Eagerly she tears the envelope across and turns the contents into her hand.

"They're Mother's," Jude says.

"Put them on," says Katherine.

"Before she died she left a note in her jewelry box that you were to be given her pearls on your graduation day. Max brought them by yesterday. With his love."

Louise lifts the strand over her head. It's so unexpected to find out that Mother had even thought about her finishing college. The pearls are beautiful. "Am I the only one who wishes Mother were here?" she asks in a challenging tone. "Even if she *would* ruin my graduation?"

"I wouldn't mind her being here," Jude says.

"Suckers," Katherine says, but the word doesn't seem to come from her heart. "By the way, why is Billy here?"

Louise had been expecting this question. She's amazed it was so long in coming. "We're friends," she says simply. "He's the best friend I've ever had." She'd prepared this answer long before Billy seemed so *much* a friend.

"Counting Jennifer?" Jude asks.

Louise nods with wide-open, solemn eyes. What she wants is for Billy to be her lover *and* friend. The way he used to be. Both can exist at the same time. She knows. They've existed before. Sisters can be friends, too. Just maybe not these three.

"How long have you been dating?" Katherine asks.

"Not long," Louise says. But then an uneasiness about Billy makes her slide into the truth. "He hasn't *been* here before today, but we've been writing each other. We're standing the test of time," she adds bravely, perhaps foolhardily.

"That's important," Jude says.

Who knows if she's being honest or sarcastic? Louise motions them out the door ahead of her. "I don't think it's so bad that you waited ten minutes to find help for Mother," she murmurs to the sister most likely to become her "sister." "I would have done the exact same thing."

Katherine looks over her shoulder. She begins talking more quickly so that she can finish before they reach Louise's room. "It wasn't bad of Jude, but it was bad of me. It showed that I was more afraid of Mother's anger than of her death."

"I think that's understandable," Louise says.

"What's not understandable is that I wanted her to be dead," Katherine says. "I wanted her to be dead rather than angry at me. Thank God, she lived through it. I would have been crippled for life if she hadn't."

"Aren't you anyway?" Jude asks in a suddenly fraternal tone. *"Joke,"* she adds.

"No," Katherine says. "No, I'm not." She glances at Louise, but Louise can't quite read what her eyes are saying. Louise makes a little funny face anyway.

They collect the men to go to the ceremony. Louise shows off her pearls, even to Daddy, who nods without looking closely. Frank says that the pearls are almost as pretty as Louise's teeth. "But not quite," Katherine adds. She hopes that the gift will make Louise just a little happier that she finished college. Jude decides that she agrees wholeheartedly with Louise: she wishes Mother were here, too, even if it meant graduation would be ruined.

They leave for the quad, Louise hurrying everyone as politely as she can.

They are sitting to the left of the center aisle in this order: Daddy, who everyone said should have the honor of the aisle seat, Katherine, Frank, Jude, and Billy. The empty chairs to the right await Louise's graduating class. Some music starts up and then stops. A tape recording of "Pomp and Circumstance" is being played through a couple of raspy speakers. They can see the chapel door from where they are sitting, but no one appears. Katherine leans forward. She doesn't mean to leave Frank out, but she always seems to forget him when she and Jude are together.

To them both, she whispers: "We didn't make a mistake. It was not wrong to keep Weezie from quitting college."

"She'll *be* glad, if she's not already," Jude says.

"You led her to water," Frank says. "*She* drank."

Billy, who has leaned forward to hear them, gives his own view: "Although she'd never tell any of you, I think she's glad to be getting a degree. She's excited about going out into the world."

Going out into the world? Jude thinks. Not quite. Louise doesn't even have a job. Louise hasn't even looked for a job. She's coming home tomorrow to live with Daddy. She gives Billy a supercilious glance, which he doesn't seem to register. Then she rolls her eyes at Katherine.

Katherine nods at Billy, letting her lip rise slightly so that Jude will know she has seen and understood. Louise *will* be going out into the world, she hopes. She's been trying to tell Daddy that he will have to give Louise a little push toward independence, but he keeps throwing up his hands as if she's pulled a gun. He says that wherever Louise wants to live and whatever she wants to do is fine with him. He doesn't know how he's hurting her.

Although she'll criticize Billy to Jude, Katherine knows that she is beginning to feel differently toward him. A couple of years ago, Billy would never have leaned forward to hear what they were saying. He would never have offered an interpretation of Louise. He seems, for the first time, unafraid of them. Katherine likes that very much. She's still unhappy that he didn't go to college. And she thinks that it might eventually cause problems between him and Weezie. But maybe it won't.

Billy also looks better. At twenty, he was still a skinny kid without any recognizable personality. At twenty-two, he's stockier, although he still has a skinny person's unattractive way of walking, hips leading. His baby face, though, has become defined by his mustache, created almost. It's a lovely mustache Katherine thinks. It's winning her over.

The graduates begin filing out of the chapel. Someone turns up the tape recorder, which gives the audience cover to talk more freely.

"Tell me what you've been working on," Jude says to Billy. She knows from bumping into him at the hardware store that he's begun designing some of his own pieces of furniture.

"I've been working on a bed," he says.

"A commission?"

"No."

"For yourself?"

He hesitates. He seems shy now that she has put him *in* the bed. "For me . . ." He seems to want to say more.

She turns her head so that she is looking more squarely at him. The line of graduates moves perpendicular to them. Jude sees Louise's face brighten as it spots them. As it spots Billy, to be precise.

"There's Louise," she whispers. Billy turns in time to wave. Louise gives a simple wave back. She's smiling so big that her cheeks seem about to burst.

Billy turns back to Jude. "I shouldn't have come," he says. "I didn't know it would be like this. The bed is for me and Lucy Payne."

Jude's eyes widen. She looks around Frank to Katherine, who is watching the arriving column of girls. Katherine turns quickly, wariness already in her eyes. Jude's face says that she has just heard the worst possible news. Before she repeats it, though, she must get further confirmation.

She turns back to Billy. "Why are you here?" she asks.

"I came to tell her," he says, his voice somber and terrified at the same time. "I thought she would want to know that everything has worked out for me."

"But you're dating her."

"I came to see her graduate and to take her out to dinner. I'd decided it would be best to leave tonight, until she asked me to be her escort for the wedding. I love Louise," he nearly cries.

"I'd do anything for her. She was my first love." Billy hangs his head.

Jude leans across Frank. "Billy's getting married," she whispers.

"Who to?" Frank asks.

Katherine and Jude look at each other, their faces expressionless. Finally, Katherine lowers her eyes. For the longest time, Jude lets Frank's question hang in the air. Then she says, "Lucy Payne," although Frank doesn't know who that is. She has said the name aloud, but it's as if she hasn't been able to get it out. It's in her throat still. It's clogging her throat. It's a name she'll never be rid of. She or Katherine either.

"Why didn't you just write her a letter?" Jude asks Billy. He is leaning forward, resting his chin in his hands. His elbows are braced against his knees. His mustache seems to curl around his frown. His lower lip quivers. He looks away and then looks back.

"I would have just written if you'd told me the truth," he says. "If you hadn't told me she was a totally different person since her trip to Paris. If you'd said she was . . . was still in love with me . . ."

"I don't know if she's in love with you or not," Jude says in a quick, arch voice.

"Well, then you're blind."

"Maybe she was just glad to see you. We're all glad to see you. She's missed you. We've missed you, too." It sounds false, she knows, and an hour ago it would have been, but now it's true, so true. Louise has missed Billy. The family's missed Billy. The family would like to have Billy back.

Louise, seated now, leans forward in her row, trying to attract Katherine's attention, but Katherine pretends not to see. Daddy is dozing. Louise coughs aloud. Katherine takes a deep breath and looks.

"What's wrong with Billy?" Louise mouths.

Katherine looks toward him. Billy has his head in his hands again. To Jude she whispers, "Tell him to sit up." She turns back to Louise. "Nothing," she mouths. "Tired?" she offers, as a possibility.

She glances back at Billy. He's sitting up now, but his chin is touching his chest. She looks again at Louise. "Get his attention," Louise mouths.

"Tell Billy to look at Louise," she murmurs to Frank. Frank murmurs to Jude. Jude murmurs to Billy. With her peripheral vision Katherine sees him lift his head. His lips are bunched as if he's trying to hold something inside. But he makes them into a smile, the hardest-fought-for smile she has ever seen. When Louise has had time to receive it, he faces forward once more. His lips knead against each other, as if one is trying to hurt the other.

"Greetings, friends and families," says the Hollins College president.

Part Three

JUDE

CHAPTER

11

Jude sits on the curb in front of her house, waiting for Katherine to pick her up. Today is All-Day Saturday, but where she is going with her sister is important enough for her to miss the time with her children. Katie and Charles are inside with a babysitter. They don't mind when she goes away, especially when she hires a girl who's willing to play with them, but if Katherine asks to go inside, Jude is going to pretend that they've been pitching fits. Katherine can notice an out-of-place ashtray and intuit that Jude's been smoking again. She can see a wad of Kleenex in a trash can and figure out that she's been crying all day. If she saw a picture off a nail or an Orange County Board of Education return address on an envelope, she'd immediately deduce that her sister is moving away.

The morning air is humid, a typical June day that will probably end with a storm. Since the beginning of the month, rain has fallen almost daily, creating a constant thickness in the air. It's been hard to keep her grass at bay. It's been hard to wear the same set of clothes all day, although she tries to, so she can keep the laundry pile low. She does change the children whenever they look really miserable.

The neighborhood where she lives, Kirkwood, is an area which began as cheap after-the-war housing but which has become a fashionable stepping-stone neighborhood. Jude lived here when she and Cap were married, and although she's changed houses, she's within two blocks of where they gave their first party—a cookout with two kegs of beer—and where she got pregnant twice. Because her present house has been a rental for a number of years, it doesn't have the appeal of the houses which have been heavily improved, but the floor plan is the same as always. Jude stayed in this neighborhood for her children's sakes. She wanted them to grow up around normal families.

In Kirkwood, everyone is married and has children. Husbands are accountants, lawyers, and businessmen. A few of the wives still work, usually as teachers, but gradually each husband makes enough money so that his wife can quit her job to devote time—obsessive time, Jude has begun to think—to the couple's children. All these people are too earnest, the men about their jobs, the women about child-rearing. On weekends they become earnest about their lawns as well as their tennis and golf games. They're *incredibly* earnest about making it to First Pres, which is where they all go, every Sunday.

Jude's neighbors are among her friends, but perceptible changes have occurred since her divorce. In their hearts, her neighbors wish she had left Kirkwood. They wish—the wives in particular—that she had moved to a condominium complex like a normal divorcée. When she was married to Cap, husbands of her friends used to make suggestive remarks to her. Cap did the same to their wives. But now—when she's told what nice legs she has—the wives no longer laugh it off. Not that she has many opportunities to *hear* compliments anymore. Though she's included in their huge parties, she's not invited to the smaller ones. Her old friends also forget to ask her to sub at bridge club. But the most unforgivable thing they do is act less interested in her children. Her children, they think, are no longer desirable. In hundreds of ways they betray her, and as a result she cares less about angering them. Last week she wore a bathing suit to mow her grass.

Either she came out of her house too soon or Katherine is late. Jude sits down on the curb about the time a car turns the corner half a block away, but it's not her sister's. The car is a station wagon with lots of wood, probably Booboo Sherrill's car. Booboo is the tennis champion at the club she and Cap used to belong to. She waves at Jude as she passes but doesn't smile. She has on her whites, so her husband, Carter, must be babysitting their three boys. Jude nods but doesn't wave. She suspects the Sherrills are the ones who put anonymous notes in her mailbox this past spring asking her to please do something about her yard. She finally decided to comply.

Katherine's red Opel finally eases around the corner. Even at such a distance, Jude feels her pulse quicken. She puts the preplanned expression on her face: a mysterious, fun-loving smile. To break her news to her sister, she is taking her to Chapel Hill, a town an hour east of here. On the way over she's going to say that she's thinking of leaving Greensboro for a while. When they arrive, she plans to treat Katherine to lunch at Aurora, Be Mine, a vegetarian restaurant. Afterward, if Katherine has been receptive, she plans to show her the garage apartment she rented sight unseen over the phone on Wednesday. She can hardly wait to get a look at it herself.

The car glides to the curb, Katherine poking her head out the window. "You're reminding me of Daddy," she says. "Do you remember? Shangri-la?"

"Shangri-la?"

"Daddy used to call Mother from the office around noon on a Friday. He told her to get packed, they were going to Shangri-la. He wouldn't tell her where, only how many nights they'd be staying and what the climate was going to be. He'd even made the arrangements for us. All Mother had to do was be ready. You look great, by the way." Jude has on a pastel-pink jumpsuit which makes her complexion glow. "I haven't seen you in a ponytail in ages. You're a teenager again. *Where* are we going?"

"Did Mother like it? Did she just go crazy with excitement? I can't imagine anything more romantic." There's so much extra enthusiasm in her voice that she's surprised Katherine doesn't notice. She slings her purse into the back seat and opens Katherine's door. "Is it all right if I drive? Part of my surprise? I'm not going to tell you where we're going, so don't ask. *Or* why, either. You'll be back by supper, and what you have on is just fine. Sorry about my tire," she adds. She doesn't mind going out of town without a spare, but Katherine does, so they cannot take Jude's car.

"Help yourself." Katherine steps out of the car, her blue sundress wet against her back. Like Mother, she's always prettiest in the summer, Jude thinks. In the month since Louise's graduation, she's added a rich suntan which makes her eyes look even bluer. It's her one vanity, something that Jude never mentions. "Can I see the kids before we go?" her sister asks. "Mother *hated* those weekends."

"Why? Why on *earth*? I would have *loved* them. Will you wait till we get back? I've already told them goodbye." Without argument Katherine heads around to the other side of the car. "Why didn't she like going away?" Jude asks, relieved.

They both settle into the car, adjusting mirrors and seats and fastening seat belts. "Think about it. Mother had to call up her friends and cancel out on dinner parties. She had to give away tickets she'd bought. All in the name of love."

"But Mother was so romantic."

"I'm not sure of that. I used to think so, too. But Mother wanted action. Not a candlelight dinner for two at some remote resort. Or dancing with a roomful of strangers. Strolling under a starlit sky. Not her style."

"Later it was. With Max."

"Was it?"

Jude pulls away from the curb. She already feels the way she felt on family vacations when Daddy drove up the last rise before they saw the ocean. How can she wait an hour to tell Katherine what she's about to do? "I still can't imagine not wanting to go somewhere special. No matter what you had to miss. I *love* new places, new people. And if I didn't meet anybody, I'd love the *anonymity*." Katherine turns her head quickly, and Jude realizes that she's already said too much.

"I don't care about places," Katherine answers. And then, in a softer voice, "I really don't even like *vacations* . . ." Jude doesn't answer. Katherine notices that she's stopped listening.

The reason Katherine was late to pick up Jude is that when she was kissing Frank goodbye this morning he mentioned to her that one of his cases has been rescheduled so they'll have to reschedule their vacation. He sees no choice but the second two weeks in July, which is exactly when she's supposed to begin Dr. Stern's summertime Eliot course. She suggested a vacation in late August instead, but Frank said he has another case planned then. Next, she suggested *no* vacation, but retracted the idea as soon as she saw his face. She's reasonable. She just hates to cancel something she's so been looking forward to. Also, Dr. Stern is expecting her. Her taking the course was his idea.

The last day of her Yeats class, Dr. Stern had asked her for coffee, calling out "*Mrs.* Borden, please see me after class," emphasizing, for some reason, that she was married. She wondered why he couldn't talk to her standing in the classroom or back in his office, but then she'd felt silly. This was college; this wasn't the world. This was where *minds* were admired. This was coffee at the student center with a professor who might want to tell her he admired her work or—she'd nearly panicked a second time—who might feel she should abandon the study of literature. How foolish she was: she had an A in his class.

But something about Dr. Stern makes her feel foolish, period. For one thing, he's so embarrassingly natural. In class when he's reading a poem, tears may come into his eyes. He yells at unprepared students. Once she thought he and Wayne Currie might even come to blows. And he'll pause for many long seconds when he's lost in his own thoughts, totally unaware that everyone is watching him and then looking at one another. He makes her feel like a fake.

Walking from the English department to the student center, Dr. Stern told her that he'd examined her permanent record the day before and noticed that she'd been taking lots of different courses. "I assume you're not dabbling, simply undecided," he said. Unlike Frank, who always paid so much attention to her, Dr. Stern's attention roamed all around them. She watched him react appreciatively to students he knew, to the nodding trees, to the mountains of clouds riding past the treetops, even to the classroom buildings—whose exteriors he seemed to regard as his own private frame. Yet she did not feel ignored.

"Of course," she said.

"Of course?"

"Simply undecided." In a rush that felt both sophomoric and honest she'd added: "I just like so many subjects. I haven't taken a course that doesn't positively intrigue me." She looked quickly at him to see if her inane language—"positively intrigue"—had offended him, but it hadn't seemed to. "I want to *be* something," she'd said. "It took me ages to figure out that much. I just don't know what. I mean, I do know what, but I don't have time to do that anymore."

Dr. Stern's face constantly changed as he listened to her: eyebrows rising quizzically when she said something he didn't fully understand, lips frowning in thought, eyes softening at words like "ages." But he didn't interrupt. "What are you too old for?" he asked.

"Well, I can't be a ballerina . . ."

"Did you want to be a ballerina?"

"No. No, I didn't. Not totally. That was just an example of what someone who's almost thirty can't be." She was happy to find such an easy opportunity to tell him she wasn't a child.

"Ballerinas, pianists, violinists—they're all prodigies anyway," he said. "You either start before you're ten and feel that your mother has manipulated your entire life, or you never start at all. What, though, besides a prodigy, which one can't determine anyway?"

"It will sound silly . . ." She wanted to ask about *his* mother, but he was speaking so much more formally than in class. The idea that he might have designs on her seemed ridiculous. "Maybe I'm only saying I wanted to be this because I can't . . ."

"Can't be *what?*"

"I don't know if I want it because I *want* it or because I *ought* to want it. At the same time, I think if I'd really wanted to be such a thing, I'd have figured out a way to be it when I was young enough. So I don't quite believe myself."

Dr. Stern, who had a loose jaunty way of walking, suddenly stopped in his tracks. She stopped, too. When he stood, he shifted his weight from one leg to the other. His eyes, impersonal until that moment, seemed suddenly to pin her to the scenery. Receiving his stare, she would have sworn that he didn't have a humorous bone in his body. She would die if one could be found.

So she laughed aloud and murmured, "I'm not being very specific, am I?"

He smiled at her, for the first time more than cursorily. His voice, however, remained cold. "Will you please name the profession you would have liked to pursue if it had occurred to you soon enough?"

His enunciation made her feel shy again and also embarrassed to admit that she considered herself smart enough and dedicated enough to have wanted—much too late—to be a medical doctor. The thought first came to her last semester in her history-of-science course. So, did she really want to *be* a doctor or did she just love the *idea?* A woman doctor. She loved the idea of being a poet more, but for some reason she wanted to tell Dr. Stern the other. She just hadn't thought of being a doctor soon enough. Did not thinking of it make her seem flighty? Insincere? Out of step? Permanently wistful about everything? She wished she were younger, so she could have grown up after whatever women chose to be was taken for granted. Dr. Stern waited for her answer. "Well?" he'd finally said with irritation.

"I'm too embarrassed right now to say," she murmured. She wished she could stop being such a fool, but she couldn't.

He'd restarted his trek to the student center, pausing almost involuntarily for her to start walking, as if he couldn't quite bring himself to be rude. Yet she somehow had become excluded from his company. He wanted to cancel their coffee, it was clear.

In a low voice she said, "I thought I should have been a doctor."

"What kind?" he asked. *He* was a kind of doctor, she remembered, although everyone knew or should admit the word's common usage.

"A physician," she said. "Probably a pediatrician." That should assuage him. A woman pediatrician seemed less threatening than, for instance, a woman surgeon. The truth was, she'd never thought about what kind of physician she'd be.

"You'd make a far better doctor of English literature," he'd said.

"Do you think so?"

It was a moment she would always remember. Dr. Stern's voice had sounded the way she always imagined God's voice would sound: direct, elegant, elegiac. It was the voice he used reading poetry, yet full of knowledge of her. She'd been suddenly readmitted to his context, where he lived and moved and had his being. It was the tone of her question that readmitted her. The tone said how much she believed in his judgment. The next thing he said was that she should sign up for his Eliot course. He'd be gone on vacation to England the first semester of summer school, but then he'd be back. She said, joyously, that she'd be in the front row . . .

The thought of moving away from Greensboro first occurred to Jude on the way home from Louise's graduation. She was riding in the front seat with Daddy, having chosen that over the normal way they sat: Daddy and Frank up front, she and Katherine in back so they could talk. She wanted to be away from Katherine. She wanted, in fact, to be away from them all. Away from her father's lack of opinion. Away from Frank's niceness. Away from Billy's stupidity for telling them before he told Louise. Away from Louise's goo-goo eyes. And, finally, away from Katherine's fearfully wild mood, so reminiscent of Mother, at the reception. Katherine explained too much to too many people: how Louise had grown up in Paris, come of age at Hollins. How their mother had died and how no one knew how the death would affect her youngest child. How Louise had come through it changed for the better. It was as if Katherine were showing everyone—Louise especially—herself at her worst, so that after the family left, when Billy told Louise he was getting married, Louise wouldn't doubt for an instant why such a tragedy had befallen her. It was because of her sisters, Jude, by association, included. Sisters were not "sisters" or even friends, Louise would think. Sisters were the worst enemies. But Jude was not Louise's enemy. Jude had only agreed with Katherine that Weezie should finish college. She'd only agreed that Billy didn't have much ambition. She'd never asked or forced their little sister to do anything. Katherine had.

Because of Katherine, Daddy, Louise, Billy, Frank, and even

Jennifer, an idea, an idea that somehow had existed long before graduation, started climbing inside Jude. After several days of thought, she broke down and called Paul Hinton, whose name she'd finally remembered. The secretary at his school said he was giving an exam. When he called her back at home that afternoon, he spoke as if he didn't know who she was and she'd had to identify herself as the girl he'd met at the Fifth Season. Having to say those words made her hang up. She waited by the phone for him to call back, but he didn't. Then she fixed supper for the kids, whom she'd put in front of the television about the time she'd expected his return call. It appeared, she later thought ironically, that she'd thwarted the development of passion in the heart of Paul Hinton. Leaving her house that night, he'd said, "I really wanted you to be different." She'd answered, "I am different." He'd said, "You're a wonderful lay . . . a fantastic lay, actually." In a freezing voice she'd asked, "Is that *actually* supposed to be a compliment?" The telephone call had been to give him one more chance.

If she had to explain to someone exactly why she's moving to Chapel Hill, she would say that a man named Paul Hinton hadn't allowed her to make a mistake. He'd predetermined what was acceptable behavior in another person and what wasn't. And one night a woman named Judith Cramer didn't measure up to his standards. If he'd been worth anything, he would have waited before passing judgment. *He* could have said no more firmly. One of them had been married twice and run around to boot, and it wasn't Jude. Paul Hinton was as capable of turning down sex as she was of demanding it.

She remembers standing by the fireplace, her hands in his back pockets, them staring at each other for long seconds. The way foam must feel rising through a beer, she'd felt rising in her the absolute sureness that things can't ever work out between a man and a woman, because they won't let each other *be* and love whatever that *be* is. Paul wouldn't allow her to make love with him their first time together. He wouldn't allow her *not* to reveal herself at first and then *to* reveal herself later. She wouldn't have made love to him their second date. She wouldn't have been drunk. He knew nothing about her. He'd made superficial decisions about what she was like, based on one encounter. But that encounter didn't define her. She *was* a different person, more different than he could ever imagine. But he'd never know. Nobody would ever know.

In the month since Louise's graduation, Jude has given up her lease on her house in Greensboro, rented through the university grapevine that exists in every sizable city in North Carolina a "large" garage apartment behind one of the mansions on Franklin Street in Chapel Hill, canceled her next year's contract, applied for nineteen available teaching positions in Orange County, and cashed in the stock she'd bought with most of the money Mother left her. The first thing she's going to buy is a cute car with a spare tire. The second, some good-looking clothes. She plans for the first time ever to live a self-centered life. On the surface this sounds terrible, but it's the sanest thing she's ever done. Her cocoon will consist of her children and herself. If someone happens to like them, fine, but he'll have to find a way to bore through her tough silky case and join the existing larvae. And he'll have to understand if none of them ever hatches.

"I called Daddy's right before you picked me up and woke up Louise," she says. They have reached the highway and she lets the car go; Katherine does not seem to object. It's an almost pastoral drive between here and Chapel Hill: fields, rolling hills, grazing farm animals, trees. Too many billboards, unfortunately. Warm fragrant wind is whipping through the car. Jude has a sudden unsettling feeling that Katherine may not like her idea. Katherine may even try to stop her.

"Weezie is such a leech," Katherine says in a voice loud enough to be heard over the wind.

"She says she needs a break."

Katherine sighs. "Her whole life's a break. Why can't she realize that she had her break when she went to Paris last year? All the jobs will be gone by the time she starts looking for one."

Although Jude has always echoed whatever Katherine says about Weezie, at the same time she wonders what's the big rush.

She's speaking from experience: as a person who graduated from college, snap!, married, crackle!, and had kids, pop! pop! So much happens to a person between the ages of eighteen and twenty-five, but then the years stretch ahead like a desert. Moving slowly through the big events, even if it's not by choice, seems to Jude most opportune.

Conversation about Louise has always been a rallying point for her and Katherine. For the last few months, they've been discussing how soon their little sister should go out into the world on her own. While Louise was in college—and Jude was getting a divorce and Katherine editing the airline magazine—they talked about how she could get the most out of her education. During her high-school years—while Jude was having her first baby and Katherine was marrying Frank—they spent time discussing Louise's looks, hoping to help upgrade her social life.

For the years of Louise's girlhood, Jude remembers the hours they spent speculating whether or not she was Mother and Daddy's last effort at saving their marriage. Neither, according to Mother during Jude's wedding weekend, when Mother became drunker and drunker with each event. Drunk but without major disaster until they reached the reception in the grand ballroom of the country club. All of a sudden Mother, who was in the receiving line, began introducing her bridesmaid daughter Louise as her "diaphragm bypass" baby in a voice distinct enough even for Cap's mother to hear. Jude had rushed to the ladies' room, Katherine following. Too young to know what Mother meant, Weezie didn't even leave the line. While they were in the bathroom, Mother asked Daddy to dance, which was what finally convinced Max to take her away. When Jude appeared with fresh makeup, Daddy led her out on the dance floor. She danced silently, thinking he wanted to confide something to her, but he'd only turned their tangoing bodies in a new direction. Finally she'd asked, "Is it true about Weezie?" A confirmation of what she and Katherine had always joked about had become of immense interest to her. Besides, she was happy again: Mother was gone, and Cap, handsome and trim, looked glad—in spite

195|

of Mother—to be married to her. She was certainly glad to be married to him. "Was Weezie an accident?" she asked.

Daddy had stopped at the end of a turn, holding position while asking tensely, "Is that what she said?"

With a little giggle Jude repeated the phrase, "Diaphragm bypass." After all, she'd just become a married woman. And she'd been drinking her share of champagne. Although it was her wedding day, Daddy was not amused.

"Louise was planned the same way one plans to make a cake," he'd said. "The ingredients were bought, mixed, and baked. Don't let your mother fool you. We were in love with each other. We were in love with each other *until*." He'd begun dancing again. In a remote yet pointed tone he continued: "Louise was conceived not to save our marriage. Not hoping for a boy. Since you've never had a child, it's something you can't understand. But each child born is born perfectly. That's something you'll learn." Daddy's explanation—the most intimate thing he'd ever said to her—had only stepped up Jude and Katherine's teasing of Louise. But they also told their little sister the truth. Two years later, when the obstetrician lay Katie on Jude's chest, she understood literally what her father had meant. In Katie and now in Charles she has something perfect herself.

They have been talking about Louise's present situation for close to fifteen minutes—saying that if Daddy doesn't watch out he'll be supporting her permanently—and although it's always like this, Jude is still surprised at the power of conversation to distract from what's really going on. *Why is it they are going to Chapel Hill?* Just kidding. She thinks that one reason she's been so depressed this year is that she hasn't spent enough time talking. Talking makes life easier. It keeps her from thinking. Even when she and Cap were unhappiest with each other, they still talked incessantly about insignificant things. Which must have had something to do with his year-long reluctance to move out. Carolyn's conversations were endless, she knew from newspaper staff parties of the past, and also so weighty. She remembers once feigning interest in one of Carolyn's conversations: the starving children of Biafra. Jude carefully absorbed the rending tales and then drank another beer so that the sunken eye sockets and distended bellies would disappear. Then she handed over twenty dollars, hardly knowing how it could help. She figured out later that the twenty dollars helped Carolyn. Because she is the "least selfish person" he's ever met, Cap wants to marry her.

Her successor is a horsy girl, not fat, but quite large. On the other hand, Jude has a nice figure: willowy legs, breasts as perfect as pillows—as Cap once told her—and pretty shoulders. She tells Katherine that Cap's car was the first to stop Saturday while she was mowing grass. "He said he was just riding by. Thought he'd check on the kids. I had on my bathing suit," she adds.

"Sort of cooking your own goose, aren't you?" Katherine asks, her eyes holding Jude's for an uncomfortably long time. Finally, Jude looks back at the highway.

"What do you mean?"

"You have the only nonmatronly body in your neighborhood—"

"I do not."

"—and you're showing it off to your friends' husbands."

"I was not."

Katherine speaks quietly: "You don't worry me, because I'm your sister. But you worry every other sweet Suzie in town."

"That's their problem."

"Not in the long run."

Jude decides to go ahead and confess everything, mainly because she's still amused with herself and not at all worried about Katherine's warning. Besides, she's leaving town. "While Cap was there, Jim Nixon and Alex Holt stopped, too."

Katherine begins shaking her head. "Mistake, mistake, mistake," she says. Katherine knows that Alex is one of the husbands Jude slept with to get back at Cap.

"I felt fine with my ex-husband, but by the time the crowd gathered, I felt naked."

"What did you expect?" Katherine's face is drawn.

"I went in and put on one of Cap's old shirts, and when I came back out, he looked really miserable. Not that I had on his shirt. But that the shirt was at my house, where he can't live anymore.

"Not that he particularly loves *me,* but I think he's finally realized what he's gotten himself into. Don't worry," she says, pausing to look again at Katherine. "I'm through sleeping with married men. In a way, though, I actually feel sorry for Cap, the way you feel sorry for a baby bird that tries to get out of its nest and breaks its neck. On one hand you think what a fool. On the other hand you think it didn't have much of a chance. Now Cap doesn't have his children. And he's got to start a new family. He should have stuck with what he started out with. I'm just not that bad."

"You're *great,*" Katherine says. She seems calmer now that Jude has made her pledge.

"Not great, but we were compatible. Perfectly compatible."

"Great, but not compatible. At least not in his view." Katherine can never understand why Jude will not accept this, but she makes sure always to say the truth.

They were compatible *enough,* Jude thinks, but decides not to pursue it. With her peripheral vision she is studying Katherine, whose face is shiny from the heat. She has a faint glow about her as if earlier this morning she was satisfied by either exercise or lovemaking. Jude's not sure, but she thinks Katherine and Frank are lovers. Not lovers in the style of Mother and Max, but lovers like Mother and Daddy must have been: gentle, slow, attentive. Now is the time to announce her plans. Katherine is going to object, but this move will not undo her. What will make the difference to Katherine is that she has Frank. The move will not undo Jude either, because she has Katie and Charles. Having just one person as your own makes you willing to let go of others. Having just one person also makes you brave. Without the kids, she doubts she would be moving anywhere.

"I think it's the worst idea I've ever heard," Katherine says. She tucks her blowing hair behind her ears, as she always does whenever she's serious about something.

Outside, the sky is clouding over, reducing the glare and making it easier for Jude to drive. She has said only this much: that she is considering moving away from Greensboro and thinks

Chapel Hill might be a good destination. She invited Katherine on the trip today so that they could look over the town together.

"It's the equivalent of running away," Katherine continues. She's leaning forward to try to catch Jude's gaze, but Jude won't look.

"No it's not. It's me doing something for myself, taking a step. If I'd needed to run away, I would have done it a year ago. I want to move to Chapel Hill because I want to start over."

"You haven't tried hard enough in Greensboro."

"How can you say that?"

"You can't find a nice guy bar-hopping."

"I don't bar-hop. And please don't remind me again that you found Frank in church. You didn't find him in church. You found him at happy hour at the Greensboro Country Club. It was a setup by the Robinsons." They are not getting angry with each other, because they have said all these things before. They each lie easily about their histories, expecting to be corrected by the other.

"The first thing I knew about him was that he taught Sunday School for the Unitarians."

"That's not the same as finding him in church."

"Almost. We went to church the next day. To pray for forgiveness." Katherine giggles, although she is only pretending to be amused. Jude has talked idly before about leaving Greensboro, but this time something is different, she's thinking. Her sister looks too pretty today. Not a fixed-up pretty, but something coming from inside. Her conversation has been unusually animated. And that ponytail.

"We've started this discussion in the wrong vein," Jude says. "I'm not even looking for a man. I hate men. I'm moving to Chapel Hill, where I don't know anybody and where I won't feel this constant pressure to *find* somebody. I don't want anybody. I wish I could get you to understand that."

"You don't hate men," Katherine says. She rolls up her window so that the car will feel more intimate. Jude rolls her window all the way down.

"I'm hot," Jude explains, but the open window is allowing

her more separateness. "I hate men more than you can imagine."

"You can't be a daughter of our mother and hate men."

"That's exactly why I do hate them. But I can't explain it, so don't ask me to." In a quieter voice she adds, "I hate wanting them so bad. I'm through with that."

"You don't hate men," Katherine repeats. "You can't hate half the human race. What's wrong with wanting them? They want us. And what pressure are you talking about? You're certainly not getting it from me."

"They're not human," Jude says. She is thinking particularly of Paul Hinton. "They don't have needs. Sure, they want us, but not very much. There's nothing that they can't live without. Ask one." No one would die for anyone, she remembers her sister once saying. But Katherine doesn't have children.

Heatedly, Katherine is asking her: "Can you say that Frank's not human? *No.* Can you say that *he* doesn't have needs? One of his needs is to have a reasonably happy sister-in-law. And the thing he can't live without is me."

Jude relaxes her grip on the steering wheel and eases her foot off the gas. She's been doing eighty. "Aren't you a lucky thing?" she asks in a suddenly calm voice.

"You know what I was trying to say."

In the silence, Jude thinks that she doesn't hate men. She just hates the ones she knows. Not Frank, she thinks wearily. But all the rest. She hates Paul Hinton for his self-righteousness.

In a soothing voice, Katherine says, "I want you to give it another year. It's too soon to make a change. The kids are barely used to Cap being gone. I don't think you should move them. I don't think you should move yourself."

"Whatever you say," Jude says darkly. She hasn't yet said that she no longer has her job or her place to live.

"Don't say, 'Whatever I say.' *Think* about this."

"I've thought about it," Jude snaps. She looks at the speedometer because the world seems to be flying by. But now she's driving slower than the minimum speed.

"If you had thought about it, you would have reached another conclusion," Katherine says. The flush on her face has been replaced by rock-hard whiteness. "You might as well move to Chicago. We'll hardly get to see each other. I won't be able to watch Katie and Charles grow up. I'll hardly know them . . ."

"You ought to be glad I'm doing something for myself," Jude says in a faltering voice. Not many people genuinely love her children. Katherine does. But being away from her could hardly hurt them. "All you're thinking about is how it's going to affect you," she adds.

"What about how it's going to affect Daddy? What about Cap? Katie and Charles won't have a father anymore."

"That was Cap's decision, not mine," Jude says in a surer tone. "As for Daddy, he hardly knows his grandchildren exist."

"He knows *you* exist."

"And I'll miss him," Jude says angrily. "But does that mean I'm stuck here the rest of my life?"

Katherine allows a long silence. She wonders if this is just an idea or if Jude has already taken action. She suspects the latter. "It sounds as if you're trying to punish Cap," she says.

"I'm not trying to punish him. But I don't see that I have to live my life for his convenience. I never did a thing to make him leave. We had a perfectly fine family."

"You keep saying that." Katherine grows quiet again. Finally, she says in a low voice, "I *don't* want you to leave me. I *am* thinking of myself. I would never leave you, and I don't understand how you can leave me. We need to be together. We're a family. We're all one thing." She's thinking that more than any of them Jude needs people she can depend upon.

"I'll be an hour away," Jude says.

"You can find a man in Greensboro."

"I'm not looking for a man. Please, listen to me. I'm *not looking for a man.*"

"Any woman with two kids is looking for a man." Katherine says this, but does she believe it? She believes it's true for Jude. Jude needs a man. Not to help with her children, but to help with herself. Katherine doesn't need one, she thinks. But maybe the fact that she *has* Frank makes her think she doesn't

201|

need him. If she were without a man, wouldn't she want one more than anything?"

"*Not me*," Jude says. Why will Katherine not believe her? Why does she think that life is lived only one way?

"Everyone wants to be loved by a lover."

Jude wishes she could explain life as she now lives it to her sister. But the life of a single woman is beyond the comprehension of a married one. You become one of two things: desperate as she used to be or, now, suddenly—unexpectedly—uninterested. There is no middle ground. "You are living in a different world from me," Jude says. "A predictable, easy world." If Katherine tries to tell her anything else, she thinks she will turn the car around and go home. Things *will* change between them when she moves. She'll become less important to Katherine and Katherine to her. She and her family won't be "one thing" anymore. But neither will she have inside her this terrible trapped feeling as they all hammer out their lives together, blow by miserable blow. Maybe being "one thing" is what she's trying to escape.

In silence they pass one exit and then another, and suddenly they are halfway toward her new home and she knows there will be no turning back. She'll promise Katherine that she'll move back to Greensboro if she isn't happy in Chapel Hill. She'll move back if she finds she can't bear to be so far away from her sister. But she has been far away from her since she had Katie and Charles. It's something that Katherine hasn't yet realized.

"Chapel Hill is a great town," Jude says.

"Too transient."

"There's a big permanent population. Getting bigger and more sophisticated as the Research Triangle grows."

Katherine intones: "You'll go there and meet someone. He'll get transferred or find another job and then you'll move to New York or San Francisco or London. And I'll never see you again."

"That's *not* going to happen."

"You'll fall in love. You'll—"

"Will you shut up?" Jude feels about to explode. "Nobody's in love. Don't you know that? Don't you talk to your friends? Marriage is the great institution of tolerance. Don't you listen?"

"Mother and Max were in love," Katherine says quietly. She could use Frank and herself as another example, but she holds back. She hates to keep reminding Jude of how great Frank is. Jude knows: it's stood between them like a wall ever since she and Frank got married. *Their* only problem is babies, and she wouldn't define that as a problem of *love*. "Passion exists," she tells Jude. "Mother and Max. Frank and me. You and someone yet-to-be." Dr. Stern and the whole world, she suddenly thinks.

For a few moments Katherine stops listening to Jude, who's continuing to talk about the nature of passion. Her sister knows so little about her: what's good in her life, what's not so good, what she thinks about when she isn't thinking about Jude and Louise. She thinks about them, she knows, so much more than they think about her. Both of her sisters regard her as someone finished. Both think she has everything anybody would want. How can she tell them that she doesn't? How can she say that she has hopes and dreams that even Frank doesn't know about? The only person she's told exactly what she wants is Dr. Stern.

"I read last week that even the most passionate affairs cool off after just two years," Jude says. She's hardly interested in the subject of passion, but she hasn't minded finding out that it doesn't last for *anybody*. What she's interested in right now is getting Katherine to Chapel Hill, where her sister can begin imagining how happy Jude will be.

"Frank and I have been married four years," Katherine says. "Nothing's changed. Mother and Max were always in love. That will exist forever: he'll never marry anyone else. You and Cap never had it. That's why you don't know about it. Maybe it's the level of passion we're talking about. I mean the desire to possess another person's mind and soul, too. Not just his body. You can possess anyone's body. And get bored in two years. I'm sure the ladies' magazines know. But how can you get bored with the combination? The world has known great lovers," she concludes.

Are she and Frank "great lovers," she wonders. Sometimes she thinks so; sometimes she thinks not. Sometimes she wonders if they're too happy to be great lovers. Don't great lovers fight? She and Frank are so careful around each other. Too careful, she thinks. Or could being careful be another way to be lovers? Mother and Daddy *and* Mother and Max fought like cats and dogs. They knew what was wrong with each other, loved each other anyway, and kept slugging it out. Frank thinks she's perfect. She thinks he's pretty perfect, too. Although she's not attracted to Dr. Stern at all, she thinks that if *they* were married, he would want to fight with her and she would fight back. It's something she would hate.

Next to Katie and Charles, the person Jude loves best in the world is her sister. She loves Katherine more than she loved Mother. Rather, she has always loved Katherine; she can't say that about anyone else but her children. When Mother was alive and healthy, she hated her more than she loved her. When she was sick and dying, she exclusively loved her, and when she was dead, she couldn't remember ever hating her. Now that Mother's been gone two years, though, Jude is glad she no longer has to put up with her. She'll always, willingly, put up with her sister.

Katherine would never move to Chapel Hill and leave her behind, Jude knows. It's how she regards sisterhood, as something fierce and absolute. Katherine loves her excessively, with a love she'll never lose. Her mother's love, on the other hand, was so tentative. At any moment Mother could turn against her, set her against her sister, shame her for all the things she couldn't be. She loved her mother, but, somehow, not as a mother. She loves her sister. As a mother? She thinks yes.

They turn off the interstate onto curvy Highway 86, which has been under construction since she's had a driver's license. Everyone she knows—whether they attended the University of North Carolina here or not—has visited Chapel Hill for years: in the sixties to try health foods; in the early seventies to buy Alexander Julian's about-to-be discovered clothing; and in the mid-seventies to taste nouvelle cuisine in one of the rare concentrations of fine restaurants around the state. Like Wrightsville Beach, Chapel Hill is a town that almost everyone in North Carolina gets to know some time or other. People *visit* Chapel Hill, she ought to remind Katherine. Friends will come to spend the night with her all the time. She won't be lonely at all. She'll keep her Greensboro friends and add a whole second city. Katherine can see her if she can manage to drive an hour.

"I *have* to leave Greensboro," she murmurs.

"Why?" Katherine immediately asks.

"I have to find what I want. Not a man. I just want a fresh start. Why is that so hard to understand? I can't stay in Greensboro because you want me to. I won't let you tell me what to do the way you told Louise."

"We both told Louise what we thought. That's all we did. I still think Billy was wrong for her, and so do you."

In a quieter voice Jude says: "And now you think Chapel Hill's wrong for me."

"Not Chapel Hill. Moving, in general."

"I wish you wouldn't tell me what to do."

"I wish I didn't have to. Roll up your window, please. So we can talk. Don't you want to know what I think? Don't you think I owe it to you to give my honest opinion? How can you not want to hear it?" After being unexpectedly distracted by her thoughts about Dr. Stern, it's hard to reengage herself with Jude. But this is more than a conversation, she's realizing. Something is being permanently decided. Katherine searches for the right approach. She cannot bear to lose her precious sister. She refuses to lose her to what is only a search in a new place for a man. If only Jude would say so.

"Louise has lost Billy, and Mother is dead," Jude says.

Katherine looks carefully at her, but Jude will not look back. Her half smile is nervous, determined. "I know she's dead," Katherine says tentatively.

"She wouldn't be dead if . . ."

"If what?"

"I've been thinking about this for a long time." In fact, it has just occurred to Jude to turn the conversation to Katherine's relationship with Mother. "You interfere too much in other people's lives," she says. "But it's what you don't do as well as what you do."

"Roll up your window," Katherine demands. With irritation

Jude turns the handle twice. "What exactly are you trying to say?"

"You abandoned Mother."

"I think it was the other way around."

"She asked you to come home and you refused."

"Oh," Katherine says, thinking she's beginning to understand. "And so you're going to abandon me."

"That's not my point."

"It may not be your point, but that's what's happening," Katherine says. "You're abandoning me. For no good reason."

"You don't need me."

"That may be true. But I *want* you. Isn't that just as important?"

The conversation has veered in a wrong direction and Jude must regain control of it. "I'm trying to show you some examples," she says in a steady, important voice. A teaching voice, Katherine thinks. "Number one: Louise no longer has Billy. Number two: Mother told me before she died that her real death began happening a long time before. It started, she said, when you wouldn't go back to live with her. Number three—"

"Did you believe that?" Katherine asks incredulously. "Have you ever considered that what Mother said was just another way of trying to divide us?" She is trying to stay calm. She thought Jude was smarter than this.

"I believe you abandoned Mother," Jude says in a curt voice.

"She abandoned *me*, Jude. I was sixteen years old. She told me to get out of the house. She told Daddy the same thing. Do you think *he* divorced *her*?"

"She asked you to come back. She didn't ask him. It's not the same. You were never sixteen years old."

Katherine doesn't speak. For a long time she sits abnormally still. "I was so sixteen," she mutters absently.

Jude watches her, surreptitiously at first and then straight on when she isn't forced to watch the road. Katherine's face is lifeless, frozen; her eyes show no emotion. Jude wonders if she's taking this conversation as it's intended: an exploration, a stretch toward the limits of their understanding of their lives, a groping for whatever the truth may be. More than anything, Jude thinks she is praising her sister, since she is telling her that she is stronger than their mother was, that she could have kept her from dying, given her life. Saved her as even Max couldn't. When you are strongest, it's your responsibility to exercise that strength. That's all Jude is saying. Who actually abandoned whom is perfectly clear to her: Mother abandoned Katherine. But at the same time Jude knows that Katherine could have stayed and survived. If she will admit that much, perhaps she will stop interfering with Jude's plans.

Jude lost her virginity only a couple of miles from here at a church camp she attended when she was sixteen. Katherine thought she'd lost it to Cap. Until their divorce, so did he. But she'd lost it to a counselor-in-training who was as ignorant and fumbling as she. At dusk one June day she and Anthony Eubanks left the campsite looking for kindling for a fire. When darkness fell, they linked hands to find their way back. "Want to kiss?" he'd whispered. It was too dark to see each other, but she knew from earlier observation that he was good-looking, if a little greasy. Had they actually done it? Although there was no blood, Jude knows that something was inside her. The day Cap admitted he was in love with Carolyn, she decided the answer was yes. One of the things she'd told him that day was that, contrary to what he'd always believed, he hadn't been the first.

They pass the sign for the camp, and she asks Katherine if she remembers the summer she was a camper here. No, Katherine says, in a still-pained voice. Does she need to explain further what she meant, Jude wonders. If she explains about Mother, the topic will be out of the way and then Katherine will want to talk about the move again. Jude will find herself listening. She's afraid to hear Katherine's arguments, afraid of their strength.

"Have I ever—" she begins, and then breaks off. She was going to tell Katherine about Anthony. But knowing about him will only lead Katherine to ask what else Jude's never admitted. Nothing, except that the garage they'll park in front of as soon as they have lunch belongs to her as of August 1. She's moving.

Nothing Katherine can say can change her mind, because she won't listen. Things are out of Jude's hands, anyway: in Greensboro she has no job and no home.

They reach the city limits and she turns right on Franklin Street, stealing a glance at her sister, whose face has not changed. Jude can tell that Katherine is not softening at all. It irritates her. People crowd the sidewalks. Not just students, but people with kids, people like her. Chapel Hill is an exciting place. It is *her* place.

"Pull over for a second," Katherine suddenly says. She's looking out the window as if she's spotted someone she knows. What luck, Jude thinks. Whoever this is will remind Katherine of how attractive Chapel Hill people are. She pulls to the curb. Instead of calling to someone, Katherine gets out of the car and slams the door. She leans inside the window, examining Jude's face. "You remind me so much of Mother," she says. She is not crying, but her eyes are puffy and strained. "You think you can say whatever you want to say and I'll forgive you. You think I won't even notice. You're just like her. You betray *me* over and over, but you think *I'll* never betray *you*. And you're right, I won't. But it's not okay with me, and I hate you for it. And I won't ever forget it. I know that you think I'm happier than you are. Maybe I am; maybe I'm not. It doesn't give you the right to treat me badly."

Waves of heat travel across Jude's scalp, down her throat, into her shoulders. Whenever she's told that an action of hers reminds someone of Mother—even if it's something so unlovely as the compulsive way she becomes when she's drunk—she's always felt a little bit proud. Who wouldn't want to display the exciting unpredictability of a mother like theirs? But this is different. Katherine, not some neurotic neighborhood bitch, is making the comparison and finding serious fault. "I was complimenting you," she says. "You didn't understand."

Katherine gazes steadily at her. She tucks her hair behind her ears, making her features seem larger. "You were not complimenting me," she says in a trembling voice.

"I was saying that you were stronger than Mother," Jude says, her voice rising.

"That's *not* what you were saying," Katherine says. "You said that I destroyed Mother. You said that you've always believed *her* instead of me. You implied that, simply because I tell you the truth, I'm going to destroy you, too. *Jude:* you can't just say on a whim whatever you want to say. That's what Mother always did. It's wrong. It's destructive. It was hate so strong we all thought it was love."

Katherine stands straight. For a moment she doesn't move and all Jude can see is her pumping midsection. Then she walks around the car and opens Jude's door. Jude scrambles over the gearshift and Katherine gets in, buckling the seat belt angrily but in the practiced way that shows this is her car. Her heart feels small and dense. She hopes Jude will not try to explain any further, because she won't be able to respond. Not for an unfathomable amount of time.

Beside her, Jude is hardly able to concentrate on her sister's hurt feelings—although she wishes she could. Instead, she is sick that they've come this far and she's not going to get to see her new apartment. She wants to know how big it is. What kind of windows it has. She knows the floors are carpeted in blue. Will the shade match her sofa?

Neither of them attempts to say anything as they begin the ride back to Greensboro. It starts to rain, big hot drops.

CHAPTER

12

The whole four years she has been married, Katherine has awakened with Frank's body lined up behind hers so that they are touching from head to foot. And when she is awake enough, he hugs her and kisses her neck and buries his face in her hair and his head in her pillow, which they are sharing. Not once has this gesture of his failed to leave her astonished at her own good fortune. Not once has it failed to suffuse her chest with warmth. From girlhood, Katherine thought she might someday be married, but she never thought she'd be happily married. To be shown love—isn't it everything, she wonders as she turns onto her stomach. She has awakened alone in bed for the first time in months, but she immediately remembers why: Frank is in the kitchen, showing her what a good father he would be.

Both doors of the bedroom are closed so that Katherine cannot hear noise from downstairs, yet there is an electric feel of suppressed sound to the house. Need—in the form of two children, Katie and Charles—has entered where before only desire was present. Katherine has only to open the door in order to be aware of the change. Jude called Frank on Thursday to ask the babysitting favor. Although Frank knows that they've had a quarrel, he told Jude that they'd be happy to keep the children Friday night, Saturday, and even Sunday if she found it necessary.

She rolls out of bed, stretches fully, and puts on her gown, which she took off in the middle of the night because of the heat. Turning the doorknob quietly, she tiptoes to the top step. Downstairs, a little ensemble—bacon sizzling, coffee dripping, toast popping up—is playing. The music even has a wonderful smell.

Katherine does not mind that her husband doesn't necessarily take her side in an argument. She does not mind keeping her niece and nephew over the weekend. The only thing she minds is that Jude forced her to participate without talking directly to her. And she minds that Frank, without knowing any details, thinks the argument was her fault. To be fair, she has only told him that they have disagreed over Jude leaving Greensboro. The rest of the argument she never plans to tell anyone. Frank thinks that it's good Jude is moving. He says the new environment should benefit both her and her children. He says that Katherine is being selfish. He, too, believes that Chapel Hill is not that far away.

She goes quietly to the bathroom to remove her diaphragm and squats in the bathtub, her gown gathered over one arm, to wash herself. Although after the United Way meeting she stopped using birth control for a while, she has begun using it again. She didn't worry about getting pregnant the first couple of times she and Frank made love because she'd just finished her period. But the third and fourth times she could hardly respond. Frank, on the other hand, seemed more engaged with her body than ever before. She felt him trying to make a baby, which she found quite different from making love. There was a striving in his thrust that ignored pleasure. Her own body tried to resist, her reproductive organs seeming to draw up as far inside her as they could. She willed Frank's sperm to be unsuccessful, wondering if her powers of concentration could prevent a fertilization. Women over the centuries would probably tell her no. Two weeks later she had put the rubber cup back inside her. She was able to breathe again. She could press her body close to his. She could lose herself once more. When Frank first felt the diaphragm, he let out a deep moan, but he hasn't said anything to her. When he smiles, though, she sees sadness in his eyes. When he laughs, he laughs with that nearly inaudible extra pitch of people who are enduring secret pain. But it's not secret.

"Good morning, everybody," she says. All three of them turn

to greet her as she enters the breakfast room. Their Irish setter, Miss Fancy, brought to their marriage by Frank, thumps the floor with her thick tail. She is safe around children but avoids them. Sort of like herself, Katherine thinks.

Charles sits in a portable chair that attaches to the table. Katie, wide-eyed, is on Frank's knee. Frank himself sits cheerfully calm as if he has been doing this all his life.

Charles is a deeply dimpled red-haired cherub with a stocky body like Cap's. Jude had warned Frank that in a strange place the baby might not sleep through the night, but unless Frank got up without Katherine hearing, he must have been fine. Her niece gazes steadily at her with wide unreadable eyes, the kind of look generally unsettling to adults. She doesn't smile the way her brother does, but Jude says it's because she's entered a shy phase. Katherine thinks Katie is a sad child. Her hair is drawn up in a ponytail set yesterday, its raggedness emphasizing the perfectness of her small features.

Katherine goes to kiss Frank, which she thinks they ought to see, and then she kisses each of them on top of their heads. Babies' fragrance is the most hypnotizing thing about them, she thinks. Frank returns to the game he is playing with Katie, pretending that each bite of French toast is an airplane flying into her mouth. A look of exaggerated anticipation fills his face. Katie squeals loudly and then her eyes go blank while she chews, the airplane only a transient pleasure. Katherine sits down to feed Charles, who has spooned blobs of cereal all over the table. At her place Frank has set a half grapefruit with a cherry in the middle, orange juice, and a cup ready for her tea. So far, motherhood seems rather easy.

"We'll let Aunt Katherine take her bath," Frank says, "and then we'll put on our costumes and go to the parade." At the word "parade" Charles begins beating his juice cup against the table; Katie's eyes widen, but she doesn't smile.

At Jude's suggestion, they are taking the children to the annual Fourth of July parade in her neighborhood, an event that attracts unicyclists, stilt walkers, one or two vintage automobiles, and hundreds of crepe-paper-wrapped bicycles. Jude has sent over costumes borrowed from a friend: for Katie, a silver-sequined majorette uniform, and for Charles, a red-white-and-blue-striped bubble suit. Adults sometimes dress up for the parade, too, and Frank plans to wear a rented Uncle Sam outfit. He's been trying to convince Katherine to wear her cheerleading uniform from high school, but she doesn't see the connection.

Katie leaves Frank's lap for Katherine's, and protesting mildly, he gets up to fix more French toast. Normally he comes to the table in his bathrobe, but today Katherine notices that he's dressed in shorts and shirt. Katie hugs her, eyeing her uncle as if he has become a dangerous stranger. "She's used to women's laps," Katherine offers. After all, Frank is the one who's been so nice to them.

"She liked mine fine until you came down."

Frank's feelings should not be hurt. This is how it is with babies and mothers, she considers telling him, but he will find out soon enough if they have their own. Children are so easily able to divide and conquer, needing only one breeding ground: parents who love them more than they love each other. Would Frank love a child more than he loves her, Katherine wonders. Would she love one more than him? Because of how much she has loved her sisters and with such unsatisfying results, she thinks not. But a child, she is told, calls forth unexpected responses. She's always been afraid of what those responses might be. But maybe she would feel only utter love. If so, she should probably have said yes to Frank about children from the beginning. By saying no, she may have only exaggerated their importance.

With a sanguine look, Frank brings her a plate. So she can eat, she hands him Katie, who vigorously wiggles out of his grasp until she is lying prone on the linoleum floor. Strangely, Katie makes no sound at all. Jude has told Katherine about this nonverbal way Katie exercises her will, but it's the first time Katherine has seen it. She shrugs at Frank—wanting them to silently agree what pains children are—and slips her chair close to the table so that Katie can't get back up in her lap. This visit may end up serving her purposes instead of Frank's. But she already knows that if it begins to, Frank will say that Jude's children aren't the same as theirs would be. Their own children will not mystify them the way someone else's do.

"Take Katie outside," she tells Frank in an encouraging voice. "Show her your garden. Let her pick a tomato or some of your beans. Tell her how they grow." He looks at her as if she is brilliant.

"More juice?" she asks Charles. Most of the juice, because Frank forgot the plastic lid, has spilled on Charles's pajamas.

"I have a surprise for you," Frank tells Katie as he walks toward the back door. Reluctantly, she gets up from the floor and follows.

Katherine rummages around in the grocery bag of supplies Jude sent until she finds the lid, refills the cup, and hands it to Charles. When she finishes eating, she picks him up and carries him upstairs, sniffing him and kissing him and tossing him in the air. She's glad he's not old enough to tell his mother how much fun they are having. She's not even sure she wants Frank to know. Charles laughs a raspy baby-laugh and vomits some of his cereal, which makes her realize she should handle him more gently after a meal. She hugs him close and touches her cheek to the softest cheek she has ever felt. He doesn't yet know how to return a hug, but he makes appreciative noises. Without question, she loves this child. If something threatened Charles, she would put her own life in the path. But deep down she knows it's because Charles is helpless and it would be her duty, not because she is willing to die for someone. She would certainly not die for Jude. Not anymore. But, to be honest, not before their argument either. Already, she would not die for Katie. Once Charles passes the stage of helplessness, she will no longer die for him, either. She doesn't think she would even die for Frank. She wonders why people are always saying they would die for someone else. Isn't it just a romantic lie? Rather, isn't it a loudmouth attempt at competing with God? Frank, though, *would* die for her, so maybe the idea is legitimate. She feels suddenly shamed, the way Mother's words when she was dying couldn't make her feel. But Frank is the *only* person who would die for her, which makes her feel less ashamed. It was a ruse of

Mother's that she would die for her children. When she'd had a chance to "die" for Katherine, she hadn't. If Frank had the same chance, maybe he wouldn't, either. And if she herself had a chance to die for someone, maybe sometime she would.

She sits Charles in the middle of their bed, taking off her nightgown and then, because of Frank being dressed at breakfast, putting it back on. She has no idea when one should stop appearing nude in front of baby boys. From the beginning? Age two? Age ten? If it's true that sexual preference is determined by age three, this could be important. While she's in the bathroom starting her bathwater, Charles rolls off the bed. When she returns, he is trying to scramble back up but succeeds only after a boost from her. He repeats this over and over and over and over.

Frank and Katie, involved in a conversation about tomatoes, are climbing the stairs. Katherine quickly folds up her cheerleading uniform and stuffs it under the bed. While playing with Charles, she'd gotten it out to see what made Frank think she should wear it to the parade. The colors—red and white—are the only possible reason. It embarrasses her now, but early in their relationship she tried on her high-school uniform for him and performed a few cheers. She did this more or less to woo him: to show that at twenty-five she was as energetic as she'd been at eighteen, but also to feed his intense desire to know everything that's ever happened to her. Frank thinks that history also tells the future. But Katherine hates to think of herself as only repeating her errors or even her successes. She's always changing, she tells him. He would not be able to predict what she will do.

Having other people in one's bedroom always feels unexpectedly intimate, and it's no different, she notices, when those people are children. Katie runs from behind Frank's legs and hurls herself onto the bed beside her brother. Charles is in the process of sliding off again, but she grabs his fat little fists and pulls him back up. He begins screaming, but she won't let go. Katie watches without expression as Katherine and Frank approach the bed. Suddenly, with a half smile, she gives a quick

215|

nod, sinking her teeth into Charles's scalp. The pitch of his scream ascends an entire octave. He pushes at his sister, but Katherine has to yank Katie away—by her feet, the first thing she can reach—to make her stop. Frank grabs Charles, whose wail has assumed the steadiness of a pumping heart, and begins tossing him in the air. Before it's over, Katherine thinks, he'll have no breakfast left.

"It's okay, little fellow," he says with a big smile. "She didn't mean to try to kill you."

"Only betray. Like her Mommie does to me," Katherine says.

"Lay off," Frank says. "In front of them."

She's surprised and hurt by his abruptness. The children have no idea what she's talking about. It's Frank who didn't want to hear what she had to say. He doesn't look at her. His face is calm. He doesn't even know her feelings are hurt. Her understanding of children becomes even sharper: they divide not only wittingly but unwittingly. Frank is trying to cuddle Charles, but with his elbows at sharp angles it's as if his arms won't go circular. They could switch children, but she thinks he wouldn't know how to discipline a girl.

She squats, takes both of Katie's hands, and tells her to look her in the eyes. "You bit your brother."

"Ax-dent," Katie says.

Katherine moves her hands to Katie's shoulders. "It was not an accident." Every time Katie makes a defiant face, Katherine applies a sort of indignant pressure. "Say you bit your brother." Pressure. "Say you did it on purpose." Pressure.

Tears begin seeping out of Katie's eyes, but her expression is remorseless. "Ax-dent," she repeats.

"We're not going to the parade until you admit what you did and until you apologize." Katherine remembers one of Jude's child-rearing methods: refocusing the child's attention. "As soon as you apologize, we'll put on your costume and your white boots and we'll go to the parade. You want to go to the parade, don't you?"

Katie appears to be thinking.

"Don't you?"

"No," Katie says with ringing conviction. Naturally. Charles hiccups and whines, hiccups and whines as he forgets and remembers what happened. Frank is boosting him up on the bed and letting him fall off again.

Perhaps, "as they say," the best way to handle children is to ignore bad behavior / praise good behavior, but Katherine can't quite believe this. She stands and looks down at her niece, hoping to intimidate her, but Katie looks back unwaveringly. She's Katie's aunt, not her mother; she's surprised Katie is not more respectful. She weighs whether or not to tell Katie how disappointed in her she is, but before she can speak, Katie whispers, "Sorry." Her big blue eyes don't look sorry at all. Her valentine mouth shows no sign of repentance. What must Katherine insist upon now? If Katie refuses to be truly sorry and Katherine has to follow through and cancel their trip to the parade, the day will stretch on interminably.

"Good," she says. "I'm proud of you for saying you're sorry." She doesn't meet Katie's eyes, so Katie will know she's not too proud. "Uncle Frank is going to dress you while I take a bath." Another indication of the limits of her pride.

"No! *You!*" Katie cries, throwing her arms around Katherine's legs.

"I don't have time." Katherine steps out of Katie's grasp, and although Katie tries to move with her, she moves quicker, separating herself. She picks up the baby, who, when he feels her embrace, is reminded again to cry. "Katie's sorry," she coos. "She asked me to tell you." It is clear to Katherine that she would die only for the totally innocent: those under two.

"Want me to dress her?" Frank asks.

Katherine nods. She keeps rocking Charles while with her fingers she probes the four-tooth indentation in his scalp. The baby reaches for his injury. Katie watches guardedly, but Katherine pretends not to notice. Frank gives her an admiring look—the baby has calmed again—which she doesn't acknowledge, either. She is thinking how an entire hour of her and Frank's life has passed with nothing at all to show for it.

217|

Since they are outsiders, they have to drive to Jude's neighborhood, park the car in her driveway, and walk to where the parade begins. Already, it's such a hot day that Katherine opens all four doors of the car to cool it off enough to put the children inside. The sky is white with haze, not bright blue as it ought to be. An occasional dull breeze makes the humidity just bearable.

Frank returns to the house to fetch something he says he forgot. "Surprise!" he calls on his way back out. The surprises are miniature American flags for each of them to carry. Since Katherine is wearing only red shorts and a white blouse, she is delighted to have something that makes her look as if she's aware of the holiday. She is obligated for the children's sakes, after all, to participate. To be a committed soldier.

"You look cute," she says to Frank while he's backing out of the driveway. Truthfully, she thinks he looks comical in his red-and-white-striped pants, navy tails, and top hat. She thinks of Uncle Sam as someone as tall as a telephone pole. Frank is not tall or thin or hunched over in an I-Want-You way. To suit his trim, well-built figure, he should be dressed like a juggler or an acrobat or a wrestler.

"I wish *you* had dressed up," he says.

He had found her cheerleading uniform, unfortunately, while he was brushing off the dirt from the garden that Katie had got on the sheets.

"I thought it was lost," he'd said in a disappointed voice.

"I lied." She walked over to where he was standing, to cram the uniform back under the bed.

"You look adorable in it," he said.

"I look fifteen."

"What's wrong with that?"

"I'm twenty-nine. I can't wear my cheerleading uniform to a Fourth of July parade. People will laugh at me."

"No one would ever laugh at you," he'd said.

One of the things she loves about Frank is that he believes in other people in such a wholehearted way. He helps balance her, who only believes in two or three. But she will not make a fool of herself.

"I won't do it. You can't make me. I totally refuse," she finally said in an extreme voice to make him stop pestering her.

She thought then and she thinks now how different they are. Frank is *for* everything; she is such a skeptic. He participates in the world; she contemplates it. When she first met him, she pretended she was the same kind of person as he. She joined in the things he liked. For six months, for example, she jumped three times a week into the never warm enough water at the YMCA, toning her body alongside his. She played golf; she gave dinner parties; she went sailing. It hadn't been a total lie: Frank's love invigorated her. And she was trying to be the happy person he wanted her to be. She's told him she'll go swimming again someday. She still plays golf once in a while, and she's convinced him that it's more fun to take people out to dinner instead of cooking for them. Somehow she's made him think that nothing's changed. For the next two weeks, though, he'll see that they have. Monday they are leaving for Sea Island, Georgia, where they'll eat, drink, swim, play golf and tennis, like they used to. She'll hate almost all of it.

Although she's started using her diaphragm again, since her talk with Frank she has turned herself back into what he regards as the perfect woman. She's been snuggly and adoring. When she first lays eyes on him at the end of a day, her face lights up like the sun. It lights up naturally—she's always glad to see him—but she causes it to light up, too. She's made her husband happy again, and unexpectedly she's felt happier, too. She's even told him that she's on the verge of deciding about a baby, but he must give her some time. She makes love to him with special tenderness. She's not being false. She feels all these things that she shows him. She just doesn't show him everything. She no longer mentions wanting to be something, and he doesn't mention it either. She thinks he ought to ask what happened, but he's probably afraid of her answer. Since she's developed an interior way of thinking that he knows nothing about, she wouldn't tell him anyway. One day, perhaps, she'll decide what she wants and make an announcement.

Independence Road, the street that the parade goes down, is

crowded with people. Katherine is leading Katie, and Frank is carrying Charles. It feels odd to have children with them. People who know them will wonder anew why she and Frank don't have any of their own. Her skin bristles slightly. She puts on a smile. Except for an insurance salesman she knows who always dresses up like George Washington, Frank appears to be the only man in costume. Children are dressed as Raggedy Anns and Andys, clowns, Supermen and Superwomen, Indians, Pilgrims. Except for a few dowdy dressers, most of the mothers are dressed in the manner called casual chic. The fathers wear Izod shirts and Patagonia shorts. Although Jude shouldn't be moving to Chapel Hill, Katherine thinks she shouldn't have stayed in Kirkwood either.

Katherine tries to imagine what a Fourth of July parade made up of patriots would have looked like. She can't say that there is *no* character in the faces she sees today, but the engravure of *personality*—a slight distinction—seems to have the edge. Of all things, too much money has most softened the national character, she thinks. As a result, everyone, herself included, has too many choices. One of the greatest impulses must be to succeed over adversity. But past adversity shows on none of these faces. What qualifies as adversity? For her, it might be having a baby. Having a baby might engrave her face. It might enable her to be a poet. Or maybe she would only have to grub out ditches. She imagines sitting down in a corner of her tiny garret at midnight, the day's backbreaking work—kids? ditches?—finally done, so empty of paralyzing choices that poetic words would spring forth in perfect order.

She turns to share her realization about hardship with Frank, but fortunately he has already started talking to some of the many people they know. She could interrupt, but perhaps these are thoughts she ought to consider before mentioning. The minute they stopped their inward trek, Frank had handed her the baby and gone off to talk to people. With Charles hugging her neck and Katie clinging to her legs, she's become like a tree for koala bears. To an extent, the children camouflage her. She's also hiding behind her sunglasses. She can be seen, of course, but she has the distinct feeling that no one really notices her. It suits her fine that Frank is moving from cluster to cluster. Frank loves crowds; she's never comfortable in them. She is not like anyone here, and she prefers not to begin to sense any similarity. On the other hand, people are always glad to see Frank, to take his extended hand. Shaking hands is the greatest show of self-confidence she can imagine. It says Frank is one of them.

She squats low to the ground to rest her back and to relieve for a moment the sensation that her clothes are being stretched into permanent shapelessness. She tells Katie to talk to Charles. She tells Charles to talk to Katie. Would they please pay attention to someone besides her? She huddles them together on the ground and stands a moment to look for Frank. He might as well be carrying Charles as he makes his rounds. It's as if she's risen briefly but miraculously out of a sinkhole. Frank is nowhere in sight. Instead, she sees Dr. Stern—what is *he* doing here?—who sees her, too.

Suddenly both children are climbing up her. A little boy, older than Charles but younger than Katie, has snatched their flags. Katherine is hamstrung, but she is long, too, and well balanced, since Frank hasn't brought her a beer yet. Even with both her legs stuck, she chases and catches the little thief with the spread of her upper body.

Dr. Stern is striding in her direction. "Well done," he says in a ringing voice. He squats as she stops to return the flags to the wailing children.

"These aren't yours," he says. He already has Charles in his big hands, examining him in an unusually thorough way. She remembers the way he examines poems and it seems less unusual. He has on jogging clothes. In the classroom he's such an imposing figure, and here it's no different. There's a largeness about him that has nothing to do with size. He has enormous legs, as thick as tree trunks.

"They're my sister's," she says.

He hands Charles back to her and bends over to tweak Katie's nose. "Aren't you a beautiful thing?" he asks. It's clear that he's appreciating them more than just because they're with her.

Katie gives him a bold smile. Dr. Stern stands straight for a second so that he can reach into his pocket. Then he holds his fists in front of her. "Choose," he says. She slaps his left hand. He turns it over and opens it to offer a piece of gum.

"What do you say?" Katherine asks, immediately hating herself for assuming the expected pose. But she does want her teacher to think her sister's children are well-mannered. Katie does not respond.

While she's opening the gum, Dr. Stern puts his hand on Katherine's wrist where it's holding Charles. If any other man at this entire parade did the same thing, it would be natural, but . . . She looks up at him and gives a purely friendly smile. He does not seem to see it. It's as if he's trying to look deep inside her. But then he lets go of her wrist and gives a friendly smile, too.

"What happened to you?" he asks.

Although she knows exactly what he's talking about, she gives him a puzzled look.

"You're not on my class list," he prods. "For the Eliot course."

"What are *you* doing *here?*" she asks. On the Fourth of July she'd think he'd be anywhere but here. She imagines him strolling through woods or lying in a hammock reading. He might even be writing letters at some handsome desk he has had since childhood. Holidays are grand opportunities to correspond with special friends, he might say. She would imagine him on a journey if she didn't know he's just returned from England.

He does not seem inclined to answer her question, and she thinks the answer to his—she'll be on vacation—is too boring. She asks, "How was your trip? You must be recently back."

"Not what I expected," he says in a grave voice. He has a way of gazing off into the distance as if his side of the conversation is continuing in his head. But then he glances back at her with those same searching eyes. She feels somehow bare.

"Oh?" It's hard to comprehend that a trip of his to England would not be the most intense of experiences. She remembers a visit she made to Asheville once when she stayed at the Grove

Park Inn, where Scott Fitzgerald sometimes wrote. Sitting at the desk in the room the hotel clerk promised was the great novelist's, she'd looked out over the Blue Ridge Mountains and felt awe. Not her awe but his. Surely Dr. Stern had felt the awe of the poets he loved so much.

"I can't talk about it," he says.

"Why not?" Her voice is far too insistent.

He grins. "I'm embarrassed," he says. She grins, too. He's reminding her of the time she wouldn't tell him about wanting to be a doctor.

"In your own good time I'm sure you'll want to tell me everything," she says. It's a forward remark but made entirely in fun.

He grows serious again. "I've made the trip many times. England always reminds me that there's a God. This time it wasn't the same."

"You weren't reminded of God?"

Suddenly Katherine is jarred by a remark spoken near them about neighborhood real estate. She glances around and sees Lou Johnson, her hand half covering the secret she is telling. Katherine is glad, so glad that she's found the one person here who can talk about something worthwhile.

"Oh, that was still there," Dr. Stern says absently. "The rest wasn't."

"What rest?"

"I guess I've been to the Motherland too many times. England's so civilized that I'm not moved the way I once was. I must need Paris. Or an equivalent. A new lover?" he adds in a throwaway manner. But then he gives her that same direct look. She blushes, but he doesn't seem to see. "I went to write, you know," he continues. "Maybe you don't know. I write poetry. I'm a poet before I'm a teacher, actually. I go to England to work almost every summer. Next summer, though . . ." He trails off.

She's so shocked that he's a poet. She thought he was a teacher. She thought he was in love with other people's words. But he makes his own. Now that she knows he's a poet, he looks different to her, but she doesn't know why. His eyes, though, have become a poet's eyes instead of a teacher's. His gestures, his dress, the same. Even his size. He's a large man already, but now he seems larger than life. She cannot ask him about his writing, at least not yet. It scares her. "Did you travel alone?" The answer to this may also explain why he is at this parade. He must already have one lover. Since he wants a *new* lover. No one but a poet would say something like that. Not in Greensboro at a Fourth of July family parade in Kirkwood.

"I always travel alone," he is saying. "Whether I'm with someone or not."

She makes a slight face. Is that a poet's language or a braggart's? Or, she suddenly—kindly—thinks, is it the language of a man who has never been in love?

"Am I being difficult?" he asks. For just an instant his face looks fragile and she cannot level her original accusation, even kiddingly. Maybe he is a lonely man. "I'm known to be difficult," he says, his expression changing. "Some people think I'm worth it." He looks away from her, his eyes showing not the slightest wonder as to whether she is one of the legion who thinks so.

She'd felt so genuinely happy to see him, to have a chance to explain about the Eliot course before next September. She's glad, too, to find out that he's a writer. He'll be able to tell her so much. But he's suddenly excluded her again, the way he did the day they had coffee. She looks angrily at him, but he's looking somewhere else. How can she dare feel so much anger at someone she doesn't know? But in some frightening way she knows Dr. Stern. Since he evidently doesn't know or want to know her, she looks around for Frank so that she can introduce them.

"So you're on sabbatical," he says in a tone that's almost mocking.

"Not at all." She refuses to tell him about their vacation. "I'm reading this summer. English novels. Lots of them." That's what she's decided to do in lieu of the course.

He whistles.

"Why are you making fun of me?" she asks.

In an almost biting voice he asks, "Why didn't you sign up for my course?" Can he be angry at *her*? Perhaps the course was under-enrolled.

Her left arm is aching, so she shifts Charles to her right side. It's then she realizes that something is missing. She looks down at her smooth, tanned, about-to-go-on-vacation legs. Katie is gone. The freeness around her knees feels about ten minutes old. The first thing she wonders is what reason she can give Frank that she has lost their niece. She feels a priori confident that in this particular crowd a known child is safe. But will he? She won't be able to say that she's been talking about God and England.

"Frank Borden," Frank says, shaking Dr. Stern's hand, and in the same breath, "Where's Katie?"

"I just this second realized she's wandered off," Katherine answers.

Dr. Stern names himself: "Eric Stern," but offers no further introduction. Perhaps Frank won't even realize that he was her Yeats teacher.

"I'm sure she's nearby," Katherine says, scouting over one shoulder and then the other.

"Katie!" Frank calls. The funny thing about his costume, she's realized, is that he doesn't *behave* as if he's costumed. Even wearing a top hat, he stands as if he's dressed like everyone else, which is what makes him so comical. *"Katie!"*

"Don't panic," she says, embarrassed. She doesn't want Frank to make a big production out of her losing one of the children, and the best way to stop him is to find her fast. She moves away in one direction, sending him with a light push in the opposite. Then she returns. "Would you hold Charles?" she asks Dr. Stern, thrusting the baby at him.

Everywhere she turns, she sees people Jude knows: Gary and Linda Birdsong, Jim and Estelle Matthews, Carol and Dick Pickle, Booboo and Carter Sherrill. They all have children but the children aren't with them. It's natural for the children not to be with them. This is Katie's neighborhood, Frank has forgotten. She knows where she is.

"Katie," she calls in a fondish voice. She does not hear Frank calling out. It's hard to look for a lost child among costumed children. She sees flashes of sequins, several silver batons, even the silver spokes of bicycle wheels, and thinks she has found her but hasn't. She reaches the outer limits of the crowd, where late arrivals are still appearing, and sees no sign of her. She goes a quarter turn of the general circle and plunges back in among the chatting groups. Soon the parade will begin, and Katie will realize she's lost. When Katherine finds her, she is going to wear her out. Spank and then ask questions, which has to be the most effective way to punish.

Thank God, she resisted Frank's urging to wear her cheerleading uniform. Thank God, thank God, thank God. A cheerleader would have looked all right except in the case of an emergency: then she would have looked like an imbecile. Uncle Sam, running around in circles instead of glad-handing everybody, looks pretty imbecilic himself, she thinks. If only Uncle Sam had thought to take one of the children with him instead of leaving them both with her . . . It's hard to be responsible for two when you have no experience. For a brief moment she thinks she understands Cap's girlfriend's nervousness.

Where is the little bitch? her mind begins to ask. She's sorry that she's thinking of Katie as a little bitch, but she can't help it. Would a real mother think that? Probably so, although Katherine is sure she'd never find one who'd admit it. Would a father? Probably not about his darling daughter, but she's sure most dads think of their sons as little brats every once in a while.

She spots Frank, who holds his empty arms wide. She shows that her arms are empty, too. Dr. Stern is nowhere to be seen, but if he's squatting down tending Charles he would be unseeable. Should she be trying to find *him*?

She feels the blank breathless beginnings of panic. What a ripe crowd this is for a childnapper. How easy it would be for a stranger to pluck Katie away from another almost-stranger, her aunt. If she has lost Katie, she will kill herself. She won't have any choice. How will Jude ever forgive her? Will Jude think she'd been careless because of their fight? Was she?

Frank darts off at a quarter angle and then quickly returns.

He's carrying instead of wearing his top hat. She's holding Charles's flag. Frank's black curls are matted to his head. He looks frightened.

"What have you done with Charles?" he asks.

What have you done with Charles? her mind repeats. "I gave him to Dr. Stern to hold. Eric . . ." she adds faintly.

"Do you know this guy?"

"Of course, I know him," she says furiously. "He's one of my professors."

"Well, where the fuck is he?" People around them startle on account of all the kids here. Blushing, she turns to face the thickest gathering. "We can't find Katie Cramer," she announces. "Has anybody seen her?" A few necks stretch, the word is passed on, but then the talking resumes. No one else knows where his kids are either. But they all live here; she and Frank don't. Frank hurries off again.

"Hallooooo," she hears over the crowd. It's Dr. Stern, thank God. Veddy British Dr. Stern. She had not doubted him even the slightest bit. Yes she had. She had wondered briefly if he could be a childnapper or even a pederast. But it was because he was at a Fourth of July parade, such an incongruous place for him to be. It had made her realize how little she actually knows about him. How dangerously trusting it was for her to hand him Charles. She had handed Charles to him on purpose. She'd needed an extra pair of arms, true, but it was more than that. She wanted to see what he could handle.

"I have both of them," Dr. Stern calls. She is relieved beyond belief. "Katie wasn't ten feet away, but the two of you were long gone. I had trouble getting her to stay with me except that I had Charles." He bends over to give his foundling a smile. "She's been taught well. More bubble gum had no effect whatsoever."

Katherine realizes that if Dr. Stern is really looking for a lover, he and Jude might hit it off. He's already crazy about her kids. He's rescued one of them, almost two. But Jude is painting her Chapel Hill apartment, and Dr. Stern lives in Greensboro. Katherine had told her she ought to stick around.

"Frank," she calls out searchingly. In her eagerness to hold the children again, she stumbles into her teacher, rubbing up against the thick fuzz on his arm. It's surprising that his skin can be warmer than the July heat. She intends to say thank you, but she can't remember the appropriately ironic remark she'd also planned. The bareness of his enormous legs makes her intensely aware of her own bare slender ones.

"You're remarkable," she says. Her language is excessive, but it's what she's thinking. Dr. Stern has in his possession both of Jude's children, when only a moment before Katherine had thought it within the realm of possibility that both were gone forever. Children do get lost; they are kidnapped; they're murdered; they die. It didn't happen today to these children, but it could have. And that's the fear that all these careful, unreckless parents at this parade live with, she realizes. The fear that, through no fault of their own, life will change. What everyone has his guard up for cannot, unfortunately, be guarded against.

"You're sort of irresistible yourself," Dr. Stern says, looking deeply into her eyes. Her face drains of color. This is not what she was leading him to say. She was complimenting him. Complimenting him for more than finding Katie, true. For the things he'd taught her in class. For being a poet. For his legs. Complimenting him whether he made fun of her summer reading plan or not. She *likes* him.

"I can't figure out why you're here," she says lightly.

"I'm patriotic," he says.

She stares at him, her eyes asking for a legitimate answer. It's odd the way she's trying to talk to him the way she talks to Jude.

"I have to be out in the world," he answers. "So I can write. That doesn't surprise you, does it?"

Before her, Dr. Stern begins to assume a strange white cast, as if he's been stripped of his blood. His eyes, though, grow bluer—a blue deeper and more intense than she has ever seen in nature. All peripheral sound abruptly halts. She can hear him saying, "I've missed seeing you. I want you to take my class. You can't imagine what it's like to teach someone who comprehends me. No one ever comprehends me." She wants to make him stop, for things to go back to normal, to substitute a simple thank-you for the word "remarkable" that she used. She wouldn't even need to say anything ironic.

From far away but in normal pigment, she sees Frank approaching. She raises her arm to signal that everything is fine, hoping that the world will heed her order and return to normal. But when she looks back at Dr. Stern's eyes, she can hardly breathe. It's as if nothing else exists, although, without looking at them, she is aware of his manly legs.

"Thank you, but we're going on vacation. For the compliment, I mean," she whispers. Frank is still fifteen feet away. "Would you hold Charles for me just one more time?" she asks. Dr. Stern takes the baby slowly from her without letting go of her eyes. Then Katherine kneels to Katie's level and, for the second time today, holds her by her shoulders. She makes Katie's eyes meet hers. The blankness of them is almost more than she can bear, but she proceeds anyway, turning her over her lap and administering two firm blows. Katie screams as if she's being murdered.

"Don't you think that's a little unnecessary?" she hears from up above. It's Frank speaking.

"I didn't want to do it. I had to do it," she says.

When next she becomes aware, she finds that Charles is in her arms and Dr. Stern is nowhere to be seen. The parade is forming, a jeep with loudspeakers in the lead. Frank is lining up with Katie. Without hesitation, Katherine lines up with Charles. She looks around, in case she might spot her teacher again, but she knows that he has gone. He's on his way home to write a poem. The music begins and Frank stands a little straighter. She feels ashamed of his simple emotions and ashamed of herself for feeling ashamed. How can he have gotten angry at her for losing Katie? Why did he not understand? With Jude's neighbors she begins marching to "The Stars and Stripes Forever." She wonders if there's any way at all to cancel the trip to Sea Island.

CHAPTER

13

Every night before she goes to sleep, Louise pretends that she is still eighteen years old. As she did then, she quietly opens the draperies of her three bedroom windows to let in the moonlight. It is really reflected sunlight, she knows, but it's so hard for her to believe that the moon's light is not its own. As the celestial presence enters the room, the blue carpet that covers her floor goes invisible. The white canopy over her bed and the ruffled skirt that covers her bedside table float in the room almost the same way that she, in her long white nightgown, does. Against the flocked wallpaper, her pieces of furniture seem to become shapes within her command. She glides around the room, passing again and again through the darkened reflection that her freestanding mirror offers. She moves an imagined vase of roses to a more advantageous spot. She turns back the bedcovers. When everything seems to be perfect, she goes to the window to wait, bringing a strand of hair over her shoulder to fondle.

This is how she used to wait for Billy, when they were both in high school and he was still in love with her. He never appeared, of course. He never walked down her driveway in the dead of night and stood beneath her window and stared longingly up at her the way she was staring longingly down. He never knew to appear because she never told him she waited. Waiting for Billy was something she did to illustrate the power of her love. She's twenty-two now and she still stands here and still feels the same, although Billy doesn't and never will. She knows that she could blame her sisters for her loss, but she blames only herself.

"I'm sorry you had to find out this way," he'd said on her graduation day.

Daddy and Jude and Katherine and Frank had just shut the four doors of Daddy's station wagon, the rear of which was packed to the ceiling with Louise's belongings. The car began moving slowly. For one brief moment Louise let herself feel an immense sense of beginning, as if Hollins College were her and Billy's home. It was a *grand* home. A home that he had built all by himself.

Then she asked, "Find out what?"

Billy's whole body was curved in apology, but his mustache—to someone who wasn't used to it—made his face totally inscrutable. Louise wanted to wipe it off in order to see what his lips really meant. A gentle protectiveness filled his eyes, but that was how he'd always looked at her.

"Find out what?" she'd asked again. She pulled her eyes away from his to see if she could still see the station wagon. Just then it rounded a curve and disappeared. Her chest heaved with relief.

"Didn't Katherine tell you? Didn't Jude?" Billy asked weakly. His mustache quivered. It didn't make him look older; it made him look as if he were in hiding.

She kept looking at his upper lip, unable to bring her eyes back up to his. She felt her own lips moving, but it was the instinctive opening and closing of the mouth of a cow or an old woman. She covered the bottom half of her face with her hands.

She asked him not to say anything else until they could get away from the lingering groups of parents and graduates. That meant walking all the way to Siberia. She still had on her graduation gown, which she was supposed to hang in her dorm room for collection by the assistant dean of students. Instead, she dropped it on the grass where she stood. She dropped her mortarboard with its black tassel on top. Billy leaned over and retrieved everything.

"Leave it there," she said in a tone of voice she'd never used.

231|

He dropped the gown but held the mortarboard and tassel. Then, under her strange commanding gaze, he disengaged the tassel and dropped the cap. Finally he dropped the tassel, too. She turned her back on the heap and began walking.

On the way to Siberia he had to support her because her legs kept giving way. It was the same sensation she'd had when Mother finally died after those seven hours of convulsions. That time, Katherine had been the one who'd kept her from falling. The weakness was terrifying: Louise felt that part of her—the part forever connected to her mother—was dying, too. She never told anyone that grief had come second, a late late second. She never said that the main thing she'd thought the day her mother died was: "Don't let me die." She'd been talking to Billy's God. She'd felt the same terror on the way to the parking lot, but she hadn't asked Billy's God for anything.

They drove to McDonald's, where Billy bought her a double-thick vanilla milk shake, which she sucked at until her cheeks hurt. He drank black coffee, which in her memory—like his unexpected smoking—he'd never been able to stand. In between taking small burning sips—she knew this because he kept blowing into his cup—he told her that he was marrying Lucy Payne.

She thought that if she'd been Katherine or Jude, she would have known how to make him change his mind. But she'd looked at him and realized that he wasn't even anyone she recognized. She had the funny wild idea of asking him to take his overnight kit inside the McDonald's men's room and shave off the mustache so that he would look like himself and everything would be all right. But then she realized that it would have to be his idea. If she suggested he shave—even if he agreed—it wouldn't mean that he still loved her. Even if he did still love her, she suddenly thought, it was too late. Billy was a man who stuck with things. Whenever he could.

She said, "Lucy Payne is a lovely person." Lucy Payne was one year older than her and Billy. She was a small woman, smaller than Louise, and in her spare time she could be seen walking the nicer neighborhoods of Greensboro with her huge golden retriever named Pal, who made her look even smaller. But the most important thing that Louise knew about Lucy Payne was that she was a college graduate, too.

"I wish I'd known," Billy said. Since finishing his coffee, he'd hunched over the steering wheel of his Volkswagen. He kept turning his hands from front to back in the space between the steering wheel and the windshield. Louise imagined the wedding ring that would soon grace his left third finger. But no. A long time ago, in another life, it seemed, Billy had told her that he could never wear a wedding ring because of the machinery he had to work with. "But you sent the pin back," he said. "You never even called me. You didn't write. I didn't understand, but I decided to respect your wishes. I know how much you hate people telling you what to do."

"Known what?" she'd asked. She couldn't explain about the pin, so there was no need even to try.

"Known that . . ." He glanced quickly at her.

In his eyes Louise could see a desire not to know the truth. The truth, after all, was what had happened, wasn't it? The truth wasn't what she *wished* had happened. She'd left Billy. That was the truth. With the gentlest expression she asked, "You don't think I'm still in love with you, do you?"

"Aren't you?"

She reached toward him but let her wrist stop in midair. Her hand looked like a cup. Might he still drink from it? "I'll always love you," she said. "But I'm not *in* love with you." She might be an actress in the last scene before the lights are cut: Billy might yet touch her hand, but time was growing short.

After a pause she said, "I'm in love with someone I met in Paris. Someone named Jacques Terlinden." She turned in her seat so that her body faced Billy's. "I really don't expect it to work out. I don't particularly want to live overseas."

Until she'd named a name, she could tell that Billy was not believing what she was saying. But suddenly a look of wonderment came over his face.

Louise gave a sad little laugh. Looking far out his side of the windshield over the golden arches and into the hills, she said, "I never thought I could love anyone but you. But I guess there are lots of people we can love. Isn't it sad that there's not just one?" Although her eyes filled suddenly with tears, she let them betray nothing to him. She was simply crying over the state of the world. She could see relief on his face. But she could also see that if it were within his power to change things, he would. That was the moment she'd never forget.

After hearing some details of how they'd become acquainted—Lucy was walking her dog in Fisher Park and he'd thought she was a child until he drew close enough to see her face—she asked him to take her back to Hollins. She said that he shouldn't stay for Jennifer's rehearsal dinner that night and the wedding the next day, since it would probably hurt Lucy if he did. He asked, could he stay anyway, and she said, no, because old feelings between them might be stirred up. At that moment he let his own stirred-up feelings make him reach for her, but with her mind firmly centered on Jacques Terlinden, whom she imagined as being tall, urbane, and untender, she turned her head. He fell back in his seat, asking her how she would return to Greensboro without a car, and she named another someone who'd be happy to give her a ride. Actual names, including Lucy Payne's, she thought, could accomplish so much. What she would have to do would be call Daddy to come back up here and get her. Daddy might even think they'd planned it that way and he'd forgotten. But she wouldn't tell Billy she didn't have a ride. He'd use it to make her change her mind—her mind might still be changed—and then there would be a mess.

Less than two hours after her family had left, Billy began his own retreat down the same winding road. The weakness filled her again and she whispered to herself that she'd been wrong two years ago when Mother died. She wasn't afraid of dying: she wanted to be dead.

When she opened the door of her room, she found Jeff and Jennifer making out on a bed. She said a brisk "Hi, guys!" turned on the radio while Jenn buttoned her blouse, and, in the name of truth, told another lie. With bright watery eyes and a trembling voice she told them, "I'm going to be Mrs. Billy Jones and happy about it."

Jennifer had shrieked, jumped up from the bed, flung her arms around Louise. "Where is he?" she shouted. "You're too prissy to bring him in here, aren't you?"

Louise walked to her dresser and picked up Billy's picture. "He still loves me," she answered. She looked straight at Jeff then, trying to imagine how Jacques Terlinden and he differed. Perhaps in "reality," Jacques Terlinden now belonged to her. Why would Jennifer need him? "Billy had to go back to work," she continued. "He sends his apologies, but he had no choice. Sometimes they work twenty-four hours a day at that shop. You've heard of golf widows. I'm going to be a lathe widow."

She could stop adding details now, since she could see by Jennifer's wandering eyes that she'd been convincing. It was Jenn's wedding eve; she could be forgiven her distraction. But Louise kept on anyway. "We haven't made any definite plans, but by the time you're back from your honeymoon, I'm sure we'll know dates and things. You and Jeff will have to come to Greensboro for a visit soon. I'll want you to be my matron of honor."

Before she even finished the sentence, Jeff started kissing Jennifer again. Jenn struggled, but not very hard, in mock embarrassment. Why shouldn't they be happy, knowing that she was as happy as they? Louise was feeling doubly devastated, though. She'd not only lost Billy, but she was going to lose Jennifer. A friendship based on absolute honesty, such as theirs, could hardly recover from such a momentous lie. But she'd say anything rather than ruin what she still regarded as Jennifer's mistaken wedding.

Louise closes the draperies. She has been back from Hollins only three weeks, yet she is able to imagine that she never left home at all. Only now she can't just live here and go to high school and do the grocery shopping and the laundry and take a few swipes at the furniture with a dustcloth. Now, since she knows how, she must provide for herself. The idea of working does not horrify her so much as the idea of never being able to quit.

Through an employment agency she's had five interviews, but the only one that interests her is managing an ice-cream store. She's always said that she doesn't care what kind of job she has, as long as it doesn't interfere with her life. But now she has no life. Could running an ice-cream store be fun? For about a week, her father had said tonight over the dinner she'd fixed. She also wanted to ask him what people do with their time when none of the regular things exists. But she'd had to phrase it so she wouldn't hurt his feelings.

"What can I do with my life?" she'd asked.

He was sitting before an empty plate, his country-style steak finished before she'd barely started hers. According to her sisters, eating quickly was a habit he'd picked up from Mother and never been able to break. Although he hasn't said so, Louise believes he's elated to have her good cooking on the table again. She didn't have time to look at her father on graduation day, but she's noticed since coming home that, although *she* hasn't changed in her four years away, *he* has. His slight amount of hair has become thinner, and the elusive sadness of his face has been set by wrinkles. It's how she someday expects herself to look.

"It's a new life now," Daddy had answered. "It's like starting over." For a moment she thought he understood about Billy, and she was filled with a desire to throw herself across the table. But then he said, "Your education hasn't prepared you to do anything. You'll have to get a new education, on the job. That's the perennial problem of liberal-arts degrees."

She didn't know there was a perennial problem of liberal-arts degrees. She thought she was educating her spirit. That's why she had to go to college, and why Katherine said she had to stay. She supposes she'll find a job, enter into a routine, and time will begin to take care of itself. Time will dribble away, in other words, because she won't have Billy or an apartment or kids or just the ordinary stuff to do when she comes home in the evening. Just more and more time to fill.

She hasn't cried yet. During Jennifer and Jeff's wedding ceremony, so that she wouldn't hear any of the words, she stared hard at the huge, dizzying cross hanging over the altar. It worked, although she didn't expect it to: that she could use her eyes very hard to keep from hearing. She supposes she could use her ears very hard and keep from seeing. She won't ever cry again, she thinks, unless something like a song or a movie catches her unaware. But she doesn't turn on the radio anymore, and her father takes a woman banker, instead of her, thank goodness, to the movies. She refuses even to read the trash novels she loves, which Katherine so disdains. Katherine would be gratified until she knew the real reason, which is that they make Louise feel so much. One night last week, when she could have watched an Australian romantic saga on television, she instead settled down with the World War II textbook she'd studied at Hollins by way of the previous owner's underlining. What she affirmed to herself was that history was no more interesting to her now than then.

The history she'd really like to understand, she thinks, is her own. All she knows is that for many years she felt unable to act. Maybe it was because she had two sisters instead of one. She might have been able to handle a single strong opponent, the way Katherine, for example, was able to handle Mother, but she could never be so much younger and so much more innocent and deal with two. *Youngest sisters of the world, unite,* she thinks, and laughs. She immediately sobers. But something inside her keeps smiling. Perhaps she's finally stumbled upon the answer.

It's a new life, Daddy said. Which is the thing that makes her wonder what, if anything, the old life meant. Not that it was Hollins's fault, but during her years there, she lost her mother, her boyfriend, and even, she supposes, the person she used to be. In fact, she would *love* to manage an ice-cream store, but now that job is beneath her. Running an ice-cream store would show the world that she has no regard for the money her father spent on her education. And that she doesn't value herself. It would make Katherine and Jude say that they'd provided her with every opportunity to no avail. Running an ice-cream store would also probably make her very fat.

"And you'll get sick of the stuff," her father had pointed out at supper. "The smell will even come to gag you. I'm thinking you should consider a job more in line with your interests," he'd concluded.

What interests are those, she'd wanted to ask. Does he think she's interested in history?

She wonders if Daddy will allow her to live here permanently. Or if Katherine and Jude are going to make him run her out. So that she can learn to stand on her own two feet. And become a self-sufficient woman. Maybe together she and Daddy can stand up to them. Maybe she's always looked in the wrong place for an ally. She found Jennifer quite by accident, although Jenn is an only child and not a youngest sister. Actually, Daddy has always *been* on her side, but maybe he'll start being on it with more guts.

After he'd made the comment about her interests, she'd asked, "What did you think about Billy?" She was just curious.

"What do you mean?" Daddy had taken a long swallow of iced coffee.

"Whether I should have married him or not."

"Did he ask?"

Her father is so afraid of starting something. That was another habit he'd inherited from his years with Mother, she could tell her sisters. He hadn't meant to hurt her feelings by his question, only deflect a serious conversation.

In a simple voice Louise said, "No, he didn't." And then she put on a blank face and ate the rest of her steak and mashed potatoes and lima beans and thought how there was no one in this entire world who was even *interested* in being her ally. The only two possibilities had been her father and Jennifer. But because of her mother, her father was afraid to talk, afraid of what might be said. And, now, a future relationship with Jenn is in doubt. Still, she knows what advice Jennifer would give. Jennifer would say to move away from her sisters, to Richmond, where their budding relationship could blossom. She'd promise to introduce her to lots of bright young men. But even if Jenn could, Louise will not leave home. She would leave it to go to Paris, but not to Richmond. She'd leave it for the promise of a new life, but not just the hope.

Could Mother have been her ally? Could either of her sisters, if she approached them separately? Could any of them have understood about her and Billy? Even now, she'd like them to know that Billy was the love of her life, not just a high-school sweetheart. She'd like to tell them that he was the sustaining kind of man, like Daddy, whom she'd wanted to spend her life with. But even if she told them how she'd stood at her window all these years and waited for him, she thinks they'd still say that Billy was not her true love. If he had been, she would never have let him go. How could she convince any strong person that she herself hadn't been strong enough? Billy Jones was her one true love, but she was the only person who would ever know it. She could never even convince him.

She finally feels sleepy. She doesn't sleep in the middle of her double bed, as most single people do, but to one side. She plumps her pillow and the pillow beside hers. Then with a hard fist she strikes the second pillow several times until she makes an indentation that tomorrow will resemble where someone else lay his head. She no longer tries to imagine Billy's face next to hers or his thin legs against her legs or his soft tongue in her mouth. It would be a sin against Billy's God to lust after another woman's husband-to-be, she supposes. For a while she had imagined Jacques Terlinden lying beside her, but then the untenderness that she'd supposed in him from the beginning had grown too intense. She'd become afraid of Jacques Terlinden. Now the face she imagines is blank.

Tomorrow she will turn down the ice-cream-shop job. Her family is not always right, but this time she suspects they are. One thing her father mentioned was that if she took the job, no one would ever hire her for a job that had to do with history. What kinds of jobs have to do with history, though? What jobs are acceptable?

In the morning she'll call Katherine and ask these questions. If she had Jude's brazenness, she'd call her right now at some time after one o'clock. But she's too nice. Katherine will probably say that she can be a travel agent or some kind of research assistant. A legal aide? Or, terrifyingly, Katherine might suggest that Louise return to school to make herself more employable. In her cool dark bed Louise's whole body suddenly turns hot. She won't ask Katherine a thing. How terrible it would be to be convinced to get more education.

The next hour she thinks about how cheerful people are who are buying ice cream, which makes her change her mind and decide to take the job. She sees herself welcoming customers at the door, offering them tiny tastes of ice cream with tiny spoons. Then she decides, no, she won't take the job, because she doesn't really want to waste herself, if working at an ice-cream store would be wasting herself. Nor does she want to get fat so young.

Finally she yields to sleep undecided and empty of confidence and hope.

CHAPTER

14

Jude has always known when she was about to make a serious mistake. In the last six years there have been two: the first, the day she married Cap; and the second, the night she conceived Charles. Both realizations came during an almost unstoppable process, yet *almost* unstoppable—everyone knows—*is* stoppable, and if she had understood more about life either time she would have managed to stop each one. But, of course, she was too young to know how to say no. She was a girl. Except for premarital sex, girls are programmed to be sweet and nod their heads. It takes forever to learn to do the opposite.

When she had the realization about her marriage, she was waiting at the head of the chapel aisle listening to the solo violinist conclude "Liebestraum." When she had the realization about Charles, she was making love to Cap without protection on their first reconciliation date. Both times she asked someone to rescue her. In the narthex she was standing arm in arm with her father, watching Cap and the rector stare at her from in front of the altar. Suddenly one very high note from "Dream of Love" pierced her brain, a flash of clear vision. She turned to her father and in the gravest of voices said, "Daddy, you've got to stop this." For the first time ever, she'd admitted to her conscious brain that something was missing between her and Cap. He thought he loved her. She was the only one who knew he didn't.

"You're just nervous, honey," her father had said. He patted her hand but not before she saw a tiny flicker of recognition in his eyes. He thought that *she* didn't love the young man at the altar.

"It's more than that," she'd answered.

She'd been only twenty-two years old. Although she knew this was not stage fright—although she knew *Daddy* knew it wasn't stage fright—she didn't know what to do. Should her father have known? Would any father, at such a moment, lead his daughter away? Hers had started walking her down the aisle where twenty minutes later she became the wife of a man whom she loved but who didn't love her. From then on, all she had to do was wait for him to find out.

On the night she conceived Charles, she had spoken aloud, too. "You have to stop, honey. I'm not taking pills anymore. I don't see any reason to take pills when we're separated." She spoke in a fearful voice that should have destroyed Cap's concentration if nothing else. She didn't know why she was letting him go so far, having decided in advance that a reconciliation visit was not going to include sex. She'd halfheartedly tried to throw him off, but he pinned her down by holding fast to the spindles of the headboard. She reached climax twice in quick succession—once more than ever before in her life—and knew immediately that she was pregnant or would be within seconds. Cap called it a "cosmic fuck," adding to her sureness. She invited him to stay with her all night long, feeling that she'd been blind to think that he hadn't at least *come* to love her. Making love to her like that, how could he feel any other way? But he'd gone back to the apartment he was sharing with another recently separated man, telephoning to ask if there was anything to worry about. In an angry voice she'd told him yes. Six weeks later he was once again in residence awaiting the arrival of their son, Charles.

If she'd known six years ago what she knows now, first she would have disengaged her arm from her father's, thanked everyone for coming to her wedding, and announced that she regretted the enormous inconvenience but that she wasn't going to get married after all. Second, which wouldn't have been necessary if she'd handled the first mistake properly, she would have fought off Cap if it meant maiming him. Both times, in other words, she would have intervened in her own life—for the sake of what she knew was the truth. Which is exactly what she's doing by moving to Chapel Hill.

Most people, as she did, *sense* what they ought to do. But few are willing to hurt themselves badly now in order to avoid hurting themselves worse later. She'd married Cap and now they're divorced. She'd conceived a child without a father to be at home to love him. Though she'd never call Charles himself a mistake—since she loves him as much as she's ever loved anything—still she knows that, in some ultimate way, having him the way she did was wrong.

At age twenty-eight, is it possible for her to make any more mistakes? She thinks not. Serious mistakes happen only before you grow up, before some combination of circumstances comes along to change everything. Those are the years you don't know who you are. The years that you can't find out who you are until you make all these enormous decisions. The years that you have to make all these enormous decisions that turn out to be the mistakes that tell you who you are. No wonder everything gets so fucked up. But she's made her mistakes now. And she's learned. And she knows that moving to Chapel Hill is going to make her happy.

While she's been thinking about the mistakes of her life and realizing that they were not only unavoidable but also necessary, she's been lugging down her driveway a huge packing box full of things she's finally decided to throw away. For the first time in a week it rained last night, a noisy, thrashing rain that made her work harder and harder. She'd pared her belongings down to the bare essentials. In one box she'd thrown things to keep. In the others she junked everything else. The morning brought crisp delicious air and a sky as lustrous as sapphires. Now a perfumed breeze is fanning her, making her feel at peace.

Katherine is following her down the driveway, carrying to the curb a broken portable television set and an old toaster oven with a burned-out element, both of which have been stashed in the attic since Cap met Carolyn and stopped fixing things around the house. "These won't be here long," Katherine announces. "Scavengers will get them. *I* might take the oven." Her face curious, Katherine begins poking through the box that Jude is attempting to fold closed. "You're not going to throw all this stuff away?" she asks in an incredulous voice. Then, remembering that—although they are "sisters" again—she is not participating in Jude's life anymore, she changes tone: "Throw away whatever you want to throw away." She digs in the box a little deeper. "That's your wedding portrait, Jude," she says in a plaintive voice.

They have been speaking to each other for three weeks, since the day Jude came back from Chapel Hill after the Fourth of July parade. Katherine and Frank had spent that Saturday afternoon feeding the children lunch, trying to get them down for naps, and avoiding each other. Secretly, Katherine had been trying to block out that inexplicable moment with Dr. Stern, the moment in which she imagined she'd fallen in love with him but was really only overwhelmed by the heat and her worry about Jude's children. In that moment Dr. Stern had appeared larger than life, but that was how things looked, she knew, when one was about to faint. All afternoon she'd refused to speak to Frank about anything except what related directly to the children. It was easy, since he was not speaking to her either. By late afternoon, though, while the children were in the breakfast nook having snacks, he began to talk. He hated himself when he got mad at her, he said. It was such a waste of their valuable time together. He was sorry he'd criticized her. Katie *should* have been spanked. He wanted to know what else she was angry about so that he could say he was sorry about that, too. He was sorry about everything. They were standing in the kitchen, apart from the children for the first time that afternoon, yet within their range. She said that she didn't want to talk about his rudeness to *her* until she got over his rudeness to Dr. Stern—her *Yeats* teacher, the man who had opened her eyes to poetry, a kind, helpful person whom Frank had not bothered to thank for finding the children, or rather, Katie.

"I wasn't rude *to* your teacher," Frank said. "I was rude *about* him *in front of* you. He didn't even hear me, so what do you care? The class is over. You got your A. At least I didn't spank my niece for something that was my own fault," he'd added.

So he didn't think she should have spanked Katie, after all. Liar, she'd thought.

"You were being rude to my work," she suddenly said, having just then hit upon the real reason he'd been so unpleasant to Dr. Stern.

"What are you talking about?"

"Frank Borden is *never* rude to people. But you were rude to Dr. Stern. You were rude to him because he's one of my teachers."

"I didn't even know who he was," Frank had exclaimed.

"I don't believe you."

"I was worried, Katherine. That's all. Sometimes I think you're nuts."

With cold glittering eyes Katherine had finally looked at Frank—the first time she'd managed to look into his eyes since she'd been trapped by Dr. Stern's. She said she needed to take Dr. Stern's T. S. Eliot course, which, if Frank remembered, started next week. Frank returned her stare. A quick coldness came to her stomach. Frank's impish expression, which no strain, no anger, no sadness could ever quite erase, was gone.

"Need?" he'd asked, but with a much bigger question in his eyes.

Just then Jude's car pulled into the driveway and Frank's voice turned thoughtful. He mentioned that he had to get some rest, couldn't she tell? He said he was tired to the bone. That was why his temper was so short. But if she really wanted to stay home from their vacation . . .

Her shame finally became total. Hushing him, she said she could wait. September was soon enough to take another course. She'd just promised Dr. Stern she'd be in the Eliot class. "So, call him," Frank had said, the coldness again in his eyes.

Just then Charles began crying. With relief she turned to him, but Jude was already inside, hurrying to her baby. Katherine spoke to her sister, eagerly, warmly. It was the first time they'd seen each other since their argument. All she'd done the day they drove back from Chapel Hill was drop Jude off at her house; neither had said goodbye. She asked Jude if she'd made much progress on the apartment. Jude, limp-looking from the heat, answered yes as she grabbed up both children in her arms. Then Katherine faced Frank. She made her face completely blank as if she'd already forgotten her request to stay home. Could he have seen something as unfamiliar on her face as she'd seen on his? Jude and she began chatting and continued talking for an hour about Chapel Hill. Her sister seemed like a pleasant stranger. On Monday she and Frank left for Sea Island. For two weeks she became a sportswoman and a lover, making him forget she'd ever suggested staying home. When they returned, Frank refreshed, she full of subdued excitement and resolve to become a friend of Dr. Stern's, Jude had already begun packing.

"What do I need a wedding portrait for?" Jude asks.

"And all your albums!"

Jude has always saved everything. But she doesn't want to keep reminders of her past in hopes that one day she'll be glad. It would go against what she's feeling now. After she moves, she'll just start saving again. She'll start new albums, for example, of their new fresh lives in Chapel Hill.

"Let me keep some of these things for you," Katherine says in spite of herself. "You can pretend that you threw them away, and then one day when you realize you want them back, I'll have them. I'll hide them. And I'll never mention them again unless you mention them first." She hadn't thought she would elect to do anything for Jude ever again.

Jude looks into the deep box. Lying loose somewhere in there is her wedding ring, although she did keep her aquamarine engagement stone for Katie. There's also the iron that Cap gave her their first Christmas together. She'd wanted him to give her something romantic, of course, but he'd thought he should buy an item they needed. Also in the box is the *best* gift Cap ever gave her, a cheap photocopy of a Mary Cassatt oil entitled "Mother's Kiss," which he brought to the hospital after Katie was born. She doesn't want any of it.

As she tries to decipher her marriage, Jude thinks that when she became a mother was the only time Cap ever really loved her. He'd been awed by her abilities, never understanding how she could assume such an alien role so effortlessly. It began at Katie's delivery when in the hospital he'd watched her with glowing eyes and talked to her about how brave she was. She hadn't even minded when in the recovery room he'd whispered, "Next time out, we'll get a boy." It had continued for months, Cap constantly asking her, "Where did you learn that?" She used books and what other mothers knew, and when she took Katie to the pediatrician she asked a million questions. But she never let Cap think her knowledge was anything but innate.

They'd had a "next time out": their mistaken cosmic fuck. She'd produced Charles. But during that time Cap changed again. Maybe he'd seen that lots of women become mothers, very fine mothers, and realized that it wasn't so special after all.

"Why don't you keep just a *few* things?" Katherine asks in a coddling tone. She picks up one of the elaborate albums in which Jude cut up pictures to create a collage on every page. "Really, Jude, I'd like to have these for myself if you don't want them. There are pictures of all of us, including some of the last pictures we ever took of Mother. You can't take them again, you know." In the naked sunlight Katherine turns to a page showing Katie's second birthday party. "You can't get this back either," she drones on. "Katie will never be two again." She keeps turning pages.

Jude sees a picture of Cap shoveling sand from a pickup truck into a sandbox, a picture of him wearing a ten-gallon hat she gave him for a birthday, a picture of them both making ugly faces.

"It hurts now, but it won't always hurt," Katherine says. "One of these days you'll think of him as a son of a bitch."

"One of these days?" Jude laughs. "Why do you think I don't want pictures of him in my new apartment?" She takes the album out of Katherine's hands and drops it back in the box. The picture of Katie at her second birthday party, though, has taken hold of her. How will Katie feel when she's grown up if there are hardly any pictures of her first three and a half years?

She knows how *she's* always felt about the fact that Mother and Daddy took so many pictures of Katherine, the firstborn, so fewer of her, and practically none of Louise. She knows how she's always promised never to let it happen to her own kids. She hasn't taken a picture of either child since Christmas, which is bad enough. Should she be giving up what she has so far managed to preserve?

She decides that Katherine is right. She'll throw away the iron, the wedding ring, the sports albums she made for Cap in high school (fuck him), the statue of the monkey sitting atop a stack of books contemplating a human skull that he gave her when he used to call her that unforgivable nickname, "Monkey." But she'll keep the family albums. And maybe she'll keep the wedding picture. Won't Katie want to see it?

She's begun selecting what she wants to save when Louise, who's been inside wrapping crystal, pokes her head out the front storm door. "Look who's taking it easy," she calls. She's wearing a sundress and had fixed her hair before she came because she's been invited to a baby shower at two o'clock, three hours from now. She walks down the steps, carrying nothing.

"What a help," Katherine murmurs.

"She tires so easily," Jude says.

Both of them know they are not to ride Louise today, Daddy's orders. They are not to ridicule the new job she's considering. Or to suggest that she ought to be moving herself. Above all, they are not to question her about Billy, whose wedding date has been postponed, ostensibly because Lucy Payne's grandmother is dying of a brain tumor. In their whole lives Daddy has never given them any kind of order, especially one which takes sides as this one does. So they know, although he denied it this morning in his calls to them, who the requests come from.

Immediately after she had hung up with Daddy, Katherine had called Jude. The line was busy, but she kept trying. "I guess she's still trying to prove that we shouldn't have made her go to college," she'd said when she got through.

"Maybe Billy has decided to marry her, after all," answered Jude.

"What?" they both demanded. Although each had received a phone call, they'd been given different information. Daddy had told Katherine but not Jude that Louise was probably going to take the job managing the ice-cream parlor. He'd told Jude but not Katherine that Billy might be back in the picture. Billy hasn't actually called Louise. But Daddy said he thought it was odd that a girl would postpone a wedding because of a death sometime in the future.

"Why can't Louise just talk to us?" Katherine asked Jude. "We're her sisters."

"Maybe we don't say what she wants us to."

"Maybe we don't," Katherine said, her voice suddenly heavy with irony. She'd waited silently.

Over the telephone Jude cleared her throat in an aware way. "I know you didn't abandon Mother. I just wanted to shut you up about my moving to Chapel Hill. I succeeded," she adds, but not proudly.

When Jude told Katherine that she thought Mother began dying when Katherine left home, she was saying aloud something that she didn't believe. Mother had always told Jude that Katherine "killed" her, but Mother didn't die for another decade. Mother had lived spiritedly with Max, Jude knew. Still, there had always been something broken in Mother after Katherine—and then she and Louise—had gone away. Her anger was less fiery and more deadly. Her provocations became meaner instead of more purely searching. Neither Katherine nor Jude had ever minded being challenged by her. They'd both been willing to search out—with her as leader—all possible meanings of all moments. The only thing they minded was being unfairly attacked. At which Mother became increasingly adept.

When Katherine heard Jude's accusation, she had lashed out at her, but also taken it into her heart to ponder. She knew that on one level Jude had simply been trying to redirect her attention from the move to Chapel Hill. Jude dealt the same way with her children. But she also knew that Jude was trying to tell her something. Not simply that she interferes. She knows she interferes. It's her responsibility to interfere: to tell the people

249 |

she cares about what she thinks. She expects the same from them. But *could* she have saved Mother? Saved her from what? *Did* it destroy Mother or start her on the road to destruction when she left? Was Katherine stronger even then? The accusations Jude posed are the same accusations Katherine has directed at herself all her life. Clearly, they are accusations out of Mother's mouth, just as Daddy's requests today have come from Louise. But Daddy *wants* them to leave Louise alone. And what Katherine did to Mother is Jude's question, too.

Continuing the conversation, Katherine had said, "I still think moving to Chapel Hill is a mistake. I still think you're abandoning me."

"Please. Give up," Jude had said. "It's too late. You don't need me nearly as much as you think you do."

"If you say I don't need you," Katherine continued, "then you say people don't need sustaining relationships. You say they can function just fine with whoever's at hand. No one is vital to anyone else. Any warm body will do."

"I don't mean that exactly," Jude answered. "But you *think* I'm more important to you than I am. You've got Frank, I keep telling you. I've got Katie and Charles. I need you in a forever sense, but not day-to-day. I only need my children day-to-day." Whether this is entirely true or not, Jude doesn't know, but sometimes there's no other way to deal with Katherine but to hurt her.

Who does *she* need day-to-day, Katherine had wondered. Who does she need forever? Her view has always been that whomever she needs forever she also needs day-to-day. And vice versa. "Frank's picking up the U-Haul at nine-thirty," she'd said briskly. "I'm going to drive a car over, so I'll be at your house a little earlier. I want to know more about Billy and his girl-friend," she added.

"Are you going to ask Louise about him, anyway? In spite of Daddy?"

"What Daddy said isn't what he thinks," Katherine said. "That was what Louise told him to think. I don't see any reason that we have to avoid all the subjects that are of any interest. If it was up to Louise, we'd all be talking about recipes and . . . ha! . . . flavors of ice cream." Both of them laughed. "I can't believe she might take that job."

She paused, but Jude seemed to have nothing else to say. "I'll see you in about thirty minutes," Katherine said. "To help you pack for a place I don't want you to go to. Because I don't need you anymore," she added laughingly. "I only want you." She made herself sound like a good sport, although in fact she was still deeply hurt, hurt perhaps the way her mother had once been by her. Perhaps this was the moment at which *she* would begin to die. If it turned out to be, she'd be sure to let Jude know.

By the time Louise meanders across the yard to them, Jude has started stacking her albums in Katherine's arms. "We heard about your job," she says bluntly. Being the first to ignore Daddy's request is a way to show Katherine her loyalty. But she's also irritated with Louise, whom before today she's been defending by not participating in any attacks. An entire week ago she'd asked Weezie to help out today. She'd asked Daddy to help, too. Where is *he*? "Congratulations," she adds, dipping her upper body into the box.

"We also heard that Billy postponed his wedding," Katherine chimes in.

Daddy had advised her not to tell her sisters about Billy's change of plans, and then when they were sitting at the breakfast table this morning, he'd told Jude over the telephone himself. It was a terrible mistake, he'd said in a pitiful voice after he'd hung up. But Louise forgave him. "Billy didn't postpone it; Lucy did," she says in a stone-cold voice. "It's for a very good reason: an upcoming death." Her ability to speak so unemotionally pleases her. "I haven't taken that job," she adds. She feels an indescribable hatred for her sisters. She hasn't realized before how much she hates them as a pair. The only time it's bearable to be around either of them is when they're not around each other. She should have known not to come over here. In fact, she knew. That's why she didn't come dressed to help. That's why she asked Daddy to wait at home, so that she can use him as an excuse to leave. If her sisters make her mad, she'll say she has to go to pick him up. Then she won't come back. Also, in case Billy calls, someone will be at home to answer the phone. Lucy's grandmother really does have a brain tumor. But since Louise heard of the postponement, she's wondered if something else could be wrong.

To Jude's ears, Weezie sounds as if she's about to cry. Yesterday she would have felt sorry for her, but today she doesn't.

Katherine only hears Louise's ever present refusal to deal with her and Jude, but she's not yet ready to give up on her sister. She *can't* give up on Louise, she suddenly realizes. Louise is about to become her only sister in town. "Dear Weezie . . ." she says.

Louise turns angrily, expecting some fakey remark, but Katherine is giving her a hopeful look.

"We don't want it to be like this," Katherine says. "I think we're all having a problem with reentry. You've been away so long . . . Jude and I have spent lots of time together . . . You feel excluded . . . We think that you don't want to be a part of us." She makes the last statement to prevent Louise from claiming that the opposite is true.

As always, Louise finds herself being seduced by Katherine's words, but now she's aware of the seduction. Maybe that's what she learned at Hollins: when she's being had. Still, this is an important moment: the first time she's been around her sisters as an employed college graduate. She didn't let Daddy tell them that she's actually taken the ice-cream job.

Breaking away from Katherine's *we's* and *us's*, Jude says, "I myself want to participate in your life, and you to participate in mine. You should have come dressed to help. I mean, how many times am I going to move?"

Louise's face clouds over again.

"Twice, I hope," Katherine mutters. "What Jude's trying to say is that we want to feel free to tell you what we think. We're not being mean to you when we tell you our opinions. We're caring about you. I'll give you an example—my friend Sharon Fifield." She'd thought of using Jennifer but changed her mind.

"You'd *love* Sharon, Louise, because she's *so* nice. When she's around, I feel great, but when she leaves I feel hollow, because I know that everything she says is some sort of lie. You want us to lie to you, but we can't. We're your sisters."

She doesn't want them to lie to her. She just wants them to be kind. But Louise tries to hear them out. Her sisters want to be able to tell her what they think without her getting angry. It sounds reasonable. It would be reasonable, she supposes, if she were ever able to choose what *she* thinks over what they think. Which makes it sound as if the problem is with her. The problem *is* with her, but what should she do? Listen to them and lose herself, or lose them? She wishes she could come back here in five years—with everything in her life decided—and then they'd have nothing to fight about.

She takes a deep breath and looks at each of them separately so that they will know she is trusting them. "All right," she says in an introductory sort of voice. The introduction to her new life. Katherine props the pile of Jude's things-to-save on the corner angle of the packing box, looking at Louise with the most open and accepting of faces. Jude offers what Weezie would describe as a wistful look. Is she sad that she's leaving home? That Katherine and Louise are to be the sisters who are together all the time?

"All right," she says again, her chest heaving once quickly in nervousness. She finds herself about to say "all right" a third time. It's so hard to actually begin speaking.

"All right?" Katherine says for her, but it's a gentle prodding. Jude is looking at her with total concentration.

She puts on a big smile. "It may make me fat," she says, "but I've taken the job managing the ice-cream store. I start Monday." Her voice is cheerful, but she feels as if she has pulled these simple words from her soul.

"You've already taken it?" Katherine asks.

"Daddy said you were just considering," says Jude.

"That's what I told him to say. I wanted to tell you both myself. Together." In a sense this is true. Mostly, though, her intention was to let Daddy warm them up to the idea. If they knew a little something in advance, she wouldn't have to face their stunned silence. All she has to face, she realizes, is their . . . stunned silence. Are they disappointed in her? They say nothing immediately, although they should, but there is no criticism on their faces either. How much time has passed? Five seconds or thirty? She can't tell. She only knows that it's been too long.

"Come back, Weezie," Katherine calls. Louise is halfway to the house. "That's wonderful news. Give us a chance to get used to it. We didn't know you'd made a decision. Now we have our very own Baskin-Robbins queen."

"Haägen-Dazs," Louise says, turning around to look fiercely at them. Suddenly her chest feels as if it is being crushed. She has done the best she can. It's never enough for them.

Her sisters stand together by the box of trash. As she's always thought, they are like one person. But it's not *because* they are sisters, because she is their sister, too. They could be any two people. What they have between them is some kind of deadly spark. They entertain each other. They excite each other. They prod each other. They infuriate each other. She's never infuriated either one of them, she realizes. She's only irritated them. And what a difference that is. She would not be Katherine's soulmate if Jude lived a million miles away. If Jude were dead.

"I think it's going to be a fun job," she hears herself saying. Questions tremble in her throat: Do you think I've made a mistake? What *should* I do? What would you do if you were me? But she doesn't ask any of them.

Instead, she looks at her watch and asks, "What time is it? I was supposed to pick up Daddy at eleven. His car broke down. He wants to help pack, but he had some work to do this morning. I'll be back in ten minutes." She walks to the house, entering and exiting as if she's actually late. She lets her car keys jingle impatiently. Jude and Katherine are loading into Katherine's car the things Jude has decided to save. "Back in a jiff," she says cheerfully, not looking at them.

"We should be nicer," Jude says, loud enough for Louise to hear, but their sister gets in the car without turning around.

"Maybe so." Katherine steps out into the street. Without a smile, Louise stares through the windshield at her. The motor is rumbling. Katherine wonders if Louise will zoom away when she walks around to the window. But she waits.

"You can't leave without a story," Katherine says.

"I don't want to hear a story."

"We've kept lots of them from you because you were too young. But eventually you'll know everything we know. If you listen."

Jude approaches the car from the other side. "We'll tell stories all afternoon if you'll stay," she says.

They are like cranes above her car, wanting to grab her with their big metal mouths. "I told you I have a baby shower to go to."

"We'll tell stories until one-thirty, then."

"I don't want to hear any stories today."

"What about a *good* story? A *good* story about Mother and Daddy."

Louise knows her sisters. If she refuses to let them tell her this story, they'll never tell it to her again. They'll remind her for the rest of her life about the time she didn't want to hear the best story of all. She looks at Katherine and then she looks at Jude. "I didn't think there *were* any good stories. I thought they were all bad." She still hasn't agreed to hear one.

"Do you remember in the hospital when Mother told us to tell Daddy goodbye?" Katherine asks. "Did anybody do it?"

"Of course not," Louise says in an offended tone.

"I didn't," Jude says.

"I think he ought to know," Katherine says. "I think Louise ought to tell him."

"I would never tell him that," Louise says. "She meant for us to tell *Max* goodbye. She just forgot who she was married to."

"She knew exactly who she was married to," Jude says from the far window. "She never stopped loving Daddy."

"Neither one of you is right," Katherine says. "She was just making trouble. It was her nature. She wanted to leave *us* with a great big question. Which man did she love? Maybe both." A gleam enters Katherine's eyes. "Maybe neither."

"People who are dying don't do things like that," Louise says.

"*She* did." Katherine straightens up from her talking position.

Jude has always thought that Mother never stopped loving Daddy and simply got carried away by something she was suddenly too deep into to reverse. It's never occurred to her that Mother might not have loved either man. How ingenious of Katherine. How *possible*. Does Katherine believe what she's saying?

Katherine leans in the window again. Jude does the same. "We're really happy for you," Katherine says to Louise. "It was mean of us to give you a hard time about the ice-cream store. Someday you may have your own chain."

"We really are sorry," Jude echoes.

Since they are on opposite sides of her and she can't look at them at the same time anyway, Louise looks straight ahead. It's safest. "No, you're not," she says.

"We *are*, Weezie."

Seeing Louise's bottom lip edge out, they shoot startled glances at each other, but then Louise bites the lip back under control. She blinks several times. Still giving them only her profile, she says softly, "Daddy asked you to leave me alone."

"Are you going home to tell him that we didn't?" Jude asks.

Louise shakes her head in a slow sad way. "What about the story?" she asks. "Do you have one or not?"

"I really don't know a good one," Katherine says. "I know lots of bad ones. But you're holding out for something good, aren't you?" Changing tones, she speaks directly to Jude: "Story of her life."

"Get out of the way," Louise suddenly cries, giving them just a moment before she presses hard on the gas pedal. Katherine and Jude each jump back. The car leaps down the street. They look at each other to see if either is angry at Louise for endangering them, but neither is. They listen to Weezie's tires squawling around the corners.

"She put Daddy in the middle," Katherine says. "She shouldn't do that."

"We'd be mean to her, anyway."

"We're not mean. We're just trying to teach her some things."

"If only she understood Mother a little better," Jude says. "Or just understood *complexity*."

"What do you mean?"

"She can't understand how someone can hold opposing views. Like how Mother probably loved and hated Daddy at the same time." Jude wonders if Katherine will agree.

Katherine ponders. "Loved and hated us, too," she says. "And, if we knew *everything*, probably loved and hated Max. Frank can't understand it, either. Maybe nobody does but you and me." She's sorry she mentioned Frank. She doesn't want Jude to think there are any areas of misunderstanding between them. "Frank is just good," she explains. "He doesn't believe that someone can be wonderful and terrible at the same time."

"Mother?" Jude asks.

"Of *course*, Mother," Katherine says intensely, although the question is rhetorical. No matter how tempted she is, she can't tell Jude that she's found a *man* who is both wonderful and terrible. Rather, the man has found her. Wonderful because he's already become everything she's ever dreamed of being. Terrible because he knows she's married and is pursuing her anyway. But even more terrible because he's pretending not to. She was not really about to faint that day, she'd realized during her vacation to Sea Island when nothing at all held her attention. She was falling in love. Dr. Stern was making her fall in love: exercising his enormous magnetism, yet pretending, in case she didn't respond, that he had no real interest in her. Though she can't tell Jude, she needs to tell somebody. What's between her and her teacher will not go any further, she's decided. And it surely won't if she can find someone to trust. The person she tells will be the person who will say to her what a fool she is. If Jude weren't moving to Chapel Hill, it might have been her.

"I don't think we should expect Louise to understand Mother," Jude says. "She never went through what we went through. And no matter how many stories we tell her, it can't be the same as if she were there herself. I don't know if she really wants to know all this stuff, anyway. I think she just doesn't want to be left out. She thinks the more she knows, the more we'll all be the same. I used to think that, too. But it's more than gaps in knowledge. It's gaps in experience. She ought to consider herself lucky. *I'm* lucky that I didn't experience all that *you* did." Jude starts walking toward Katherine's car. In a new tone she asks, "Are you really going to tell Daddy what Mother said?"

"I think he has a right to know. I don't think I should deny her last wish."

"Why haven't you done it sooner?"

"I've only just started thinking about it."

"Because . . . ?"

"I never thought she still loved Daddy. Until recently. I've been thinking, that's all. Maybe she loved them both."

"I'm not sure he'd want to know," Jude says.

"So you think I shouldn't tell him?"

Jude shrugs.

Their conversation subsides rather than concluding, and the time ticks and ticks and ticks away as they wait for Louise to return with Daddy, who lives only five minutes from here.

They finish packing Jude's memories in Katherine's car with only one argument—about the iron. Katherine thinks it's ridiculous for Jude to throw away a perfectly good iron. She points out that Jude doesn't have a job yet.

Jude says she doesn't plan to iron again, anyway. Why should she do *anything* she doesn't want to do, except for things that relate to her kids? No ironing again ever, she promises herself. Her excitement about her move is flaring again. Off and on, she feels herself about to burst.

This newest episode with Louise has brought Jude and her closer again, Katherine realizes. Is now the time to ask Jude what she really thinks about her and Mother? Is what she thinks of any value to Katherine? Could it ever alter what Katherine herself feels? Katherine has always preferred that everything be discussed and rediscussed and discussed again. It's the only way she begins to understand what has happened. But has she been listening only to herself?

Katherine, Jude, and Frank have been loading the trailer for forty-five minutes when Weezie's car reappears. Cap, who has charge of the kids for the day, has stopped by with them to watch. Katie is in the process of retrieving all her broken toys from the trash pile. Each time she makes a discovery, she lets out a brand-new wail. Charles clamors for his mommie, and Jude gives Cap a withering look. When, she wonders, is he going to figure out that he ought to leave? She has been all the way around the truck with Charles, letting him blow the horn, showing him his packed crib, talking him once more through the move, the way the book said she was supposed to do.

Daddy gets out of Louise's car alone. For an instant he stands beside the car, not approaching them, which makes Jude think Weezie tattled. His stomach pokes forward slightly like an old man's, although he is just sixty.

"I knew she'd go home crying," Jude murmurs to Katherine, who with Frank is loading the box springs of her bed.

"It wasn't a real bet," Katherine calls back. Weezie failed to return, but who knows whether or not she told? Daddy probably won't say one way or the other. One thing they know she *didn't* tell is Mother's dying words.

Daddy approaches Cap, whom he hasn't seen in over a year, and asks him what he's been up to "other than eating." Cap and Daddy always got along, appreciative of each other's sense of humor, but Jude is still surprised her father can be so friendly.

"I finally quit smoking," Cap is explaining. "I've got this girlfriend who's really against it." Daddy doesn't even seem to mind the mention of a girlfriend. The part about the smoking, though, rankles Jude, who spent five years of her own life trying to get him to quit.

"Cap, honey," she calls in what she hopes is a sisterly-sounding voice. He turns around, eyebrows raised, his face a picture of complete serenity. How can he not feel out of place? "I can't get a thing done with the kids here," she says. "I really can't. I know you'd love to visit with Daddy, but we've got a lot to do."

"Why don't you call a babysitter, and I'll stay here and help?" he asks. He picks up a floor lamp that's ready to be loaded.

"Not a good idea," Jude says.

"Don't be such a stick," he says fondly.

Katherine and Frank are struggling with the mattress, and Frank gives her a look that says he could use a stronger back. But Katherine imperceptibly shakes her head. The idea is insane, their eyes agree—typically Cap.

"Thanks anyway," Jude says. "The best help you can be is to get out of here with the kids. Really. Come on. Go. This is not a family reunion." Maybe it's because she's so glad about what she's doing that she doesn't feel angry at him anymore. She's talking the way she used to talk to him when they were married: wry indulgence of his unwillingness to grasp a situation. Why was such a bright girl as Carolyn attracted to him, she wonders. Why had *she* been attracted to him? It was because she had started with him so young and never thought about anybody else. And because she'd thought the life they would have together would be so clear-cut and normal. Maybe Carolyn thinks the same thing.

Cap is not angry about her move, which is another reason she is regarding him with benevolence. He even made a small donation to her moving fund over and above his normal responsibilities. He's taken the kids one day of every weekend since she announced her intentions. And he says he will drive to Chapel Hill regularly to see them.

She takes Charles to Cap's car and buckles him in his car seat. Then she goes after Katie, whom she assuages by loading three of her broken toys in Cap's trunk. She puts Katie in a seat belt and still has to summon him again. This time, though, she points out that the children are about to suffocate, which finally starts his legs moving, albeit slowly. It's Cap and her father who ought to be married, she thinks patiently.

"I'll pick you up tomorrow afternoon," she tells the children. "Your new rooms will be all ready." Charles starts crying for her again. Katie remembers a doll still in the trash, and Jude promises to save it. "Go," she says to Cap. "Now."

He props his arm on the back of the seat and lowers his head slightly so that he's looking up at her in the boyish way that used to make her sympathetic to whatever he wanted. "It's just too late, isn't it?" he asks.

"Too late for what?"

"Too late to start all over."

"Us?" she asks with a choke of laughter. "You've got to be kidding." Is this serious stuff, or is he just fishing to see what she still feels about him? She can honestly say that she feels nothing but sadness and fondness. He should be flattered that she feels fondness. It's the best way a thwarted love can end up.

The goal of her life, she once told her friends at a junior-high-school pajama party, was not to be rich or famous or even happy. The goal was to be safe, and what she meant by that was never to get a divorce. Until she spoke, all the other girls at the party had spoken on behalf of happiness. After she spoke, they all agreed that they, too, wanted safety above all. Now she knows that there is no such thing. She wonders if her childhood friends know yet. "I wouldn't be interested in you anymore," she says.

Cap grins as if he doesn't believe her. "*I'd* be interested in *you*," he says. "In those great boobs . . ." he adds jokingly.

Too much, she thinks, aware of the halter top that is showing her off again today. She stands straight, bangs the top of his car half-angrily with her hand, and waits for him to drive off. The last view he has is of her bounteous chest framed in the passenger window of his car. Dream on, my ex-darling.

As they continue packing, Daddy seems content to stand at the tail of the truck and give Frank pointers about the most efficient way to stack furniture. When someone needs a final boost over the edge, though, he pushes. Frank's movements acquire a machine-like quality and he stops chatting. Jude, serious, straining to help, is silent, too. She smells the sun on her skin. Everybody's shirts are wet in wide swaths.

Both Katherine and Jude wonder, off and on, about Louise,

261|

but neither of them asks Daddy where she is. Jude is too occupied with the work at hand. Katherine is wondering when she will see Eric again, and what she will say when she does.

At two o'clock, just the moment Louise should be arriving at her baby shower, Frank closes the truck and they all stand still for the first time in hours. Jude notices how slumped everyone's shoulders are. She asks her father, "Why didn't Louise come back with you?" In a befuddled way he says that he thinks she had a baby shower to go to, but he's not sure. Then he tells them goodbye, saying that he's sorry he couldn't be of more help, but they know about his back. What about your back, Jude almost asks, but decides to save the question for Katherine. To her knowledge, Daddy has never had back trouble.

Five minutes pass and everyone's shoulders begin to rise the slightest bit. The three of them are to drive to Chapel Hill, where they will unload, and then drive home. She is spending tonight in Greensboro at Frank and Katherine's. Tomorrow she will pick up the kids and they will go to their new home. She wonders if tomorrow is when she will feel sad or whether she will just not feel sad at all.

Part Four

KATHERINE

CHAPTER

15

The poems are exquisite, of course. Small. Energetic. Intense. They read as if they've been labored over, not for days, but for weeks. Two of them are about her. The one dated in May—the last day of class—is titled "I will not be the same," and is about how someone can make someone else into a better person. In it is an allusion to a paper she wrote for him. And the words "someone who comprehends me." And a description of her thick hair, which the writer longs to touch. The one dated July Fourth must be the one he wrote after he left her the day of the parade. Technically, it is her favorite, but "I will not be the same" is the one which moves her more.

Katherine touches her hair. It's soft and abundant. She pulls a strand to her nose and sniffs. It has the heavy fragrance of lilies, thanks to her shampoo. She has never thought much about her hair except as something else she has to take care of. But the poem has made her feel as if it is special hair, even beautiful hair, hair that a man, a certain man, would love to crush between his fingers. But, so what? Frank loves her legs.

The air-conditioned waiting room, so welcome when she first stepped out of the miserable August heat, has become uncomfortable. But she seems to be one of the few who are cold. Most of the women—many of whom are in various stages of pregnancy—appear at ease. A couple are even fanning themselves. This morning, Katherine brought a urine specimen here. She is back this afternoon to be told the results. She shuffles through Dr. Stern's poems until she finds her third favorite. A nurse with a rote smile and a file in her hand sticks her head out the door, looks directly at Katherine, and calls someone else's name. Katherine had begun folding the poems closed but then opens them again. She has her three favorites memorized. How many days, weeks, months, years will she be able to recall them?

After a while the door opens again: another nurse, another smile, another file. This time her name is called. She folds the poems, sticks them back in the mailer in which they arrived, and looks once more at the ragged printing where he wrote her name and address. On the way through the door, following the nurse, she dumps the small packet in the trash can. Although she doesn't really need to, she is here to make it official. That's what people do. And who is she to behave unlike everyone else?

Long ago, she and her husband, Frank, went on their annual vacation together. They picked Sea Island, Georgia, because Frank had never played its golf courses before and because she never cared where they went when they were going on vacation for sport. At Sea Island they slept late every morning, jogged, ate enormous breakfasts, and teed off around eleven. Late afternoons they took Scotches out on the beach and cooled their feet in the tepid ocean water. Evenings they showered and made love or made love and showered—depending on Katherine's mood—and went to the dining room for dinner for two by candlelight.

All week she'd been strangely quiet, though she made an effort to talk. She was inattentive, though she tried to pay attention. She introduced subjects and forgot them. She saw a look in Frank's eyes and tried to make herself the way she used to be. She couldn't remember how she used to be. She couldn't remember what she ever talked about. She played golf every day and never saw a ball. She swam but did not feel the ocean.

She decided—though her mind was too far away to make a decision—that when they returned to Greensboro she was going to tell Frank she was leaving him. It was only fair that she not waste any more of his time. They must separate quickly before more damage was done.

She wrote to Dr. Stern from Sea Island, during two afternoons—instead of the one she'd thought it would take—while Frank was getting massages. She'd expected to dash off a couple of lines and take the envelope to the front desk for mailing, but she rewrote her original words over and over. She'd thought it was hard to speak in his presence. It was infinitely harder to form sentences on a piece of paper, sentences that did not seem utterly idiotic. Without explaining the hotel stationery, she asked if he would mail some of his poems to her home. She also said "Thanks again" for his help when she lost Katie, hoping it would erase in his mind that she'd once called that same help remarkable, rather, that same helper. She was sure he knew she loved him. She kept her note matter-of-fact so that he would not guess how much. She said she'd see him in September.

The poems were waiting for her when she got home. While Frank was unloading the car, she put the envelope in an out-of-the-way drawer. That night when he went to bed, she said she felt like reading. Usually, she did late-night reading in the guest bedroom, but that night she went downstairs so she'd have enough time to hide the envelope in case Frank got up. There was no letter, only the poems. At first she was disappointed, but then she realized that the poems said everything. She read them all night long, deciding slowly on her favorites. She read them silently. With moving lips. In the barest whisper. They were the most wonderful poems she'd ever read.

The next morning she woke up the same as always, with Frank's body curved close to hers. He seemed like a stranger to her. Why was she not a stranger to him?

As soon as he left for work, she dressed to go over to the university. She was going to find Dr. Stern and ask if she could audit the last five weeks of the Eliot course. She wished she'd thought of asking it in her letter. As she was walking out the door, the phone rang. It was her father calling to welcome her back. How was the golf, he asked. Fine, she said. Louise has started looking for a job, he said. That's great, she said. Judith's really excited about her move, he said. Great, she'd said again, but with markedly less enthusiasm. It was the first time since she left on vacation that she'd thought about either sister. Jude was leaving for Chapel Hill next weekend. Katherine and Frank were to help her pack. Then she'd be gone. It was sad.

"I was just on my way out the door," Katherine had finally told her father.

"Errands?"

"Yes," she'd answered, her voice almost sharp.

"Things back up when you go away."

She'd waited silently, so ashamed of herself, but she couldn't bear to talk to him thirty more seconds.

"Come by and see me, honey," he'd said. "I've missed you."

"I will," she'd answered, knowing that next to Chapel Hill his office was the last place on her list. But then she'd driven straight downtown. She realized she had some things to talk to him about.

She'd had every intention of telling her father that she was no longer in love with her husband, that she was in love with one of her English professors, that she intended to leave her husband immediately, that she saw no reason not to. Could he think of one? Thinking of Frank as her "husband" rather than "Frank" made it easier already. She was going to point out to her father that there were no children, that she wanted no alimony, that she simply wanted to be honest . . . and free. No, she was not sexually involved with Dr. Stern. No, she didn't know whether anything would work out between them. But it didn't matter. Her honesty to Frank—to her husband—was the most important thing at this point. If she were this willing to get involved with another man, it meant she didn't love the man she was with. And she was this willing.

On the drive into town she'd further planned to say to him that he needed to listen to her predicament with an open mind. That he was not going to like what he heard because it would so clearly echo something that once happened in his life. But he was the only person she knew to turn to. Didn't he think she should leave somebody she didn't love? Even if she'd made the mistake of marrying the person? Even if the person was wonderful? Even if nothing was "wrong"? She was just looking for something more right.

Her father's secretary had been on break, so she'd walked

straight into his office. He looked up from his desk, his face shy with the unexpectedness of seeing her. Hadn't she a little while ago acted as if she didn't have time to talk to him? She'd hugged him and sat down. He complimented her on her tan. He said it had been lonely with Jude in Chapel Hill working on her apartment and with her on vacation at the same time. With Louise pounding the streets . . . It was the second time he'd mentioned missing her.

"I know I don't see you so much when you're here," he'd added as if in explanation. "But when you're gone, I always know it. I think I think about you more."

It always faintly amused her to see him sitting at a desk. He was not staid enough to belong at one. He took off his bifocals and asked her something. She didn't hear what.

"I said did Frank have fun? He said he was looking forward to getting away with you."

"He had a great time." *But I'm leaving him.*

"You chose well, my dear. Frank is a fine man."

"I know." *I don't love him, though. I love somebody else. A wonderful terrible man. Like Mother. A man who may not love me. Although I think he does. But it doesn't matter. Even if he doesn't love me, I still don't love Frank.*

Her father had looked at her, just the barest question in his eyes. Why was she here? She hasn't said. "I haven't seen you in so long, I wanted to see what you looked like," she said sweetly. She'd looked at him then and he'd looked back. She'd thought how people never do that. They steal long glances at one another, but they never look at each other at the same time. She'd never looked at her father like this in her life. The sadness in his eyes was so palpable that she could have commented and he would have admitted that it was there. What was his view of Mother's and his separation, she'd wondered. Katherine knew that at one time Mother was passionate about him. Even on her deathbed she mentioned him.

"Did you know that?" she'd asked.

He looked at her very strangely.

"Sorry. I'm not thinking today. I just got back from vacation. Still in slow gear. But do you know what Mother said to us right before she died?"

His eyes went unreadable to her. He offered no indication that he wanted to hear anything.

"It's nothing bad," Katherine said in a subdued voice. "She just said to tell you goodbye."

"Thank you," Daddy said.

"I think she—"

"Thank you," he interrupted.

"Don't you want to know what I think?" she'd asked. She was partly hurt but also irritated with him.

"Really, I don't. I just don't. What you think doesn't matter. What she *said* doesn't matter. Try to understand." He'd stood. "I have a meeting," he'd said. "Thank you for coming by. Am I still invited for Sunday?"

"You always are," she'd answered. "I just wish you'd accept more often."

She had not gone to the university. Instead, she spent the day driving around Greensboro. She drove into all parts of the city—down public streets in the rich section of town that looked like private driveways, down oiled streets in the poor section of town that were public streets—and even out into the country, where the roads seemed too narrow because of the tall rye grass on both sides. She drove many times past Dr. Stern's house, which stood in a bohemian section, if such could be said to exist in this conservative town. The house, a two-story frame one with a front-porch hammock, appeared unoccupied.

She thought about her father. It was the first time that she'd ever thought about his life. She'd always regarded her mother as the sufferer, not him. But it was because Mother had talked so much about her suffering. But is the person who says so the only one who's miserable? In all these years she has never heard Daddy complain about how Mother had hurt him. For a long time she'd thought he *hadn't* been hurt. He *realized* how inadequate he was in the face of her power. He *knew* they should not have ever married. But could that not have been the case at all?

Her mother had betrayed her father. No, she couldn't say that. They'd been ill-suited for one another, a mismatch. She was a fighter; he, a man of peace. And they had not worked it out. But she and Frank *were* well-suited. They'd been lovers; they were friends. If she left him she'd be doing something far worse than her mother had.

"I hope this is good news for you."

A physician's assistant, a sweet-faced woman with blond ringlets—not her doctor, who's busy with a delivery—walks into the office where earlier Katherine had been ushered. Genuine joy fills her face. Katherine remembers where she is and assumes that if babies are your business, you're bound to be delighted by each new conception. "You never know how women—even married ones—are going to take this news anymore," the woman confides, evidently sensing from Katherine's demeanor that she is happily pregnant. But then she pauses.

Katherine knows she should say something but doesn't trust what might come out of her mouth. She doesn't want to cry, not here, but her eyes are brimming. She is not surprised, she keeps reminding herself. She knew she was pregnant. She'd been trying to get pregnant. But hearing the words is so difficult. Everything is changed forever. There's no longer a chance she was wrong.

"Some first-time mothers are overwhelmed," the assistant offers in a kind voice, but then her expression shifts slightly. "Are you going to continue this pregnancy?"

The question finally wakes Katherine. "Of course," she says. She nods vigorously. "Of *course*." The assistant shows a renewed smile.

Katherine submits to an examination and finds that her uterus is properly enlarged. She lets blood be taken. She presents another urine specimen. She hears suggestions about diet, weight control, consumption of alcohol, and exercise. Everyone at the office says congratulations; she beams at them. She schedules her next appointment. She'll be coming here once a month until the ninth month, when she will come once a week. She has a while to get used to the news, since she hasn't told Frank what she suspected. The way he's been after her, she doesn't think he's guessed.

She leaves the office and decides to cruise around town, the way she did the day after they got back from Sea Island. She thinks that if she tried to explain to anyone what she's lost, no one would understand. Certainly not Jude or Louise. Certainly not her father, whom she hadn't even been brave enough to tell about Eric. Would her mother? . . . What she has lost is her separateness. In losing it, she's lost her right to change. It began happening when she married Frank four years ago. It was totally accomplished about an hour ago, when her pregnancy was confirmed. In between, she'd come home from a summer vacation ready to end her marriage and begin an affair with another man. And then she took a look at her father.

She turns into Irving Park, the place where most of "old Greensboro" lives. It's a beautiful area: mansions surrounding a handsome golf course, well-tended lawns, stylish automobiles, prettily dressed children. In a way she feels as artificial as all these carefully tended items. She, after all, is an item, too. A wife. A wife pregnant with her husband's child. This is not the life Frank has had. Frank knew from the beginning that he could choose whatever he wanted. A woman. A career. He could pick whether or not to have children, although men always pick to have them. It's an easy choice.

She has not had the same control over her destiny as Frank. But then she wonders whether *Frank* thinks he has control over his destiny. Could *he* feel powerless? Was he trapped by the woman he picked—her? Was he trapped by his career? Now he can't be anything but a lawyer. And a husband. And a father.

Maybe no one feels totally in control unless he's totally alone. But is even Dr. Stern in control? He wants her but can't have her. Even if she ran away with him, wouldn't it be the same old story? She'd find herself entwined with someone else's life. Perhaps she'd find herself pursuing a doctorate in English literature. But whose idea was that? Didn't she really want to be a poet? She might even find herself having yet another man's baby. Dr. Stern clearly adores children. Maybe *trapped* is the human condition.

She pulls over to the side of the road near a park, turns up the air conditioning, locks the doors, and lies across the seat, bawling. She'll never be alone again. Such knowledge would make most people ecstatic, but not her. Yes, Frank, she is going to have it all. She isn't going to miss anything.

While she cries, she begins to wonder about the consciousness of her baby, and even while her shoulders are still heaving, she begins to pat her tummy. She is "with child." Is the child "with brain"? By now it must have some brain. But whether or not it does, she knows that it's aware of her misery. Already in the womb the end of innocence begins.

She raises her head from the seat, her neck hardly able to support its weight. She looks in the rearview mirror and sees her swollen eyes, dripping nose, puffy lips. She sees anger and self-pity and looks away. She tries to think about her blessings. Maybe a baby is one of them . . . Maybe a baby is one of them . . . Maybe a baby is one of them . . . Thirty minutes pass, thirty minutes in which her swollen face finally begins to look normal. Soon she'll be able to go home.

She's parked beside Elmwood Park, a small neighborhood playground that contains plaster sculptures of the tortoise and the hare. The park is empty, so she gets out of the car, her body stiff from sitting. Two dogs are chasing each other through last year's autumn leaves. The heat is oven-dry, searing, barely breathable. Even the insect sounds are muffled. Someday she will bring her child here to play and tell him how she used to visit this park when she was pregnant, dreaming of the day they could visit here together. It will only barely be a lie. She'll sit with him on the back of the hare and tell its story about being fast but ineffectual. And she'll sit with him on the back of the tortoise and tell its story about finally getting somewhere slowly. She wonders if the lessons of life are first learned when someone begins to try to teach them. If so, she will attempt to absorb what she says. All the way home she practices a tender smile.

As she turns into the driveway, she sees Frank's car. It's time for him to be home from work. He has every right to be here. But she wishes he wasn't. Or she wishes that he wasn't always here. That just once the car would not be in the driveway at five-thirty in the afternoon. She slides the gears into reverse, thinking that she will ride around a little longer. And then she pictures Frank inside the house. He'll be sitting at the breakfast table reading the afternoon paper, drinking a St. Pauli Girl beer. He will have poured her a glass of wine. He'll probably have started supper. He'll stand up and kiss her when she walks in. What is wrong with her that this does not utterly please?

Frank doesn't even wait for her to come into the house before he is at her car door, opening it, helping her out, standing close to her, wanting a hug. Could he somehow know? She flashes him a smile but only pretends to look at him. Since midsummer—since Dr. Stern and since she stopped using her diaphragm—she has not been able to look straight into his eyes. It makes her wonder if she was wrong not to abandon him. Even without looking at him, though, she knows that his face has changed. It is no longer wholeheartedly cheerful as it once was. She cannot bear to see what it is now. What it is is her fault.

"I've been thinking about you all day long," he says. He has changed out of his suit and tie and into Bermudas and a club shirt. His vacation tan has faded from his face but not his arms.

"Isn't that a coincidence?" she asks sweetly.

He enfolds her in his arms, nuzzling her ear with his nose. He is trying to awaken her, she knows, but somehow she cannot hear the summons.

They chat as they walk through the back door. "Where have you been?" he asks. She offers a vague "running errands." She asks, "How was your day?" In imitation of her flat voice he says, "Fine." And so they cover their eight hours apart in twenty seconds.

She hates herself. And then she hates herself more because the veal is floured and ready for the bubbling butter and the asparagus is steaming and Frank strides across the kitchen to catch the rice just before it boils over. She lays her purse on the breakfast-room table, where a St. Pauli Girl bottle sits beside the open newspaper. In their refrigerator Frank stocks six kinds of beer to take care of everyone's taste.

It is the St. Pauli Girl bottle that makes her turn around and in a not totally calm voice say, "I'm pregnant."

What she knows he would like to do is shout, throw her up in the air, turn a cartwheel. But he contents himself with grinning, although the grin keeps growing until his narrow face can hardly contain it. He reaches for her hands and pulls her close to him in the most careful way imaginable. She feels the badness inside her rise up and then fall back and then rise up again. In a husky voice he says, "I'm the happiest I've ever been."

"I know you are," she says. Suddenly the badness seems to race out of her body—chased by the goodness of Frank—and the body that was stiff and unyielding suddenly yields, and Frank laughs because he feels it happen, and she begins to cry because to be shown real love is all she's ever wanted anyway.

He is talking to her about child care. She has heard him mention the phrase now about five times. They have finished dinner and are sitting in the dining room. To celebrate her announcement she draped the table with a pink cloth and lit one of the three-armed silver candelabra she inherited from her mother. Frank's cooking was delicious. She'd been so famished that she ate what was left on his plate. Now they are finishing a bottle of wine. Both of them agree that her half bottle shouldn't affect the baby at all. She was told today how much she can safely consume, she told Frank, but she doesn't remember the amount. It was because she was so excited. Yes.

Already they have talked about which room will be the nursery, about taking an early vacation next year, about whether or not to try to resurrect Jude's baby furniture, about Lamaze versus Bradley, Spock versus Brazelton, about breast-feeding—which he thinks doesn't matter in the long run but she knows does.

"Are you listening to me?" he asks.

"Yes," she says, too quickly.

"I want you to start lining up help now."

"Now?"

"I want you to know how things are going to be, so you won't worry. I want you to be able to plan your time. The only way you can plan your time is if you have help. I've looked into this, and I know what I'm talking about."

She finds it both quaint and a little beyond belief that before she was pregnant he had actually discussed child care with someone. For some reason she doesn't want to know with whom. What if it was Anne Bedingfield? The thought makes her feel slightly sick. Or maybe this is the newest symptom of her present condition. She is no different from Anne Bedingfield. No different at all.

"I'm worried that you're going to feel trapped," she suddenly says. "By me, by this baby . . ." she adds as if this age-old concern applies only in its age-old way: to the man and not the woman.

"Trapped?" He gives a small patient chuckle. She can't fool him that the question is not two-sided. "I would never use that word," he says. "Because I'm happy to be trapped. I would choose to call it highly involved. The real question is, do *you* feel trapped? And I know that the answer's yes, because that's all you've been talking about for six months. Except your thinking's screwy. You have the idea that if you eliminate everything from your life, you'll be able to pick which things you want back."

"That's not true," she says.

"You say you want to be something, but what, you don't know. You say you don't have time to have children because you want to be something. I don't even think you want to be married very much anymore. For some reason you think I'm in your way, too."

She ought to grab him and emphatically negate everything he's said, but she can only manage to say again, "That's not true," in a faraway voice.

"You don't realize it, but if you keep on like this you're not ever going to be happy," he continues. "I guess I keep thinking you're going to come to your senses. I guess I must be sure you will. But right now I don't understand you. You have a husband who loves you. You have total freedom to do whatever interests you. You're pregnant with your first baby. Lots of people handle all those things. You have up to sixteen hours every day."

Do you know why I'm pregnant, she wants to ask. Do you know that I *have* made a decision? For *you*. But these are things she can't ever say. She doesn't have to be happy *too*, does she?

Frank's face is clouded over, but he's not visibly shaken as he's been before when they've had this discussion. It's because she's pregnant. It's because he knows that—almost apart from her—everything has been decided.

The woman sitting beside her in her Twentieth-Century Poetry class has been writing the initials "P.A." all over a sheet of paper ever since Dr. Stern started class. Katherine thinks that probably they are her boyfriend's initials. She writes them in magnificent curlicues, in block print, in lowercase letters, in two dimensions—every way she can think of—all around the margins of the spiral, where occasionally she jots down a note on what is being discussed. Only fifteen minutes of class time have passed and already the page looks as if it's been tattooed. If Dr. Stern happens to glance at her, he will notice. But whenever he looks toward this side of the room, his eyes bore directly into Katherine's.

P.A.'s girlfriend is somewhere near Katherine's age, not necessarily her chronological age, but her interior age, which, depending on her mood, can range currently from twenty-five to sixty. P.A.'s girlfriend, in other words, is a woman—not a wet-behind-the-ears graduate student—the first woman who's been in any of her classes. Already she's looked at Katherine several times and made a face that Katherine thinks is supposed to be a smile. Usually she's done this when Dr. Stern has made some sort of wry remark. P.A.'s girlfriend is very pretty in a wholesome manner. She wears no makeup but her eyes are big in her face anyway. She has a real nose, unlike so many women Katherine knows, and what seem to be naturally surly lips. She wears her coffee-black hair tucked behind her ears. It's blunt cut at her neck as if she does it herself. Her eyes are dark and quizzical and roaming. Katherine is not the only person with whom she's made silent contact.

Katherine returns her attention to her teacher, who is describing the melodic difference between nineteenth-century and twentieth-century poetry. All one need do, he says, is read a number of poems aloud and the difference becomes immediately apparent. Even if one did not know the English language, he continues, one could still intuit the nihilism of the twentieth century simply from how the words sound. He turns as if he's looking out the classroom window, but he's looking at her again. He announces that he's going to read several poems so that they can hear what he's talking about. His harsh voice makes her skin respond in rolling chills.

This is the first time Katherine has seen Dr. Stern since the parade. She'd almost decided not to take any courses this fall because of morning sickness, but Frank promised the nausea would end, and two weeks ago it had. She'd decided against taking a course from Dr. Stern at all, but twentieth-century poetry has always attracted her, and besides, she's pregnant. It's not that she thinks she won't remain attractive as a pregnant woman: Jude was her most beautiful ever. It's how pregnancy proclaims you as belonging to someone else—to two someone elses, in fact. There's no escape from the enlarging womb, which stands in the way of all possibility anyway. As soon as Dr. Stern finds out she's in a family way, his interest in her will end. Which made it all right for her to take his class. Her interest in him, of course, will not end, because it's just the same as it ever was: a friendly interest. She admires his poems. The only thing she'd like to avoid is listening to him read.

While Dr. Stern is looking up "The Love Song of J. Alfred Prufrock," P.A.'s girlfriend turns to a fresh sheet and writes P.A. in page-high letters. She gives Katherine a long sideways look, her mouth widening in a curveless smile. Could she have interpreted their teacher's frequent glances? Katherine has decided she'll try to get to know the woman, at least attempt a conversation when class ends, so that she can avoid talking to Eric. He's angry with her, she's realized, but is he angry to see her or angry because he hasn't seen her? Dr. Stern begins to read. She doesn't need to hear him; she can read the poems herself. She can read them quite eloquently herself.

P.A.'s girlfriend begins talking to her with her face, just like

Jude does. She looks down at her doodling and then inclines her head in Dr. Stern's direction. Katherine asks with her eyebrows what "P.A." means. The woman mouths something, her lips bouncing comically against each other, but Katherine can't tell what. Dr. Stern's reading voice slips into her ears, but she immediately shuts it off. She scribbles her finger in the air, asking the woman to write down what she said. On a clean paper in bold letters the woman prints "Pompous Ass." She smirks. She is talking about Dr. Stern.

Katherine smiles a smile that is neutral, yet because it is a smile can be read as agreement. The center of her body hurts as it might after a quick punch. Her eyes veer away from the woman and alight on the man. His mouth forms an enormous frown. His eyebrows hang heavy over his eyes. As if he is Eliot himself, he is reading the last few lines, his tone mincing when it needs to be and then full. He begins staring at her midway through, the last of the poem memorized. To the class, he appears to be gazing out the window.

Shall I part my hair behind? Do I dare to eat a peach?
I shall wear white flannel trousers, and walk upon the beach.
I have heard the mermaids singing, each to each.

I do not think that they will sing to me.

I have seen them riding seaward on the waves
Combing the white hair of the waves blown back
When the wind blows the water white and black.

We have lingered in the chambers of the sea
By sea girls wreathed with seaweed red and brown
Till human voices wake us, and we drown.

If she does not find something else to concentrate on, Katherine is going to burst into tears.

Within seconds after Dr. Stern announces that class is dismissed, her classmate, who is perhaps a P.A. herself, bounds out the door in her purple Nikes, not even taking the time to meet

Katherine. Young female graduate students are surrounding their handsome teacher. Katherine need not have worried about his having the opportunity to approach her. She notices particularly a serious-faced blonde who's wearing a white ruffled blouse and a straight skirt. She's rather young to look so prissy, but then Katherine wonders if she herself is too old to look like a slob. Not a slob exactly: she's wearing jeans and a snug-fitting sleeveless turtleneck, aware as she passes by the crowded podium of how these clothes mold themselves to her body. She is not yet showing. She feels Dr. Stern's eyes on her but doesn't turn her head. Another set of eyes are on her, too: those of the blonde, another brilliant student, no doubt.

"Mrs. Borden?" He is calling her. She takes one more step without responding, which she immediately realizes is a mistake. The female students will know that the delay was intentional.

"Yes?" She does not like this overdressed blonde, who is still watching her.

"May I see you in my office?" There is an odd silence from the graduate students, a silence that Katherine knows she caused. She couldn't help herself. She'll soon be fat. A better student is about to take her place. And she's near tears over someone calling Dr. Stern a pompous ass, over his great sadness—shouldn't *his* sadness as well as Frank's be considered?—over human voices waking us and we drown. And this is what's happened in the last ten minutes.

"Certainly," she says in a brief, polite voice.

"I never gave you back your Yeats paper," he calls after her, as if to explain why he's singled her out.

She thinks of calling back, "You can keep it," since he seems to need an excuse to see her. Then she could simply go on her way. But his mouth has a vulnerability, though not his piercing eyes, that she has never seen. She walks out the door and down the hall to his office. Instead of going inside, which she knows is perfectly acceptable, she takes the chair outside the door. One by one the students come out of the classroom and walk by her. Katherine smiles at each of them. Last comes the blonde. So she will not have to speak, Katherine buries her face in a book. Close on the girl's heels is Dr. Stern, who does not even seem to notice the small wiggling ass only steps in front of him. For just a moment Katherine is relieved.

He walks past her into the office and goes behind his desk. She doesn't leave her seat. "Would you come in, please?" he calls.

The hall is empty. She rises slowly. She is never afraid of anybody, but she's afraid of him. A hardness sheaths his eyes, protecting him from her: he's afraid, too. She'd like to weigh what she says, but words are coming out of her mouth: "I've missed seeing you." Halfway through the sentence she manages to make its tone cheerful.

His shoulders droop, he leans slightly forward, his face seems to reach out to hers. "I didn't expect you back."

"How could I miss a course of yours?" she asks lightly.

The hardness appears in his eyes again. "I decided that you're a dabbler," he says. He stands straight again, which gives her a brief illusion that he is another species. When he looks like this, so large, so harsh, so distant—as he so often does in class—it's as if he's not human. "Did you read all those books, by the way?"

She would like to be able to say yes, she read the books, but she won't lie to him. She lies to Frank; she's always lied to Frank so that she could tell him what he wanted to hear: she's always lied to all men. Nice, complimentary lies. Lies to make them feel more special, more unusual than they are. She had always thought the lies were harmless, but so much of what Frank thinks exists between them is based on falseness. She will never let it happen again. Even with a friend. A friend like Dr. Stern.

"I only read five novels," she says. "All in June. I couldn't take your summer-school course because we went on vacation. But I'm not a dabbler. I got pregnant. After that happened, I couldn't read. I haven't done anything for the past six weeks but throw up and think."

One paragraph of short, practically spat-out sentences has

told everything there is to tell about her current situation. She feels sunk in her own stinking puddle of misery. It's hard to lift her head, but she forces herself to.

As she expected, Dr. Stern's face has closed even tighter against her. They could be strangers. She could be the blonde in the straight skirt. If she were the blonde in the straight skirt, she would get a more intimate look than this. She doesn't want to be strangers with him. They aren't even friends yet. But she loves him. She has always loved him. As she watches him shrinking further and further away from her, she knows she will always love him.

"You don't seem to be throwing up now," he says, a clinical detachment in his voice. "What about your work?"

Perhaps they are merely lamenting that she may no longer be a Ph.D. candidate in English literature, and for a moment she freezes, wondering if this could be all it is. They hardly know each other, after all. But there is magic between them. And anger. And love. She knows it and so does he.

"Eric," she says, sitting down. A fine Nordic name. The only time she will ever get to say it. She stretches her arms across the desk. Her fists look small, her wrists no bigger than a child's.

He steps from behind the desk and closes the door. Without coming near her, he returns to his place and sits down in his chair. He lets his large hands barely touch the edge of the desk. Almost involuntarily, though, they move toward hers. They retreat. Then, as if against his will, they move toward her again. They enfold her wrists. It's as if they are swallowing her. His face is stricken with pain. "I want you," he says, not looking at her. "You know I wanted you. Why did you let this happen?"

He is not speaking in the traditional terms of physical desire, she knows, although her wrists lie smothered beneath his hands. He has somehow *decided* on her. Why her, though, when there are so many others? At least one willing pretty girl in class today. His hands are hot and moist, and they knead her bones so hard it hurts. They are trying to draw in her entire self. She wants him, too.

Suddenly his hands calm. "I don't understand," he says in a quiet voice.

"Why I'm pregnant?"

"That."

"Why I didn't come to summer school?"

This seems to be the only way they can talk right now: he hinting at his feelings; she putting them into words. She doesn't think she could ask a question on her own.

He nods once.

"Why I'm taking this poetry class?"

"Yes," he whispers hoarsely, as if that's the least explicable of all.

"I couldn't stay away," she says in a low taut voice. "I already told you that."

"You think I'm a good teacher," he says stonily.

"Of course," she says. His eyes flutter. His hands grip her wrists harshly again.

Should she tell him now that she loves him, or should she leave the words unsaid? Which would be easier? Doesn't he already know?

"I've been in love before," he says, beginning gently to massage her wrists. "But I've never loved someone who was like me." As if to himself he adds, "I don't know if I've ever met anyone like me." He looks up suddenly and catches her almost curious gaze. "You think I don't know that much about you, but I know everything," he says in an imperious tone. "We're alike. It's as if we're brother and sister. Or father and daughter. Our origins are the same." His voice grows firmer. "Except that you give yourself. And I don't." He pauses. "Until this summer I thought you might give yourself to everybody. Some people are that open. But at the parade I realized that you were giving yourself just to me." His voice softens. "And then I didn't see you again." His eyes glisten for a brief moment. Or maybe the light has just caught them.

His words overwhelm her. Finally she asks, "How *could* I see you?"

"How could you not?"

283|

"I'm married, Eric. I'm pregnant."

"Neither of those things matters," he says. "I'm talking about something totally apart. You know what I'm talking about. I'm talking about what's eternal. I'm talking about *our* truth."

She is silent for a long time. Then she says, "Some truths cancel others out."

She thinks about the face he is looking at so fervently and how it is not such a handsome face as his. Her face is all right, better at some angles than others. She only looks truly pretty when she smiles; when she is crying, she looks dreadful. She remembers how, with her boyfriends in high school and college and even as late as Frank, she would always turn her face to the angle which flattered it most. She would use her hands and her eyes simultaneously to distract and attract. It made her wonder if the people who loved her loved her because they didn't see the real her. Now, if she ever smiles again, it will not be because it makes her prettier. She wants Eric, and everyone, to see her exactly like she is.

A great deal of time may have passed or only a few seconds. She knows only that her attention is alerted by how the office is growing dim, as the sun passes some last roof line. She hasn't looked at Eric while he's been watching her, her eyes fixed on a stack of correspondence, probably his poetry submissions. For the first time she is uninterested in his poems. It's as if she's been traveling for a long time on a road that she believed was going to take her somewhere, and suddenly the road ended. What can be said? What can be done?

She tries to think about Frank, but his image seems that of a stranger. Her mind grasps for a picture of her home, where she cooks, where she sleeps, where she makes love with her husband. The home where she was happy. But she can't conjure what it looks like. She *knows* Frank. She does not know Eric. But she feels that she could discard Frank, discard her house, and never think about them again. She would not even go back and get her clothes. The only thing she cannot discard is her own body.

"I should withdraw from your class," she says in a voice

that sounds nothing like her own. "I will withdraw. It's not fair."

"You won't do it."

Where her voice has been trembling and tentative, his no longer shows any trace of uncertainty. His is almost arrogant, as if he's scored a victory at a faculty meeting. She looks at his face. His eyes make her tremble. A flicker of triumph shows at the edges of his mouth, or perhaps he is merely smiling at her. She's not insulted: he isn't an ass, but he is pompous.

He begins speaking slowly, reciting:

> *Each night I climb from the fire*
> *Still cold.*
> *Yellow tongues lick after me:*
> *My garments smell of burn;*
> *But my flesh is unravaged, continent.*
> *I stand before you, waiting.*

He is reciting the poem he wrote on the Fourth of July. "Virgin," it's called. His voice is almost more than she can bear, but his eyes hold fast to hers, keeping her from turning away. Suddenly she joins the recitation. He seems not at all surprised that she knows the words.

> *I long to burst into flame*
> *—Apparent self-immolator—*
> *Inhaling the singe of my hair,*
> *Suffering the char of my flesh.*
> *I long to join with you completely.*
> *Side by side in the pit is not enough.*

The brief duet is over. She quickly averts her gaze.

"You won't always be pregnant," Eric says.

She cannot bear to hear words like these, because they claim that only the present is to be considered, that past and future do not exist. She wishes they did not. But they do.

"Yes, I will be," she says. "In a way I always will be. I'm talking about what has been, what is, and what will be." She sounds so sure, yet she's begun to wonder if it's possible to have

285|

a baby, to keep Frank, and also to love Eric. But the answer is no. The answer has to be no.

He stands and comes around the desk directly to her and takes her in his arms. She lets herself be kissed, a long hard kiss. And then she lets herself be held. He slides one hand under her hair. He whispers to her that she is irresistible and that he loves her. She continues to listen even after he stops speaking. She can hear his soul. Finally she disengages herself and says that she must go. He touches his hands to her thickening waist and then steps away.

CHAPTER

16

It's like a party-all-the-time at the ice-cream shop, which is the last thing Louise would have expected.

Just when she sits down at her desk to figure out whether all the tubs of ice cream have yielded seventy scoops, as they're supposed to, somebody else she knows is waiting out in the store proper, wanting to tell her hello.

"It's a guy," Carilee, her best scooper, had leaned into the minuscule office to say.

"Tall or short?" Louise had asked.

"Tall," Carilee answered, so Louise knows it's not Billy. Except that the way the counter is designed, almost everybody looks tall from this side.

Everyone is so interested in ice cream, so eager for ice cream, so delighted by ice cream, that she feels like a minor celebrity. In the three months she's been working, she's seen more people out of her past than she saw the entire four years since high-school graduation. Those of her acquaintances who didn't go to college seem to have everything under way: jobs, marriages, kids, as well as a seen-it-all expression on their faces. If they've been to college they sport a pseudo-sophisticated air: yes, they've been away, combined with a telling eagerness: no, they haven't lived any life yet but want to ASAP.

Her sisters have visited the store, too: Jude, home from Chapel Hill last weekend to borrow Daddy's 35-millimeter Argus from the thirties for some new boyfriend to see. And Katherine, who keeps mentioning that, with Jude gone, she and Louise need to be seeing more of each other. Each sister walked directly into her office without asking anybody out front if it was all right, which Louise had thought very forward. At the same time, though, she appreciated the show of intimacy. She especially appreciated it when Carilee said how much she wished *her* sisters liked *her*. Louise comforted her by saying that usually these kinds of friendships between sisters don't develop until your twenties. Like all the girls who work for her, Carilee is still in high school.

Her father also drops by occasionally on his way home from work. He stands beyond the counter, jiggling coins in his pockets, waiting for her and then chatting endlessly as if—again—she is not actually at work. She's had to excuse herself from him at least five times.

Even Lucy Payne comes here. Louise first recognized Lucy's enormous bronze-colored dog tied outside the plate-glass window, and then noticed the top of Lucy's head, which barely cleared the counter. Pal is so much larger than most dogs that at first glance Louise felt uneasy. Lucy bought a dish of macadamia-nut ice cream for herself and a sugar cone of fudge ripple for her dog. When she ordered, she spoke to Louise as if they knew each other, although in Louise's memory they've never been introduced. Deep in her heart Louise had hoped never to have to acknowledge Lucy as a person in this world, but that hope had been dashed. Louise expected Lucy and her dog to make a mess right outside the front door, but she saw Pal actually licking around the cone as Lucy held it. The dog's head came up past her waist. The difference in their sizes was very show-offy, Louise thought. Exactly how Lucy must look with Billy.

Now that Lucy's grandmother is dead, the word is that she and Billy are to be married at Thanksgiving.

When Carilee came to tell her about her visitor, she'd also reported that they'd just run out of Cookies and Cream, so Louise stops by the freezer for a new tub.

"Out of my way," she calls out as she comes through the door. The containers are not so heavy but very cold, and she can get chilled for fifteen minutes by carrying one twenty feet.

Carilee removes the empty tub. Louise plops the full one in its place, quickly drying her hands on a towel.

"Cookies and Cream, anyone?" she asks, raising her head to look over the counter. She's not so tall herself, but at least she can see her customers. This customer, whom she's kept waiting for ten minutes, is someone she doesn't know.

"Hi, Weezie," he says. As if to aid her in recognizing him, he stands perfectly still, a small smile on his face. "Don't you remember me?" he asks, but not in an accusing way.

Her mind is racing to think who he could be. Only people who also know her sisters ever call her Weezie. He is half bald, which has to be a clue: when she knew him, he had hair. He has caterpillar-thick eyebrows and a matching mustache, which apparently stand out more than they used to. An orderly, not unattractive set of complexion scars crosses his forehead. She cannot come up with even a possibility of who he is.

"George Morales," he says, relaxing his stance. He reaches over the counter to shake her hand.

"Hi, George," she says brightly. "I drew a blank."

"You still don't remember me," he says.

"Of course I do."

Since there are no other customers, Carilee is out in the seating area wiping down tables, her back to Louise. Suddenly she lowers her head and looks at Louise from underneath her armpit. Her face is upside down. Is she frowning or giggling? For a second Louise can't tell. She must think this guy's a weirdo. Although lots of weirdos visit doughnut shops, Louise has never seen one in an ice-cream store. But George knows her nickname.

"It's all right that you don't remember me," he persists. "I've changed a lot. I don't have hair anymore, as you can see. And after twenty years of living with him, I finally took my stepfather's last name. I used to be George Akers." Although this name means nothing to her either, she won't further insult him by pretending that it does. "My father left our family before I was born," he adds in an explanatory tone.

"Anyway, you and I had classes together starting in the seventh grade. Civics, algebra. And when we were seniors, we had the same English and world-history teachers. But it was a big school. And I didn't talk much then. I always sat on the back row."

"I wish I could remember," she says. "If I could look you up in the annual . . ." The uncomfortable truth—would it be all right not to pursue it?—is that she must never have noticed him. He's realized it, too.

He shrugs. "It doesn't matter," he says. "I'd heard that you'd come back home . . . and gotten a job . . . and I wanted to welcome you . . . back. I've been away myself—" He breaks off, seeing her questioning eyes. "I guess if you don't remember me, you're finding this visit pretty odd."

She doesn't know what to say, although he's waiting for her to say something. "I'm glad to see you. I'm glad to know you," she offers. "Where have you been away? In school? Would you like some ice cream? Do you have a job?" She could chatter on and on. She could probably chatter him out of the store if it became necessary. But he doesn't seem dangerous. He doesn't even seem weird.

"I'm getting ready to go to college next semester," he says. "I've been in the Army. I'll have some ice cream if you will."

When they first began talking, the counter between them felt like any comforting barrier, but suddenly to Louise it seems to be blocking true communication. She feels as if she doesn't have a body. She feels as if George doesn't have one either. Heads all by themselves talking to each other feel odd, she thinks. In other words, she'd like to walk around to his side, since he can't come to hers. Then she remembers that she's the boss.

"I know because this is an ice-cream store that it's hard to think I'm working," she says. "But I am."

"I know you're working," George says, looking behind him. "But nobody's here. That's why I asked."

"People think all we do is scoop ice cream, but there's a lot more to it," she says. "We even have a computer. I have to weigh all the ice cream every day to make sure we're not over-scooping. Can you believe that I've had someone working for me who only got forty scoops out of a tub that should yield seventy? She was fired, of course." Louise suddenly lowers her eyes. "This is boring," she murmurs.

"All jobs are boring, except to the people who do them," he says. "All vacations are boring unless you went. All other people's kids . . ."

She gradually realizes what he means, but not before she feels a sharp surge of anger. At the same time she begins blushing for responding so strongly. She accepts that he's making a kind of joke. She laughs.

"I'm slow," she offers.

"You're just sensitive."

"It's because of my sisters. They think my job is beneath me. It's not," she adds simply. She feels a small prick of guilt. Katherine has been very interested in her job lately. Maybe she keeps her sisters just as trapped in her mind as they keep her in theirs. "You must know Katherine or Jude," she says. "Katherine Borden? Judith Cramer? They're the only ones who call me Weezie. What flavor do you want?"

George orders Swiss Almond Chocolate, still her own favorite after all these weeks of working here. She fills a sugar cone with more than the allowed four ounces, planning to add fifty cents of her own money to the till. Since she took over the store, it's been averaging sixty-five to seventy scoops per tub, near-perfect, the owners have told her.

"That'll be a dollar five," she says, handing him the cone. He gives her two ones and a dime.

"*One* dollar five," she repeats.

He grins at her without explaining.

"I'm working," she says. "If the owner came in and I was eating . . . You know . . . Plus, I eat this stuff all day long . . ." She doesn't know why she said that except that it makes her seem curiously thin when she should be fat. Efficiently, she rings up the sale and lays the nickel change on top of the extra dollar bill. Shall she keep standing here? Shall she go back to her office? She wipes a drip off the counter. She puts the dipper back in the dipper well. Carilee is cleaning windows where some teenagers made ice-cream handprints a little while ago. Cleaning windows and listening.

George showed no sign of recognition when she mentioned her sisters. *"How* did you know to call me Weezie?" she asks.

He smiles broadly and the scars on his forehead flatten out a bit. "You probably don't remember this either, but at the beginning of the seventh grade you announced to Mrs. Rigby, our homeroom teacher, that you wanted to be called Weezie from then on instead of Louise."

Suddenly she does remember. She squinches up her face. Until that first morning of the seventh grade, Mrs. Rigby—tall, big-bosomed, jolly—had been her most admired teacher. Ragbag, as everyone called her, didn't mind poking fun at the principal, who was rumored to have an eye for his secretary, or at certain teachers, who in her opinion emphasized grades at the expense of learning, or, evidently, at female students, many of whom, like Louise, were fascinated that year by the prospect of somehow altering their names.

"Mrs. Rigby said just what she thought," George says, looking behind him again. "She asked why in the world you wanted to be called a squeaky name like Weezie when you had such a lovely name as Louise. I'll never forget the pitiful little face you made. From then on, I thought of you as Weezie. Of course, you never got called that."

"Except by my sisters," she says. Although she'd cried in the bathroom over what Ragbag said, she's always liked the name Weezie. It's a sweet kind of name, one that people say fondly. Evidently, George Morales feels the same way.

George makes a couple of passes at his ice-cream cone. He has a big flat tongue, squarish instead of pointed, and he eats his ice cream by licking around its entire circumference, sort of the way Pal does. Tongues—which Louise had never before noticed in her life—and styles of ice-cream eating have become of immense interest to her. There are very red tongues and very white tongues; broad, flat ones, and narrow, thin ones. The kind of tongue she finds most attractive is the color of the inside of a cherry and small and pointed. Most of these tongues belong to women. The most attractive male tongue she's seen is pink and muscular-looking. Little tongues tend to dart out at ice-cream cones; big tongues seem to wipe them. Some people don't use their tongues at all, she's noticed. They bite the ice cream with their lips.

George is eating his ice cream all at once, like lots of people do. She likes to let a thin layer of melt form and start licking right before it begins to drip. He might eat differently, though, if she were eating, too. It's always awkward to eat in front of someone, especially an item that so involves the mouth. She'd walk away and let him eat in peace, but then he might leave. Her curiosity has been stirred. What else has someone she never even noticed noticed about her?

He throws away his cone without eating it, the way lots of men do, and then licks one of his fingers, which she finds mildly disgusting. She's thought for some time that ice-cream parlors ought to offer something damp to clean up with instead of flimsy paper napkins. She knows, though, that it would not be cost-effective.

"What will you be doing between now and January?" she asks.

Carilee leans against the sink, a disinterested expression on her face. Louise knows that she's already formed some firm opinions about George. Carilee has firm opinions about everybody, especially people she doesn't know.

"Looking for a job," George says. When she gives him a funny look, he waves his hands "no" in front of him. "Not dipping ice cream." He laughs. "Warehouse work. Something I can make a lot of overtime doing. I learned how to operate a forklift in the Army. That will pay. I've got education money from the government, but I need money to live on. I like things around me to be a little nicer than they were when I was nineteen. Sheets on the bed. Milk in the refrigerator. Those kinds of things."

She looks amused. It must be that George was so quiet in high school that *no one* noticed him. He certainly would be noticed now, she thinks, especially by the girls who wouldn't have dreamed of noticing him then. Not that George is particularly handsome, but he has a disarming openness. Also, he's willing not to be mad at you if you never knew who he was. Unlike everyone else, Louise hadn't actually known him and turned up her nose. Instead, it was as if George weren't there. Maybe she should never try to explain it, but she's beginning to think that one day she might have to. George apparently means to be here.

Two mothers with three little blond boys between them stroll into the store. Louise likes to wait on toddlers because she can help the store's scooping average with them. They're not being cheated, because they never eat whole servings anyway. The mothers seat the children and approach the counter. Carilee has already sprung into action, a dipper in hand. The mothers are engaged in a private banter which sounds like a conversation about having sex with their husbands. No actual words make Louise know this for sure, but when she glances at them, they immediately start talking behind their hands. She hates this kind of rudeness.

Although he is standing five feet away from them, George still takes a couple of steps back. His mouth wrinkles and then smooths. He gives Louise a thumb-up. Then he slides out the door. It's almost as if they are crowding him out.

Once outside, he stands for a moment at the plate-glass window, steady again, in control of where his feet are. He smiles sadly at her, the way someone who really cares about animals might do before a cage.

He'd like to be back in here with me, she interprets.

But it suits her fine that he is out. She knows just enough. Now she wants to scour her high-school annual, find out who he was back then. She may even call up some of her high-school friends who have been in the store. Ask them whether or not they remember him. And do they know him now. She wants to find out all she can by the time he comes back.

When next she glances outside, George is gone. The mothers have taken ice cream to their boys, turning the store quiet. She waits for Carilee's opinion.

"What a drip," Carilee says, as she bangs the dipper roughly against the sides of the dipper well. "I'm sorry," she adds, shrugging her shoulders at Louise's disappointed stare.

In her heart of hearts Louise doesn't think she should be doing this. But it's three-thirty in the afternoon, and she's dressed up in the first dress bought with her own money, and George should be ringing her doorbell any minute. They are going to Billy's wedding.

"Essential," Katherine had said last week at lunch. "If you don't watch him get married, you'll never believe he actually did it. It's like seeing the body of someone who's dead. You need the confirmation." It was their first lunch ever without Jude, a surprisingly pleasant, friendly occasion. Katherine seemed less effervescent than normal, though, her enlarging abdomen somehow weighing her down. She still had plenty of advice to give, but Louise felt privileged to hear it, she didn't know why.

"This is a small town," Katherine had continued. "You won't be able to avoid seeing them forever."

"It could be that I might *never* see them," Louise said. "I haven't seen Billy in seven months."

Katherine pressed her lips together tightly. "You know the number of months without counting," she said.

"Of course I know the number of months. It's how long I've been back home." Louise lifted her shoulders once and let them drop.

"You only know the number of months because of him."

"Don't be ridiculous," Louise said, although Billy *was* the only reason she'd ever counted anything, starting with the number of days between her monthly periods and continuing with the time between college vacations. But the answer she'd given Katherine appeared to be satisfactory.

Katherine leaned forward confidingly, but then, before saying anything, she sat up straight, the coming baby, Louise imagined, forcing her good posture. "Billy will be comforted when he sees you with another man," Katherine said. " 'Relieved' might be a better word. He feels really strongly about you. He probably loves you more than he loves Lucy."

Louise was cutting her first bite of quiche, which had arrived too hot. She stopped her fork for a brief second and then made it continue. "I don't think that's the kind of thing I need to hear," she said.

Katherine looked directly into Louise's eyes and then on beyond them to her own personal horizon. Her face wore a busy expression. Suddenly something—a flash of Louise's iris, a flicker of her lashes—yanked her back. Louise laid her hand on Katherine's wrist. She made sure that her eyes did not beg.

"I'm sorry," Katherine said. She must have said it without thinking, because a look of surprise crossed her face. The very fact that the words seemed to be said accidentally, though, comforted Louise. Katherine had a basic sorrow in her heart for keeping her apart from Billy. What more could she ask?

Louise drew her hand back to her lap. "Losing Billy still hurts so much," she whispered. "My heart feels dead."

Suddenly Katherine's eyes grew hard. "It shouldn't," she said. "You dodged a bullet. That's how you should always remember Billy."

They had eaten in silence for several long minutes, Louise yielding to her sister the decision about when the conversation would resume. Finally, Katherine began to talk. The subject was whether Jude's children were suffering from being so far away from Cap. Well into the discussion, Louise commented that it was too late to change things anyway, since the move to Chapel Hill had already taken place. "Anything you do is reversible," Katherine countered. "That's what makes life so complicated." Her voice was almost fervent.

Louise fiddled with a piece of pineapple on her plate. "You mean that Billy might change his mind and marry me?" she asked.

"Goddamn, Weezie. I'm not talking about you and Billy. You and Billy are the *last* people I'm talking about. Don't you know yet that it's over?" she asked, her voice hot. "If he were going to reverse himself, he would have done it at your graduation."

In a calm voice Louise said, "At my graduation I told him I didn't love him. What else could he have said? I told him I was in love with a man I met in Paris."

Katherine gave her a long, assessing look. "As I said, you dodged a bullet," she said with careful seriousness. "Maybe you dodged two. What was *his* name?"

"I made it up," Louise said softly. "I don't know why. I don't know what might have happened if I'd only told the truth. I don't know why I *didn't* tell the truth. For some reason I was being loyal to Lucy Payne."

The doorbell rings and Louise checks one last time the red felt hat with the saucy black tail feathers that Katherine has spent hours on the phone this week trying to convince her to wear to the wedding. Although she bought the hat herself—it was on the manikin with the dress she fell in love with—she's still not sure about it. Manikins are tall, slim, and beautiful. What they wear doesn't always translate to real people. The only way she would know for sure that the hat looked good was if she bought the dress *and* the body.

She opens the front door boldly. Although George would be incapable of going to a store and picking out a dress for her, she thinks he has good enough taste to say whether or not something looks good. She has to look up to find his eyes. For some reason she was looking on the level that Billy's would have been and missed his first reaction. "Hi," they both say.

Like most men without much hair, George always looks the same because he can't look tousled. On his face is the resilient look he always wears. He's not jealous of Billy, he's said. He doesn't mind going to Billy's wedding. Somehow George thinks he's locked in to her: after being too nervous to speak to her for ten years, he dates her for three months and thinks everything is decided. But it's not. Kissing him doesn't excite her. Up close he looks funny because he doesn't have any hair on his head. It's as if she's kissing somebody who's upside down. He thinks she's just being careful about committing herself too soon. But she doesn't love him.

She's always thought it silly to compliment men on their clothes—especially first—but George stands as if he's presenting himself. He wears the same navy blazer that she's seen every Saturday night since they've been dating, a white shirt, a muted red tie, and gray pants. "You look nice," she hears herself say. If he doesn't quickly mention *her* appearance, she'll refuse to go to the reception with him.

"Your dress is gorgeous," he says. George has an effeminate way of slurring certain words—adjectives, particularly—that amuses her but also, if anyone hears, embarrasses her. It's the only thing she's been able to find wrong with him that he can help. "I don't know about that fancy hat," he says.

"You don't know about the *hat?*" she cries. She turns on her heel and races to the foyer mirror. "The hat's perfect. The hat *makes* the dress." She snatches it off her head.

"See how plain?" she asks at the same time he says, "Much better."

Here she is, caught again. Katherine thought that the hat looked great. George doesn't like it. What does *she* think? It would be so easy if she knew, but some basic defect in her emotional makeup keeps her from being able to decide anything. Is she happy; is she sad? Does she like her work; does she hate it? Does she love her sisters? Did she love her mother? Of course, she loves them all, but does she *love* them? Is her father happy having her home? A college graduate ought to know some of these answers. She's been very nervous at work the past ten days. Is it because of Billy's wedding? Does she like George or not? She likes him fine. But what difference does it make whom she *likes?* Liking, as Billy used to say, is basically inconsequential. *Does this hat look good or doesn't it?* Would someone who really knows please tell her?

She takes off the hat. George is behind her. *Without* the hat she looks . . . well . . . nice, like everybody else. The cowl neck and dropped-waist style of the dress make her look both thin and buxom. A miracle. *With* the hat she's on the edge of something. Is it exquisite taste? Or embarrassing flamboyance?

"What's the only thing worse than being talked about?" she suddenly asks George's reflection. The hat is back on her head now, a little cockeyed, but she'll fix it in a minute. "Come on. Take a guess." An interesting thing about talking to someone in a mirror is how you can't keep your eyes off your own reflection. You keep glancing back—George is doing it, too—to see how your face is acting out your thoughts and words. George's eyebrows are jumping.

"The answer is *not* being talked about," she says. It was one of her mother's favorite jokes. "I've always hated the whole concept. I don't know why I find it so appealing today."

"Everybody likes to be different once in a while," George says.

"That's not true. Everybody wants to be the same. They want to be *thought* of as different but *be* the same. I had a roommate in college who was a perfect example." She's never mentioned Jennifer to George. George would insist on driving up to Richmond one Sunday to meet Jennifer and Jeff. "Jennifer had this wonderful affair with this French guy she wasn't brave enough to marry," Louise says. Using the word "affair" so glibly sends a small thrill through her. "So she married her hometown sweetheart."

Suddenly Louise doesn't see how this fits the question of her hat. Except that, although Jennifer wouldn't marry Jacques, she *would* wear this wacky hat to his wedding. She'd wear it to remind him of how special she is. Of how that unknowable exciting part of her has been lost to him forever. Perhaps she is being perverse, but Louise wants Billy to long for her today, to long for that special private her that he alone once knew and that no one, not even he, will ever know again. He could not have predicted the hat, which will make him wonder what else about her held surprise.

"I hope you don't mind," she says sweetly. "But I do like this hat. Katherine thinks it's right. Hats are very stylish right now. I *won't* be the only one wearing one."

If she can accurately predict, she would say that Billy would probably refuse to leave this house with her wearing her hat. But, then, if she were still with Billy, she wouldn't have thought of buying it. She and Billy were going to have a very plain life. It would never have occurred to her to want anything else. A sudden sense of irony fills her. Her sisters have always wanted her to be not-plain. But she's not doing this because of them.

George helps her into her coat, opens the door for her, guides her down the front walk, and puts her into the car, which he's left running so it will be warm. The day began sharply clear—she checked as soon as she woke up—but high gray clouds have been forming since late morning. The car feels toasty, but just as soon as the heater blows away her chill, she feels herself starting to sweat. George swings into the car. She quickly turns off the fan. She takes the hat off her head to let heat escape her body.

George smiles. "I knew you wouldn't wear it."

"I'm wearing it," she says. She puts it back on, though she would rather leave it off until they get to the reception. She decides not to explain about being hot. Besides, now she's cold again. She reaches to restart the fan.

In midair, George grabs her hand. "Anything wrong?" he asks. He could be angry at her sauciness, but he's not. He really hasn't been angry at her in the entire three months they've been dating. Rather, he's gotten angry and then dismissed it. Something clicks in his face, as if a certain part of his brain is reminding him to stay calm. His eyebrows even go limp.

From the beginning she's known—found it hard to believe, but known anyway—that dating her has been the pinnacle experience of his life. It's what he's wanted since they were in the seventh grade, he keeps telling her. But somehow their relationship doesn't deepen. She knows more facts about him than she knew at the beginning, but they haven't shared any secrets. It's as if possessing her is all he wants.

"I guess I'm nervous," she says. It occurs to her that she doesn't want her first fight with George to take place at Billy's wedding.

"If you take off the hat, you'll be less nervous."

"If I take off the hat, I'll be mad at you."

Billy and Lucy are getting married in a small family ceremony at the apartment where they're going to be living. Rumor has it that Lucy wanted Pal to be there, so a church service was out of the question. The reception, which is what Louise "and Guest" were invited to, is being held in the apartment complex's clubhouse.

Louise reads the time, four o'clock, from a Paine Webber sign. She also notes that the stock market, which is where George believes all big money is made, is down ten points. By now, Billy and Lucy are probably married. They may have been agreeing to love, honor, and cherish each other the same instant she snatched the hat off her head. By now, too, the pictures have been snapped. Lucy has even had time to take Pal out to pee. Does it worry Billy, Louise wonders, that the dog is so important? After college George is going to brokers' school. Someday, he says, he wants to be filthy rich. His plan is to borrow ten thousand dollars from a bank—not her father's—and create a fortune.

The clubhouse is a modern building with sharply sloping roofs. George drives under the covered entranceway to let her out. A bright green indoor / outdoor carpet leads up the steps.

"Go on," he says. "I'll catch up with you in a second. I need a cigarette."

She does a double-take. George does not smoke, but she's told him the story about Billy lighting up at her graduation. He grins at her.

"It was a joke," he says. "My favorite girl *hasn't* left me."

"Ha," she says.

At first she'd wanted to go in alone; next she'd hesitated about it; but now she jerks open the door and gets out. In her anger she forgets to check one last time whether or not her hat is on straight. She turns around, but George is driving off. She places her fingertips on opposite sides of the brim. She can't tell whether the hat is straight or not, but she makes a small adjustment anyway. Someone pulls up behind her. Without looking around, she ascends the steps and opens the wooden door. Through more closed doors ahead of her sift piano music and the dull roar of a crowd. She walks bravely toward the noise. She'll kick the dog if it jumps up on her or even if it sniffs where it shouldn't. She promises herself that she'll do at least that.

When she opens the door, she turns her left shoulder slightly forward, bracing herself against Pal's possible onslaught. Her eyes sweep the room. Near the door is the receiving line, although at the moment no one is going through it. Across the room is a buffet table, and against the right wall is a pianist with mounds of white hair. She doesn't see a dog.

A downward grin fills her face. To think that she expected Pal to be at the reception, too. If he *had* been here, she would have kicked him whether he jumped up on her or not. She would have found him and kicked him.

She feels the entire receiving line looking at her and smiles a right-side-up smile. A white dress which must house Lucy stands in the middle of the line. Otherwise, Louise cannot distinguish anyone. A waiter with a tray of champagne walks up to her. She wants to ask him to stand here while she drinks her fill, but she can't because everyone in the line would see her. She takes a glass. She takes a sip. She takes a step. She stumbles and spills part of the champagne on the floor. Someone will have to bring a towel so that no one will slip and fall.

"I'll get that," a voice at her ear says. It's Billy, of course. He quickly kneels at her feet, swabbing the spilled champagne with his handkerchief, and, just as quickly, rises. No, it's George. George has a dark mustache. Billy's—if he still has his—is blond. She cranes her neck over her shoulder toward the line. Finally she finds the eyes that she's been looking for ever since she arrived. She smiles, seeing only Billy. He has on a tuxedo, which she never thought she'd see on him. But he won't be wearing a ring. She often used to ask him how all the other girls would know he was married if he didn't wear one. He'd answered that it would just be obvious.

Now that she has her champagne, it is only good manners for her to step up and greet all the happy people. She starts forward and then remembers George, and then she forgets George. She changes her direction away from Mr. and Mrs. Payne and heads toward the middle of the line. Billy is the closest friend she's ever had. Every rule of justice says that she may speak to him before she speaks to anyone else.

Although she doesn't have on the wedding dress, she still

feels like a queen approaching him. She knows Billy hasn't forgotten how soft her skin is and how sweet she smells. Mother always said that Louise never lost her baby scent. Her shoulders are erect, showing off to him the prettiest little figure—his words—that he's ever seen. Lucy's childlikeness includes her body, too, Louise first noticed at the ice-cream store.

Like an entourage, moments from her and Billy's past together seem to accompany her: when they put the lining in her jewelry box, when she let him pin the wings pin just above her breast, when they took walks to get away from her family, when they made love in his car, and on and on. She feels drawn to give some sort of sign to the images that float behind her, so she nods her head—a large generous nod. But what is in her mind are not visions of the past but visions of the future they were going to share. Most of all, she thinks of her and Billy and a baby.

She stands before him now, not knowing how to begin. His face is exuberant. He's looking at her with such simple kindness that she thinks she might start weeping and never say anything at all.

A very loud word suddenly sounds in the air between them. Two large hands take her upper arms from behind. And then a small childlike hand hooks inside Billy's elbow. The word is "Congratulations." George Morales said it.

She is not able to speak. She looks from one to the other of the three people standing with her, but she can no longer find the eyes she knows.

A little voice says, "I like your hat." The person talking, Louise realizes, is Mrs. Billy Jones and happy about it.

She'd forgotten about her hat, but quickly she finds Billy's eyes for his opinion. She can see him reassessing, yielding to Lucy's view. It's a great hat, she knows. He's a man with no taste. All at once she grabs his hand and pulls it up in the midst of all four of them. "Show us your rings," she says.

Lucy places her left hand in the air beside Billy's. They wear matching rings, four narrow ropes of gold melded together. As she focuses on them, Louise's throat becomes a stake inside her body. She tries to compliment the rings. The word that comes out is "Pretty." It's too dangerous for Billy to wear a ring. Doesn't Lucy know? She takes her hand from underneath Billy's, but he doesn't let it drop. Instead, he and Lucy keep looking at their hands. They remain absorbed until new people coming down the line force her and George onward.

"Goodbye," Lucy calls. "Good luck."

CHAPTER

17

Clomping up the metal steps to their garage apartment is Jude's babysitter, Darrow Whitfield, a tall, big-boned, good-looking, heavy-stepping redhead, a junior Russian-studies major who dates a local black attorney who handles important real estate deals in Chapel Hill. Since Greensboro is still so much a part of her perspective, Jude thinks there's a lot of incongruity in all these facts. Someone who babysits also dates seriously. Someone who babysits for her dates someone whom Jude could feasibly be dating. A twenty-year-old white girl dates a thirty-year-old black man, and it's socially acceptable for both of them. This just doesn't go on in Greensboro. But it goes on here, and nobody thinks a thing about it.

Darrow lets herself in, calling, "Am I early?" and then starts looking for Katie, who always hides under the breakfast table whenever anyone's coming. Charles is once more dragging all the cushions off the sofa and chairs, after which he will demand that Mommie put them back right. Jude has done this ten times since four-thirty. It's now five o'clock and she hasn't had a chance to get dressed yet.

"You're early, but thank God," she says, coming around the counter where she and the kids eat. Darrow's cheeks are bright with health. She's someone whom in Greensboro Jude would never have thought attractive—so different-looking from the standard beauty there—but here in Chapel Hill, with her peasant garb, no makeup, and hair that may never have been combed, Darrow is exotic.

"Would you mind fixing supper?" Jude asks. "I bought

Stouffer's spaghetti, and salad stuff is in the fridge." Darrow has found Katie and is wholeheartedly on her knees under the table with her.

Jude met her babysitter in line at the post office the first week she was here, and Darrow has been helping her out ever since. Part of Darrow's agreement with her parents since she was fourteen years old is that they will pay for everything but her clothes, which she must earn the money for. What her parents didn't anticipate, she'd told Jude that day in line, was that she just wouldn't care about what she had on. But since she has to wear something, she felt lucky that she'd just met someone who could give her occasional work.

Jude goes into her bedroom and brings out her outfit for tonight, so that she can dress and talk at the same time. She has a regular teaching job now and she's made a few friends, including her widowed landlady and a young male writer who lives in the basement of the big house, but she tries not to miss any opportunity to have a conversation with an adult. She sits down to put on a pair of wild paisley stockings while Darrow reaches for a pot.

"I'm going to the People Sampler," she says.

"I did that last month. You'll love it," Darrow says from under the table. "I met an artist, and I was going to go see his paintings, but I knew what would happen if I did. Hal's not so relaxed about that kind of thing."

A People Sampler, invented by a woman in Huntington Beach, California, is a three-hour party with a number of ground rules. All ages of adults go. You select a new someone to talk to every twenty minutes, male or female. There are suggested topics of conversation like nuclear war and abortion and children's rights— things that help you know right away whether or not you can deal with the new someone. By the time the party's over, you've met approximately nine people, some of whom you're bound to like.

"Should I try to meet men first or women?" Jude asks.

"I'd try not to plan it one way or the other," Darrow says. She stands up, Katie in her arms. They're making faces at each other. "I wouldn't always try to be the picker either," she continues. "Let someone pick you."

Jude pops her head through her black turtleneck tunic. She bends over and brushes her hair vigorously from her nape. "I was thinking about trying to make some women friends the first couple of hours and then pick me out a nice man at the end. But maybe all the good ones will be paired up by then," she muses.

"I think you're missing the point," Darrow says. "You've got to let it be spontaneous for it to work. Remember, the whole *party's* overstructured. You can't add more structure or you won't have fun."

She knows what Darrow means, but at the same time she wants her twenty-dollar admission fee to yield a return. Twenty dollars means something to her. But maybe tonight she should pretend that it doesn't.

She lives only half a mile from the Carolina Inn, where the People Sampler is being held, so she'll walk. That way she won't have the encumbrance of a car if someone wants to take her out afterward. She's still planning. Maybe she *should* have the trouble of a car. Maybe it would be "not cool" not to have a car, as if she'd anticipated leaving the party with someone. And if no one asks, she will feel awfully dreary walking back.

"Should I take my car?" she asks, although she's beginning to feel embarrassed about asking a twenty-year-old how to run her love life. However, the twenty-year-old seems to know what to do.

"Of *course*," Darrow says.

Jude flinches.

"You're in the old days," Darrow says.

"It's not the old days." How can someone who's twenty say that to someone who's only twenty-eight? "It's just different in Greensboro. There's more of a pattern. There are expectations. Like you're dancing." Darrow gives her a blank look. "Formally. A minuet. No, not that bad. A waltz."

Darrow seems not to know about the old way of relating to a man: passive aggression. But she does seem to have what she wants. Reaching the point that you can take or leave men must change everything.

She goes to each of her children and kisses them. Already they love Darrow, so it's no problem to leave. But even if they didn't love her, Jude's departure wouldn't be so wrenching. Something has happened between her and her kids. She's not mad at them all the time anymore. Of course, she's happier and that's part of the reason, but something in them seems suddenly appreciative of her. Don't ask how a two- and a three-year-old can appreciate anything, but maybe they have some extra sense that Mommie needs tender loving care right now.

"Bye, my little darlings," she says in an adult voice that they won't hear. She waves at Darrow, slips out the door, and walks down one side of the steps so they won't bounce back and make noise. She carries her car keys but still has not decided whether she'll walk. She likes to walk. What's wrong with walking? It makes her look as if she's interested in her health. The parking lot at the Carolina Inn is always full, anyway. And besides, the kind of man she wants to attract is not twenty. *Her* kind of man probably *responds* to passive aggression, since it's the only thing he knows.

She swings out the gravel driveway onto Franklin Street. The autumn sky is a faded blue with a tiny white sun hanging like a leaf. The trees are half bare of their foliage. When she walks, Jude likes to really walk, taking big steps, swinging her arms, moving to a beat inside her head. It's a great feeling to walk: like a kind of gentle sex.

Ahead of her on the sidewalk is a guy walking a bicycle. He has short hair, but she can tell by his age and his clothes—a fatigue jacket and blue jeans—that he's one of the sixties hippies who never left here. Some of the hippies have become entrepreneurs, as chefs or real estate men or even lawyers. Some, like this man, have made a fad into a real life.

"Hi," she says without slowing. She could easily have a conversation with him—it's that relaxed in Chapel Hill—but she doesn't have time.

"Pretty lady," he says softly after she has passed.

She could go with him. No question that he'd have an interesting story. But he probably doesn't have a place. Also, she's paid her twenty dollars.

She never imagined that coming to a new place could make her feel so free. But that's how she's felt since she moved to Chapel Hill. For weeks after they arrived, she'd wake up in the morning, and as she realized where she was, she would actually have the sense of restraints falling away from her. Then one day she woke up and felt nothing fall away at all. Except for a few lingering attitudes, she was totally free: Greensboro—her past— was gone.

She's tried to feel skeptical about this feeling of freedom. She's tried to think that as soon as she developed a history here the same old smothering feeling would recur. But she's decided that she may never have a history. She and her two kids will just live their lives. She'll exist one day at a time instead of living half the time in the past and half the time in the future— especially the elusive future—the way she used to do. Already she has to force herself to think about her family. If she hadn't written it down for months ahead on her calendar, she might forget to call them. Even Cap never crosses her mind except once a month when she meets him on I-85 with the kids.

She doesn't completely know Chapel Hill yet. But people she has met have told her that, unlike other places, you can be yourself here. You can do what you want, be friends with the people you find attractive, and go to bed with whomever appeals to you, no matter how offbeat they are. But she wonders if she could find the same freedom anywhere she moved. Maybe becoming faceless is all that happens to people who change towns. She's been told that men in Chapel Hill are seriously looking for someone to fall in love with. But maybe in every new place men want to fall in love. Women certainly do: 7.3 million more of them available than men, according to a report she read in last Sunday's newspaper. The men, the report commented, are getting awfully spoiled. Fuck the men, she thinks. And then— she can't help herself—she laughs aloud. When she lived in Greensboro, that statistic would have made her take a drink.

When she laughed, she was passing Hector's, a hot-dog place where Chapel Hill teenagers hang out. They are not her favorite crowd. If she walks home alone tonight, she'll have to take the other side of the street. Several of the kids step out of the group to leer at her. One boy, who can't be more than fourteen, aims both his fists in her direction. A girl whose hair is wildly teased imitates in a screeching voice Jude's laugh. As a group, they look as if they could suddenly pull her into their midst and make her disappear. Although hands reach out at her, she doesn't slow her pace. She keeps her eyes frozen on the young boy, her neck swiveling as she passes. The fists come closer but she doesn't draw back.

"Creeps," she says loudly, snapping her head forward to cross the street. Without her eyes protecting her, she feels more vulnerable. They could probably kill her. But she's called their bluff.

Something flies past her shoulder and lands ahead of her on the asphalt. It's a pencil. She stoops, picks it up, and puts it behind her ear. It's laughable that they've thrown a pencil, tool of learning, at her. But she won't laugh at them. She hadn't laughed at them to begin with. Narcissistic morons.

A little breathless, she steps up on the side of the curb where the old brick post office is. It's as if she's swum ashore. But then that's how she feels about Chapel Hill in general. The long sidewalk, where all the old-time stores still do a thriving business, stretches ahead of her. It's filled with people, mostly singles but here and there a couple with a stroller or a toddler on a leash. The Carolina football team plays at Maryland tomorrow, so the town is free of the university's gluttonous alumni. Students, faculty, residents each think they have first claim on this town, but everyone agrees that alumni have the last claim of all.

The sun drops even with the store awnings, simultaneously blinding her and warming her. This was the first town she ever visited that thinks pedestrians are more important than drivers. All you have to do is step into the street at a designated crosswalk and all traffic halts. When she was in the seventh grade and her class came to see the Christmas show at Morehead Planetarium, she crossed the street three times in a row before the teacher stopped her.

She decides to stop traffic now. She crosses, looking neither to her right nor to her left. She's grown up now, so other grownups will not be so indulgent if she immediately crosses again, so she waits. The power of the individual! She loves it. She steps into the street again. *They* must watch out for *her.* She's not required to give any signal at all.

Where Franklin Street intersects Columbia, there's a Texaco service station called the Happy Store, where students buy beer and snacks. She has an idea. Since she's going to be meeting at least nine people, she's going to buy nine favors. She'll give each person she meets a treat.

Inside, she decides on Reese's peanut-butter cups. The clerk, a slick-haired townie in a Texaco uniform, starts to bag them, but she asks if she may put them inside her purse instead.

"I'm having a chocolate attack," she explains.

"Not unusual," the clerk says. He works quickly, ringing up another sale before she has a chance to get out of the way.

It's a good idea. It will make people remember her. She was the girl . . . woman . . . who gave out the candy. If she meets someone she thinks won't appreciate the gift, she'll just withhold it. No, she won't differentiate. She'll let her personality speak for itself. She's a person who likes to give tokens. Are you a person who likes to receive them?

The time is five o'clock. The place is the Carolina Inn in Chapel Hill, North Carolina. The occasion is a People Sampler, a party which brings lonely people together. Jude is a lonely people, plural because she's lonely more than the way one person is lonely. Her loneliness is manifold, like the loneliness in a rest home.

Carefully printed signs direct her through the simple chandelier-hung lobby, down a hall, and into a large cypress-paneled room. The room is oblong, with a narrow stage at one end. Chairs are arranged in groups of five. On a table are scores of name tags. Jude finds hers and puts it on. She also sees a stack of something labeled "phone slips," which she quickly understands are to be given out to people she likes. She fills out five. For a minute she hesitates. Then she writes "chocolate" on the back of each slip. Behind her she feels a sudden momentum. Unlike a normal cocktail party, everyone is arriving at once.

Two people appear to be in charge, a man who's directing those with name tags toward the groups of chairs—five strangers per group—and a woman wearing an extravagant blue-sequined dress and a strong, caring smile. The man—Joe Richardson, according to his name tag—takes Jude's elbow and the elbow of a woman just a couple of feet away and sends them toward the middle of the room. The woman is blond with black eyes. She has on black pants and a white blouse with an intricate collar that extends to her shoulders.

"Is this for real?" the woman says with a sideways look that does not engage Jude's eyes. She has on perfume. Her nails are fixed. She has a practiced way of walking, her ass stuck out like a dancer's.

"Who knows?" Jude says companionably. "Let's give it a chance." She glances behind and sees that Joe is sending three more people in their direction, another woman and two men. The new woman, who looks about fifty, is underdressed compared to the rest of the crowd, in a plaid flannel shirt and jeans. Jude's eyes trail down to the woman's shoes, well-worn brogans laced with rawhide. She doesn't seem to fit a People Sampler, but she's just the type of woman Jude was hoping to meet.

The two men, dressed informally, are both reasonably attractive. One is about six feet tall with such blond eyebrows and eyelashes that his face looks bare. The other is stocky and dark-featured and has on rimless glasses. They're talking animatedly as they approach—the subject is Carolina's poor football record—and they continue the conversation until they're seated.

The bare-faced-looking man stands back up, names himself, and shakes hands with all three women. His name is Ted Grasty. The stocky man doesn't stand but holds up one finger. He smiles when he says his name, Jack Nicholson, adding, "Not the real Jack Nicholson." The blonde is named Saralyn, and the farmer is named Maud. Jude offers her own name. She wonders who in the group will be interested in whom. For her, it's Maud. The two men will probably like Saralyn. Jack may attract Maud, since he seems less self-absorbed than Ted. Saralyn will like Ted.

Just as it becomes clear that no one in their group knows what to say next, the lady in the blue-sequined dress climbs the stage to the microphone. "Good evening," she says in a hearty voice. She's a top-heavy woman with a grand way of looking around her. "My name is Dixie Armfield." The crowd slowly hushes. "I'm happy that so many of you have so much to talk about so soon," she says, smiling her strong smile again. "We want to proceed with our evening's schedule. I thinks it's appropriate that the early birds get to sit together and the stragglers"—she glances toward the registration table—"get to do the same. You're already naturally selecting yourselves, don't you see? One of the things that drove me craziest about my, I think, second husband was his punctuality. I like to be *late* for church," she suddenly purrs. "Who else does?" No one raises a hand, still shy in this forced situation. Give it a chance, Jude tells herself again. She surreptitiously surveys the four members of her group, *none* of whom seems interesting anymore. Saralyn has a glazed expression on her face, almost as if she's about to go to sleep. Jude wonders whether she had some drinks before she came, since nothing is offered to eat or drink until the party's over. Ted and Jack appeared interested in what Dixie was saying only when she began to purr. Only Maud seems genuinely attentive.

"The first thing Joe and I want you to do tonight," Dixie continues, "is find something within your group that you all have in common. You'll have to talk about yourselves to do this. You'll have to ask questions, explore, discover, and, most of all, *reveal*. I know it's hard to expose your true self to strangers. Some of you may even be wondering right this moment why you're here." Dixie seems to look directly at their particular group. "Some of you may feel so shy that you're about to get up and walk out." Dixie looks quickly at a grouping to her left where someone is standing up. *"Don't,"* she says loudly. The young man quickly sits back down, waving his hands over his head that he had no intention of leaving. Scattered laughter comes from the crowd. "It's *normal* to feel uneasy," Dixie says. "Everyone *here* feels uneasy. You're not alone. That's what the purpose of the People Sampler is: to show you that you're not alone."

At the doorway Joe is still organizing groups of five and sending them to the last few empty chair groupings. Almost all the chairs are filled. Jude wonders if some crowds are better than others. What was the crowd like when Darrow came? It had an artist. Does this crowd have an artist? She makes quick guesses about the people in her circle. Saralyn is a court stenographer. Maud raises Arabian horses. Ted owns a small textile company. Jack is an assistant professor of psychology. Would anyone guess that Jude in her crazy paisley stockings and tunic dress is a teacher? Maybe people are thinking *she's* the artist.

Dixie repeats the instructions and steps away from the microphone. Flashes from her sequined dress keep reaching out. It's hard to stop looking at it.

"Let's start with our names again and what we do," Ted says in a faintly resigned voice. Jude is sitting across the circle from him. He looks briefly over her head as if he's spotted someone more interesting in another circle. "Someone else go first," he says.

"*You* go first, Ted," Maud says. She has a friendly but penetrating look on her face. Jude smiles involuntarily. She feels everyone in the group but Ted do the same thing.

But Ted's a good sport. He smiles, too, that Maud has so unmistakably kidded him for proclaiming himself the group's leader. "Okay," he says. "I'm a research chemist for CIBA–GEIGY. I've done a lot of work on Binaca toothpaste and Binaca breath spray. I've lived in Chapel—"

"I've seen Binaca toothpaste in the drugstore," Saralyn interrupts. She has a high, sweet voice with a slight nasal twang. "But I've never bought any. I think you need to improve the packaging. It's so dull. And change that horrid name." Saralyn pulls nervously at the collar of her blouse but doesn't take her eyes off Ted.

For a moment Ted is silent. "I have nothing to do with marketing," he says quietly.

"I know just where you should go," Saralyn says excitedly. "I'm in advertising. I've just gotten in, so I'm on the ground floor. Girl Friday, which includes getting everyone's coffee." She shoots an apologetic glance in Maud and Jude's direction. "But these guys I'm working for—Mayo and Teller—are tops. They could take your toothpaste and make it famous." Saralyn looks around the circle. "Do any of you use Binaca?" she asks. "Or is anyone else involved in advertising?" It's as if she thinks their group is in a race with the other groups, Jude thinks. *Dixie, our group wishes to announce that we have in common Binaca toothpaste.* Saralyn grins. "I forgot to say my name. I'm Saralyn Reynolds Dickstein. I used to be married to a Jewish guy." She lowers her eyes shyly. "But we didn't break up because of religion." She gives a little giggle. In a soft tone, quite unlike her earlier voice, she says, "I guess I'm doing what Dixie said to do: reveal yourself. Somebody tell me if I'm telling too much."

Maud has an amused but kindly look on her face. "You're not telling too much. Ted might think so, but not me."

"What's *your* business, Maud?" Ted asks sharply. The atmosphere within the group suddenly changes. Ted has an openly hostile expression on his face, but it's directed at everyone within the circle, not just Maud. "And what about you?" he says, looking at Jude with the same hot eyes.

Jude thinks of standing up and announcing to the room that a fight is about to take place. It's unbelievable that it could happen so quickly. She's glad she came, if only to reaffirm to herself how insane people are. Thank God Ted is not a blind date of hers.

But no fight. Maud has a surprised look on her face. "I was teasing you, Ted," she says, in an unintimidated voice. She takes her attention away from him. In advance of speaking of herself her eyes begin to twinkle. "I do two things. I teach kindergarten and I'm a potter." She holds up her hands for everyone to see. They are blunt-nailed and permanently dirty. "Either job would make them look just like this," she says. "Judith?"

"Is that all?" Jude asks in mock alarm. "I want to know more. I already know about me," she adds. She and Maud exchange a glance of tentative mutual admiration. She could learn from Maud Hinshaw, she already knows. "I also teach," Jude tells the group. "I have no experience with Binaca toothpaste or advertising. Maybe Jack Nicholson"—she smiles—"holds the key."

Jack leans forward and presses his palms tightly together. Everyone watches as his knuckles grow whiter and whiter. "Good evening, folks. My name is Jack Nicholson, no kin to the actor, although tonight I am an actor of sorts." Jude glances at Maud but Maud does not notice. "I'm not really here of my own accord. I'm a guest of Dixie's. I came tonight rather than stay at my hotel and read. But since I'm not from Chapel Hill, there's no reason to try to connect with me. I'll be gone tomorrow." He separates his hands.

"I wouldn't say you're acting at all," Saralyn says. "If you were acting, you'd *act* like you meant to be here." Saralyn makes the most astonishing statements with the most innocent face. "Why don't you leave?" she asks plaintively. She must have liked Jack best, Jude thinks. "You didn't even pay, did you?"

Maud interrupts. "Does this group have *anything* in common? Anything at all? We know we're not all Jews. Are we Protestants?"

"Catholic," says Jack. Saralyn looks at him disdainfully.

"Born in North Carolina?" asks Maud.

"Texas," Ted says.

"Vermont," Jack says.

"Republicans? Democrats?"

"Independent," says Saralyn proudly. But then her face turns in on itself as she tries again to think of something they might all share. Jude is watching her when the idea hits. "I've got it. Not that we can be proud. Or that it's even something you *want* to have in common. Everybody's divorced." Her face has a luminous quality. "Aren't you, Jack?"

He nods, and no one else objects to their own same status.

"Can't we think of anything more positive?" Jude asks.

"I don't think so," Ted mutters. He sits forward on the edge of his chair and looks at the empty stage. Dixie is at the registration table talking to Joe.

"What do you do, Jack?" Maud asks.

Jack puts his hands together. "Actually, nothing," he says. "Well, actually, I manage money. Except that it's mostly already managed. I mean, I'm not a professional investor. I just *pick* the professional investors."

"Oh?" Saralyn says. She seems confused as to what he means, but her anger at him for not being a true participant seems to be gone. They begin talking. Ted is still gazing far out of the group.

Jude leans in front of Saralyn to whisper to Maud. "Is it always like this?"

"Don't ask me," Maud says, her shoulders quivering in silent laughter.

Without stopping her conversation, Saralyn stands up and with a firm hand guides Jude into changing chairs. Jack is talking to her in low private explanatory tones.

"I don't tolerate bullshit too well," Maud says. "But then, on the other hand, I can't stand to see people's feelings get hurt. Everybody bullshits. What I hate is when someone is pompous about it."

A sparkle of sequins catches Jude's eyes. Dixie is climbing the steps to the stage, her round ass prominent, to send them on to their next encounter. Does every man here really want Dixie? Jude sneaks a look at Ted, who begins to applaud. Others around the room begin applauding with him. Saralyn is clapping and so is Dixie's friend Jack. Dixie smiles around the room. "So you're all enjoying yourselves?" she whispers throatily into the microphone. The applause quickens.

"Do you have a phone slip?" Jude asks Maud.

"I didn't pick any up," Maud says. "But give me one of yours. If I don't get up with you again tonight, I'll give you a ring sometime this weekend. Also, if I lose it, I'm in the phone book."

"I'm *not*," Jude says. "I just moved here." She reaches under her chair and unzips her purse. She pulls out a phone slip, hesitates, and then pulls out a pack of Reese's peanut-butter cups. She hands both items to Maud. Maud's eyebrows rise questioningly. Mustering her courage, Jude says, "You're neat." Is this all right to say in Chapel Hill? Does she need to explain that she's not a lesbian? Probably not to Maud.

The squarish, kindly face lights up. "You're a woman after my own heart," Maud says. "Chocolate and ice cream. They're my downfall." She leans back in her chair to show her healthy girth.

"We're going to be great friends," Jude says just as the applause dies out.

In a way Jude would like for her and Maud to get up and leave arm in arm, chatting, giggling like girls, their faces bright and smiling. Wouldn't it be a literal endorsement of how well a People Sampler works? But she doesn't want to appear rude, even though, in her view, the People Sampler is truly unsuccessful because the men are so disappointing. Is everyone here a loser? Not her. Not Maud. But where is a *man* who isn't? And will *she* happen upon him? Or will Saralyn?

Dixie is explaining how the rest of the evening will go. When she gives a signal, everyone is to begin milling around until he or she sees someone interesting. You stop that person and talk to him for ten or fifteen minutes. The subject of the first conversation is to be how difficult it is to initiate a conversation with a stranger. The person who picks is to explain to whomever he picks why he picked him or her and why he is psychologically able to pick. Darrow told Jude not to do all the picking, but it seems much wiser to pick someone who's attractive to her rather than to be picked by someone unattractive.

Dixie asks everyone to stand up. The crowd seems to give out one large, barely suppressed groan. It rises, but reticently, not as the earlier applause would have led one to expect. Jude quickly looks around. No one seems eager; everyone seems uneasy. A better way for grownups to engage must exist. But what?

People begin walking. Jude sees a face that's shy, a face that's scornful, a face that's above all this, a face that's open to anybody, a face that's looking at no one, a face that's nervous. She picks the face that's nervous because—although she thinks she has a confident smile on her face—she's nervous, too.

"Hi!" she says with enthusiasm.

A look of relief crosses the face. It's a man's face, not a good-looking man, but who wants a good-looking man?

"I'm Judith Cramer," she says. "And I don't want to talk about why I picked you, except that you looked as nervous as I feel. Plus, this circling is terrible. I feel like a piranha, or the leg that a piranha's after."

"I'm Marty Diamond," the man says. "I was just about to pick you when you picked me." Marty Diamond is a short thick man with closely trimmed hair. He has on part of a suit—the vest and pants—but has left his coat somewhere. His best feature is a blunt jawline which—now that his nervousness is gone—looks almost forbidding. He's wearing his Phi Beta Kappa key.

Jude waits for him to say something else, but he's looking at some point in space. Most of the crowd is still circling. Dixie announces that she will have to begin a countdown if people don't go ahead and make up their minds. "You don't have to marry this person," she announces, which is the first thing she's said that's made Jude smile.

"I'm new to Chapel Hill," she says.

"Are you?"

"From Greensboro," she says, nodding.

"I have some friends in Greensboro," Marty says. He reaches up and absently strokes his key. Evidently he is someone who will have to be drawn out.

"I see that you're very smart," she says.

"Oh." He looks at his Phi Beta Kappa key, turns it over, lets it resume dangling outside his vest pocket.

The noise level of the room suddenly takes a dramatic leap. Pairs of people stand all around, some smiling politely, but some in lively conversation, too. Jude sends a prayer in Dixie's direction. If it gets any worse than this, she is going to walk out.

"What do you do?" she asks.

In their last thirteen minutes together she finds out that Marty

319|

is a general surgeon and that today he cut off a leg, removed a ruptured appendix, and operated on someone's large intestine. Surgery had always seemed so glamorous to her until this man explained what he actually had to do. Like the members of her first group, he was also divorced. His wife and two children still lived in Ohio. He'd moved here a year ago. He said he couldn't stand watching his wife poison his daughters' minds against him.

"Don't you think it would have been better to stay?" she asks. It's the only personal comment she's made.

"You don't know that woman," Marty says, his voice lowering to a growl. "She's a monster. A Scylla or a Charybdis. Whichever one has the snakes for hair."

"Medusa," Jude whispered, but he didn't hear.

His diatribe was cut mercifully short by Dixie's announcement that it was time to meet someone new.

"Nice to have talked with you," Jude says.

For the first time Marty seems to come awake. His anger toward his former wife seems to melt away. "I didn't find out anything about you," he says. His face has become a different shape, the jaw softer, the tight lines around his eyes relaxed into a sort of wistfulness.

"We didn't have enough time," she says generously.

"Stay with me for the next session," he says. "No one will know."

"That's not fair," she says.

"I insist."

She does not want to be unkind, but the desire to preserve herself, which she felt for the first time following her evening with Paul Hinton, is rising within her. Marty cups her elbow in his palm, which is hot and slick. "No," she says firmly, drawing her arm away from him and up under her breast. He looks stung, and out of kindness, she puts a smile back on her face.

"Let me take you home," he says.

"I already have plans." He is hounding her. He will not let her escape. And so she turns her shoulder toward him and suddenly slips through the multitude of singles who have begun milling about again. She only stops when she can no longer see him.

She finds a woman with a tired face and tilts her head to see if she is willing to talk to another woman, but there is a deft shake of the head. Jude moves on. She sees Maud but decides at this point not to risk another rejection.

She begins to mill about, too, her eyes bright and alert but not focusing on anyone. She feels as panicky as a young animal.

Someone stops in front of her. She nearly bolts. The person says hello. The person says that his name is Mickey Mickleberry. The amusing alliteration of the name is what manages to settle her down. She looks at him. He has the first regular face that she's seen tonight. A light shines in Mickey Mickleberry's eyes.

"You look a little shaken," he says, leaning forward to peer into her face. "Are you all right?"

She takes a deep breath, her chest shuddering slightly. Her heartbeat begins to slow.

"Are you an artist?" he asks. "You look like one. But that's no guarantee. I take pictures, but I feed myself by waiting tables at the Wild Flower Kitchen. Have you been there? Do you like the food? Would you please say something?"

"I'm a teacher," she says. "I have two little children. I just moved here. I don't know anybody."

"On occasion you can meet people at these People Samplers," Mickey Mickleberry says. "But you have to be a hardy soul." He wrinkles his nose. He is as slender as a shoelace and slightly stooped. She can easily picture him beneath the curtain of an old-fashioned camera. "This is not the best group I've seen at one of these things," Mickey says. "But who can tell about groups? If you want to meet people, you should come for an early supper where I work. You can always meet people there. And it's a smart crowd." Jude thinks about the Phi Beta Kappa key holder. "But laid-back," Mickey continues. "Of course, there are assholes everywhere. Maybe just a lesser percentage out-to-eat in Chapel Hill."

She likes Mickey Mickleberry and he likes her, and when it's nearly time to change partners again, he suggests that they leave. Her immediate inner response is no, not because she doesn't like Mickey but because—even after all this proof—she still has

321|

hope for the unknown. The next person might be the right person. If she leaves, she risks consciously turning her back on the man who might love her and cherish her for the rest of her life. The evening has hardly begun. She has time to meet six or seven more people. She paid. She bought peanut-butter cups to give to people she liked. She'd expected to like them all.

Mickey Mickleberry may be her age, but, as usual, he's young. His hair is longish, untended, and he's wearing a warmup suit, not a sissy velour one but one that he obviously uses. He could be bisexual or even gay, although why she considers this she doesn't know. Maybe it's because, unlike all the straight men she knows, he's so nice. But there's no point in leaving with him, even if he's the most avidly heterosexual man here. Someone who hasn't been married and has no children is just not worth the investment of her time. That's why each generation of people, with the same kind of experiences, basically reorganizes itself within its own pool. Mickey, who she would bet her life has no kids, belongs to a different club.

"I'd like to meet your children," Mickey says. "It's early. Let's go get them and take them for some ice cream. This is not my scene tonight. How about it?"

"I ought to introduce you to my babysitter," Jude says.

Mickey gives her a funny look. He has a direct way of looking at her in which his eyes come right up to her face, take a dive and swim underneath whatever current mask she's wearing, and then retake her on, bare eyeball to bare eyeball. "How old do you think I am?" he asks.

"Thirty?"

"What do you think my interests are? Do you believe you have me completely pegged?"

Dixie announces that it's time to change conversation partners again, but Mickey keeps asking questions. "Why do you think I would like your babysitter instead of you? Why do women think that men are all alike? We're certainly not allowed to think *you're* all alike." Mickey puts his hand in the center of her back and begins guiding her toward the door. "You assume that I'm not interested in your children. Well, I am. We're going to go meet them. It will certainly be more interesting than hanging around here. Maybe I *won't* like your children. But then maybe you won't like mine either."

She gives him a chastened look.

"I don't have any kids, but I love kids," he says without looking at her. "Just don't make so goddamn many assumptions."

Jude is giggling almost uncontrollably as they pass the stage. She glances up at Dixie. It must be the angle, but the light bouncing off Dixie's sequins almost blinds her. Part of the unwritten rules of a People Sampler must be that the cream of the crop can't leave at seven o'clock.

"Where do you live?" Mickey asks.

"On Franklin Street, past Hector's."

"Did you walk or drive?"

"I walked."

"Then let's walk. Do you have a car that we can go get ice cream in? And then will you drop me off here so I can pick up my car?"

"All the answers are yes," she says. She likes the way that sentence sounds. She likes how it implies so much about her and her view of the world. It *is* her view of the world.

Mickey hears more than most men hear, she thinks, because he heard what she said and is smiling into her eyes with great affirmation. He puts his arm around her neck and holds her tightly as they walk. He has a long stride like hers. He smells of fresh soap. She tries to look up at him but because of the angle she cannot see his face. What does he look like? She's forgotten. But in a moment or two she will have a chance to find out again, and then she will begin to memorize him. It doesn't matter what he looks like. All that matters is that for some reason they have connected. They like each other. They may like each other forever.

"Do you know how sexy you are?" Mickey whispers into her ear.

She smiles. "Not as sexy as you." Maybe she *can* go to bed with someone immediately and feel passion. Maybe her problem has been one not of situation but of person. Paul Hinton was simply a son of a bitch. Mickey Mickleberry is someone she could take her clothes off in front of ten minutes from now and not feel one bit embarrassed.

They have reached the hotel lobby when she opens a package of her Reese's peanut-butter cups and hands him one.

"I can't believe this," he says in an exaggerated voice. "How did you know? This is my favorite kind of candy. I would fall on a hand grenade for one of these." In some larger sort of way he means everything he says. She can tell.

CHAPTER

18

"I bought it last week," Jude says. "With my inheritance."

Weezie and Katherine are outside her apartment circling Jude's cute new station wagon, which has replaced the rattletrap she's owned for years. A floodlight from the top of the garage brightens their path.

"I'd been holding on to that money," Jude adds. "Waiting for something to come along that would be worth spending it on. Like a trip somewhere. But then I started thinking that I'm *on* my trip. Besides, anything glorious for me is going to have to involve two people, and if there are two people, *I* won't be paying." She laughs at her joke. Her eyes have a sort of unspecified warmth to them, a contentedness, Katherine thinks. She and Weezie laugh, too, at what, these days, seems an obsolete idea of moneyed men. Of moneyed men willing to spend their money on women. Do they still exist?

It is a cold moonless night in Chapel Hill, the Sunday after Christmas. Jude's kids are at the top of the stairs. Katie is jumping up and down on the metal landing, making it make loud popping noises. Charles is in the arms of the babysitter, a tall unkempt redhead whom Katherine and Louise met when they arrived. The three sisters are having dinner together, since they'd had no time alone during the holidays. It was Katherine's idea after she'd finally forgiven Jude for leaving so early on Christmas Day. Only Katherine and Louise had gone to Mother's grave; Jude had been in a hurry to get back "home." At the grave Katherine told a story about the night Mother played the piano— the same song, "Everything I Have Is Yours," over and over—

until dawn. Without Jude there to listen, though, the story had no power.

Jude continues, "Of course, this boyfriend of mine doesn't make much money. So I probably won't be going anywhere. But where I do go, I'll be going in style. At least people won't look at me and my two kids anymore and feel sorry for us. No one objects if I drive, do they?"

"Not me," they both say.

New boyfriend. Not much money. These are things that Jude mentioned to Katherine over Christmas, but with no elaboration. Katherine wants to find out if this new relationship is serious. The only other information she has about it is from Louise: Jude borrowed Daddy's Argus to show the new guy. So he must like photography.

Jude's car has bucket seats up front, so they can't all sit together. Katherine opens the back door, leaving the front seat to Louise. If Jude had asked her about buying a new car, she would have suggested hanging on to the old one until it fell apart. Jude doesn't know when she might really need Mother's money. The Naugahyde smell rushes out, making her feel slightly ill, though her morning sickness has long been over. Jude's old car smelled like baby pee and spilled coffee and cantaloupes. It reminded Katherine of Jude. But this new car reminds her of Jude, too.

After the flurry of waving goodbye to the kids and their enthusiastic babysitter, everyone grows quiet. It's the time of year for reflection, Katherine realizes, but somehow the usual urgency that they all feel when they're together is missing. Now that Jude has moved, the number of times they are in each other's company has declined precipitously. Perhaps their individual calmness could be interpreted as some new sign of maturity, but Katherine senses that there's a lack of interest on everyone's part. Jude's and Louise's new lives, perhaps even her own secret life, seem not quite to preoccupy them, but have kept them from giving each other serious attention. Or perhaps this subdued atmosphere among them only has to do with its being Sunday, the least festive of the weekend nights. It was the only evening Jude didn't have plans.

Louise turns halfway around in the front seat. "Are we going to tell Mother stories tonight?" she asks in a cheerful voice. She is plumper since she began working at the ice-cream store, which in some inexplicable way makes her seem more of an individual. On the trip to Chapel Hill she'd been the most talkative Katherine can remember—a kind of chattering, though, instead of serious conversation. It seems that after eight months she has finally heard from Jennifer, and she and George Morales are going to Richmond next weekend to visit Jennifer and Jeff. At least Katherine thinks that's the story. Whenever she's traveled lately, she becomes so introspective that she hardly pays attention to anyone she's with. Fortunately, Louise never notices such lapses.

"Let's talk about us instead," Katherine says, speaking distinctly so they can hear her from the back. She notices how deftly Jude handles her new car. "Since we haven't been around each other—just the three of us—in so long, I'd like to find out what everybody's been thinking about. What you've been doing. About your boyfriends." She feels a twinge of irony. But even if she were willing to talk about her life to her sisters, they'd never take the first step: asking. They think, as they've always thought, that her life is known, that no surprises lie ahead, unless, of course, something terrible happens to her or Frank or the baby. But they don't anticipate tragedy, either. If they did, they'd feel happy for the happiness they think she has now.

Although she hardly feels she's their mother anymore, like a mother she cannot confide the true story of her heart. They could never forgive it. But what she'd like most to confide to her sisters is not the story of Dr. Stern at all. She'd like them to know how much she wants to be a poet. Dr. Stern is over and done with. And not part of reality. They would hate her for him, too, the way they'd all hated their mother for Max. What was the true story of their mother's heart, she wonders. Was it much more than Katherine ever knew? Would she have forgiven it? Not until now.

"I hope Mother's not listening," Louise says. "She's not used to being left out."

"So do I," Katherine says.

Jude does not comment.

"I think we'd better talk about Mother *and* us," Louise says. "I don't want her to be angry."

"I wish she could be angry," Katherine says. "That would mean she knows what's happening to us. There are so many things she's missed. At least she knew about Jude's babies. She never knew I was even thinking of having one."

"Neither did I," Jude says dryly.

Although it's mild, Katherine is pleased that Jude has expressed some emotion. Since the move, it's as if Jude doesn't know them anymore. At Christmas she was almost crazy to get away—to return to a place where she's spent twenty-four hours a day since July. Katherine hadn't told Jude last August she was going to try to get pregnant, partly because Jude had just abandoned her, but more because she'd thought she'd have plenty of time. Who would have expected she'd succeed the first month she tried? Even now—five months into it—she still doesn't always believe she's going to have a baby. And, apparently, she's not the only one. Every time she walks into her poetry class—which, as Eric predicted, she did not drop—he looks at her with waiting eyes that seem to match her waiting body. It's as if, despite what she told him so many weeks ago, he expects that things are going to change. In the classroom he has been more brilliant than ever. He has a way of anticipating the class's prejudices and correcting them—sometimes angrily, sometimes kindly, but always with a genius that everyone, except perhaps P.A.'s girlfriend, feels. Katherine no longer simply admires him; she adores him. The class is drawing to a close and she's trying to decide whether to take a new course in the spring. She can only audit, since her baby will arrive in April, but she'll still have three months of study. She wonders if she dares take a course with Eric. But she also wonders how she could possibly miss one.

All these weeks she's avoided seeing him alone. When he scheduled individual conferences to determine term-paper topics, she didn't sign up, but without approval of her subject he gave her an A. Underneath the A, though, as if it were her grammar grade—in case, she supposed, she'd had to explain to

Frank—he drew a question mark. She has not stopped by his office to offer any answers. Of course she can't see him. She's married and she's staying married. If she were to answer his question, though, she'd answer it with one of her own: isn't it enough that she loves him? that she will always love him?

Because she's pregnant and has legitimate mood swings, she's managed to make Frank believe that everything is all right. Because of her discomfort when they make love, though, they are now more friends than lovers. She cares for him in the warmest way imaginable. His excitement about the baby is boundless; she tries to make hers match his. Although she does not feel "at one" with the growing fetus, as do so many mothers-to-be, she is looking forward to the day the baby arrives. Often at night, though, her racing heart awakens her. Typical of pregnancy, her doctor says. Also typical of terror, she knows.

"I do wish Mother were alive," Katherine continues in a subdued voice. But maybe Mother doesn't need to be alive. Maybe she *knows* what's happened in her oldest daughter's life. Before she died, she may have anticipated it. Perhaps she was even the cause. Katherine cancels her last thought, which strikes her as a little too convenient. "But I guess it's better if she's dead and just listening," she says. "Then she can't talk back."

"There you go again," Louise says, for once apparently unoffended.

But, casting a quick look toward the back seat, Jude says, "*Please,* Katherine."

Katherine stares hard at the back of Jude's head. Her sister has let her hair grow since she moved here. A French braid lies against her neck, the rest of her hair hanging past her shoulders. "Why did you mind that?" she asks, genuinely quizzical. "It's no different from the way we've always talked. What's Chapel Hill doing to you?" Her tone is changing; she can't help it. She takes a quick breath. "Other than keeping you from visiting Mother's grave?"

"Chapel Hill's doing nothing to me but *great* things," Jude says coldly. "It's not keeping me from Mother's grave. I had a date. Mother wouldn't have minded."

"But *we* minded," Katherine says.

"Am I supposed to be visiting her or you?"

"*Both*," Katherine says.

"No more arguing or I'm getting out," Louise says. Do either of them care enough to stop her? But the car becomes utterly quiet. She isn't particularly surprised that they've stopped arguing. They probably each wanted to, and she gave them an excuse. Still, it pleases her that they've seemed to listen.

Jude is silent. For a reason she's been unable to pinpoint, she has been dreading this evening. She loves her sisters; she really does. But they're making her think of the past. Although Katherine would say she's being self-deceptive, Jude no longer feels as if she has a past. She's no longer the person she used to be. The person she is when she's with Mickey Mickleberry is not anybody they've ever seen. She's had a chance to start over with him, to be—for the first time—the person she's always wanted to be. Being with her sisters, though, makes her forget who she is and remember who she was. She doesn't want to get the two confused.

She'll gladly talk to them about Chapel Hill. She'll even talk to them about Mickey. But she doesn't want to talk to them about Cap or about her kids—except how they'll be from this point forward—or about Mother. She's decided she no longer wants to compare notes about Mother. Her and Mother's relationship was separate from her sisters, and unique. It's buried now deep inside her. She doesn't want it dug up. Each person you know, she'd like to tell Katherine, is what *you* see in them or what they are or have been to you. If you try to understand them through someone else's eyes, you'll only be confused. She simply can't look at their mother the way Katherine does. Mother did not destroy Katherine; she created her. She didn't abandon her; she set her free. And she taught Jude everything she knows. Of *course*, Jude had wanted to come back early to Chapel Hill on Christmas Day. Mickey had been cooking a duck for her and the kids. But Mickey's cool: he would have waited. She hadn't gone to Mother's grave with her sisters because she didn't want to hear anything that might conflict with everything she's figured out.

Until Jennifer's telephone call this week, Louise has felt herself waiting for Katherine somehow to indicate that they are going to be sisters. They had one pleasant lunch together in November and Katherine has come by the shop lots of times. But all she's shown Louise is surface niceness. Louise has no desire to argue with Katherine—she'd never win—but she's realized that she doesn't want their relationship to be happily meaningless either. "Happily meaningless" is the phrase Carilee uses to talk about every relationship in her family, including her parents'. She admires how Louise and her sisters "deal" with one another. And Louise has begun to see its value, too. Carilee just doesn't understand *how* honest everyone is.

Although Louise loves her sisters, she realized after Jenn's phone call that *true* feeling is reserved for friends. She *likes* Jennifer. Liking is not "basically inconsequential," as Billy used to say. It's the best thing you can feel for somebody else. Even after eight months of no communication, she likes Jennifer so much. On the telephone she'd immediately told the truth about Billy. Jennifer was brokenhearted, but at the same time touched that Louise had kept the devastating news to herself. She said it was the most unselfish thing she'd ever heard of anyone doing. Louise not only likes Jennifer, she loves her. She feels only love for Katherine and Jude. But love has a place.

Next weekend she and George Morales are going to Richmond to visit Jennifer and Jeff. Although George is not wonderful like Billy, she knows he'll make a good impression on her friends. He meets people well; he has goals that others identify with; he's, in fact, a man with a future, just like Jefferson Davis Miles III.

"Here we are," Jude says as she glides the car into a parking place right in front of the restaurant. The fact that she speaks relaxes everyone. The restaurant has large windows which reveal tables of diners cozy in candlelight. Louise gives Katherine a hand out of the back seat. It's an evening that seems hushed because it's so cold. The streetlights barely light the street. Jude locks the door and then starts ahead of them up the front steps. They glance at one another, eyebrows raised, and follow.

When they are seated at a perfect corner table, Katherine, who is treating, asks Weezie to select the wine. Whether or not the reputation is deserved, everyone says that Louise knows more about wine than anyone in the family because she has lived in France. Jude waves at a woman across the room and then excuses herself from the table. Although the sisters have only a couple of hours together, Katherine refrains from saying anything. If their first dinner together in Chapel Hill is too unpleasant, she thinks they might lose Louise for subsequent meetings. They might even lose Jude. And then there would be only Katherine, the sister who would always show up.

"That was a great new friend of mine," Jude says when she returns to the table. "Maud Hinshaw. A potter and a teacher and a very funny woman."

" 'Great' is an oft-used word around here," Katherine says in an affected voice. The wine, a rich-looking Bordeaux—too heavy for her taste—is being poured by an Oriental girl. "Tell us about 'great' Chapel Hill."

Jude looks directly at Katherine. She'll try to explain although she knows that Katherine will not seriously try to understand. Her sister's mind has been made up for months. "Moving here is the most important thing I've ever done," she says. "I don't mean that the way it sounds. The way it sounds makes me sound trite. The real most important things I've done are get married, have two kids, and get divorced. But that was all part of a program. A sort of downhill slope I found myself on. The only thing I've ever done that was totally right—thinking of no one but myself—is move to Chapel Hill. It's not because of Mickey that I'm happy, although I'm crazy about him. It's because it's *not* because of Mickey. Can anybody understand?"

"I can," Louise says. "And I'm so happy for you." Katherine glances at Louise: her young eyes have tears in them. Suddenly Katherine's eyes well up, too, but not because she's happy for Jude. She's lost Jude. Jude is never coming back. Jude doesn't even want to come back. And Jude is free. Why can't *she* be free?

Jude looks at each of them. "You aren't mad at me?" she asks in the seductive tone they each employ from time to time. It was a tone Mother had mastered. She touches her sisters' wrists and then picks up her glass of wine. "You don't think I've deserted you?" Her last question is directed only at Katherine, who for the sake of pride would shake her head but cannot.

"We understand," Louise is saying. "You couldn't stay in Greensboro for your family. People get stuck in places," she adds, aware before she speaks that she is one of those people. Except that she doesn't mind being stuck. She would be afraid not to be stuck, unless she finds out that Jennifer was serious so long ago about her moving to Richmond. Would she do it? Haägen-Dazs is opening lots of new stores in Virginia. It would be easy to get a transfer. Especially with her record.

"But why here?" Katherine asks. "I still don't understand. Please don't say it's because of the people. Every place *anybody* likes is because of the people. Unless you like *places*." A little jab. "Every place you *don't* like is because of the people."

"If you really want to know . . ." Jude says. She's already finished her glass of wine and signals Louise to pour her another. She doesn't want to get drunk, but she wants to reach a certain mellowness that will keep her from examining anything Katherine might say. Katherine *is* always right; Jude just doesn't want to hear it. She speaks slowly: "Because it's new. Not because it's Chapel Hill. I could be anywhere as long as I'm not in Greensboro. I don't hate Greensboro. Greensboro just happens to be where I've been.

"There's no question that Chapel Hill is special," she continues. "It's small and libertarian and open, much more open than home. But for me it's special because here I have no past. My life began in August. Katie and Charles are my past, of course, but they're the only things I can't forget. Fortunately, Mickey likes them. And I like them, too. More than I ever have. So I was right."

Louise's eyes are shining. Katherine assumes a pensive look. Jude doesn't want them in her life, but Louise didn't even hear her. Everything Katherine said last summer is true. Jude's search was simply the search in a new place for a man. But she found one. Katherine can't fault the process. If Jude had stayed in Greensboro, though, she might have had Dr. Stern. It would have been almost as good as Katherine's having him herself. She's happy that Jude is happy, but she thinks her sister is operating under false pretenses. The past can't simply be discarded. It's inside Jude like her soul.

"Tell us about Mickey," Louise says. She knows that soon the time will come when she'll have to tell about George Morales and disappoint her sisters. She doesn't love George, even though he's on his way to college to become a famous stockbroker. She's not going to marry him. George doesn't like her in the right way. He doesn't even know her. He only remembers her from when she was a girl in Mrs. Rigby's class. *She* never knew *him* at all.

"Mickey is nobody's type but mine," Jude says. "He's wickedly smart and he makes me laugh. I've never been with a man who makes me laugh. We never stop laughing, except sometimes." She looks teasingly at them. Her eyes are less focused. Katherine refrains from reminding Jude that what she liked most about Cap was that *he* made her laugh. People remember the past, but no one ever remembers the truth.

Jude leans loosely against the back of her chair. Her eyes scan the art hanging over Katherine's and Louise's heads. She knows she's hurt Katherine's feelings by saying the kids are the only things she can't forget, but she wants to tell the truth. Also, she doesn't want her sisters *here* all the time. It would suit her fine if Mickey never met them, if he never had their perspective of her, if she remained his only source of information about her life. She is here to start over. The way to start over is to pretend you've just been born.

She continues: " 'Are you serious about Mickey?' you ask. No. Not yet. I used to think you had to be serious so soon. But he hasn't let me. I don't quite know how to explain it." She pauses to finish her glass of wine. "It has to do with what he's willing to talk about and what he isn't. I go to bed with him and everything. It's special, but it's different from the way I've gone to bed with guys before. It's secondary. We didn't even make love for the first three weeks." She adds that for Weezie's sake. She's never acknowledged in front of her little sister that she's gone to bed with anybody, even Cap. She has no idea whether or not Louise slept with Billy.

"Mickey was working at a restaurant when I first met him," she says. "He works a while, saves his money, then takes a sabbatical to do his photography. When he runs out of money, he starts working again. Don't worry," she says, her eyes on Katherine. "I'm not supporting him, and I don't intend to start." In fact, although she's asked him to, Mickey won't live with them. He thinks it would be bad for the kids. They divide the expenses of dating.

Katherine doesn't care whether Jude supports her boyfriend or not, although she's clearly expected to disapprove. A *mother* would disapprove if her daughter was supporting a boyfriend. But Katherine isn't their mother anymore. She *thinks* like a mother, she'll admit, but she's trying to stop talking like one all the time. Jude's car is *Jude's* business, she told herself ten minutes ago. Louise could find a better job, but at least she found the first one. *Not* commenting is a small step, isn't it? How can she let them know she's taken it?

Her sister Jude is a lovely woman, particularly enticing tonight in a pink sweater outfit which makes her complexion glow. Her face is a grownup face, no longer an extension of Katherine's own. Her sister Louise is pretty, too, a youthful pretty, the most delicate of the three. They are both adults. Does she really realize it? They don't depend on her anymore. She'd always expected this to happen, but she thought something new, something better would emerge.

"I'm looking forward to meeting Mickey," she says. It's completely inadequate to be able to think of nothing else to say. Can she only communicate when she's telling them what to do? She does hope that Jude and Mickey will be happy for a while. That the kids will grow and prosper. And that someday Jude—not broke—will come home for at least a lengthy conversation.

She hopes that Louise will find someone like Billy, but with a college education.

Jude catches her eye. With a sudden break in tone she says to Louise: "How about it?" Before Louise can catch up, she continues: "Is George a good fuck? Was Billy?"

Louise's face drains of all sweetness. She stares at Jude for a brief moment and then looks at Katherine equally angrily. What caused this? In a dry voice she says, "It's really none of your business, but since you're my sisters . . ." Louise has never talked about sex with her sisters, never wanted to. They must think she's finally old enough. It occurs to her that in Jude's own weird way she may be complimenting her. "Maybe I can't think of any reason *not* to tell you," she adds in a musing tone. "I'm old enough to do it, don't you think?" she adds lightly. They're grinning.

"I don't sleep with George," she says, wondering if they'll make fun of her euphemism. "Neither—you'll both be happy to know—am I a virgin."

"Hurrah," Jude says, making a sort of wild gesture with her wineglass. Nothing spills. She can tell from Katherine's expression that she already knew about Louise. She can also tell that Katherine thinks she's drinking too much. Fuck Katherine, as always.

Louise continues: "Billy and I had a special relationship that I don't ever want to talk about. He was the one, of course. And nobody since. Neither of you ever appreciated him, so don't start pretending you did. But he was a wonderful guy, and I wish I'd married him."

"I wish you had, too," Katherine says in a quiet voice. Neither of them looks at her. She wonders if she actually spoke.

A waiter wearing a big loop earring arrives to take their order, but Louise holds up a finger for him to let her finish what she's saying. "I'll tell you this much about George. He's a nice guy who's crazy about me, but I'm not going to marry him, because I don't love him. I'm not moving out of Daddy's house either, so don't try to make me. I'm glad you talked me into finishing college. I really am. Thanks very much. But please let that be all." The waiter, who's been watching her patiently, begins clapping. In a sweet voice she asks him to come back in five minutes.

"I want to go to the ladies' room," she tells her sisters. "Feel free to talk about me while I'm gone, but when I come back I want you to include me when you talk about me. You can say anything you want. Just don't leave me out." She weaves among the tables, Katherine's and Jude's eyes following her.

When she is out of sight, they look at each other. "She's getting a little plump," Katherine says.

"But tougher," Jude responds. "A lot tougher. Do you see much of each other?"

"Yes." Katherine would like Jude to think she sees Louise more often than she does. "We've gotten closer. Weezie's really a dear." Although these moments are probably the only ones she'll have alone with Jude, Katherine opens her menu. She loves her sister, but she no longer knows how to reach her. If only it could be as it used to be. When Jude listened to her and respected her. When Jude worshipped the ground she walked on. She doesn't know what subject to put forth. Is there time, really, for anything? Before she can decide between Mother, Mickey, teaching, or Jude's kids, Louise is back in her chair.

"All through?"

"We didn't talk about you," Jude says. "Katherine was trying to decide what to order. I was drinking some more of this great wine."

Louise and Jude begin chatting about Jude's new teaching job: how bright all these professors' kids are. But it's not just the professors' kids. Everybody in Chapel Hill is smart. The waiter returns for their order. Katherine asks for an extra glass of water. Although with this beach ball in her lap it's hard to imagine that she could forget she's pregnant, for a few moments she has. She promised Frank not to drink more than two glasses of wine this evening, so already she has to slow down. The baby has recently quickened. She feels him kicking now, but it's a casual kick to let her know he's there rather than to say he wants to get out. She prays the baby will be a boy. She'd be terrified to have a daughter, to have to try all this again.

She feels tears on her face. It's happened only a very few

times in her life that tears have existed before she knew she was crying. Once she remembers dreaming that her father was dead. Another time was when she and Eric recited the poem together. She sits very still now, until they notice her simply because of her stillness. Weezie's jaw drops slightly; Jude's eyes, heavy-lidded, open wider. Jude takes a swallow of wine without losing the connection of their gazes. Louise looks suddenly as if she might cry, too.

"What do *you* have to cry about?" Jude suddenly asks. The wine is affecting her, making her hostile. "What *in the world* do you have to cry about?"

What *does* she have to cry about? She has to cry about the loss of her sister. About how her husband is no longer the man she loves. About how she has spurned the man she loves. About how, soon, her studies will end. "Nothing," she says, blotting each cheek with her napkin. "Nothing at all. My life is perfect. Nothing bad has ever happened to me. I'm happy beyond belief. Without question I'm the happiest person here."

Jude is glaring at her, but Louise's face has a look of startled curiosity. No, she's never imagined that there is anything about her sister's life she doesn't know.

Katherine takes a new tone. "I have a lot to tell you both," she says, although she is still unsure if she'll proceed. It's so dangerous to lay open your heart to someone. Yet, it's the only possible way she can have her sisters. She's known it for a long time.

"About Mother?" Louise asks. She is trying hard to understand, to not be left behind, but confusion fills her face.

Katherine speaks gently to her: "I think we know enough about Mother. We need to move on."

"I've already moved on," Jude says. She is still refusing to listen. To her, Katherine is still the mother.

"There's so much *I* haven't been *told*," Louise blurts.

"We need to move on to us," Katherine says calmly. "What's the most important thing to you, Louise? Not what *I* think, but what *you* think. What do you hope for? Who do you dream about? I know you dream about Billy. Jude: Who are you now?

What's happening with your kids? Are you in love? Do you want to be married, or are you happy just being with someone? And what about me? Neither one of you knows anything about me."

"Not true," Jude says.

"It's not your fault," Katherine continues. "You don't ask me anything about myself, but I don't tell you anything either. I've never been honest with you. I've always kept the things that matter a secret. I've only been honest about *your* lives . . . not about mine. It hasn't exactly been fair."

She pauses. They are waiting for her to continue, attentive to her as she does not remember them being. Attentive not like daughters but, perhaps, like sisters. "Last summer . . ." she says. It's so hard to say this. It's the hardest thing she's ever had to say. "Last summer . . . I fell in love with another man."

The looks they give her are looks of incomprehension. A sort of horror roams in their eyes. She's going to have to go all the way back to the beginning. To when Mother died. But back even further, to when she was sixteen, and even before that. She has to admit to them all the times she's been wrong. She wants to ask them some things, too. She doesn't believe the answer is always yes. Do they? Next week, after she takes Dr. Stern's final exam, she's thinking of walking out of his classroom forever. Won't they agree that she should? What is their advice? She's always wanted to know what they think about things, and now, finally, she will ask.

They are back at Jude's apartment, sitting on the floor, their shoes off. Jude's children are asleep and the babysitter has gone. Louise is yawning. They are tired, but Katherine has asked that they not disband quite yet.

At dinner the whole story of her and Dr. Stern unfolded so unexpectedly quickly that she was embarrassed. "So, nothing really happened," Jude commented. "How can you still be in his class?" Louise asked. At first Katherine wondered if they were being deliberately obtuse, but then she realized how little they had to go on. She would tell them more, if there was more to tell. But nothing *had* happened, except that her heart now seemed wrapped up and put away forever. She understood the relief on her sisters' faces: she wasn't going to lose Frank, after all.

Louise unfolds her legs to bring them each a fresh cup of coffee. Since she waits on Daddy, they also let her wait on them. Jude has put on a comfortable nightgown, but not to rush them away, she said. She wishes they'd planned to spend the night.

Louise takes the coffeepot back to the kitchen and returns, refolding herself on the floor. The first silence since Katherine's confession occurs. Katherine lets it drift a while. No one seems to want to disturb it. Finally, in a low magnetizing voice, she begins: "Once upon a time our mother was a little girl."

The room is suddenly more silent than before. Her sisters are afraid of what she's going to say. They need not be.

"She was a beautiful child spoiled by her parents—our grandparents, and by her teachers—did either of you know she was a straight-A student?—and even by strangers. Mamaw used to tell me how, when Mother was a girl, people used to stop her on the street and hand her nickels.

"Always beautiful, she never went through a gawky stage. Boys began paying close attention to her from the time she was twelve. She married the sweetest one—our father—when she was seventeen. The attention of men, however, did not stop when she got married. Mother had charisma. People flocked to her because of how good she made them feel. She had something that wasn't considered possible back then: men friends. On her twenty-first birthday she received a roomful of bouquets."

"*Come* on," Jude interrupts.

"Just listen," Katherine says. "It's a story. I'm making it up, but it's true.

"She was pregnant with me at the time. Beautifully pregnant. Never had there been such a pretty pregnant woman. She had me and then she had Jude the next year. It was hard, but she worked hard. She carried off motherhood the same way she'd always carried off everything.

"One day she went to mail a letter. A man who saw her on

the post-office steps turned around and followed her inside. He engaged her in conversation while she was in line. It wasn't unusual. Men had always followed her.

"She loved her husband deeply, and had always kept potential suitors at arm's length, but this man was different. He began by telephoning her. He had a quick wit and a sharp mind, sharper than her husband's, and he engaged her for months in simple conversation. In a way, it was like an education for her, since she'd decided against college in favor of marriage. She began reading certain magazines he mentioned so that she could offer more points of view. She read books. They even talked about God. Except on weekends, he called her every day for a year at two o'clock.

"The Monday he stopped, she thought that something had happened to him and she called his office. He was busy, his secretary said. Every time she phoned, the secretary gave the same answer.

"Finally, on Friday at 2:01 p.m., she called a babysitter for us and went to his office. He received her, taking her in his arms as she walked through the door. He explained that he hadn't been able to stand it any longer. He loved her. He couldn't live without her. She said she loved him, too. They went to a hotel because there was no need to wait. And he made love to her like she'd never been made love to before. They were enjoying a year's worth of stored-up passion, he whispered.

"At home late that afternoon she waited for our father. She was angry at him for marrying her so young. He'd always been so nice to her: she was angry about that, too. Max was never careful of her feelings. But when the family was gathering that evening in the kitchen, her words stuck in her throat. She did not leave him for ten terrible years. There was one flurry of reconciliation which resulted in Louise.

"Mother fell more and more in love with Max: their love, she agreed with him, was fated. He loved her, too, but he was angry that she wouldn't leave our father. For days he wouldn't speak to her. Then she would meet him somewhere, and he'd once again turn her body into something powerful. It was their bodies that won her. With our father she'd been a receiver, but, slowly, Max taught her how to act in a great drama starring two.

"For a few years she was able to keep her relationship with him contained. First, it was what she did to please her mind. Next, it became what she did to please her body. Finally, she began to love him with her soul. She was ashamed, though. And so she began showing the people she loved how terrible she could be. Making them hate her was the best way to punish herself. And so she hurt her children. And so we hated her. When she'd done enough, she left Daddy and married Max . . ."

There's a long silence. No one looks at anyone else. Then Jude speaks: "I guess it didn't work. Because I don't hate her."

"Neither do I," Louise says.

Katherine says, "I don't anymore, either." Tears run down her cheeks, but she doesn't wipe them away or try to make them stop. She takes a steadying breath. In a bare quiet voice she asks, "Do you both hate me?" She's not asking just about Dr. Stern. She's asking about everything that's ever happened. Her sisters' eyes say that they understand the question.

Neither of them answers. They just come to her, first Louise and then Jude, and hold her close.

On April 17 Katherine gave birth to a son, Matthew Patterson Borden, eight pounds, eleven ounces, nineteen and a half inches long. There were no complications.